Skara

Andrew Appleby

* * *

The First Wave

Published in 2017 by Skara Books
Fursbreck Pottery, Harray
Orkney, KW17 2JR

Typeset in Freight by Lumphanan Press
www.lumphananpress.co.uk

Back cover photograph of Andrew Appleby taken by John Welburn ABIPP

Final edit by Chris of First Editing

Printed and bound by Airdrie Print Services

ISBN: 978-1-9998611-0-0

Dedicated to my wonderful wife, Sigrid

Contents

Acknowledgements

I would like to thank my wife, Sigrid. Without her constant encouragement, *Skara* would not have been completed. It was while we were looking at Grooved Ware pottery from Skara Brae in Orkney that she spotted the head of a Great Auk on a large shard. This unique discovery gave so much inspiration for the story.

Professor Ari Berk for his support, friendship and literary encouragement. He kindly wrote the preface. We have spent many happy hours visiting Skara and other Orkney sites.

Ronnie Simison: farmer, discoverer, protector and excavator of the Tomb of the Eagles, South Ronaldsay, Orkney. This site is the inspiration for Shala's Lee Holme. Ronnie's intuition into stone artefacts and their uses threw so much light into the dark past. Sadly he didn't live to see *Skara* published. In his honour I slipped a broken stone axe into his grave. It rests by his left hand.

John Hedges, archaeologist at Tomb of the Eagles. I have walked over many sites with John and made remarkable discoveries with him. We observed and interpreted the landscape around the Tomb of the Eagles. I'm fairly sure I have spotted where Lee Holme could still lie.

My grateful thanks to Nick Card and ORCA (Orkney Research Centre for Archaeology) for allowing me access to the excavations and finds at the Ness of Brodgar.

My daughter Ruth Colston and her husband Mark, who encouraged me from the first pages to the last.

Caroline Wickham-Jones for her information on rising sea levels and her confidence in my staggering discoveries under the waters of Harray and Stenness Lochs.

Erik Meek, RSPB, for his liberal sharing of knowledge and confirmation of the Great Auk on the Skara Brae shard: also the Dunter, or eider duck, which accompanies the Auk.

Joanna Buik, who helped so much in formatting my work.

Errol Fuller, who wrote the definitive book *The Great Auk*, and explained that the oldest representation of the Great Auk was from a Spanish cave and dated to 40,000 BC. Sigrid's discovery is the second oldest, dating from around 3000 BC.

Antonia Thomas and Dan Lee for allowing me to dig on their Neolithic 'town' called Braes of Ha'breck on the Island of Wyre. The is the inspiration for the House of Croo. I was so fortunate to be allowed to excavate in the 'midden', where I found several beautiful stones and artefacts. My personal belief is that these items actually dropped from a collapsing roof. It also provided the scene for the brewery fire.

Merryn Dinely for sharing her knowledge of Neolithic beer brewing. Her excitement is infectious!

Dr Stephen Harrison for his collaboration in OPPRA's Neolithic Grooved Ware experiments (OPPRA: Orkney Prehistoric Pottery Research Associates). I studied in detail the pottery from the Tomb of the Eagles with him. This gave me the scenes of the Ancestor Tales and the visit of Shala and Wrasse to the tomb.

Dr Tim Palmer, Chief Pathologist for Inverness Shire (retired) helped me with positioning the arrows for the death of Rush and the paralysing of the Bald Head's victims.

Martha Johnson, whose geological knowledge was so valuable.

Professor David Sanderson for his expertise on blown sand, storms and tsunamis.

Trevor Cowie of the National Museum of Scotland for encouraging Sigrid and my research into Skara Brae's ceramics.

John Ross Scott, editor of *Orkney Today*, for constant encouragement, and publishing Sigrid and my earlier stories (Now and The Notes and Letters).

Alison Sheridan of the National Museum of Scotland for her time and assistance.

Professor Colin Richards for our important dialogues on Neolithic Orkney.

Christopher Gee, discoverer of Smerquoy's early Neolithic houses.

Mr Aitkin, custodian of Skara Brae, who allowed my brother Malcolm and me free range to explore the wonderful Neolithic houses on my first trip to Orkney in 1963.

Dr Steve Dockrill and Dr Julie Bond, who allowed me total access over their Shetland excavations at Scatness Broch. Although Iron Age, it still gave me great insights into human lives of the distant past.

Julie Gibson, Orkney's County Archaeologist: her lively spirit and fresh approach to archaeology is so rewarding.

John Adams, the pilot who flew us over the Isles. From his plane I could see the old landscape beneath the ripples and photograph much of it. He allowed me to fly the plane over the Hoy Hills!

Daphne Lorimer, who discussed bones and burials with me.

Victor and Henrietta Poirier encouraged me to think hard about life in the past when we designed a television series.

Shayla Spenser, visitor to Orkney, who has amazing theories on the spiritual past.

Keith Hobbs, who constantly asks how the next book is coming on.

Ronald (Bingo) Mavor, writer and my wife's first husband, who advised me on the early chapters. He wanted to kill Wrasse off because nobody would expect that, but I reprieved her.

Christopher Jones, my dear friend who tragically died in an archaeological accident.

Willie and Sandy MacEwan for allowing me thinking space at West Manse on Westray.

Ben Short, who was my English teacher and mentor.

Kerrianne Flett, my workshop manager, for listening.

I thank my cousins Jennifer Copley-Mey and Emma Boden for their huge encouragement, help and understanding.

A major thank you to Alison Williamson for patiently, expertly and enthusiastically copy editing the first editions of *Skara*.

Also to John and Sarah Welburn for their huge input with photographically reproducing my illustrations.

Why I Wrote Skara

*

Since the late 1970s I have yearned to write a Neolithic epic set in Orkney. I began it after a Christmas Eve walk on Birsay Beach with my wife, Sigrid. We watched the redshanks running in the ebb across the wet sands. I said, 'At last I have the beginning and end of my book. It starts with a tsunami and ends with one.' I began Skara that evening, introducing Shala, her family and fellow villagers. By then I had decided that the first great wave would be described as a race memory in later storytelling. This is where the powerful character of Wrasse appears. Two days later, the huge tsunami hit Indonesia.

Skara, with Shala and Oiwa, is the first novel in this series. It sets the scene for momentous movements in knowledge and political power in Orkney. But the islands were suffering from inbreeding, so before these developments could take place, these dangers had to be countered. Hence the spiritual insights of Shala and Wrasse – I firmly support race memory and the predictive force of dreams, having experienced these in abrupt and physical ways.

From Skara Brae or Birsay, gazing west across the Atlantic, the next stop is unimaginably distant. This is from where I chose the hero,

Oiwa, to travel. He had his reasons, as you will discover, and undergoes terrible yet wondrous adventures.

My inspiration for the series has been my lifelong interest in archaeology. I have always believed that Orkney was a great centre of knowledge and culture, influencing world thinking at a time when early civilisations were about to burgeon, but there is virtually no material evidence to back this up. Only when you think deeply about the sites, the dates in world history and how the islanders were modern people in their time, at the forefront of technical advances and natural wisdom, does the notion become plausible.

The skills of people who use early technologies also fill me with inspiration. Their efficiency of movement, style and concentration bring spectacular results, and the simple yet effective struggle for mere existence becomes a rich, rewarding lifestyle. I always tend to look at evidence with an alternative view, and my experiments in ancient pottery, cooking and material culture have given me skills and knowledge of the past. I enjoy putting flesh on ancient bones, brains in their skulls, hunger and satisfaction in their bodies and, of course, love and lust in their hearts. I feel that many archaeologists tend to de-personalise the lives of people from the past and misinterpret perfectly ordinary discoveries as ritual. My characters are intensely practical in the way they live. Cult is there, but takes second place to real life.

There is an old Orkney expression, 'If it's hard work, you're doing it wrong.' We look back assuming everything in the distant past was difficult and survival was tortuous. Yet, as the great explorer John Rae discovered, if you take your example from the locals, there is always a right way, and a time and place to work miracles.

Andrew

Skara Characters and Places

Orkney Characters
Shala... Red-haired, pale green eyes
Gull... Shala's mother
Juniper... Shala's older sister
Flint... Shala's older brother
Partan... Shala's grandfather and father of Gull
Quernstone... the neighbour who is always baking
Reaper... Quernstone's husband
Dale... Drummer, 10 years old

In the Solstice Tales and Legends
Longo... The First Man
Guman... Mother Goddess from Caves (Gumar in Oiwa's clan)
Tuman... Father God from the Stars (Tumar in Oiwa's clan)
Karnal... Son of Longo
Jurt... Daughter of Nistor and Karnal. Became Aiva
Wrasse... Hag and Shala's Mentor
Tangle... Mother of Several

Cullen... Girl knocking limpets
Seaguard... Seal wife
Gill... Seal party leader
Gurnard and Vacar... Fore-Folk heroes
Rod... Reaper's nephew.
Waret... Rain spirit.
Grool... Fire spirit (Greil according to Oiwa)
Kull... Wind spirit
Weir... Wrasse's first love
Crane... Lee Holme girl
Fallow... Lee Holme girl
Tangle... Lee Holme girl, daughter of Tangle

Oiwa's Goose Clan
Oiwa... Youthful hero in Canada: goose spirit ... Pronounced Whaa
Quil... Oiwa's mother
North Star... Oiwa's father
Honey... Oiwa's sister
Petal... Oiwa's other sister
Mica... Oiwa's oldest brother: spiritually a bear
Bark... Oiwa's middle brother: spiritually a lynx.
Tine... Oiwa's youngest brother: spiritually an eagle
Barb and Ripple... villagers with twins

More Orkney characters
Hornfisk... Ancestor builder
Sable... Female neighbour from Char
Sprig... Sable's young son

More Goose Clan characters
Grayling... Firemaster in the Sweat Lodge.
Rush... of the Caribou Clan: spiritually the Moon
Lichen... of the Caribou Clan: spiritually a stag

River Journey Characters at the Stork Clan's Village

Farrnar... Legendary Slayer of Gunnal

Buzzard... Chief of the Stork Clan

Fall, Marsh and Rail... Grayling's sons

Gale... Buzzard's daughter. Loved by Fall

Ember, Plover and Rainbow... Buzzard's wives

Catfish... Buzzard's Brother

Stella... Wife of Catfish

Birch Skin... Buzzard's nephew

Snaaaaar... Birch Skin's partner

Dew... Snaaaaar's daughter

Jay... The girl who loses her boat

Scale... Jay's father

Moss... Coiffurist and lover of Oiwa.

Sleeke... Couffeurist and lover of Mica

Lizard's Toe... Masseur

Minnow... Small son of Sable: red hair

Phantom... Minnow's pig

Knotwood... Sable's daughter

Timber... Sable's oldest son: red hair, falls in love with Shala

Hoof Tracker... Stork Clan hunter

Fang... Hoof tracker's dog

Musk... Wolf Clan leader

Claw... Musk's sidekick.

Eyewhite... Musk's wife

Bristle

Heng

Day

Vulpese... Wolf deity.

Scurran... Vulpese's wife

Peach Leaf... Claw's wife

Marten... Claw's nephew and astronomer

Char... Chief of the Baldheads

Limpet... Char's wife

Sether... Char's brother
Smolt... Char's dead father
Gneiss... Son of Char and Limpet
Thrift... Daughter of Char and Limpet, lover of Oiwa
Skellig... Tomb Keeper
Birch Twig... Sether's wife; red hair
Ugruk... Innu chief
Sgeir... Ugruk's wife

More Orkney Characters
Fernfold... Wrasse's sister
Dilly... Wrasse's lost child
Copse... Sable's husband
Gum... their dog
Carve...Copse's mate
Timber... Red-haired son of Sable

The Northern Crossing
Drake... Seafaring friend
Guillemot.... Seafaring friend
Heather... Drake's Wife
Sprang... Chief of Shepherd's Tongue
Osprey... Sprang's dog
Selk... Seal god
Orci... Whale god
Spindrift... Dead mother
Reel... Spindrift's son
Erica... Sprang's wife
Sea Shadow... Mythical whale
Otterman... Fisherman
Sprat and Mackerel... Otterman's children
Brill... Otterman's wife.
Morning... Otterman's adolescent daughter
Night... Otterman's adolescent son

Lintel... Wrasse's sister
Cran and Mire... Wrasse's other sisters
Pike... Man from Otter's kit
Clart... Pike's wife
Roach... Pike's son
Lily and Velvet... Priestesses at the house of Croo
Ebb... Eunuch singer and Wrasse's grandson
Dilly and Spider.... Young brother and sister catching frogs
Shearer... Dilly and Spider's chaperone
Cherry... Boy reed cutter
Scanner... Chief of See More Hill
Fox Glove... One of Scanner's wives
Rose... One of Scanner's wives
Clam.... Scanner's first wife
Spar... Commander of Tarmin
Garnet... High Priestess of Tarmin
Cairn... Queen of Tarmin
Spar... Garnet and Cairn's butler
Cliff.... Wrasse's son
Mire.... Wrasse's sister
Moth... Wife of Spar
Old Purse... Cliff's predecessor
Tapstone... Stone robber of Tarmin.
Cleat and Shank.... Crewmen of Seastar
Maiden Gallow... Gallow's wife
Grace, Favour, Luck and Charm... Gallow's other children
Breeze... Dale's wife with deformed child

Oiwa's onward journey
Ice Crystal... Albatross clan woman
Foaming Wave... Albatross chief
Moon Sky... Foaming Wave's head wife
Sharpened Tooth...... Great hunter and prince of Albatross Clan
Greill... Oiwa's name for Grool, the Fire God

Falling Star... Oiwa's Albatross mate
Spring Leaf... Falling Star's friend
Span... Older boy actor
Musk Bone... Ugruk's brother
Sange... Albatross's God of Eternal Life
Little Moth... Ugruk's daughter
Ungrin... Sea monster
The Hot Rocks... People of Smoking Mountain
Longspoot... Hot Rocks 'Prince'
Cove.... Longspoot's Friend.
Summer Fox... Chief of Hot Rocks Clan
Taiga... Granddaughter of Summer Fox and Oiwa's lover

* * *

Places: Orkney
Lee Holme... Shala's village
Char... Sable's village
Tarmin... Wrasse's home village
(Rousay, Midhowe)
House of Souls... Midhowe cham-
bered cairn
Flow Burn... Flows to where Scapa
Flow is now

Loch of Scap... Where Scapa Flow is now
Tannus by the Marsh... Stenness now
Bore Brig... Sluice and Clapper Bridge between Stenness and Ness
of Brodgar
Stone Road... Cobbled track towards the Sight Stone
The Slumbering Mother... Hoy
Seaforth... Carve's Boat
Cutlip Bay... Possible landing place
Shepherd's Tongue...Township and landing place

The Auks' Passage
Auk Island
Whale Arch... Drake's Village by Auk Island
Porpoise... Drake's dingy
Eagle's Noust.... Stopping place
Rouse... River at Shepherd's Tongue
Rouse Lake
The Harpoon... Otterman's dugout
Sparrow Hall... Village
See More Summit... Where Morning was conceived
Top Loch... Loch above the Rouse
Black Cott... Official residence
Gare Head... Cliffs At Skara
Virgin's Cock ... Stone stack and rock
Forest of Kaime... Tangled woodland on Hoy
Pissing Pony of High Hump... Waterfall off Hoy cliffs
Mountain's Bowell... Rackwick Bay
Island of Vaar... Home of Gallow and Russet
Bay of Calm... Gallow's home

Oiwa's onward journey
The Sand Kisser... Oiwa's 'borrowed' boat
Echoing Caves of Black Island.
Upper Hill... Where Bloodstone comes from
Skullar's Point
Ormer... Sharpened Tooth's kayak
Orca Fin Bay
Fallow Fell... Valley of myth and healing
Fluke... Weir's kayak

Foreword

*

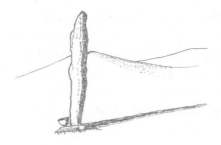

The first time I stepped foot on Orkney, I felt as though I was walking into a song, a sort of chorus of stone, sea, wind, and time. Reading Andrew Appleby's *Skara*, I can hear a continuation, a new verse, of that same song.

It is perhaps Andrew's familiarity with the earth of Orkney that gives *Skara* its honesty and its characters their believability. It is always a challenge to create a world from far-distant ancient cultures, especially from those that have no written epics to carry their feelings and fears to us directly. Nevertheless, Neolithic people's lives can be read, subtly, in the fragments and clues they've left behind. We can see archeology and a strong imagination at work in *Skara*. Both are required to make the past of Orkney speak, and Andrew is that rare writer able to read the palimpsest of stones and summon with them.

The well-limned folk of *Skara* bring the past once again into the circle of the sun. Though their world exists across a considerable chasm of time, they feel as sure and real as the land beneath our feet, even now. *Skara* is an inviting world, a world much smaller than our modern one, yet far vaster in its vision. It is a place where the elemental gods walk close beside the people of place; where word and spell give name to innumerable aspects of sacredness and make thin the boundary between human and animal; it is a world where ancestors are not lost in death, but honored in tabernacles of stone that render family and clan eternal. In its sacred honoring of family and memory, and of the sea, *Skara* presents a world that has much to teach our own.

It is no accident that *Skara* was written by a potter. Indeed, Andrew's novel and his ceramics share a considerable frontier. In both, he gives form to what Ovid called "scumbled elements," working ancient clay into new vision; layers of earth and archaeological strata are both given elegant and enduring expression. In *Skara*, truly, we find an extraordinary tale, thousands of years in the making, shaped by a master's hands.

Ari Berk, Ph.D.
Professor of Folklore and Mythology
Central Michigan University

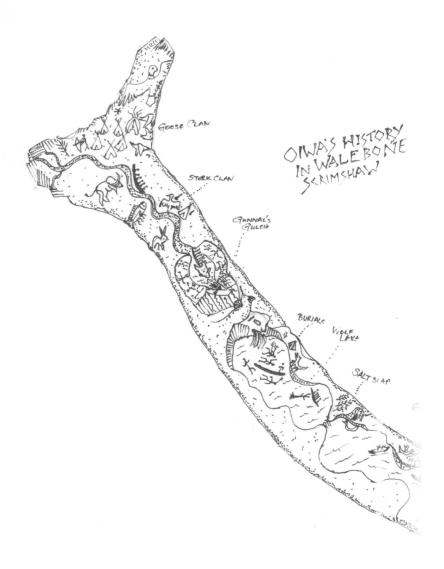

OIWA'S HISTORY
IN WALEBONE
SCRIMSHAW

GOOSE CLAN

STORK CLAN

GUNNAL'S GULCH

BURIALS

WOLF LAKE

SALT SLAP

NORTH RONALDSAY

PAPA WESTRAY

DOUNBY

WESTRAY
PARTENE

SANDAY

EDAY

(DUNMALLOW)
CALLING HILL
BURGS HEAD
HIGHLANDS
SWART STANE
WEST MAINLAND
TARMIN
ROUSAY

STRONSAY

SPARROW HALL
CROSS
SHAPINSAY

AUSKERRY
SHEPHERD'S TONGUE

SKARA DUNE
ANNA POLLLS
GAREHODE
BRODGAR
STENNESS LOCH
BORGKERS
TANNUS
SANEN BAY

WEST MAINLAND

EAST
MAINLAND

DEERNESS

CUTUP BAY

WHALE ARCH
ANA ISLANDS
STACK BAY

FOREST OF KAME
SEVENS

HOY

BREDAM

FLOTTA

SOUTH
WALLS

SOUTH
RONALDSAY

CHAR

ANCESTOR HOUSE
LEE HOLME

VAAR

LILLE SANDS

SHALA'S
ORKNEY

AJA

BIG LAND

FLOATING FOREST

KEY

ORKNEY AS IT IS NOW

NEOLITHIC ORKNEY

DUNES

:- TANNUS :- REPRESENTS NEOLITHIC NAME

DOWNALL

Chapter 1

*

Shala's Story

Redheaded Shala watched from high on the Skara Dune, searching with her hazel-green eyes through the misty spume blown from the barrage of tidal waves. Was that a speck of humanity far off on the raging sea? Could this faint vision be the core of her quest approaching from that vast, dangerous distance?

Momentarily, the flashing redshanks' flights, searching the churning beach at the foot of the great sandbar, distracted her: she was taken inexorably back to her earliest memories.

* * *

Shala was late. She always was, despite the excitement of the Ancestor Tales. Her northern world had short winter days. When you are a four-year-old girl, on a bright afternoon with the sea gently lapping on that vast expanse of sand, you just want to stand and watch. Her bird friends, the redshanks, dibbled in the tiny advancing waves, searching for wee crustaceans, casting long shadows in the low Orcadian sunlight. Her footprints were scarcely larger than those of her favourite birds, and she sported a similar redness of leg as her little limbs chilled in the zephyr from off the sea.

Her village was at the head of the bay; she turned towards the wispy smoke trails drifting inland. The main house was closer to the shore than the others. It was big and strong, its stonework sturdy and tight. The wonderful reed-thatched roof pointed up to the very skies. A shimmer of warm air venting from its high pitch told her that her home was warm. Shala waved to her redshanks and ran back. At the high-tide mark she caught her mother's watching eye, making her even more aware of those midwinter stories. Shala's keen eyes flashed over the lines of flotsam. To her right she spotted an amber nugget. Stepping sideways, she garnered it; its glinting, rough-hewn shades matched her finely plaited hair perfectly.

Shala had been dressed for the storytelling for seemingly ages. 'Why does everyone else take so long?' she thought. Her mother beckoned to her, not going down the stone steps to meet her lest she scuff her new shoes. Shala skipped over the pebbly foreshore to nip up the treads to her mum. She held out a small pair of newly braided booties for her. Shala gripped them with her left hand as she opened her right, exposing the amber.

Gull picked her up. 'Amber,' she said kindly. 'It will take on your character. It will polish in your hands. If you are rough it will scratch. If gentle, it'll polish. All its colours, nature and hue will grow as you do. But hurry, dear. We're off to the storytelling.'

Her older brother, Flint, and middle sister, Juniper, were waiting at home. Gull put Shala down on the slab threshold as she called for Jasper, her man. From their door, many neighbours appeared, stooping slightly as they emerged from the great house into the flagstone courtyard.

Everybody was so well turned out. Shala was amazed. 'This happens every year,' Gull said. 'So if you fall asleep during the tales, it won't matter – you'll catch up next time.' Gull lifted Shala and carried her to the raft on the loch far up behind the village. Shala watched as her mum's shell earrings glinted blue and pink as they swung on beaded loops from her pierced lobes.

When the raft had filled with villagers, it was pushed out gently across the lochan. The journey was lovely. The short midwinter day soon turned to evening. As the sun dipped, the water took on a pinkish shimmer with gilded frills. Guiding the raft to the stone-paved slope at the far end, the polesmen sang their solstice songs. The raft nudged the flags and was roped to two stubby standing stones marking the way to the Ancestors' Hall.

Shala was put down on the paving. Everyone leapt to dry land without wetting shoes or hems. The women adjusted their hair as Gull straightened Jasper's feathered headband. She wiped Flint's face. He'd chewed a messy drake's wing on the voyage. Juniper, always neat, smoothed her reddened hair back smartly. In a warm hustle and friendly bustle, the villagers circled left along the cold, shaded path beside the tall mansion. They veered further as the walls lowered to an adult's waist height. The neat masonry stopped abruptly, ending in a standing stone even taller than Shala's father.

Their procession rounded the monolith. A breeze ruffled Shala's feather band. In front of them was a vast hide awning. Inside were neat piles of smouldering ox bones. Resting on the glowing femurs were the largest pots Shala had ever seen. The huge round-bottomed vessels steamed appetizingly.

The light faded. Behind her the cliffs, and the lapping sea: before her, cauldrons of simmering meat and fish. Past them a great arching wall with an imposing central doorway. 'It's like ours, but under the tent roof,' Shala thought. Reflecting the glowing fires, the lintel's polished surface shimmered brilliantly. Through the dark opening was the portal to their past. Within that shadow, Shala's ancestors dwelt.

Though it was her first time here, she had heard about it from Flint and Juniper. 'All you could ever wish to scoff,' Flint would say with dreamy eyes.

'Everyone looks so bonny and happy,' Juniper said as she twiddled with her blouse.

Everything Shala had heard was true. Everybody in their best paints and splendid hair. A wonderful spread too. Folk mingled, delighted, until it was time to start. They dipped strips of fish on sharp sticks into savoury, simmering water, then pulled them out moments later. 'Here you are, Shala. Yours is in a scallop shell. I'll blow gently to cool it,' Gull said as Juniper and Flint dipped theirs.

'Have some of your favourites... Steamed oysters, Gull,' Jasper said. 'And I think little Shala is ready for some mussels.'

'Thank you, Daddy... I love them.' she responded.

The fish pot had limpets with wild chives as flavouring; samphire and seaweed gave body to the bree. A crab or three were seething, and had seethed long enough. They were shared round and others popped in to take their place. The meat was for later. Its wafting steam filled the air, giving a richness that only well-hung auroch produced.

The party evolved. The children played. Hot little drop-scones were handed round as the first part of the Solstice Celebrations entered the second. The chatter of adults subsided. A small glimmer of light showed from the dark of the ancestors' portal. A huge horn blast echoed from within. As this subsided, another resounded, then a third. In a quicker succession, a fourth and a fifth. Shala jumped, clasping her ears. The trumpet sounded again even louder as others joined it from that darkness. Auroch, mountain goat, and rams' horns, were all blown from the innards of the house. Suddenly it stopped; only the reverberating stones retained the frequency of the diminishing blasts. The arching wall echoed, enhancing the effect, enshrouding the partygoers in its acoustic thrill.

The crowd hushed; mouths opened in wonder. All stared towards the entrance. As the inner silence of the dark tomb grew, so did theirs. Moments elapsed like eons as the company began to relax. The flutter of an eyelid, that unconscious movement of someone just thinking of another drop scone was the signal for an uproarious clatter. Deer antlers, auroch shins and hammers were invisibly striking the erect stone slabs in their sepulchre. The resting stalls for those past souls were uttering their annual hammered shriek, calling the New Year forward. The woman who had been so intent on the drop scone stood stock still, mouth agape, shaking.

'Nobody told me it would be like this,' Shala whispered.

'No, dear,' came Gull's answer. 'If anyone had, you'd have been too scared to come.'

'Oh, Mum, no. It's wonderful. Will they do it again?' Shala asked, beaming into her mother's eyes.

'Not that, but there will be many more things. We're going to listen to our stories. There are many, and they remind us of who we are.'

'Who are we then, Ma?' the tot replied.

'You'll find out,' Gull assured her.

In the shadows, Quernstone, Reaper's wife, reached for that tempting scone once again. Her brave decision calmed all tensions, which Shala had totally missed. Although the clamour from within the ancestors' abode was part of the ancient ceremonies, the drama of it never lessened. Someone from within the antechamber signalled the best moment to crack the first auroch shin against the polished upright for dramatic effect.

A large leather barrel was brought to the throng. The secure lid was eased, fizzing as it loosened. The contents of the bin smelt delicious. Malt, honey, autumn aromas of juniper, blackberry and a sense of apple were ladled into rounded pottery cups that had been warming beside the fire. The warmth matured the brew to a soothing mixture, making it a delight to imbibe. There were parent-sized vessels, youthful measures, and small cups for the wee ones. Some of the big ones disappeared into the darkness under the lintel.

The flaps at the back of the leather awning were lowered, cutting out the world of sea, cliffs and the gathering dark. A nearly full moon hid behind a clouded sky. It broke out occasionally to dapple the translucent roof in lighter and dimmer shades of parchment. The air warmed. Jasper took his precious heron leg-bone flute from his quiver. Placing it to his lips, he played gently. The variation of notes, highs and lows, shrill and soft, called on the Ancestors to emerge

from their haven; to yawn and wake, to stir, to remember and to tell...
A muffled belch came from far within the tomb.

Vertical framed parchment panels were lowered a couple of feet in front of the great facade, just leaving the portal in view. Behind these frames a line of small, stone grease-lamps were lit at the base of the slate foundation. Gradually, as people were enjoying a second or third cupful of ambrose, the glow of the lamps increased. They lit up the hides to a warm yellow.

The heron bone obeyed the lips and breath of its master, issuing tunes of joy. Dale, a dark-haired lad of nearly ten, knelt beside Jasper. He had a large cauldron, tightly skinned with a stretched seal hide, its centre painted with a birch-pitch roundel. Suspended from the braided belt on his hare-hide tunic was his drum beater, a shank of springy, dried tangle stalk. He took it in his right hand. In his left he held a mallard's wing. Kneeling at the bowl, he struck the tight skin with the tangle root. The drum boomed. As he struck again and whisked the feathered limb over the surface, the sound of waves and the crashing sea were summoned. The music began rousing the ancestor spirits from slumber.

From within the black void, Longo leaped. He was thin, ancient, naked and dark brown. This aged figure gyrated outside the tomb door, white bones painted on one leg and on the opposite arm. The fleshed arm sported a skeletal hand; the opposite side of Longo's face, a divided skull. Only one side of his pelvis was human flesh, the other white pigment. Alternate vertebrae were shown stemming up from it. Every other rib moved free of his disjointed vertebrae. They flowed around his chest with a life and death of their own. This ancient being leaped in the light and the music.

Shala gripped Gull's hand. Between them they pressed on the warm amber lump. It had never left her grip for a moment. It was becoming hers, part of her. She watched intently as Longo performed his 'Twixt Life and Spirit' dance, leaping behind the screen, casting vast, sharp shadows on to it. The assembly drew in sudden breath as his silhouette was projected forward at them. Jagged movements darted as a startling, spiky-haired figure took the opposite screen.

Other drums played. One skinned pot, with strings stretched across it, was rapidly twanged. As the dervish dancers leaped on, lads and lasses rhythmically rattled smaller drums with shells and nuts inside.

Suddenly complete silence reigned. The music stopped with one bang on Dale's drum. The figures vanished. The heron bone fell silent. The rattle drums stilled. The silhouettes vanished. Nobody moved. Only the blank screens glimmered gently. Tiny wisps of lamp smoke rose behind them. A woman's deep chant came from the dark terminals of each screen. They crouched like sheltering hares. They arose slowly, arms outstretching, every finger showing jet black. They inched towards each other as their chants grew like crying seals, eventually reaching the door to lie like basking selkies.

From high above, Longo dropped to the floor twixt the silenced seals... signalling hush. From behind the doorjamb he reached behind for a long, ornate stick. He leant on it.

Nothing stirred. Longo stood gazing at his congregation. He boomed, 'This is Longo's story. Listen and learn.' Those words hadn't altered for centuries, nor the rest he'd recite: they had been told and retold by generations of Longos.

'Before there was anything, there was *Nothing!*' he began.

'Then there was a Presence.' He pointed to all in his audience with his staff. 'Guman came down from the Stars.' His skeleton hand reached heavenwards. 'Tuman came from the Deep.' The half skull peered far down as his bony foot scraped the solid stone. His look described a place many leagues below. 'Guman and Tuman met in a great cavern.' The staff, clenched in a bone hand, arched to show the enormity of that cave. His voice boomed on every utterance. After each statement he paused. After every movement he waited. His flesh and bone remained stock still.

'Guman and Tuman fashioned a clay Man,' he yelled out mystically. Longo's bony, agile, frame walked round an imaginary figure and admired its many features. The congregation murmured appreciatively. Shala watched Longo's foot lift. His heel bone shifted, showing Longo's skeleton arch and toes.

He spun on this deceased foot. 'Guman and Tuman dried Clay

Man by their fire until he was hard,' he sang loudly, miming tapping gestures on the imaginary figure with his staff.

The audience repeated, 'Hard. Very hard.'

'Guman and Tuman drank ambrose in delight.' The onlookers sipped, nodding appreciation.

'Guman and Tuman slept for thirty days.' Longo made exaggerated snoring sounds.

'Guman and Tuman woke from their dreams.' The old man rubbed his eyes; a bone knuckle sank into the flesh eye, a flesh knuckle into skull.

'Guman and Tuman pissed on to their clay Man.' Longo peed on the ground where the imaginary figure stood. A yellow stream twinkled in the dim light. An arched shadow was cast briefly across a screen.

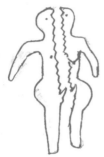

'The clay image of Man parted and softened.' Leaning on his staff, Longo gazed at the stone floor.

'One side was Man.... the other, Woman.'

Longo chanted, 'The man fell near the warm fire and felt desire stir in him.' He stroked his own skin and pulled his curly red pubic hair.

'The clay woman fell away from the fire and stayed cold.' Longo shivered in sympathy.

'Man went hard, and Woman stayed soft.' The ancient actor twirled on his heel.

'Hard Man felt Soft Woman. Man felt sad for Cold Woman. Hard Man lay next to her and mated inside Soft Woman, warming her.'

Longo paused. He stared at his riveted audience.

'Soft Woman woke. She felt life inside. She spoke to Man and called him Husband. Man's first word was 'Wife.' They danced by the fire.'

Behind the shadow screen two naked figures salsa'd as Longo chanted, 'Guman and Tuman were pleased. Guman and Tuman drank ambrose in delight. Guman and Tuman slumbered for two hundred and seventy seven days and nights,' recited Longo.

'Husband and Wife loved life. Husband and Wife embraced. Husband and Wife mated oft. Husband and Wife felt good.' Longo sang out.

'Guman and Tuman Woke from their slumber. Guman and Tuman heard Baby cry. Guman and Tuman shared ambrose with Husband and Wife. Husband and Wife sang to Guman and Tuman of their loving for each other and for Baby.'

Longo's listeners sang, 'Aaaa, aaaaah, baby.'

At Longo's bony-fingered signal, they ceased. 'Husband and Wife named baby LONGO!'

'Aaaaa, aaaaah, Longo. Aaaaa, aaaaah, Longo,' the chorus climaxed.

'Guman and Tuman went to other places. They made more images with different clays. They drank ambrose. They pissed on the figures. They liked what they did and saw.' Longo danced a dance of joy and creation on his drying sandstone flag. 'Guman went back to the Stars. Tuman returned to the Deep.'

He then screeched, 'I am Longo. Son of Man and Woman.' A brightly painted wooden screen dropped in front of him with a loud crack. He vanished abruptly.

Dale drummed briskly with his fingers to shrill blasts from the heron flute.

An echoing shout of, 'That was Longo's tale,' was yelled from deep within the Ancestors' House.

The remains of the fish stew were shared. The reddened crabs broken up and enjoyed.

'I want to learn drumming,' Flint confided to Shala. 'It's brilliant.' He wandered off and spoke to Dale, his older cousin. Dale happily showed many tricks. They tapped away together as the chatter and feasting continued.

Quernstone and Gull removed the large, empty bowl. Quernstone lifted the last cold scone, thinking, 'Reaper might like it. If no, it'll do for something.' Jasper held Shala and Juniper's hands. They wandered in the crowd, chatting. Juniper fiddled with the heron flute, wiping a glob of spit from it. Reaper and his mate Quartz put wood on the fire to smoulder gently. They adjusted the bones then placed a flagstone on three scorched rocks over the fuel.

That thick slab of level stone warmed and steamed gently. The fine blue smoke from the embers mixed with steamy vapours like rising gossamer. More ambrose appeared to disappear behind this veil through the Ancestors' portal.

The footlights behind the screens glowed. The air became expectant. Flint raised his tangle stalk. *Bang!* it went. He swept the gull's wing over the selkie hide. Jasper placed his lips on the flute, breathing shrill music into it. Their playing was soon accompanied by a rhythmic hum from the womenfolk; then a sonorous male dirge. Shala was wide-eyed, taking in every sound, every note. The amber in her fist warmed. The duo fell silent, the voices ceased. The steam cleared, leaving only pale blue smoky wisps.

Auroch horns resounded from within the Departed Ones' Hall, accompanied by a clatter of bones. In one leap, out from the entrance shot a younger, tall, red-painted man. No bones were painted on him. Instead his internal organs were shown in shades of grey and white and pale limestone yellows. He, fuller in body, was stronger looking: a dramatic sight. His right hand gripped a long, polished leather tube. He stepped forward. In the glow of the fire, Shala noticed his red hair. 'Mum, that's Partan,' she blurted.

'Shhhhh,' came Gull's reply.

'But Mum, it *is* Granddad.'

Gull looked down saying, 'Yes, we know. Rub your amber and watch.' Partan's role demanded fast heel spins and high splits. Shala saw the black entrance loom from beneath him. The leather tube remained gripped fast in his hand. He repeated the acrobatics many times. He juggled the tube from hand to hand. Sometimes in front, then behind, between his legs and over his shoulders. To Shala, he wasn't Granddad Partan any more. He became spirit, like Longo.

Partan ceased whirling abruptly. His scrotum swung still. He gazed with his wide eyes, whites glistening against the hematite greasepaint. His deep blue irises fixed those gathered before him. He knelt to reach

Longo's staff from the paved stage, his gaze keeping his audience anchored.

Partan began Karnal's story in deep, powerful tones. His agile feet spun as he gyrated. Each word projected to the audience in the time-honoured dance.

'Longo lived for 247 years and became dead.' He boomed and spun again. 'Karnal' removed the cap from the tube. He pulled out a long bone. It shone in the goose-fat lamplight. He leaped back onto the heated stone, dancing on his toes and heels.

From behind the screens, Longo's silhouette walked to and fro. At the word 'Dead,' Longo's shadow fell writhing to the floor and lay still. A final twitch and deep death rattle indicating his end. The audience bowed their heads in respect.

Karnal stood still on the slab, 'This is Longo's leg.' He waved the femur around for all to see. He tapped it with the staff. Clack, clack it went. 'Vulture took this sacred bone from him.'

A dark, swooping bird crossed the screens. The shadow-vulture ate Longo's thigh. It dragged his leg bone away and flew off with it. Squawking came from deep within the Ancestor House. Longo's venerated bone dropped loudly deep within.

'Longo was 94 years old. Guman and Tuman saw him in his cavern,' Karnal recited.

Longo's shadow arose and stood behind the parchment. Karnal leaped off the stone. Reaper's hand cast a dish of water on the heated slab. Steam rushed upwards. Two hazy figures emerged from the door to eternity. One hailed, 'I am Guman.' The other, 'I am Tuman.' They became shadow figures beside Longo.

Karnal continued the history, 'Guman and Tuman said to Longo, 'We made Man-Woman from clay. Man mated inside Woman. It was good.' The female Guman and the male Tuman silhouettes mimed the words. A shadow figure of Longo nodded at the images of his visitors. The yellow light accentuated his spiked hair. The congregation nodded.

Karnal jumped on to the steaming stone. The air was refreshing and different. Vapour hung mistily over his head. He smiled widely at his gathering; his teeth gleamed white, his tongue red. On his forehead, a pattern of vivid grey spirals: his brains. His red hair, bright as a cooked crab, gave him his name Partan, also meaning crab. This mat thinned in the middle. When he bowed the same grey spirals could be seen painted on his crown. Karnal's ochre blended beautifully with that tousled crop. His smile closed. Behind him the shadows continued their discourse.

Karnal spoke: 'Guman returned from the stars. Tuman rose from below the Earth. Together they made many clay images and pissed on them. They liked this... It was good... The figures split... making Man and Woman. Man mated in Woman. Guman and Tuman were truly happy... Many babes breathed.'

To Karnal's right, shadow images raised themselves behind the screens. Karnal peed into the fire. Steam, ash and sparks rose in another cloud, obscuring him in mist. The risen images behind him split in two and tumbled to the ground. Karnal stepped down in front of the glowing embers. He too became a silhouette against the firelight. He held Longo's femur and the staff up high. He lowered his arms, leaning towards his rapt onlookers. He bowed, pointing those totems closer to the folk. Some reached out to touch as they swayed past. Karnal's brain was clear for all to see.

In one elegant move, he straightened, reversed on to his hot platform and said, 'Guman and Tuman told Longo that there were many beings they had made from different clays.'

The audience repeated, 'Many beings made from different clays.'

'Guman and Tuman instructed Longo that he, the first born from Man and Woman, must wander and mate with the daughters of those from other clay beings.' Karnal said this slowly, deeply and deliberately. 'You Longo! Leave your home and mate within daughters of clay.'

That was Guman and Tuman's command. Partan had acted this role for some years. His understanding of the History was immense. In time he would become Longo, when Longo's present actor entered the Mansion of the Spirits.

Karnal stood again on the hot dais, forcing strange muscular movements on his left breast. There beat his painted heart. His great toes gripped the edges of the stone. An ember glowed.

'Guman and Tuman,' he sang in a high tone, 'told all the first sons of Clay Man and Woman to go and mix their clay blood. They must mate and multiply with the daughters of other clay women.'

Karnal's feet twitched, changing position. His movement seemed like dance, but the film of heat-protective ash and fat under his soles was virtually gone. He shifted to the cooler back of the stone. Karnal moistened his lips. His white teeth gleamed. Below his navel were twists of whites, greys, yellows, creams and greens, depicting his guts. A darker brown, outlined in black, described his liver. Just above his neatly groomed pelvic beard, pale yellow showed his bladder.

Karnal chanted on. 'Guman and Tuman say it is right for Men and Women to mix blood. It is bad if they do not. It is therefore forbidden that no more than two generations shall pass without this happening... This is Guman and Tuman's command and mating law.'

Karnal rested on his heels. The shadow pictures mimed every word and action, from left stage and to right. The lamps glowed ever brighter.

Karnal's last lines were delivered. 'Longo told Guman that he understood and would obey. Guman and Tuman returned to their domains. Longo left to make his first babe. His name was Karnal. That is I. I am he. I am Karnal,' he shouted, placing the bone of his father on his leg.

Partan, completing his role, released the remaining contents of his bladder into the ash and embers. Through the reek and steam, he took a final bow.

Shala fell asleep. Gull put her into a reed-woven hammock. The acts continued, illustrating endless history. Each generation represented eons. Race memories were being passed down by means of theatre, poetry, mime and music, along with song and chorus. The character of Jurt was still to perform and tell of Karnal's life.

The screens darkened. No light shone from behind them. Only a bright yellow glow, beaming from the tomb's entrance, faced the

clan. Flint and Dale watched a twisted straw carpet lower over the
doorway. It blocked the light. Only tiny chinks of brightness escaped
through its thick layers. This blind was ancient: straw strands fell as it
was raised to show the silhouette of Jurt.

Jurt's high voice screamed out, 'I am Jurt, daughter of Karnal. I will
tell you his story and then mine.' Her voice rose to a high, enveloping
pitch from the tunnel mouth. The space behind her echoed, enhancing the shrill tune her larynx played.

'I tell you of my father, Karnal. My mother was Nistor. My father
travelled to mate as Guman and Tuman told him. He mixed his blood
among many. Karnal found the great cavern. There my mother and
her sisters greeted him like others who passed among us. He shared
ambrose.

'Guman and Tuman came to Karnal and Nistor. They shared
ambrose too. Guman and Tuman announced, "We drank ambrose
with you. It is now for Man and Woman, Woman and Man: all the
bloods, waters and clays of human have been mixed by the milt of
Man and the grace of Woman."

'They turned to Nistor, saying, "Men have done Men's work." They
anointed Nistor with honey. They put feathers in her hair. They told
Nistor, "All knowledge of life is for you to hold. Your Daughters will
inherit that knowledge to guard forever."

'Guman and Tuman said, "We depart now. We shall remain only in
your memory and not return."'

Jurt moved forward. Her silhouette met the light. She was adorned
in feathers from lots of breeds of birds. They lay close, as though
perfectly preened. Candles shimmered. When she moved, that glow
was reflected. The colours of the many species took their place and
part on her: sea eagle, sandpiper, gannet, chaffinch and razorbill.
Puffin beaks ringed her neck; ducks' feet hung from her wrists; goose
feet covered her toes, shining and glistening.

Jurt's voice fell on her listeners, 'Guman and Tuman were seen no
more,' she repeated over and over. 'Guman and Tuman were seen
no more.'

Jurt recited on. 'Nistor, my mother, took the knowledge and became bird. She flew with Guman and Tuman as they parted from this world. "Mothers will see all," was the last ever heard from Guman and Tuman. Mother returned to the depths of her cavern. She mated with Karnal. I was born of that tryst.'

Jurt raised her winged arms. They shone with the dark shade of raven, the grey of goose, the black of auk. 'I, Jurt, grew and became Aiva. The Bird, who knows of land, sky and the depths of the waters: Our flocks soar and remember.'

Aiva turned, vanishing into the tomb. The straw mat descended.

Silence reigned. The Ancestor House was quiet. The entrance went pitch dark as the screen lifted. Quernstone swallowed to choke on a scone crumb. Another fell and lodged between her breasts. The tales were at an end for that night. Reaper handed her a draft of ambrose. Her choking ceased.

The throng of Lee Holme sang on as Shala slept in the comfy hammock.

Chapter 2

*

Spring Tides

Shala had grown. Partan stood tall in his finery. He'd hardly aged. The Telling Stone cast its shadow again at his feet. He began importantly. 'The size of the moon and the shadows from our Telling Stone inform us we will have an extra low tide this spring day.' All applauded the chief as his mace tapped the sacred monolith. 'This will be a great bonus for us.'

'I love low spring tides,' Shala thought, 'We always gather shellfish and catch spoots.' She put her arm round her mother's waist. 'How are you feeling?' She asked.

'Much better now, thanks dear. It was such a blow for me losing the twins. You have all been so good.'

Shala felt the lump in her throat as she recalled the sickness that took her little brothers.

'The first spoots of the year, though, always make me feel good. And I'm looking forward to oysters too. They lift the spirits,' Gull said quietly.

'Come on,' called Flint, grabbing a basket of smoothed rib-bones in one arm and gripping Juniper's hand. 'The tide's going out. let's go glean.'

'I'll get oysters, dear,' Jasper said, smiling at Gull, caressing his short red beard against her cheek.

'There you are, redshanks,' Shala thought, feeling comforted. Walking backwards, she spotted a small fountain of water spurt from the sands. 'A spoot,' she shouted, jabbing her rib-bone deep into the sand. 'Got you! That's stopped you diving.' She pushed her hand down the rib, grabbing the razor shell. 'A slow heave and out you come. Here, Mum, in your basket.'

'We are doing well, aren't we?' Gull commented later, jabbing down herself. 'Got one!' she exclaimed. Triumphal cries rang out everywhere. Gull stood watching her youngest for a moment, grateful how she'd grown. Shala threw another spoot in. The redshanks flew over, calling out shrilly, 'Teeeeeeeooooooo. Teeeeeeeooooooo.' They landed by the receding water's edge, searching out crustaceans. Shala watched them feeding as they coursed their zigzag search.

Partan, with Flint, Dale and Jasper, called Tangle's family. 'Quick, there's dozens here.' Tangle's brood skipped over. Heads down, creeping backwards, they hunted, stabbing their ribs deep into the giving sand.

Juniper sprinted to the west side of the bay to look for velvet crabs in the rocks and seaweed. She joined other girls gathering winkles. Cullen, the eldest, knocked limpets off the stones by swinging an old walking stick. Clack it went, striking a limpet. 'You've got to surprise them,' Cullen said, 'or they stick like ticks in your armpits.'

The Ancestor House looked down, watching over the bay. The sea eagles perched on top, drying their wings, as did cormorants on the cliffs.

As the tide receded to its lowest, Jasper and Partan went to the east side. There, large oyster rocks protruded from the seabed.

Shala's basket quickly filled. Her amber amulet dangled on a thong from her neck. The murky, translucent nodule had taken on a hue. 'I'm so weary,' Gull moaned. 'Let's carry this weighty burden back and rest.'

'Okay,' Shala agreed.

Reaching the boulder bank, Shala caressed her amber pendant, then finally confided. 'Mum, I'm always dreaming of the sea. Each night I wake up when everyone's snoring. It's like I'm coming from the edge of the sand with the redshanks. They speak to me in their shrill tee-ooh tones.'

They put down the basket and sat on a vast pebble. Gull asked, 'What do they tell you?'

'I don't know. They fly around me, or run ahead just as they do when I'm on my own down here. But in my dreams, I know they are talking to me.'

'Do you just hear them, or do you really listen?'

'Not exactly. Next time I'll concentrate.' They watched the tide beginning to turn. Pink sunlight rimming the bay's reflections; the redshanks combing the waterline; the beach harvesters return- ing laden. Half way up the sands, tied lines with baited hooks and flapping flounders stretched. Flint harpooned other flatfish in the shallows, and it was time for home.

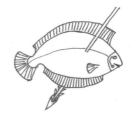

'That was the most memorable spring tide – a low ebb indeed!' remarked Gull.

Partan caught a lobster well beyond Oyster Rock. Juniper and the girls gathered huge scallops, letting their smaller ones free.

Later fires were lit on the beach; charcoals were fanned in the houses. Spoots slid from their shells in the heat, winkles simmered, and Gull had her oysters steamed. There was feasting to do. Most evenings there was singing and music in their house, but this night 'Tide Tales' were the essence. Folk gathered to listen. Their fire glowed as limpets cooked on their backs in the embers. A quick slurp from the shell, a wee chew, and they were gone.

Jasper began. 'One of my old grandfather's tales was of Farn. He told how he went to the distant rim of the sands. The tide was much further out than any had ever, ever seen. There he found a gigantic lobster, far bigger than Partan's. It lived in a chasm in weird black rocks. Its huge claws flailed at him, trying to crush his ankle and trap him. But he escaped. He prised the lobster out with his massive staff, smashing the rocks with boulders until he finally got the beast. Farn bent low, hauling the heavy old bugger out from its wrecked crevice. Its tail lashed and flashed, but Farn held on tight. Then he noticed the stones it hid in were strange. They weren't heavy: they smelt of old pines. Aged Farn carried the angry lobster home. He dragged some of those weird rocks back in his bag. He dried them by the hearth and, blow-me-down! They caught fire! Burning so hot that he cooked the mighty lobster over them. How's that for a story?'

Everyone remembered it, and different versions too. Cullen's was that it was a monumentally vast crab. Quartz claimed it was a huge whirling squid, but all met the same hot fate.

'My grandmother had loads of that rock,' Reaper added. 'She polished it and made beads. She's buried with them and a lobster shell necklace.'

'That's mad,' remarked Jasper, 'Farn lived a long, long way from here.'

'She had some,' he affirmed.

With that, Quernstone said, 'Time for bread and cockles.' Gull and Juniper got up to serve.

Dale stood, cup in hand. 'I sailed to one of the Far Isles with the Selkie Stalkers. We went way out on the sands, further than ordinary men tread. There, basking on a blackened, waterlogged tree trunk sticking out of the sand, was King Selkie. He stared at us, barking menacingly like an angry dog. His wives swam a little beyond the ebb. Other dead tree stumps stuck out. Selkies sat on them singing their shanty songs. The huge King barked violently again as the tide changed. It turned towards us as if commanded by that hulk of a seal. As we hurriedly left we saw a huge heap of great, blackened bones reaching up to the King's front flippers. He growled threats from the depths of his throat. The water rushed in, and his treasure was hidden again.' Dale cleared his throat for a long draft of beer. Licking his lips slowly, he continued. 'We ran. The sea returned, filling deep gullies in front of us. We were cut off! This was the King's doing. Finally, old Sea Guard, emerged from her hut by the dunes. She guided us shorewards. She knew the ways of the water, the seals and their King. When we reached higher sand, Sea Guard yelled, "Have any of you killed a seal?"

"'No" we answered. "We'd heard of their greatness and tested ourselves by getting as close as we could."

"'So you didn't hurt one? I need to know. Come with me," she yelled. We followed her to her house. It was stone, like ours, smaller but very tall. There were three floors. She took us up to the first floor with her clay hearth. She warmed cheese over a charcoal pot and dribbled honey on it for us seal men. As we ate from scallop shells and licked the warm honey, she went to her shelves to pull out something dark. Light streamed in from a lookout on to her old hands. She gripped a black bone and displayed it. "This is part of Kelp's treasure. He's the Selkie King, The Great Kelp. He watches his ancestors' bones when the tide takes the ocean away. My man took one. This one. He shouldn't have." She put the knuckle in our midst. "He never reached the tidemark. I wrested it from his dead, cold hand. The female seals sang, and King Kelp roared."

'Gill, leader of the Seal Stalkers, sniffed hard: We shifted awkwardly. "You will pull your boats in and sleep here," she ordered.

'We stayed a day and another night, learning lore of the seals. "There are even greater, more ferocious ones with huge tusks. They dwell in the far north, where ice stays all year," Sea Guard told us. "Only the very strongest and bravest of hunters can kill them. They are the giants who are made of ice themselves.'"

Dale took a final drink from his beer bowl. All eyes were on him. He burped, lowering his head for applause. As it came, he pushed his dark hair back. His contrasting white stripe in the long braids flopped to one side. The shell ring that pierced the top of his ear shone in the lamplight.

Gull asked Juniper to pass round more beer and Quernstone's famous scones. Shala helped. Dale tapped his drum; the sealskin reverberated. Jasper warmed oysters on a hot stone. The shells parted. Gull enjoyed what she craved.

sat in a darkened corner. She listened with the crowd to endless stories. She lived on the edge of the village. Her house backed on to the dune, sheltered from the ocean. She had been there for decades. Wrasse arrived when she married Gravel one midsummer solstice. Their first son was returned to her old home when he was twelve. Over the marshes to Tarmin he went. It was arranged that he would later share his bloodline with a lass from further north. They had to raise their family there. This had been chosen for them. New blood could then spread in Tarmin.

Gravel's effigy was in the Ancestor House. His spirit awaited its next passage. Wrasse was old, but as tough as the fish she was named after. Her low voice eventually crept from her throat, powered by that heaving breast of hers.

Wrasse's Tide Tale, the climactic one, was always heard with trembling attention. The words never changed. When the time came she stood, booming, 'The Fore Folk once lived and bred in a beautiful place.' Wrasse looked round, making certain she had all the attention. 'They had sea, sand, fresh water and bountiful hunting.' Her voice smashed the leisurely atmosphere; everyone became intent on her fixing gaze. 'They were like us, but we never knew them,' she called out. 'For so many, many turns of the sun, their hearts had huge happiness at Skara.' Her voice then became soft and as gentle as a sigh. All could hear her in their own silence. 'The land, the sky, the sea, the ebb and the flow brought them all their needs. They sang each day of their joy.'

Wrasse cleared her throat. In a vast voice, propelled from her depths, she declared, as always, 'Then from the Ocean came the Winter Auk. Winter Auk mustered his kind. Winter Auk strode past the Fore Folk up. Up. Up.' Wrasse drew fresh breath. 'The auroch beat their path too.'

Everyone in the house of Partan, Jasper and Gull chanted in chorus, 'And the auroch beat their path too. And the auroch beat their path.'

Wrasse's wet eyes glistened in the weaving lamplight. 'The Fore Folk looked to the waters from where the auks so unseasonally arrived. The redshanks flew from the shore as high tide was urged swiftly to low, then drawn to lower, and even lower.' The old woman shifted her heavy thighs and untucked a sweaty pleat of her skin skirt. Silent wind issued from her behind. Comfortable again, she continued. 'The Fore Folk wondered at the expanse of the rich seabed. A hidden larder afore them and one escaping behind.' She mopped an eye on a dry knuckle. 'The Fore Folk were caught by a seaward tempest as they chose baskets to gather ebb-fruit. Beasts of the depths appeared stranded. A luckless bounty.'

Wrasse's eyes glanced above to a horizon unseen. 'Gurnard was Auk Shaman. Vacar Auroch Shaman. They took the birds' and beasts' path high up to the Sight Stone on Harrar's Top. There, Gurnard and Vacar stayed. They watched their totem animals and birds pass further inland. They looked down low-wards to the sea as auk and auroch passed. The sucking breeze closed, whispering on their backs. 'Doom and despair to your people will be wrought this day,' that wind called Kull informed' The old dame's perspiring hand tugged a long, white lock in her dark hair as her voice rose tempestuously. 'As the wind sucks, so it blows. As waters fall, so they rise. As men harvest, so they are reaped!'

Wrasse stood like a vast, blackened cliff, her arms white like surf, as she beckoned her audience. She became Waret of The Water. Those in that room, watching, glanced behind themselves for salvation. Wrasse's powerful hands summoned the great wave in all their minds. It came crashing forward to them, as from a distant but terrible dream.

'The stricken Fore Folk,' Wrasse wailed, 'peered past the rocks and sands to a tumultuous cliff of tide. The billow raged. The sucking wind rose and grew. The men, women and children pulled to that mountainous wave by the vile moods of the changing air. Their bounty baskets emptied as they were dragged ever seawards. That rush of wind changed. Spray turned on them. Their baskets flew back at them. The rushing mountain screamed! A green and white firmament rose;

its feet swirling rocks; its shins shingle; its thighs tortured sand; its torso a turbulence of wrenched water; its shoulders solid retribution; its head, wild, white, rage; its breath, cold anger. Its pity, none,' she screamed. 'NONE!'

Wrasse drank deeply from a brose bowl. Her throat restored, her eyes bulging, she continued amid the silence of the clan. 'Only Gurnard and Vacar were left to witnesses the waste. Only they remained as Fore Folk. Their grief, bitter. Nothing was to be as it had been. The land before them became sodden ocean.

'Gurnard and Vacar called to the distant auks and aurochs. Their reply was, "When there's an ebb at Skara, there'll be skate on the Harrar Hill. Run, follow us! Catch the Geese!"'

'They looked down from the Sight Stone to a swirling pool of tormented sea. Skara was no more. Not silence, but a still, cold, quiet cocooned the throng.'

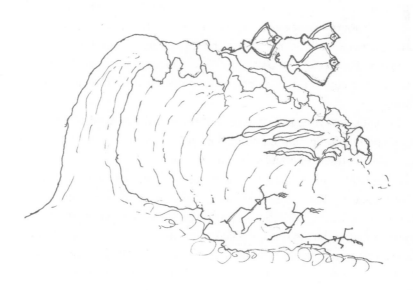

Chapter 3

Tee-Ooo's Tales

'I must go up to my bed. The eaves call me. I love my warm nook with sounds of sea and breeze. I know the rest of the legend: how Gurnard and Vacar left, searching for a new place far, far away, returning each year as a pair of geese to graze on the auroch-clipped grass, to sleep on the safety of the lochs and marshes.' Shala thought.

'I usually lower the hide flap to shut the world out. Tonight I'll leave it up and listen. The muted music's so atmospheric, a lovely backdrop to the other tales. I know I will slumber soon.'

Deep from within her head came the dream; slowly at first, then more clearly. The redshanks' legs were like crisscrossing sticks running, reflecting on the wet surface, their splayed feet leaving marks of their dance in the rippled sand. Red-scaled flashes splashed in the foam, their beaks feeding in frenzy as the birds gossiped.

'Tee-ooo, tee-ooo. Tee tee tee-oo oo,' Shala heard in her slumber. They flew in darts around her hair, then skipped up the beach and back. They glided to her feet for an instant. They circled her in a dance, tee-ooo-ing.

Within her dream she heard Gull's words. 'Listen, don't just hear. Listen.'

'I'm listening,' she dreamt. 'Your high-pitched notes are softening slowly. Are you humming? But you're growing, or am I shrinking? Now you jump to flight, but glide gracefully round me. Your shining eyes meet mine as I turn with you. I'm in your world. I hear you. Your clear voices are in my head. You're speaking from the inner depths to me. "Shala, Shala, Shala?" you are saying. "We, the redshanks, are leaving this shore. We, the redshanks, have news. We, the redshanks, know of the great forest."

'What forest?' Shala asked. 'Listen, listen, listen and dream on,' Gull's words assured her, as the tee-ooos swooped, saying in turn, 'The great forest of trees comes closer. We can eat the barnacles on them. We can suck the worms from their holes. We can ride the sea on their trunks. We can seek the shrimps delving in their cracks. We can ride the waves. We can meet our friends. We can gossip as the forest floats. It will come here. You will see.'

The dream was fading: just sounds of water lapping and a distant trill of the birds chattering far out to sea. 'Oh, do come back,' Shala pleaded as she drifted into a deeper sleep.

It was a dull day when Shala finally woke. Grey clouds obscured the sun. She washed her face in cool water from the large bowl by the door. Her hands rippled her mirror image in the still liquid. Outside there were no shadows; none either from the Telling Stone at the end of their courtyard. The tide was midway down. It was not a pleasant day for gathering sea fruit. The boys who'd set lines the evening before were bringing home strings of plaice and dabs. The sea eagles were digesting an early catch as cormorants sat tightly on rocky clefts. Some swallows flew back to Lee Home, the first of the spring. They circled the houses, approving nests of earlier years.

Shala took herself over the stony foreshore to the damp sand. Puffins flew from cliffs in flashing darts. There were no sounds, nor sight of her tee-ooos. Not one forked footprint. No running patterns of little birds to amuse her and keep her company on that driech midday. She only heard their words and voices in her head. 'We are going to the floating forest.'

Shala, bereft, sprinted back up the beach. She clutched her amber, making it hot. She ran up the stairway. Gull was reaching for dry reeds stored under their wide eaves. 'Mum, Mum,' she shouted. 'My dream, My tee-ooos. My redshanks. My friends. They've all gone!'

Gull took the reeds and squatted by the door. 'Sit, dear. Help me to split and plait these into thatch cord. What's all this about your redshanks, then, Shala?'

'I listened to my dream, as you suggested. They told me they were flying to the Floating Forest far out to sea. They are going to eat the barnacles, worms and shrimps that live on them. Where are they going to nest, Mum? What's a Floating Forest? Why have they gone?'

'These questions I can't answer, Shala. I didn't dream the dream, did I?'

'No, Mum.'

'But, Shala, you listened. When you dream again, you may hear more.'

'Okay,' she replied, thinking of what Gull had said. They spent much of that damp day together plaiting. Wrasse called by on a rare visit, chewing leather she was softening. Her teeth were worn from working hide that way.

Shala told Wrasse her dream. It reminded her how she'd dreamt of things that came only too true in Tarmin. 'That was all such a long time ago now. The autumn geese arriving, not in the usual arrowhead pattern, but in the shape of a man. I worked that one out,' she thought to herself privately.

Three days later Shala was on the beach again. She walked backwards and watched her footprints form from her heels to her toes. The lapping tide washed some away, leaving others clear and complete. The breeze came from behind. Her red hair fluttered in strands past her face. 'Tee-eee-ooooo. Tee-eee-ooooo,' she heard all around her suddenly. 'Tee tee-oooooooo.'

'You're back!' she said out loud as they crisscrossed her footprints with theirs.

The tee-ooos of the redshanks became distinct and ordered. Their sounds beat a tune in her head as the birds flitted close. The notes intensified as they whirled around her. They ran about her toes and piped their tunes up to her. The rhythm of their song sent pictures and patterns into her thoughts. Her mind listened. The birdsong changed into words that vibrated within her. 'We've returned to nest. We've come home to brood,' Shala heard. 'The forest is coming, bringing food.' The redshanks whirled away and returned. 'The forest is coming, so lots of wood,' the little birds shrieked together, vanishing seawards.

Shala walked to the west shore and climbed up the low cliff to the grassy top. Tiny bracken shoots showed through. Birch saplings had swelling buds. The cliff rose to its highest point further out towards the great sea. The land was quite narrow there, and the cliff edge swept back to show a rocky bay stretching further west. She saw boats from her village of Lee Holme hugging the shore. She  could make out Dale creeling. Seals lay on the rocks, others bobbed about in the waters, two of them close to Dale. The white flash in his dark hair showing him up. Partan's red crop was busy at the prow of the closest craft.

The High Hills, tall and dark, peered at her from across the distance. Their sombre shapes, like a sleeping giantess, dominated the view. Smoke drifted from houses and villages far into the distance. Shala thought about the tee-ooos' words that ran in her head. 'We've come back to nest. We've come home to brood.' She looked to sea and saw their dark, darting shapes speeding to her beach. They landed above high-water line to search the dunes. Their words, 'The forest is coming, bringing food. The forest is coming with lots of wood, to rebuild your nests too, maybe,' lodged in Shala's head.

She walked back to Lee Home. The bracken shoots gave way to primrose clumps. An early bee buried itself in a pollen-laden stamen. Another flew low on its route to its queen. The cliff edge lowered until it met the dunes that edged Shala's village. The grass growing there was perfect for basket making. She took her blade from her belt pouch and cut some. All the time the redshanks' words revolved in her head. 'I'll tell Mum when I get back. I'll let her know they are home to nest and their year is beginning.'

Chapter 4

*

Redshank Revelations

Shala found Gull by the stone tank set into the floor of the women's chamber. She'd given birth to her family there. It was screened from their living space by large upright flags. There was a narrow entrance, which led in turn to a store at the far end. There, the Ancestor House awnings and ceremonial tackle were kept.

The women's birthing chamber had a sacred atmosphere. It was built long before Partan's great grandparents were born, and was the oldest part of the house. Gull found it a fine place for meditation. Scented auk-oil lamps and a pot of glowing charcoal lit the aromatic space. The polished uprights glimmered, reflecting the clear, smoke-less flames.

'Mum,' interrupted Shala gently. 'My redshanks have spoken again, but not in a dream.'

'What have they said?' Gull asked seriously, removing herself from thoughts of her lost twins.

'They say a floating forest's coming. There will be lots of trees, bringing them food, and wood for us too. They've gone to nest in the shelter of the dunes. I'm so excited. I've never seen a floating forest.'

'Neither have I. None of us have. It could be so useful: new boats, firewood, rafters and beams. Are you sure it's coming?'

'Yes, Mum. I have to believe my friends.' Then she asked, 'Mum, are you all right?'

'I am really, dear. I was just remembering having the twins over our birthing tank. How Wrasse helped and cut the cords with her white knife. Do you remember Quernstone and her constant offers of baking? It all seems such a long time ago now, but when I am here, I remember them so well.'

'Yes, Mum. We all do, especially Dad, who kept the water warm. You were so happy that they were perfect. Quernstone pointed to her hare lip and then to the twins and said they were good babies, didn't she?' Shala consoled, wiping tears away.

'That's right, Shala. It smelled so wonderful in here with Juniper's steeped herbs. I don't think I'll have more children now. It will be up to you younger ones to find the right fathers for yours. That's where Wrasse's important. She knows all the bloodlines.'

Shala considered as Gull continued. 'Juniper will be going to the Learning Cott. She will understand more of Women's Law then. You will go later.'

'Would you like a drink, Mum?' Shala asked.

'Yes, please. But can you get it fresh from the spring please? I'd love to rinse my face too.'

Shala went to their source behind the house. It welled up gently in a stone tank just before the shingle bank. There was only a whisper of a ripple on the surface. It barely marred the reflection of the high sky. She knelt on the worn turf and edging stones to fill her sheepskin flask. Her tee-ooos called, 'Look down to the surface.' They flitted and vanished. Shala dipped the skin towards the pool, reflections of clouds and blue sky dispersing in tight ripples. A skein of geese was reflected on the water, changing formation. The images swirled above the fissure in the base of the cistern, where the rising water eddied. The shapes of the skeins were clear. One was a man flying in the air, the other, the usual arrow. 'I wonder if the geese will pour out into Mum's cup?' Shala thought.

They didn't. Not even into Gull's wide bowl for rinsing her face. Only the sound of the tee-ooos came to Shala as the liquid gushed.

Juniper ran in. 'That Wrasse woman is coming over. What does she want?'

'Well, just be polite, Juniper. Ask her in. You don't have to stay.'

'Good, because I don't like her. She's...'

'Juniper... Don't.'

Wrasse made her way past the great hearth to the chamber. She edged through the upright entrance stones, paying no attention to Juniper's attitude.

'We are just having spring water, Wrasse. Will that do you?'

'Thanks, Gull. Perfect,' she replied, taking a seat on a whale backbone.

'I'll get you the shiny black bowl. Here, Wrasse,' Shala said, handing her the cup. 'Ah, still no geese,' she commented as she watched it fill from the flask.

'Geese?' Wrasse asked.

'The ones reflected in the cistern.'

'But this isn't their time,' Wrasse stated.

'But,' Shala replied, 'I saw their reflections in the wellspring. I just wondered if they'd pour out into your cup? But no.'

Wrasse fell silent, peering into her drink. Then she asked carefully, 'How many geese?'

'Oh, lots. They divided either way from the crack in the bottom slate. They weren't the same, though. Although they seemed high up, it was as if one skein looked like a man, a hunter. In the other, all the geese looked like wee men.'

'Are you certain?' Wrasse demanded.

'Absolutely. Just as sure as how the tee-ooos tell me that there's a floating forest coming here from across the wide sea.'

Gull nodded to Wrasse. 'She told me that just a few moments ago, but never mentioned geese.'

'Well, Mum, you told me to listen to the tee-ooos in my dreams. Now I even hear them when I'm awake. And I see geese in the well too. I can't help it.'

'Men as flying geese?' Wrasse asked again. 'That was just like my dream from years gone.' Her face tightened. There were questions yet, but for another time...

As spring got warmer and the days longer, Shala asked, 'Mum, shall we go and get sea grass in the dune?'

'Why not?' Gull replied. 'I'd like to go over to Lille Sands too.'

'I'll get the sharp shells to cut the grass and baskets too,' Shala said.

They walked past the dune's foot towards the point. The sandy path was a favourite way for folk and sheep. The two paced pleasantly onward. Nesting birds warned shrilly, 'Don't tread in our nests.'

'Steer clear, Shala, or they'll mob us,' Gull warned as the sand slipped between their toes. The dune ended above the west beach where the track became earthy. Sheep dung spattered the cropped grass above the low cliff. On they ambled towards the point where the High Hills and open sea to the south and east could be seen. To the west were the lowlands and waterways. They clambered to the spine of the promontory and looked over its shoulder. Rocks stuck out from scattered gorse bushes. Sheep trails led them further along to a view over Lille Sands, the small sandy bay. 'Look Mum! There, stranded on the beach – two trees. And look there to the southwest. See, in the distance. It's a line of dark spars snaking towards us, weaving their way from the distant horizon. Are the tee-oooos' words coming true?'

They ran down to the beach through willow bushes and birch saplings. Huge pig-sized pebbles were strewn at the high-tide mark. 'The roots look vast,' Shala exclaimed as their toes dug into the sands. 'The bark's almost scraped off; the upper branches are gone. Only busted, worn joints jut from the trunks. There're the barnacles and tiny mussels my tee-oooos want,' she sang as she touched them. 'Look, Mum.'

She stroked the upturned roots and fondled their abraded ends. She traced those worn anchors back to the bole of the tree, where they joined the great mass like twisted limbs. 'There are still stones gripped in the roots. See, a lump of pink granite and a rounded quartz pebble.'

The redshanks flew past, scudding low across the water before landing on the larger tree.

'Wood for *your* nests, Shala.' they twittered clearly in her head.

'It's wonderful, Shala,' Gull exclaimed. 'It's just as you said. There's another trunk washing in. Listen to it grinding the sand.'

'Yes, Mum. More and more trees appear. Thud! Another. There's others crunching together over there. It's miraculous!'

'Quick, let's run back to Lee Holme and tell,' Gull urged. They sprinted to the dune path. There the soft sand slowed them. Gull needed rest. Shala ran on shouting, 'Floating forest! Trees, trees, trees.' She got to the village. Wrasse was in her doorway. She heard the news. Others gathered round. Shala's dad listened keenly. Dale, Flint and Partan appeared too. Gull caught up shouting. 'Wood! Wood! Wood! On Lille Sands,' she panted.

'Follow me,' Shala called. Everyone ran after her. 'There's one passing the point,' Shala yelled as folk charged up the dune path and others belted along the shore. Lille Sands was filling up with trunks as yet more glided past and into Lee Holme's bay. All knew what a bounty this was. 'I'm so thrilled.' Shala thought as she spurted on. Then she remembered their ancestral saying, 'Rising tides deliver as lowering ones take.' Keeping those trees here could be the real challenge.

All down the coast trees were arriving. Other villagers watched with wonder as they heard the grinding and thudding of wooden treasure on their shores. Stone axes were sharpened, and others begun. In Lee Holme the flurry of preparation started as soon as the wonder  had been absorbed. Tree upon tree grounded. High tide would be in little more than two hours.

Partan took control. 'Juniper, you and your friends go back to the village. Get all the ropes you can muster. There's plenty for thatching and net hauling. Get help. I want those ropes at high-tide mark.' Shala stood next to him as the bay filled with tide and more trees drifted towards the beach. 'Word's gone round that you predicted this, Shala. Is that true?' Partan asked.

'Yes, Granddad. Well, actually it was my friends, the redshanks. They told me.'

'Well done, redshanks,' he chirped.

Folk launched their boats and rowed out to the incoming fortune. 'We must get as much as we can as far up the shore as possible,' Partan explained. 'We can use the ropes to lash them, stopping them floating away as the tide lowers.'

'That won't be easy,' Shala added. 'Those lodged at Lille Sands are more likely to stay put. They can be roped to the huge boulders. It's the ones entering Lee Holme that could escape.'

The prevailing currents drove the floating forest round the point as Lille Sands filled. The sound of waves and grinding wood was powerful. Everybody was filled with intense excitement, especially Shala. Her redshanks flitted past. To and fro from the wooden harvest they went, intent on finding shellfish as the logs rolled in the surf. The first trees began to nudge their shore as they floated over the flat sands. The roots began grounding them. 'Tie the ropes to the tree-tops,' Partan yelled. 'Pull them round parallel to the shore. Be careful. Don't get crushed.' Men and boys went in up to their waists in the rising water. This tactic worked. The rolling trees were unpredictable, but lots got stranded higher than would have been as the tide rose. Further trees floated in, battering into the earlier arrivals. These newcomers pushed their leaders further in. Their rough, worn roots dug into the beach, lodging them tight until the rising water floated them up even more, to be grounded again in a higher, safer place. Nobody then worried if trees floated past Lee Holme. They might well land at a neighbour's, providing for new houses there too.

The tide rose to its full. 'The power of water is immense,' Partan told Shala.

'We must get organized, then,' she answered. The weight of wood in the sea broke the rhythm of the waves. Shala lunged forward into the briny, and Partan followed. 'Everyone,' she shouted at the top of her voice, 'wade in. Tie them together.'

'Follow me,' Flint screamed excitedly. His mates did, skipping over the stranded trunks, helping pass ties through and under them. Partan urged them on. 'We need as much wood up the beach as possible, before the tide slackens.' The weather was thankfully calm and bright.

Afternoon wore on, and the evening loomed. The redshanks circled around Shala. Wrasse watched the growing girl intently as she waded and clambered on to the stranding trees. Shala's bare feet felt the sharpness of the clumps of strange barnacles growing in fronds from the salt-soaked wood. Her tee-ooos tickled her toes as they pecked around them, filling their crops with the sea bounty. 'Eat before the waves rise,' she heard them say. 'Dine before destiny dashes them.' She saw them tease  out the fleshy insides with their deft red beaks as the tree they were on swung, bumping others before ploughing the fertile sand beneath. She leaped to another. It slewed. She ran along it as it too turned, rolling with the inexorable force of moon-dragged water. Screaming gulls descended on the tide-drawn forest, seeking nourishment too. Their noise drowned the voices of Shala's avian friends, who piped, 'Tonight we must huddle. Tonight we must nestle. We lay our eggs in the raging dark.'

The wooden mass got firmly stuck on the shingle. The trunks still floating and tied were perhaps safe. 'The trees in the ripples of the returning waters might drift off,' Partan shouted. 'All hands. Catch the ones that still float free. Lift the lighter ends over the stranded ones and lash them. This'll push their roots deep into the sand beneath, anchoring them fast.' His red hair bobbed about like a beacon. His tall, elderly shape took him on to the logs. 'Get the levers here,' he shouted up the beech, 'Hurry!' Shala repeated his commands. The mighty stone-shifting poles worked on their stranded brethren. 'Lever one floating trunk over a stranded one, tie it and pull it up.

Let the water work with you.' He and Shala went round encouraging
everyone. 'Pile them up and they'll stick fast in the sand.'

Sea and man do not always agree, however. The tide sagged. Everyone was weary, and the garnering ground to a halt. As Shala headed
back towards the smoky wisps issuing from the houses with Flint,
Juniper and Dale, she realised that her knees were bruised and her
fingers blistered.

Quernstone had been busy. Her baking rocks were warm: scones,
flatbread and suet cakes browned. Life's food was a continuous
procedure. Cured salmon and trout were taken from the high rafters;
riested mutton and ham too. Thick tranches were cut and beaten into
thin wafers, then rolled round soft cheeses. The salmon and trout
set on boards. Folk relaxed in the courtyard. From doorways baskets
of steaming morsels appeared. A warm breeze picked up and stirred
the ashes in their communal outdoor fireplace. There fuel glowed,
offering warmth in the shelter of Lee Holme's dwellings.

Wearied folk sat on stones or crouched around the fire. Juniper and
Flint fetched heavy flasks of beer. The sunset sky shone down as they
all arrived from the toil. Streaks of white cloud, like flights of swans
broke unnoticed from the eastern horizon. Shala's tee-ooos huddled
in their sandy nests in the dune. Talk and tales were the order of
the encroaching evening. Jasper and Partan discussed how to save
the timber, weighing the pros and cons of ways to raise the heavy,
sodden wood up the beach. Reaper joined in with his young nephew,
Rod. They hatched a plan. Shala listened. Her heart beat proudly as all
around her took on the responsibility of her predicted harvest.

A natural pause in the eating and drinking arrived. Dusk gave way to
moon and starlight. Partan sent Juniper to fetch his otter-skin cloak
from its hanger by his stone box-bed. The fur was smooth and firm. It
shone in the lamplight. The two mounted heads showed their bared
teeth. Black polished pebbles with painted circles replaced the stifled
eyes that once observed fish in dark waters, eels reaching from their
muddy lairs, and finally, the glint of a swiftly advancing spear.

Juniper draped the trophy over his shoulders. Gull stroked the tails;

together they arranged the feet around his arms and hips. The fire was raked. The embers reflected on shiny claws. Partan maintained his position as Jasper handed him his lance. He cleared his throat audibly, beginning, 'I want you all to know that we have had a memorable day,' before allowing a dramatic pause to enhance the villagers' awe. 'Shala foresaw a Forest on the Sea. She, bless her spirit, was right. Never before, even since the Fore Folk, have we seen such a miracle. These trees have been sent to us. We must keep hold of them. Just as the geese arrive and the mackerel, sillocks and courthes... these timbers have come. But they only come once, unlike our fish and game. We can build better, safer houses, make more boats and store fuel. We can split trunks for planks, hew troughs, make levers, bridges and roads into the marshes.'

Partan poked his lance-butt into the embers. Sparks spiralled upwards to be caught by a higher draught. They wafted to the west then died, ashen in the night air. Partan used his long spear to explain. 'We should use our luck. We can lever trees as the tide rises again. We can roll other logs up and over them.' A cool zephyr flicked the tails of his otter cloak as he spoke on. 'We will chop off some of the root stubs. We can align the beams parallel to each other and lever more up the shore. It will be hard, but not impossible.' His remarks met with loud applause and were toasted with ambrose.

Shala heard only the cheer. She'd slipped away to the beach. 'I think I'll go to my tee-oo friends. They'll be flitting on the trees in the moonlight for barnacles.'

As she arrived, they were twisting them off with their beaks. They spoke to her. 'See. We told you. See, we told you.'

Shala sang out, 'Thank you, thank you, tee-oos.'

'You're welcome. You're special,' they said in Shala's head. 'We will nestle again before the fast air flows.'

'Look, tee-oos, the moonlight reflection from the sea sets my amber glowing,' she said, straddling a trunk. 'Its soft warmth makes my heart leap with joy. Okay, tee-oos, fly off to your eggs and chatter away there. I can just see the wee shrimps hiding in the splinters.

Here too, where the branches have snapped. The wood glimmers as if it's a salty skin. I can feel it all the way down to its torn roots. I wonder where they all came from? It seems so solid in its stillness, stuck in the sand.'

A seal crooned as Shala clambered on to the bole of the straight pine. 'The clefts between the roots are darkened in shadow. There's still worn bark clinging between them. I can feel how the water has scoured around. I wonder what flowers grew round you? What birds nested in you? Where have you come from? How long have you been in the ocean? What put you there with all your family?

'Your crevices smell strongly of resin. I can just see glints of it shining in the moonlight's shadow. What's this I see, lodged and hiding there, glinting in the moon? It's a pearly white lozenge, like a shining teardrop. It's hard, crystalline, scratchy; no longer than a thumb joint. It's so tightly embedded, I'll use my bone knife.' Taking the knife from her belt pouch, she delved. 'The softened bark gives way. I see it better now. Just few more scrapes and I can wiggle it out. Wow! It's a broken arrow point. It sparkles like mistletoe in my palm. It's not even flaked like ours,' Shala realized. 'It's not our stone either. As I stroke it I hear distant wind in high trees, strange birds calling and the quiet tread of a large beast. I'll wrap this precious thing in suede and stow it carefully in my pouch.'

Chapter 5

*

Disaster

Shala returned. Menfolk joked by the courtyard fire. 'It's been a great day. Did you hear what Granddad said about you?' Gull asked by their door.

'No. I went and stroked the trees in thanks of them coming.'

'Here's a hug, Shala,' Jasper said, embracing her. 'Congratulations on bringing the trees, Shala. I'm just fetching a skin of my special brew for the men.'

'Thanks, Dad. I'm so tired, though. I'm going up steps to bed. Good-night each.'

Her head touched her bed end. She was deep asleep in moments. Much later the men doused the fire with their pee, pulled the logs apart and drifted off to their homes. Steam and exploding ash rose into the night to be caught in a finger of wind. Similar steam rose from other villages, and those tiny fingers joined, forming a waving hand. The hand began to close, slowly clenching to a fist.

Those swan skein clouds, portent of storm, sent their messengers ahead. Wisps of steam beckoned the easterly wrist, which came closer over the sea. The birds huddled in the dunes, protecting their eggs.

Seals sought sanctuary in the sea-lochs. Lobsters marched on the seabed to deeper water.

The windy arms reached out to the islands. Their knuckles banged on the portals of Lee Holme with mighty blasts. Ashes blew clear away. Embers, unperturbed by urine, rekindled. They churned skywards like a million stars. Some settled in thatch to smoulder. The moon had descended. Only stars gave light. Dune sand lifted into the night in a whistling cloud.

Partan woke, running from his curtained bed to the door. The gale's fist punched another hefty blow. The otters' teeth bared themselves on his shoulders. He ventured into the courtyard, only to be thrown aside. The force blew a great clart of seaweed at him. The windy fists struck again as Partan fell back. Jasper caught him. 'There's nothing we can do... The tempest is too strong,' he shouted, feeling the force push down his throat.

Jasper charged through the house. 'Juniper. Flint. Shala. Wake up! Into the Women's Room.'

In Dale's home, terror struck. In Quernstone and Reaper's too, as a fifth volley of punches hit. A pair of logs on the courtyard fire rolled together. Like drunken brothers they glowed in their own company. The wind their wine, the gusts their glory, the embers their story. Reaper saw the glaring glow. He held his lintel, waiting for the rising hurricane to abate. It didn't. Sparks flew high and dark. One, somewhat heavier, took a lower trajectory, lodging in Wrasse's reed roof.

Reaper retreated into his home. Taking two deerskins, he ran into the blasts. He was knocked sideways on to the fireplace. There he wrapped a log in a skin. The other blew away. The remaining glowing brand blazed. He wrenched his jacket off, wrapped its arms round his hands and grabbed that last log. He ran with it through the tempest to his own door, putting it safely on their fire inside. He shook ash and scorching charcoal from his torso.

The log in the deerskin burned. Jasper dashed out, meeting Dale with similar thoughts. Dale bounced in the gusts, getting there first. He struggled with the rekindling log. Jasper helped to smother it. The tempest rose again. They dragged the brand inside, where the draft was less. On their hearth it behaved.

Outside, the windy fingers of the storm phantom, ominously named Kull, clenched into fists, guided by powerful arms. His shoulders and torso followed from far below the dark horizon. The tide was turning. The wind quickened. Seaweed and sand flew. The livid ember in Wrasse's roof kindled, sinking fiery fangs deep into the  thatch. Fingers of wind teased, giving it flaming children to hold hands, rejoicing in wicked flame. The coal had caught just below Wrasse's gable. Her pride was the magnificent reed goose, wrought by her long-dead husband Gravel, that crowned it. It was his finishing touch to the thatch. The faded golden fronds were strung round a core of birch twigs, pegged firmly to the pitch of the roof. But now the famished flames plied the figurehead's plumage, ringing the bird's neck. The head drooped, and the gale tossed it aside to roll down and back across the thatch. The scorched head and blazing beak fell below the eaves. The hot, angry teeth bit deeper into the thick, dry thatch, and the roof was soon fully ablaze.

The body of the storm joined together out at sea. It gave extra strength to those pointing fingers. The feet of the tempest were dipped in the ocean, kicking, splashing. The moon made her circle of the heavens and began her tidal pull again.

Lee Holme knelt at the merciless fury of Kull. His corpse was rising after sombre sleep. Sometimes Kull yawned, stretched, farted and scratched. At times Kull sighed. He could also roll over, shouting in his slumber. This time he had been cursed in a dream and woke in rage. He'd endured that vile nightmare before. It left him fitful and angry. His powerful left arm punched out in wild tantrums.

Wrasse smelt smoke driving into her upper floor where she slept among memories and a wealth of old objects. Things she just couldn't bear to pass on or clear out. Clothes, shoes, hair ornaments, boxes of wool, Gravel's tools and all the bric-a-brac of a long life. Her children's toys, their first booties and drawings on beach stones. It was all there. Below were masses of slowly perishing nets and a store of old leather that she and Gravel had tanned together in the old, long-forgotten tank sunk into their floor at the back end of the house.

Wrasse charged down her ladder and ran to her door, but the wind was far too fierce. Bushes and reeds blew past. A coracle spun, crashing on to her doorway. Her neighbours were stuck in their dwellings. There was little chance of rescue as more debris blew against her door. She turned and fell over her wicker trunk of special shells, cursing her grazed shin.

Gull and Jasper levered up their huge threshold slab, blocking their door. So did those in other households. They just had to sit it out and hope in the strength of their tight masonry and reed roofs. Wrasse's house was dark, but she knew every inch. The sound of the fire increased and the first small glowing hole appeared. 'Doomed,' Wrasse thought, sure the house would be ablaze imminently, and she with it. She ran to the far end where she'd have a little time to dwell and pray. She could just see from the light of the glowing roof. She trod on the dried leather from her and Gravel's final tanning. She stamped her foot in anger and grief, stubbing her big toe on the stone slab that covered the tanning trough. The slab wobbled, and a dank smell rose from the pit.

Then, in the midst of her panic, Wrasse had an idea. 'I'll get down into our old cist and close the lid on myself. I'll either be broiled like a pig and make a fine supper, or survive.' She swept the mess of skins aside. Gravel's stone-shifting levers still lay on top of the slab, exactly where he's left them long ago, with the smoothing stones and hammers. She prised open the slab up and propped it. The pit had not quite dried out, and stank powerfully. Flames entered the house. The draughts they created sent them searching, suckling for food. The rafters were licked, and tasted good. Grool, the Spirit of Fire, was sating himself on Wrasse's home.

Wrasse stuffed mouldy pelts into her coffer and slipped in after them as the first sparks fell to the floor. Taking a final look at her burning house, she pulled one last skin and a hammer in over the edge of the cist, and knocked the prop away. The slab fell into place. She forced the hammer handle under the stone, raising it slightly for air. A blazing beam crashed down. She was entombed.

In Shala's home fear reigned. 'In all my years, I've never known such wind. I implore you, Kull,' Partan cried out, 'stop this tirade.' He knew it was futile.

Jasper, taking control, shouted, 'Rescue our precious things from above. The hurricane's increasing. If our roof blows away we can at least save them. This means clothes...'

He stopped under the tempest's roar. Juniper and Flint climbed the stair post. Shala shinned up another. Flint was back up there in a second, Juniper followed. Partan took the ladder. Fishing poles, nets, paddles, clothes and pots were shifted down. The lamps flickered, giving a glimmer to see by. 'Something heavy has hit our roof. The beams shudder. My screen's collapsed,' Shala yelled. Juniper's combs and collection of shiny shoes lay scattered in the turmoil. Flint's drum and  Jasper's flutes descended rapidly. A heavy hide box of ochre paints was carefully lowered. Piles of belongings lay in confused heaps on the flagstone floor. Gull tried to order them, but it was noisy and difficult. Juniper was scared, Flint and Shala too. They escaped to the room past the birthing chamber where the great Ancestor House awning was stored. Beams above creaked, but this was still the strongest part of the building. Partan wrapped his otter skin cloak round himself tightly, quaking at Kull's rage.

Flint took his little perforated pebble from his pouch. He blew across it, making sounds of whistling wind. Juniper tapped shells on her necklace. The music helped remove some of the fear. For a few moments the wind dropped. They played on until they heard the conflagration of Wrasse's house. Jasper went to the back wall, sniffing. Their reeds were tight on top of it. No light came through. 'Burning, burning,' he uttered, trembling should their house catch. Then came the rumbling, roaring vibrations through their stone floor.

Kull risen, flailed his arms in mighty rage, hurling the sea violently. Lee Holme Bay filled with cruel billows. The trees resting on the shore smashed together. Their thuds, deep rumbles, crashing and splintering were heard in every house.

Wrasse lay in her tomb. The earth and stone encasing her told her the story. The crashing of the seas; the huge rolling boulders of Lille Sands; the tumbling trunks from a distant land. She felt them all tossing like toys. Each thud vibrated through her. 'I'm glad I don't have animals in the blaze just above. The smell of burning swine isn't sweet.' The glowing beam above her heated the stone cap. Wrasse sensed it through the tiny gap she'd left. Scorching ash blew in, seeking refuge in the still of her catacomb.

In her constricted space she aggled her body to one side. Squashing up the side-slab, she dragged a skin from beneath her. By pulling her knees and her arse up, another was freed. She twisted again in utter darkness, her thighs pressed against the warming cover. Heat penetrated her garments; not hot enough to raise dough, but that could change. It did. A great swathe of burning thatch fell. The soft thud told Wrasse just what had happened. Fine threads of light, like minute red stars, floated in her cocoon. Some stung her sweaty nose and face. She jerked, bashing her forehead hard on the heating capstone. A curse, hotter than the smouldering beam, passed her drying lips.

Reaper saw the raging inferno. Quernstone was devastated. Rod and Dale knew there was nothing they could do for Wrasse. Her blazing roof was collapsing, wrenched by Kull's temper. Burning thatch carried to the hills. Gorse ignited then scrub. Pine trees sported flaming crowns. The Ancestor House high on the hill was silhouetted black and orange in the reflected flame of Grool's wicked light. Quernstone prayed for Wrasse's spirit, pleading to Kull's mercy. A futile act, but it helped her. The crashing of wood was heard over the roar of Kull's sport. His feet kicked deep in the sea. His splashing made clouds. His wet, windy hands washed waves under Lee Holme's garnered forest. With sand and seaweed, the far-travelled flotsam lifted, only to be hurled at the threshold of Jasper's door. Along the face of Lee Holme, a tree barricade crashed.

Like twigs, Kull delivered his heap. Water spewed through trunks, surging in as frothy spume. It ran through the courtyard and their doors. White foam flew as horizontal welts of rain pelted their dwellings. Dale's peering face, blasted with heavy drops, looked at Quernstone in silent pity. Another battering breaker swelled over the high water line, forcing the piled trees smack into the centre of the village. Their drenched progression ground them past the dwellings' walls, distorting their expert stone coursing. Eaves shifted and drooped. Long rafters lost their anchorage, sinking to floors on the seaward ends. The hurricane peeled Jasper and Reaper's roofs away in slow, suspended minutes.

Wrasse covered her sides with the deerskins against scorching cinders, inhaling hot fumes. She buried her face in the damp sludge over her tanning tank floor, only leaving her nostrils scope to inhale. The invading smoke rose to her crypt's ceiling. The only breathable air was at the very base. Wrasse took control. 'Inhale slowly, sparingly, counting five. Then to twenty-two as I exhale,' she told herself. The cool of the tanning sludge was a comfort, but the stench was intolerable. To soften the leather we tipped in piss, ash and dogshit. 'That's my sodden mattress now,' she thought. 'I'll cook like a slimy fish in here.'

Her guts rumbled. She blew off gruffly, recalling the ancient saying, 'Every young man loves the smell of his own farts.' Well, what about an old woman's? She giggled like a little girl at her fleeting triumph as her stink countered the pit's pong. Crash! Another beam hit the floor.

'Wind eases as rains begin.' Like tears over a mournful night, the persistent downpour began. Peering past Reaper's doorjambs, Rod

saw the glowing remains of Wrasse's home. The walls below the eaves
stood. Within them was a bed of fire. Towards Jasper and Gull's house
he could see invading piles of trees, dumped like butchered bones.
Paving was ripped up and strewn in disorder; sea foam, dirtied with
mud spray, blew into corners.

Wrasse realised with dread that the flag lid was heating up, and
tried to flatten herself away from it. Her air hole was blocking too,
forcing her to breathe more slowly. She remembered an old mantra
she used to hum. With no breath for humming, she imagined the low
notes, getting longer and deeper as they relaxed her mind. She felt
herself drifting into a black space far inside her body. She dreamed of
a dark yawning chasm, then oblivion.

Morning dawned, cold and grey. Lee Holme's scars showed. Huddled
in sheltered corners, folk consoled themselves. Partan climbed over
the smashed end of their house. Grim light streamed where it had not
shone before. He took his rescued goat's horn and shakily placed it to
his whitened lips. He blew a pathetic note. Anger at what he saw gave
him second wind. The next note erupted, violent as Kull's screaming
tempest. Waret, the Rain Spirit, whose deluge turned to heavy drizzle,
slept. Steam rose from the ashes of Wrasse's dead dwelling.

'I must look for Wrasse!' Shala burst out. She picked her way
through the tilting walls and sagging remains of their home. She
climbed the piles of trees heaped in the courtyard to Wrasse's ruin.
She heard blasts from Partan's goat horn, summoning everyone.
Slowly, the young, the old, the tired and shivering clambered over the
Kull-strewn trunks to his dwelling. The far end of his house was still
stable and sheltered. A small fire glowed in the damp air.

Partan spoke. 'Some must search for Wrasse's bones. Others will
begin stabilizing our roof remains here.' Quernstone burst into tears.

'I'll go,' Reaper said. Gull joined him. They went over to the hissing
timbers where Shala was searching. Blackened thatch, smouldering
and wet, covered the far end. 'She'll be here,' suggested Reaper. They
pulled at a charred beam. Sparks glowed. Drizzle spat. Shala's arm got
scorched. Sooty sludge streaked her ankles. 'We have to clear this,'

Shala said. 'The seaward end is burned out.' Through dunes of blown ash, shrunken by rain, they searched. Nothing resembled Wrasse's skeleton. Near the hearth, Reaper spotted two whitened shins and scorched ribs. 'That's not Wrasse. It's her bacon bones that hung in the rafters.' Shala told them. 'She's not dead. She must have escaped. She can't have died like that.'

Reaper cleared scorched thatch with a hayfork. The reeds rekindled, exposing collapsed rafters. Youthful Rod joined them, saying, 'I'll look for the old hag with you.' They levered beams from the mat of thatch. New fires ignited, even in the rain. 'If we shift these sheaves they'll burn out harmlessly over there. We might find her underneath?'

'Right,' Rod agreed.

'I'm sure we'll find her,' Shala said.

In that blackness below her floor, Wrasse dreamed. Through her deep sleep she ached. Her spirit felt trapped, bound in a cocoon. Her coffer, which had saved her from the fire, had become her trap. Through dreams she heard voices above. She smelled fresh fire. 'They're searching. For my bones?' Wrasse could have laughed, but alarm took hold in her stupor. It was like one of those terrible past dreams: the nightmare of being chased by an auroch. That dream where she could not move nor run, or call for help, always tormented her. The mighty beast thundered down on her until its bovine breath blew on to the nape of her neck. This was when she woke, terrified, never facing the beast.

The dragging of beams above pierced her dream state. Shala's 'Ouch!' when she got burned, muffled its way through the stone lid. Grunts of 'Reaper', and 'Silly loon, Rod,' drifted down. 'Like that terrible auroch dream,' Wrasse thought, 'I can't move a muscle or even call help.' She drifted into a state of conscious catalepsy. The fire was burning out. With her protruding leather and lever crushed, the roof of her living tomb had settled, leaving only the finest of fissures for breath. Face down she remained stuck and forlorn. Her bladder emptied. The hot pee stung her legs, adding to the slime beneath her. She coughed involuntarily. None above heard.

'There's no sign of Wrasse,' Gull sobbed to Partan. 'She must have been burned to ashes and blown away.' Partan sounded his horn. Work ceased.

Wrasse heard it from below her cinder-covered coffin. 'That's his bloody trumpet. He'll be telling everyone I'm dead now. Ignorant fool!'

'Together,' she heard, 'we shall make an effigy of Wrasse and place it in the Ancestor House along with Gravel's'.

Chapter 6

*

Rebuilding

Shala's home had lost half its roof. Waret sent clouds from the rim of the vast sea. Cold air seeped around Lee Holme as the Rain Spirit's new tears shed. Kull was tired and slept. Clouds gathered, casting their sodden baggage.

Partan blew his horn, summoning all to their house. He began. 'We in Lee Holme have suffered disaster. Only yesterday we rejoiced in fortune. Shala predicted a floating forest. It arrived. It's sad she hadn't foretold the wickedness of Kull's harsh breath.' Shala felt devastated by her grandfather's sentence.

'What?' she thought, 'I wasn't told of the storm.' She left immediately to wander aimlessly in the wreckage of Lee Holme.

'We've lost one of our elders, Wrasse.' He wrung his hands dramatically in the beating rain. 'Look at our broken houses, the blocked courtyard. Our village has never seen such wreckage.' All edged in under Partan's roof for what shelter they could get.

Shala reached the far side of the courtyard by climbing over the tumbled trees. Some rocked frighteningly. For consolation she fondled her amber and gripped the broken quartzite arrowhead. She couldn't hear Partan's words of solace.

'We can't blame Shala,' he continued, 'Maybe her bird friends didn't know the storm was coming. Even if she was told, would we have listened?' The gathering nodded at Partan's theatrical address.

Shala splashed through the downpour in her sodden reed shoes. For an instant she glanced downwards. Suddenly she saw the image she'd seen in the wellspring, but coming from a wet courtyard stone. Geese flew high in a forked skein; then more in the formation of a man. They passed. She blinked and stared amazed at the black, shiny flag. The vision vanished. Only rain fell, gliding away from the surface in minute wavelets.

Partan's speech became a rallying call. 'Lee Holme has to change. In the past we were many folk. We had large houses to hold our families. Look at us now.' All knew what he was getting at. 'Our bloodlines are too close. Guman and Tuman warn of this in our legends. We cannot much longer have families without our children being affected by inbreeding.' Shoulders slumped in the crowd, knowing what had to be said.

'It's time to decide... Do we rebuild Lee Holme? Or do we abandon and move to where we can find fresh life-blood for our children's veins?' He mopped his brow. 'I'm not speaking for myself. I'm old. My wife, Beeswax, is long dead. My son, Jasper, remains here. My other young left for different towns and villages. But even there, bloodlines are close. Too close for another generation of healthy humans.' Partan looked at Quernstone's face. He said nothing. Her enlarged eyes and strange lips attested to her family's inbreeding. Reaper's awkward gait and twist in his spine signified this too. All their children had failed.

Driving rain pooled on Wrasse's capstone. Water, cold as fish pee, seeped down the edges of her lidded grave. Wrasse's catalepsy endured. Her breath was low, rasping. Tiny bubbles bobbed from the sides, removing her vital air supply. The aged woman's mouth was forced shut by the pressure of her head, one nostril blocked with mire. The first runnels of water entered her ear, then her clear nostril. Her lungs working weakly.

Shala's grass cape was sopping. Each raindrop dripped in turn from her hem to the paving. She stood spellbound at the rectangular flag. The splashes cleared. She gazed through the film of water. A shimmering face slowly appeared: a young man. Was this a vision she had seen in a forgotten dream? 'He's looking up at me,' she thought, before a wicked gust punched the apparition away in violent ripples. The wind stopped, and the slab cleared.

'We live now,' Partan stressed, 'dwelling in modern times, but you must all ponder our plight. Think about yourselves and what you want for your future.' He paused, leaning meaningfully on his ornate staff. 'The one we've lost is the one we need. Wrasse knew all blood secrets of Lee Holm and around. Her young went wandering, taking her wisdom abroad.' Partan sighed. 'We don't know where.' After a silence, he continued. 'She and Gravel came here long ago to bring new blood. It hasn't been shared. Their children have families elsewhere. Where? We will probably never know.'

Wrasse felt her enclosed space flooding. Rainwater mixed with ash. It entered her right nostril. The pull of her weary lungs drew a drowning breath of ancient tanning residues and recent pee. She sneezed then choked. The tank's fumes stirred the bile of her stomach's pit. Windpipe and lungs convulsing, her bowels retched. Wrasse's eyes opened wide in the pitch dark of her cell. Water gushed in a torrent around her. Her life and death flashed before her.

Shala peered deeper at the watery stone. A new image had appeared: long dark hair with a white streak. The pebbly eyes riveted her. 'I'm drowning! Get me out now!' she heard from fierce, aged lips. 'She's in a tanning pit. I can smell it,' Shala immediately realized, bolting straight to Wrasse's home. In the grey light she found the coffer. 'Are you in there?' she shouted.

Wrasse spluttered back, choking on sludge, demanding, 'Yes! Get me out.'

'I'm trying to lever up the cover,' she called down, picking up an old hammer.

'Help!' Wrasse yelled again.

'I'm running home for it! I can't do it myself.'

All silently pondered the future. Reaper wanted to speak, but couldn't. Dale tapped his damp, tuneless drumskin. Its dull thud echoed Lee Holme's thoughts. The girls who'd knocked off the limpets mused about their place in the world. Flint glanced towards Rod. He was wringing out his straw hat, wondering if there were any honey cakes in Quernstone's larder. Quiet reigned.

'Wrasse! Wrasse! Wrasse!' screamed Shala, skating over the timbers. 'She's alive! I have found her.'

Gull leapt up, shouting, 'Where, Shala?'

'In her tanning pit. Drowning,' she gasped, clambering back over the trees straight to Wrasse's soaking sepulchre. Her struggling fingers tried desperately to release the solid slab. It was sucked in with the soaking leather. She welted it with a wet, charred log. It bounced back, sealing the stone tighter.

The men arrived. 'Get her out,' screamed Shala. Wrasse heard her voice amid the clamour above.

'I can't get a grip. Smash the thing, somebody,' Jasper demanded.

To Wrasse, the time seemed endless, like in her auroch dream. She faced that repeated nightmare, but could not finish it. She heard again the thundering hooves of the violent beast vibrate through the Orcadian stone and clay. It forced the young Wrasse to the cliff-edge. The enraged beast panted and snorted. 'This time I'll finish this cursed dream,' she told herself. The bull's arching horns encompassed her. 'I see myself in its piercing eyes, looking deeply into mine. He's inching forward. I'll step back. The turf's giving way. Heeeeeeeeelp!' she cried out in terror.

That shrill yell traversed the slate lid.

'I'm falling so slowly... There's nesting gannets, guillemots and puffins. A juniper bush, hawthorn, lichen, spume, the rocks...'

That's when Jasper gave the slab an almighty welt with a smoking rafter. Dale grabbed a pitchfork.

'I've hit bottom. But I'm alive swimming under the surf.'

Jasper's hefty swipe forced a web of fissures into the cap. Still dreaming, Wrasse watched a gigantic whale breach. 'I'll follow,' she told herself. With the power of the bull and the rising whale, she threw her back upwards. Another crashing blow from Jasper smashed the stone. Wrasse rose. Her wide bum arched. Her heavy spine burst through. A rocky shard blackened Dale's big toe.

The crowd watched astonished. She raised her head through rubble, growling furiously then collapsed suddenly to sink back into the quagmire.

Reaper and Quernstone, as everyone, stood shocked, silent. 'Help her,' Shala demanded. Eventually Quernstone and white-haired Reaper knelt. They gently shifted the dead weight of Wrasse's torso. The stones subsided around her. She was cold, heavy and still. Jasper and Partan heaved her by the armpits. She emerged. Her filthy head lolled. Her lips turned blue. Her tongue hung limp. Shala lurched forward. Rod stepped sideways, accidentally tripping her. She landed on Wrasse's back. Wrasse coughed, farting simultaneously. Wrasse's head moved, her eyes opened, she glimpsed the ruination around her. Breathing in, she laughed hysterically.

'I can't move,' Wrasse eventually commented.

'Careful now as we lift,' Jasper said.

Rod used his brain. 'Dale, let's get poles and leather from the Ancestor Awning for a stretcher.'

'First sensible thing that loon has ever said,' remarked Wrasse shakily.

'I'll come too,' Flint put in.

They scrambled over the litter of trees. Dale limped.

'I'll clean you up.' Shala said while mopping her face with her cape.

'Here we are,' Flint said moments later. 'We'll wind the hides round the poles. It'll work fine.'

'Lie still. We'll lift,' Gull said.

Quernstone, Reaper and Jasper moved Wrasse. Partan watched as though he was in charge. 'Hold the poles tight. Don't let them twist,' he said to the bearers.

'Juniper, help me cover her,' Shala asked. She agreed, even if she despised her.

'Up gently,' Partan instructed when they reached the log pile. 'Over now. Mind your feet,' he said. The rain pelted again. 'Don't slip,' he advised as he clambered over the trees. 'Take her down sideways, or else she could slip out,' their chief added hastily.

Wrasse's breathing eased as she was carried to Partan's hall. 'Get her under the roof remains. Fuel the fire.'

'I'll heat a bowl of water on the embers. Where's that flask?'

And how, Shala wondered, did Wrasse become like she is over the years?

Chapter 7

*

The Cleaning Of Wrasse

'I'm soaked to the skin,' Wrasse stated from the whalebone stool in the Women's Room.

'I'll put wood on the fire. We can certainly spare it,' Gull said. 'Shala, take that busted bowl and put embers in it to warm her back. Top up the brazier too with charcoal. There's some on the ox-shoulder shovel.'

'I don't take easily to pampering,' Wrasse complained.

'Well,' Shala stated, 'You'll just have to put up with it now.' She didn't know how those words tumbled from her, but they did. Wrasse could be fearsome indeed. Juniper looked askance.

'We'll have to take all your clothes off,' Gull explained. 'Your tunic's sopping and the suede shirt under it is drenched. Never mind the smells.' Wrasse grunted grudging approval.

The men were at Reaper's house assessing the damage. The roof posts were in place, but badly split. The house, like the others, sagged dangerously.

'Juniper, fetch Grandma's clothes coffer, the reed one you rescued last night.' Juniper complied. 'These will do fine,' Gull thought proudly. 'Here's her knotted grass blouse, a long skin skirt with stripped reed petticoat and flaxen socks. Hang them up, Juniper dear.'

Wrasse's garments loosened. Her sagging body revealed distorted tattoos of bright red, blue, yellow and green. Juniper giggled. Wrasse glanced at her. She froze. Shala soaked bog-cotton pads in warm water and began the clean-up.

Gull found her flask of beer-vinegar and egg-white hair wash. 'Juniper, would you do Wrasse's hair?'

'Yes, Mum. But please, don't let her look at me like I'm some turd.'

Wrasse grunted, amused still at the power of her glance. Shala began at her neck. The old woman's naked form, broad, gross and sagging, responded to the warm water. Small rivulets eroded the grime of months to reveal pale skin and her wrinkled tattoos.

Juniper rinsed Wrasse's matted hair from the crown down, washing away the vile muck from the tanning pit. Wrasse's head nodded weakly in approval.

Partan addressed their neighbours. 'We must make this home safe and cover the damaged end with the Ancestor House awning. All of us can then bide there while our other buildings are repaired. We can discuss our future too.'

Quernstone arrived with a bowl of oxtail stew and dumplings for Wrasse. She put her hand up in polite refusal. 'I'll eat when I am cleansed.' Quernstone put the bowl by the fire. The aroma wafted through the room, partially covering the stink of Wrasse's entombment.

Shala washed her tough, fat arms. 'Can I do her back now?'

'Okay,' Juniper whispered. 'I'll move round.' Wrasse sat stock still.

Shala doused her wide back with warm, scented water. The grime moved downwards, revealing a huge tattoo of a goose in flight, each feather picked out in black ochre. Behind its beak, a bearded human face looked upwards to her neck. Shala showed Juniper in silence.

'So, you've seen my goose?' Wrasse said. 'You watch. He'll fly.' She rolled her shoulders up and down whistling hollowly through her stumpy teeth like the wind in its feathers. The great bird's wings flapped as Wrasse's flesh heaved.

Gull swabbed Wrasse's wide face. Her broad wrinkled forehead revealed a tiny yellow ochre star tattooed just below her hairline.

'Her hair's so matted and tangled I'll have to do it from the ends up,' Juniper complained. After patient effort Wrasse's long streak of pure white hair emerged. Juniper combed it from her brow to the bottom of her neck. Wrasse closed her eyes. Gull dabbed her wrinkled cheeks.

The room warmed. Shala scraped more embers into the broken pot.

'I'll do your feet,' Quernstone said kindly, kneeling on a thin leather pillow. Wrasse stuck out her grubby left foot with its huge, horny toenails and eased it into a bowl of warm, fragrant water, sighing appreciatively.

'Excuse me, Wrasse, may I do your, er... front?' Gull asked. She then rinsed those once huge breasts that dangled like wrinkled kippers. The smell of stale skin spread in the atmosphere. With fresh cotton pads, Gull began the fronts of Wrasse's breasts. The moisture revealed faded colours in the lamplight: the left breast, pale yellow to white, the right yellow and red.

With eyes closed, Wrasse explained: 'My left showed the full moon, my right the sun. They were done before they grew. It was painful. Torture, in fact. That is when I learned my mantra to take my mind away from pain.' Wrasse sucked the aromatic air over her worn incisors and made the sound, 'Tssssseeeee.' She held it in her vast chest then let it out gradually, 'Hhhaaaarrrmmmm,' Her humming vibrated through the stonework and creaking timbers. The bowl of warming water rippled. The onlookers' spines tingled.

The long note faded, and Wrasse said, 'When these breasts were young, the sun and moon looked wonderful.' Her grooms were impressed. Gull began on Wrasse's portly belly, Quernstone, her other foot. Later Gull asked, 'Will you lean back?' She did, exposing her nethers, the old pubic hairs, thinning and grey. Gull washed as Shala hummed tunelessly. The sort of embarrassing hum someone knapping a stone tool might make when they're not sure where to strike.

On the inner sides of her legs, tattooed fish looked upwards. They were her namesakes, the wrasse, searching for a cleft, seeking a rocky haven in the cliff face; blue, green and red scales sparkled from her wobbling skin.

The granite pebble for the flag-lined birthing tank had been heated. The sisters rolled it on to a wet reed mat with an ox rib. They dragged it to the brink. Steam shot into the chamber as the boulder rolled in. Whale-oil lamps issued a misty glow.

Quernstone said, 'We'll help you to the seat over it, Wrasse.' Gull and she hoisted her by her sweat-free armpits. 'There you are,' Quernstone comforted her. 'We can wash your bum now.' The heat and steam engulfed her. Her old pores opened. Fresh sweat oozed from her skin. The salty liquid, like meltwaters from deep snow, cascaded from her shoulders.

Quernstone rubbed auk oil over her skin. Another hot, pink granite pebble rolled from a mat. The steam obscured Wrasse. She sat, eyes closed, the briny rivers running from her scalp over her eyelids.

Jasper spoke. 'Partan, We must round up the cattle and goats. The sheep will look after themselves and the pigs are safe in their pens.' The ducks waddled back and inspected the new puddles. 'Flint, come with me. Call Mutt to bring in the strays.' Their clever dog coursed the hills and herded scattered groups. Their heels got nipped if they didn't go just where she intended.

'Reaper, Dale, come with me. We'll get the awning out,' called Partan. They arrived eagerly outside Wrasse's washroom to face Gull.

'Partan?' she said. 'You can't come in here. We're bathing Wrasse. It will have to wait.'

'We need the Ancestors' House awnings,' he said, grinding his teeth.

Reaper added, 'We're setting them up over the ruined end of your house.'

'Well.,' Gull said, 'You'll have to be patient.' She glanced behind her into the sanctum, then looked back at the men. 'The awning rolls are way past the chamber. Wrasse is recovering. I don't want her disturbed.'

'Who's that? What do they want?' asked Wrasse wearily. Gull explained.

'I don't give an urchin's anus. If they can put up with me, I can with them,' she replied.

Gull turned to Partan. 'It's okay. Make a chain and pass the stuff.'

'Right. I'll get a team together. Thank you, Wrasse,' he said respectfully. He heard no answer.

Outside, the rain had ceased, the sun shone, and only a gentle drying breeze wafted.

'What is going to happen in Lee Holme now?' Wrasse asked. Quernstone braced herself.

'Partan says that because our bloodlines are too close we must decide if we stay here or move,' she replied, 'I'm afflicted. I understand. So does Reaper.'

Wrasse groaned. Her shoulders rose and dropped. Shala saw the gander flap again. 'I shall speak, when it is time,' she growled.

Partan ducked past Wrasse to the store behind the steam room. His team nervously entered. He passed scrolls of hide to Crane, she handed them to Fallow who in turn sent hers to Tangle. Quarts reached through the mist and Tangle passed her load to him.

Flint and Jasper returned with the goats. The kye were safely grazing, so they joined in the chain.

Another stone slid into the tank. Mutt sniffed at the doorjambs. She saw two great feet reaching towards her. Wrasse looked directly into the dog's eyes, transfixing them. Wrasse stared at her toes. Mutt followed that gaze. As though sheep stalking, she crept across the floor, pinned by Wrasse's glance. She inched forward to lick a wrinkled foot. The hard skin of ages softened, peeling away on Mutt's rough tongue. Wrasse smiled appreciatively. The bitch's agility found every crevice. It tickled terribly, but Wrasse grew accustomed to it. As Mutt slavered at her feet, the four nursemaids scraped her down with sheep-rib strigils. Her tattoos shone.

'Now the rumpus with the awnings is over and the dog's finished, can I have that stew, Quernstone?'

'Of course,' she replied eagerly.

'I knew you weren't dead.' Shala told Wrasse. 'I heard you and almost saw you commanding me to save you through a wet flag in the courtyard.' Wrasse stared at Shala as she explained, 'You broke another vision: a strange male from far off. His face formed in the ripples after the geese vanished.'

Wrasse's stare turned into a glare. Shala stopped.

Flint and Dale clambered in the damaged rafters. 'Tie the awning sheets over them,' Partan instructed. 'Tight, I say, and tighten them again.'

'It's all right, Partan. We know what to do,' Flint responded.

'Jasper, Quarts, organise the men to anchor them over the eaves. Weight them, wedge and tie them,' Partan stressed. 'That'll keep the weather off while we're rebuilding. After all, we've had the whole village in here for festivals and events. We'll cope.'

Evening came. Everyone brought food. 'I've got bannocks and matured cheeses from my underfloor cist,' Quernstone announced.

Flint sucked a goat's rib while Partan stood by a flickering reed lamp. 'People of Lee Holme,' he began. 'Have you considered our options? Do we rebuild our village, or do we move to where we can mix with new blood?'

Wrasse stood, banging a staff on the stone floor. Her new clothes shone in the light of a shell lamp. Her eye whites contrasted with her basalt irises. She drew breath. 'It is no use us moving.' She looked around. 'Where to?' She asked. 'How? Yes, our bloodlines here are far too close for safety. Shala and Juniper will not be able to have good children from anybody in this village now, nor the towns. The other girls, too.' She paused allowing this to register. There was plenty more to come.

'I came with Gravel to bring up our children here in Lee Holme.' She looked around her audience. 'See my white streak of hair?'

'Look at Dale; he has one too. His father, Quartz, is of my bloodline. You look all round our lands.' She turned her head as if peering into the distance. 'All of us are too close. In some way we are related. So I secretly sent my own children far away. There is only one other answer.' The folk of Lee Holme winced uncomfortably as she spelled it out, 'We need new men to mate with our women. Even if those women are already wed.'

The men looked shocked. The wives surprised.

'Shala,' Wrasse called. 'Stand up and tell of your visions.'

Shala felt embarrassed and worried.

'Go on,' Wrasse urged her kindly, giving a supportive glance. Shala held her amber amulet tight and stepped forward into the light. It shone on to her face; her lengthening reddened hair, in thin tight plaits, swung around her. She looked about the room, into the darkening places, catching folk's eyes. She'd watched Partan doing that.

'Someone is coming,' she announced. Everyone concentrated on Shala. Even Rod stopped scratching his scrotum.

'I have seen the signs. Twice now,' she added.

Partan looked straight into Shala's amber eyes. She turned, speaking to him, but still addressed everyone. 'I saw it in our wellspring. A skein of geese, and then others, flying in the shape of a man.' She paused. 'I have told only Wrasse and Mother of that vision.' Shala waited dramatically. Wrasse looked into her aura. 'I saw it again in a black slate in the courtyard. The geese flew in a skein and then in a man formation.' Shala allowed this to penetrate.' Then I saw *his* face in the slab.'

Everybody looked stunned.

'He has fair hair, yellow, like bere straw. He's got hazel eyes. He has a strong, kind look.'

'What happened then?' Partan demanded as Shala paused.

'He vanished. Wrasse blew him away. She appeared in the stone in his place.' All drew breath. She clutched the sharp quartz point,

'Wrasse shouted to me through the rain over that slab. "I'm drowning. Get me out," she yelled. That's when I ran to the old tanning pit where she was. That's how I knew where to take you.'

Shala waited for calm. 'I know he will come here: the one who I've seen. Others too. The amount of geese foretells it.'

Shala looked back at Wrasse. Her glance was returned.

* * *

'Good, you're back, Oiwa,' said his mother, Quill.

'Yes. Here's fish from the traps... and,' he added with distinct pride, 'the beaver.' It flashed through his mind how he'd watched the dark waters of its pool; the flight of his first arrow slipping below the water, then the second one he'd sent from his bow to intercept its underwater path. He visualised again how the flights slowly surfaced from the impenetrable dark of the deep. The final attempt it gave to reach its castle as it gave up its feelings for life. 'I've gutted it. Is North Star home yet?'

'No, Oiwa. Your father and brothers aren't back. Honey and Petal are getting cook-pits ready.' His two younger sisters arrived from behind the wigwam.

'Hello, Oiwa. Good hunt?' little Petal asked.

'Great, thanks. And I got a brace of partridges for Ripple.' He pointed to her tent on the other side of the circle, closer to their river. 'She's promised to cut me arrow flights with the wing feathers,' Oiwa added.

Returning geese flew in forks high overhead. 'Winter is ending,' Quill observed as those high fliers spotted a vast distant lake to descend upon. The evening air revealed its chilly fingers as North Star arrived back, leading Mica, Bark and Tine, Oiwa's three older brothers. They carried stretchers of caribou meat between them. Their tightly stitched leather clothing strained with the weight. The feathers, arranged in their sleeves and headbands, broke the line of their features, blending them with the undergrowth of the pine and mixed forests.

'Oiwa.' North Star greeted his young son with a hug. 'I see you've been hunting too.'

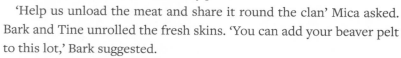

'Yes. Fish from the traps in The Dun – and your favourite, Dad, a beaver from Mirror Ponds.'

'Splendid. We can eat by the glow of the rising moon and listen to Geese fly past.'

'Help us unload the meat and share it round the clan' Mica asked. Bark and Tine unrolled the fresh skins. 'You can add your beaver pelt to this lot,' Bark suggested.

'Okay. I'm just going to skin it and remove the thigh bones.' With that, Oiwa knelt with his grey flint knife and eased the skin off his beaver. The bare body from within bore none of the grace of the former animal: just an elongated red corpse. He cut the bat of a tail free, then tackled the legs. His deft, practised movements of the knife stripped the flesh from thighs. 'Here, Honey,' he called to his sister, 'burn these two bones.'

'I will,' she answered, catching them from Oiwa's pitching hands. A blue jay gave its evening call.

'Here's a hunk of caribou,' Tine said to Honey. 'Cook that too.' She knew just what to do. Into the hot pit it went. She covered it with wet pine needles and stones. There it sizzled and poached.

Oiwa spitted his beaver and placed it over the hearth where its femurs blazed. The acrid smell wafted up over the tall pines. Oiwa uttered the old prayer in his mind. 'May your legs burn so your spirit can't chase me. May their smell strike fear in my animal foes. May your ashes blow and blind my pursuers. And may you nourish me so I'll hunt forever.' He pictured his brothers doing the same after their hunt, longing to join them one day. 'Honey, would you turn it for me? I'm going inside.'

Oiwa entered their wigwam, leaning his bow by his sleeping place among the floor furs.

'That bow of yours is very short, Oiwa,' said North Star.

'Aye, Dad. It works fine, though. I got you a lovely beaver with it. Honey's turning it on the spit now,' he replied.

'Ah,' Mica put in, doffing his feathered cap. 'You've grown. Before you come with us, you'll need a bow that fits, and longer arrows.'

Oiwa's eyes grew in amazement. 'I thought it would be ages before I could,' he replied to his tall brother. 'Can I borrow your axe to cut the wood tomorrow?'

'Yes, Oiwa, you can, but choose it carefully. It might take some while to find the right piece. It usually does, especially when you look too hard. And,' he suggested, 'we can knap some new arrowheads when you return.'

The geese gaggled high above as another skein flew over.

'Lets go out and look,' Bark suggested.

Tine agreed, 'We can think of our forefathers,' he said, leaning on the frames stretching the last winter furs and gazed up. 'How they followed them, I just don't know.'

'Oiwa, where's the North Star?'

'Up there, behind our tent. Dad always pitches ours in line with it when we return.'

'Yes, just testing,' said Tine.

'I'm going for a pee,' announced Oiwa. He wandered towards the North Star. The half moon was rising as he found their place. A small tributary of the Dun weaved through the new reed shoots. Oiwa stood on a rock and looked down to the dark pool. He fiddled awkwardly with his penis while getting it out from his buckskin leggings. 'Ouch!' He squeaked, catching his recent hairs. 'The urge has gone,' he acknowledged as he gazed down at the moon's reflection. The skeins flew too in the darkness of the pool. They separated and went in different directions. 'There's father's star,' he noticed leaning forward, 'now me reflected back. That's better, pee's coming. But my face has gone. Someone else's, someone I feel I know is there. Who is it?' he called to behind him. 'Odd, I'm quite alone. All gone. Now I'm pissing froth,' he remarked to himself.

* * *

'So, we rebuild.' Partan concluded. He went over to Shala. 'I'm so proud of you, dear. I so hope this is true. I do believe I can trust your vision. We can now wait, sure that someone is arriving, and others, perhaps. It gives us hope and purpose.' He leaned closer in the smoky light. 'I am so relieved we don't have to move.' He paused thoughtfully, adding, 'I hope I'm still living when this man arrives.'

Gull heard, and looked at Jasper's ageing father. 'You surely will be,' she encouraged.

Shala, gripping her broken arrow point while she spoke, then opened her palm. 'Can I see that?' Wrasse asked urgently, as she was stuffing it back into her pouch.

'I dug it out of one of the tree roots,' she said, passing it to her. Wrasse's dark eyes stared. She felt and stroked it. She put it to her lips, kissed it then handed it back.

'Keep it safe. It might be useful one day,' Wrasse said seriously. Then her voice lightened as she asked, 'Would you bring Gull to me? She's with Quernstone, excited about the future.'

'Mum, Wrasse wants you.'

'I'll be right over.'

Wrasse sat on a leather bolster, Gull perched next to her and Shala stood. She felt taller and much different. 'Gull?' Wrasse asked. 'If I'm staying here, and, thank you, by the way, I want Shala to be my attendant.' Shala's eyebrows rose as she stared at Wrasse.

'Juniper's older,' Gull suggested.

'No, Shala's fine.'' Wrasse demanded.

'Very well. Yes. We can give you the room above the Women's Chamber. But can you manage the ladder?'

Wrasse held her hand up. 'That ladder's fine. My only request is for you to make a hatch in the roof so I can look out.'

'We can see to that, Wrasse.' Gull agreed happily.

'I'm grateful,' she said, relaxing a little. 'It's been such a long day. I'm weary,' she admitted as she rose to go outside. The sky was clear and the stars reflected in the damp stones of the littered courtyard. Her old house still smouldered. She uncovered a huge pottery vat under the eaves and peed, then replaced the reed mat over the toilet. She adjusted her clothes, returned inside to the foot of the ladder then climbed slowly to her new room.

Everyone chatted on. Beer and ambrose were shared. Wrasse snored deeply. The eventful day ended. New bed places in cramped spaces would be shared. There were no thoughts of mating that night, or for some time after.

'Now it is a new day,' Partan importantly addressed his general council, which consisted mostly of those who would listen and agree. 'We must redesign and rebuild. We have had problems with rainwater from the roofs. We must make better drains to cope with that. Our eaves seem to be too low. We need higher walls to prevent this. Then we can pile extra firewood beneath them, have better outside work-places and store drying pots and the like.'

'That sounds worth working for,' put in Quartz encouragingly. 'After all, we have a new future to look forward to.'

'As Chief of the Council, I will make myself responsible for the over-all organisation. For example, all the old, damaged thatch has to be stored carefully. We can use it to fire pots. We have new reeds stacked, but we have to allocate our growing reedbeds to certain uses. It was Hornfisk, Gurnard's father, who built the last house here. Now we have to think about the whole village. Hornfisk's walls were measured up from his heels to the fingertip of his right hand. The footings of the walls were from his left shoulder to his other arm's forefinger. The thickness of the tops of his walls were from his thumb tip to his armpit. His house was very well measured. The heights of his roof, he calculated using the staffs he had made to keep the measurements. If you all agree, we can make new rods and staffs from my arms, legs, feet and thumbs. With these we can modify all our houses to the same scale. Then when we do get a new, growing population, we can forever plan houses with the same proportions. We have huge trees for posts and, after all, I am the tallest in Lee Holme.'

Shala heard all this from her new place beside Wrasse, who slept deeply. The toilet pots had been emptied on to the ash heap by the dunes and covered with sand. The daily round of work had to be done, despite all the damage.

Later that afternoon Sable, from Char, walked down the brae to Lee Holme. She brought her four-year-old son, Sprig. She wanted to see Wrasse. Gull met her instead. 'How are you all?' Sable asked.

'Okay,' replied Gull, 'but damaged: And you at Char?'

'Much the same,' Sable replied.

'Come to Quernstone's. She's got refreshing warm rowanberry juice from last autumn.' Sable admired the litter of logs. Gull said, 'Shala foretold the arrival of the wood, but she didn't know about the storm.'

'Ahhhhhch well!' Sable said, 'It's an ill wind.'

They nodded in agreement at the old saying.

'How are you all coping?'

'We discussed the future and decided to rebuild here. We talked frankly about breeding. There may be an answer, but it's too early to say. Come in. I'll tell you what happened to Wrasse.' They sipped the cordial thoughtfully. Gull added, 'I think Wrasse will change and become closer to us now.'

'It's time for that, indeed. She has great wisdom.'

Wrasse opened an eye and saw the inside of the awning gently flapping. She lay on a split birch bed. On that was a thick straw mattress in a reedwork casing. 'I hate comfort and fuss,' Wrasse acknowledged to herself. 'And folk with inane chatter. Of course,' she reflected, 'I've now been dragged from peril into plenty. I'll maybe now have to learn to put up with it.'

Shala had been up long before, cutting strips of cold smoked mutton, warming them with sorrel over a pot in a sieve. 'Maybe this and a cup of well water will be a fine late breakfast for Wrasse – sharp and tough,' she thought.

Wrasse rose and scratched. Shala passed her a string-handled pot to pee in. She lowered the contents below to be taken away later.

Wrasse chewed her breakfast, dwelling momentarily on her now burnt mutton in her old home. 'All I had is now ashes, apart from memories. They are clear as the water I'm sipping. Shala, come here.'

Shala sat on a small suede cushion next to the old woman. Wrasse lay in bed on her side. It creaked as she moved. 'I need you to be with me because I can tell you things. First, Shala, I want to change your name.'

'What?' Shala said in surprise.

'Shala is a child's name,' Wrasse said quietly. 'You do not have a child's head on you.' Shala looked away. 'Look at me,' Wrasse demanded. She glanced unsteadily back. 'Shala is what you are used to, but your real name should be Aiva. The Bird's Spirit.' Shala continued looking into Wrasse's hypnotic eyes. 'You, my girl, have a bird's affinity. You can hear what they say, can't you?' Shala nodded very slightly in agreement. 'Can you speak back to them?'

'I don't know. I've not tried.'

'Well, never mind that for the moment.' Wrasse said.

'Wrasse? Would you leave my name as it is, please? I'm not ready yet.'

'Well, for the time being.'

'Thank you,' Shala said, relaxing slightly.

'"Tell me all about your Geese visions.'

Shala did with passion.

'Have geese ever spoken to you?'

'No."

'Did the man in the stone speak?'

'No. But, he was just about to move his lips when you looked at me from the pit and pushed him away in the ripples.'

'Oh, pardon me,' Wrasse returned. 'I was only trying to save myself. Well, my spirit was.' She thought momentarily. 'He may look at you again. Possibly within a dream, Shala.'

'You have a lot of questions, don't you, Wrasse?'

'Yes, I do. Important ones, and there could be more.'

Shala drank warm honey water. She took a hard-boiled duck egg from the steam pot, shelled it, mashed it up in her bowl with her stone knife and mixed salted butter with it, then rolled it in a cold pancake. 'Do you want some, Wrasse?' she asked.

'No thanks, the mutton's fine,' Wrasse answered, sucking her teeth.

'I have a question for you, Wrasse.'

'Go on.'

Shala paused, gathering courage. 'Why have you got a goose tattoo?'

Wrasse shifted, blinking uncomfortably. 'The whole story?'

Shala nodded, noting Wrasse's gravity.

'Then I shall tell you, but whole stories are not always pleasant. Let me sip my water first... When I was a little older than you, I became aware that someone was travelling from afar over the sea to Orkney. How that happened, I didn't initially know. It was when the geese were flying in it became clearer. Come closer, Shala.'

She obeyed, leaning against her bed, sniffing the sharpness of the sorrel and scented ewe meat.

'Every day I went to the shore, waiting as the geese returned. Sometimes they flew past strangely low. Their skeins became fewer and fewer. One day there were none. I waited all that day. As evening began descending, I saw a final skein flying very low indeed over the cliff at the edge of our bay. This skein behaved so oddly. It came near to our shore, then circled, returning to sea. I called my sisters who came to look. As the geese returned, rounding the cliff a flight of swans joined them. We had never seen the like. The birds made an enormous noise. Then, slewing sideways round  the cliff, a small boat appeared. It was nothing like one of ours... I'll have to stop.'

She gulped, drawing breath at the memory, before continuing. 'The tide swung the craft past the cliff's foaming teeth. I have to stop, Shala. Forgive me a moment,' she interrupted herself, 'It righted, and the cliff-top birds swooped down over it. I shouted to my sisters to run up to our nousts and haul down a boat. The clamour brought the whole village out. More boats went scuttling down the stony slope and into the surf. My father waded in, pushing his dingy. I paddled out with my sisters. We were the first to reach the strange canoe washing in. We saw slime from the sea and barnacles clustering astern. A wave brought the craft closer. A terrible stench hit us. Mire, my oldest sister, cast our weighted rope to the boat; the stone on its end caught. We pulled it close. That rotting stink intensified.'

Wrasse relived that whole experience, remembering her breasts were fuller then. The sun and moon stretched widely behind her blouse; the wrasse between her legs searched for their noust, never quite reaching that sacred cleft.

Shala shifted and handed her the black cup of water. 'Thank you,' Wrasse nodded, heaving her flat bosom and drawing a long breath. 'The birds glided around us as though they were in frenzy. The geese flew higher, circling. I was the first to look into the boat. A hide covered most of the craft. I expected to see a rotting body beneath. Instead... Instead, I was looking into the face of a hooded man. He stared at me over his tangled beard, past the sagging trim. Our boats bumped. He winced painfully. His straw hair lay over his forehead. His hazel eyes fixed mine in a look of waking agony. His jaw clenched and that fearful smell rose.'

Shala looked long at Wrasse, whose voice softened. Only Shala heard. This story was for her alone. Wrasse, who had dwelt in Lee Holme seemingly forever, talked at last. Everyone knew about Gravel, Shala remembered. Wrasse's children, her life. How Gravel died long before I was born, lost in a seal hunt. A bull seal, hiding in a cleft, charged him. The men with him fled. He slipped, falling backwards, cracking his head open on sharp, limpet-covered rocks. A wave took his body, floating it past his comrades to where it got caught in a tidal current and drifted to sea. Pink foam washing the rocks. Brain sliding from the points of limpet shells.

'We towed his hide canoe ashore,' Wrasse suddenly continued. 'We carried it with him inside to our house. It was extremely slippery from being afloat for a very long time. Many hands helped. The geese landed noisily on the loch below our House of Souls. We pulled the canoe through our door, tilting the craft slightly. We got lamps and looked into the boat. The rotting stench rose.' Wrasse wheezed and heaved at the memory.

'I saw his right arm. He was just conscious; he glanced at it too. The bone on his forearm showed through the skin and flesh. Yellow pus oozed from the fetid limb. It was horrible, Shala. Mire threw up. I held myself together. Mother, horror-struck, ran for Coutou. She had been helping with a difficult birth up at Crest and had just returned; they ran back to our house.

'Coutou looked closely at the boatman. "He's not dead yet, but then again, not far off. My knives are warm from slitting that girl to deliver her boy. Get a bed ready by the fire where I can see." Wrasse coughed nervously, then spoke on. 'Coutou told us to grab a foot and a leg each. Dad held his head and I slid my hands under his good shoulder; Coutou supported his right injured arm and shoulder too. "Hold the canoe still and lift," Coutou said. We lifted as if we were one. He gritted his teeth as we lowered him on to a firm leather mattress. He moaned and fell into unconsciousness.'

Wrasse began to pant. She felt the memory of her young body fill her old sagging one as she relived those moments. Shala waited for Wrasse to continue. Her breath eased. 'Coutou raised his withered hand. At his elbow there were several cuts. "The sinews are severed," she said.'

Wrasse paused for several long breaths. Shala remained silent. Slowly she began her story again. 'Coutou sighed and shook her head. The smell worsened, pus ran from his forearm; well, what was left of it. Coutou looked round at us all, saying in slow amazement, "He's tried to cut his own arm off." We were all shocked and confused.' Wrasse closed her eyes, seeing it all just as it was decades ago. Then she resumed.

'"Right," Coutou commanded.' Shala jumped at the sudden change in Wrasse's voice. '"I will need hot water. I want the clay room-heater loaded with the best charcoal. Get me as much dried meadowsweet as possible – and fresh moss. I want gut cord to stop his blood. I want apple vinegar in my water to wash the knives. Find me a flint blade core. I have one somewhere in my bag, but it's nearly done."

'We were totally in her command,' Wrasse reported. 'Even *he* seemed to relax. Coutou put her hand on his forehead; it came away shining with sticky sweat. She washed her hands and told my mum to cut his coat and vests off. As she cut the seams with her jasper blade, my father eased his skins away. I remember the sinews popping as she cut. There was a big bruise in his ribs under his right arm. This had yellowed with time and the broken ribs beneath had grown back together. He'd been injured for weeks, Shala.'

Wrasse put her hand out for a sip of water. Shala shaking, handed her a brimming cup. Some spilt as it passed from hand to hand. Wrasse drank.

'"First," Coutou said, "we'll finish the job he began." She took her grey flint knife. Its blade was polished for a cleaner cut. Coutou raised his arm gently. She asked for some rosemary fronds. Someone ran outside to pick a bunch. She told me to push his hand down slowly. I could barely look, but I did it. The smell was horrid, Shala, but I had to put it to the back of me. Coutou placed the knife at the bare bones of his elbow and cut the sinew. She pulled his arm towards her and with a sharper tawny flint blade, parted his blackened flesh. Fetid, clotted blood oozed from his veins. My father tightened the loop of gut round his upper arm.'

Wrasse sighed, and sipped her water. 'Coutou pressed some long blades from the flint core and put the razors on a broken potshard. She placed it over the charcoal brazier and blew. Sparks appeared, slowly the broken bit of pot heated dull red. The black flint flakes gradually turned grey, then, just as they were becoming white she took the crock off. They cooled slowly. She took the first fresh blade. It slid through his flesh easily. With just a few expert movements and twists, the man's forearm lifted free.'

Shala wiped her own brow with the back of her hand.

'Coutou said to him, although he couldn't hear, "That is done, Sea Angel. Now for the rest." She gently placed his limb on the fire. It hissed as it burned. The terrible stench eased. "He won't have felt a thing," Coutou said. "It's the next bit I'm bothered about."

'He slept. Coutou went to her house. She told me to watch him and sing softly. We all hummed and crooned. Dad played his flute so softly. The Sea Angel's face relaxed into a deep slumber.

'Coutou returned with her medicine cup and spoon. She had so many different things in her house. She brought a soft skin pouch of dried leaves and flower heads. She crushed them in her mortar with a pebble and mixed a little hot honey. She stirred and poured this into her medicine cup. It smelt pungent yet sweet. She washed the mortar with hot water and rinsed that in too. She stirred with her mussel shell spoon. "Wrasse." she asked, 'lift his head. I will open his jaw; that is if it will still open." She sighed with relief as she eased his teeth apart. I saw his tongue, Shala. It was white, blotchy, and ulcerated. His lips were scabby and his teeth seemed loose. I stroked his hair back from his forehead and saw his star tattoo, just at his hairline.'

Shala could see how much all this meant to Wrasse. 'Go on,' she urged quietly.

Wrasse sipped again. 'My sisters made up verses: *Sleep, sleep, sleep, Sleep deeply, our Sea Angel, Sleep deeply and rise for us, Rise when you are well.*

'It was a very soft song. I can hear it now. Coutou spooned her brew slowly into his mouth. He choked a little and his eyes opened. He looked at mine. I smiled at him. He tried to smile too. *Later*, I thought and hoped. Coutou slowly administered the draft. The Sea Angel swallowed gradually. Coutou kept on spooning from the shell until he fell deeply asleep.

'"We must wait." Coutou said. "Now I know you won't really want to do this, but you have to cut the rest of his clothes off." They giggled. I shivered. "You must gently wash whilst my draught takes effect. The washing will soothe him. Build the fires up and bring another brazier and more charcoal. He must keep warm while I cut his arm further. I also want to see if he has further injuries."

'Coutou looked at the wound under his upper arm. "He's been stabbed; looks like an antler tip. Never mind, it is healing and not oozing."

'I watched as his leather seafarer's breeks were cut down the seams to his feet. The front side was peeled away to show his navel, then his penis, crotch and legs. The sisters concentrated their gaze on his manhood. Extremely disappointed they were, too. His stomach was hollow and wasted, his pelvis stuck out and his little tool was shrunken into his faint, tangled hairs.

'My sisters lifted his bum and withdrew his breeks. The fur linings were strange to us. Although they were matted like felt, they were different from anything we'd seen. Those garments came off like a lobster shell. I held his head so the last of his draught would go down. I watched my sisters clean him. I was jealous of them, but I had my part to do. As his legs were washed we saw his tattoos. They were like fine fish netting all down to his ankles.

'Coutou arranged a headrest for our Sea Angel, then asked me to wash and comb his beard. "Wrasse," she said to me. "This is very important. You must bathe his cheeks and make his whiskers soft with warm water. Use moss. Then rub ewe's milk on to his cheeks. Then with this blade" – she handed me one of whitened ones – "shave his cheeks. Do not shave his chin or top lip," she went on. "I have to cut more of his arm off and I do not want dirty whiskers getting in my way if he struggles. So you will have to untangle his beard meticulously and wrap it in a binding of soft goatskin. When you have done that, he should be in a very deep sleep. I will then shave his oxters off."

'All this I did. I noticed that even in his deepening sleep his hazel eyes were searching under his eyelids. I held up the rest of his arm. I had moss in my hand to rest it on while Coutou shaved his armpits. A covey of strange lice failed to escape her notice. They burned on the fire with his shaven straw hair.

'His armpit was not blighted. Coutou was very relieved. "I thought I was going to have to cut the rest of his arm off at the shoulder. Instead, I can leave a stump of bone. That's better."

'The Sea Angel's eyes stopped their search. Coutou saw that. She took the second whitened blade and carefully cut just above that rotting flesh over his elbow. She exposed his big veins, but never severed one. Coutou sweated. She steeped her long, grey serrated knife in the vinegar water with a frond of her rosemary. She cut to his bone. I watched while my sisters washed his legs. The fragrance of the water filled the warm room.

'Blood dripped from his arm, but we kept the gut tight. Coutou raised it high. His face winced once. She cut a flap of skin and left it dangling from his underarm. She teased his flesh away from the bone and still left the big veins uncut. She pulled that sickening stub of meat away. It fell limp, like rotting liver on the floor. Coutou signalled Mum to burn it. Ashes and embers were heaped over it, stopping the smell.

'So, Shala,' Wrasse went on. 'Do you want me to finish this or shall I stop there?'

'I think you should finish. I believe I need to know what happened, whether I like it or not.'

'So you do; so you do, young lady, so you do.' Wrasse sat up. The smells of cooking, grain being milled filtered into the chamber. The sound of builders chopping wood, grunting as the trees were shifted, masked their conversation. What Shala heard was not hers to share with others. She was to keep it safe, locked away, hidden.

Wrasse sipped, beginning again. 'Coutou had sent him into an unconscious sleep. She removed her great flint knife from the heating water. The blade steamed and dried. She placed it on the bone and began to saw. Progress was not fast. She picked one of the hardened white flakes. With the back of her big knife she pressed out little notches along its sharpest edges. Between her forefinger and thumb, she held the ends of her tiny saw. She wedged it in the bottom of the cut in his bone and sawed. Alternating with knife, she cut all the way round the bone. Its end joint still shone with pus.

'Coutou stopped and pointed to the whale backbone they used for butchery. My father fetched it. Coutou placed it under his shoulder so the arm bone was sticking up. "Hold his shoulder down tight," she said. "Keep a grip on his body," she told us girls.' Wrasse wiped her brow; her eyes were wide open as if she were actually there. 'Coutou jerked smartly down and the Sea Angel's bone broke clean. Marrow slipped out and rested on his flesh. Coutou wiped it away. His limp arteries and veins dangled on the slab. She tied a knot in each one; just like the baby's cord she'd done earlier. She took the blade with the sharpest point and dug holes through the Angel's flap of skin. Coutou then threaded the tied blood vessels through the fleshy side of the flap. She fumbled in her bag for her needle case and took her slimmest one, cut from a gull's wing, and stitched his skin flap up to his shoulder with bog-cotton threads.

'Coutou looked silently round at all of us, and then gazed at our Sea Angel. "That's all I can do," she said. "Time will see if it works." Shortly after that, she said, "You will watch over him, Wrasse. You found him. He's more yours than anyone's."

'Shala,' Wrasse admitted. 'This has tired me greatly. I need a rest. Will you get me some fruit-bread and honey?'

'Certainly, Wrasse.' Shala went down the ladder and asked Quernstone.

'How is Wrasse?' Gull enquired.

'She's telling me things, but she is very tired now.'

'What things?' Quernstone said, her ears flapping.

'Things.' Shala answered.

That was enough. Quernstone knew not to ask again. She handed over raspberry bread, honey and warm milk in a bowl.

'She didn't ask for warm milk, Quernstone.'

'No,' Quernstone answered. 'That's for you.'

'Thank you,' Shala replied with a smile, and scaled the ladder with their snacks.

When Shala returned, Wrasse was sound asleep. She sipped her milk, dipping the honeyed fruit bread, and sat silently thinking.

'Play where you want, Sprig, but come the moment I call,' Sable told her son. 'Leave Mutt in peace now. That bone's hers. Now, Gull, the purpose of my visit... Is there anything you need from us over in Char? If there is, then do ask. We have come off better than you. We are sheltered by the hill. I pity those over on Netland Head. They will have got the full force of Kull.'

Partan assumed complete charge and directed operations. 'That whole roof must come off,' he said as they began on Quernstone's house. We will have to take any loose walling down, then rebuild higher. Leave the door jambs – they are fine.' Then he asked Reaper, 'Can I have your old hazel poles from up there? You know, the ones that supported the earlier awning. They will make good measures.'

'Fine,' came the reply.

'Dale, climb up and fetch them. Run them round to my wreck of a house.'

'I'm glad to see you hard at work, Flint.' Partan commented.

'I'm chopping the roots off this pine. Then we can split it into planks.'

'Rod, you be more careful with that axe,' Partan advised. 'Go gently or you'll bust it. I'll select the uprights, Jasper. Can you mark off the ones for spars?' Partan took of his jacket. 'The sun's come out. It's going to be nice,' he added, as Jasper marked a tree with his axe.

Wrasse awoke slowly and looked at Shala. 'She is Aiva actually,' she thought to herself, 'but only she will know when to be called that.' She glanced at the tray of bread and honey. 'May I have a chunk, please?'

'Certainly.' Shala said. 'With milk or without?'

'With, please, and make sure it's creamy, not like ewe's piss.'

When Shala came back up with a cup, Wrasse asked, 'Do you want me to go on, Ai – Shala?

'Yes, please, Wrasse. I only asked you about the goose tattoo, and I haven't even heard anything about it yet.'

'Shala, some things have much behind them. Answers to short questions aren't always simple or indeed easy.' Wrasse cleared her throat and mopped her chin with a swab of moss. 'I will go on. Sea Angel lay on his sick bed. It was like this one, slatted so the sweat runs through. He slept long and deeply. Us sisters had to get the birthing room ready; much like the one you have. We did that and made it fragrant and warm. Coutou told us to take him through when it was done. Only dim lights could be lit. We each took a corner of his litter and carried him in. He never stirred. I stayed alone with him. My sisters went to their beds and spoke of men and giggled for ages. They had been to the Women's Lodge at Farsee. I hadn't, but I knew about men.' She moved and the bed creaked. 'I sat through the night listening to his shallow breathing. His throat rattled sometimes and bile crept from one corner of his mouth. He looked better in the low light. His beard cast a strange shadow. Our dog came in and lay by me. In the early hours Coutou came back. She listened to his chest and looked at the wound under where his arm was. It had healed, but she was still very concerned about it. She wiped bile from his lips, smelt it, and I took it to the fire.

'"He might live," she said. Crusts of fresh, good blood had oozed from the skin flap and formed scabs. There was no sign of infection on his arm any more. She removed his bedclothes gently and looked at the colour of his skin. It was less pale. She was happier. She did say, "Those feet of his could do with a good dog lick, though." That's why I enjoyed mine. It brought some of it back.

'I slept, and Coutou watched over him. Then my mother did for a while. It was my turn again. I didn't know how long he'd been sleeping. Then I heard him stir. He coughed up bile. It stank. I wiped his mouth and leaned him forward. He coughed and vomited up more vile stuff. I called Coutou. She helped me clean him, and then he choked. She leaned him out of his bed and climbed over his body and, from behind, pulled him up by his stomach. His arse rested under her chin. From his gaping mouth came streams of muck and mucus. He stopped choking and began spitting. His eyes opened. He drew in vast gulps of air. We cleaned him up. We put a pillow behind his back and he looked at us. He then closed his eyes tight and said,

"Naarwaaaaaaaaaarl!" in a long, low, frightening growl. Then he fell into another slumber.'

Shala listened, gripped by Wrasse's story. She sat closer and Wrasse went on. 'The next day he woke for a while. Coutou and I fed him beef stew. It had cooked slowly on and off for two days and was beautifully tender. I can smell it now, the dried mushrooms, the big pieces of rib and tail. The meat was very soft and he could chew gently and swallow. We cooled it, so his ulcerated tongue didn't get burned. His scabby lips were clearing up. His eyes brightened. He seemed to be more at ease. Coutou was pleased.

'Earlier, my parents had searched through his canoe. They found the white stone knife he'd tried to cut his arm off with. It must have fallen underneath him and he couldn't get it back. It was the same stone as your broken arrow, Shala. There were a few fish heads on some bone hooks and lines. He must have fed himself by fishing and drifting. There was a leather cover for the canoe, to stop the sea coming in, but it was rather rotten. It was amazing he'd remained afloat, but it had been calm after the equinox gales.

'The only word he would say was "Narwhal". He was getting stronger, though, and ate more. I cleaned his shit for him. I didn't mind. I'd done worse things. Coutou was called to a small house away up the burn. I stayed with the Sea Angel.

'He had seen the stump of his arm, he nodded to me. I told him my name was Wrasse. He smiled. He pointed to his chest. "Weir," he croaked. I was so happy. He smiled weakly again. I fed him and put my arm round his shoulder, and my sun breast touched his amputation.

'"Wrasse," he said.

'"Weir," I answered.

'I lay there and held him for some while. He coughed so I moved to wipe his lips. Then I showed him my tattoo of the fishes. It was very dim light, but my skin shone. He liked them. I took his bedclothes away to look at his decorated legs again and saw his penis had changed. His balls had dropped from their receded position too.

'While he was unconscious, my sisters had washed him and combed his hairs there. They had curled prettily and shone in the glimmer of the lamp flame. I saw his little trunk roll to one side and grow. He stood firm as his foreskin swelled. Sea Angel looked into my eyes, then to my breasts. His eyes veered with mine down to his groin. He smiled kindly to me and nodded. I was trembling, Shala, I was shaking. I crawled over him and my big sun and moon breasts touched his nipples. I felt the tip of his penis touch me somewhere moist and warm, where those fishes pointed. I pressed down on him as though it was forever and endless. He moved within me very slightly upwards. I felt an enormous pressure. I moved forward and back as he kissed the top of my head. I moved up and down gently and firmly as he responded. Weir held me down on him with his good arm and I felt a great rush of warm wetness flowing into me as he pressed upwards. It was all so wonderful.'

Wrasse shifted on her bed; it creaked again as she remembered lovingly.

'As I lay there on him, his arm moved on my back. With his sharp forefinger, he scratched deeply into my skin from my neck to my arse. He slowly scored the image of a goose. I did not resist. When he had finished, his arm relaxed and I sat up on him and gazed down on to his beautiful face with his bandaged beard. He looked at me, and was forming my name with his lips when he coughed. He coughed once more, and a great clart of blood hit my  chest. He coughed and coughed violently; more blood and bile came gushing out of his mouth. He collapsed back on his bed, and he was *dead*.'

Wrasse burst into uncontrollable tears. Her breast heaved and she wailed. She pulled her greying hair and scratched her scalp. Everyone in Lee Holme heard those desperate cries from her depths. Cries that had never before been released turned into a flood that could break all dams and riverbanks. Her salty tears flowed freely from her. Wrasse's wailing and screams of woe rose. 'I loved him so,' she managed to say through her distress. All work stopped on the village. There was a great silence. Folk gathered around the house and gazed up. Gull ran in the door, rushed up the ladder to Wrasse's chamber. She saw her engulfed in emotion. Shala was supporting her as she shook with her torment.

Gull returned below and stood at he doorway. Shala held on to Wrasse. She stroked and comforted her. The stress of years of hidden grief had been released. Wrasse tried to speak, but she could not. She wept on as Shala said, 'There, there. There, there.' The comforting words her mother used; it was all she knew to do. Gradually the salty sobs decreased in power. Wrasse relaxed a little and began to slump backwards on to her bed. Shala reached for another pillow. Wrasse put her shaking hand out for a drink. Shala handed her the cup, saying, 'There, there.'

Wrasse sipped very slowly. The small gulps of water eased her tense throat. But she still could not speak. Shala sat silently, steadying the cup in her hand. Wrasse, as in a dream, remembering so clearly her trauma, slid into deep slumber. 'There, now,' Shala said. 'Sleep, Wrasse, sleep.'

Chapter 8

*

A New Sensation

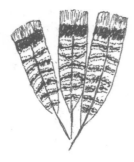

Oiwa's family gathered round their outside fire, just like so many others of the Goose Clan. His father, the chief, was a respected hunter: Mica, Bark and Tine were taught well by him.

'Take what you need,' Tine said to New Moon, the first neighbour coming for meat.

'Thank you, Tine. Please come by. I have pinenut cakes.'

'I will. You are kind,' he replied as she left for her hearth.

'I love beaver meat,' extolled North Star to Petal, who pulled a hind leg off for him. 'It tastes of the smell of water lilies. It has the essence of unfolding leaves of a spring birch. When I eat it I hear honey bees and birdsong.'

'Yes. We know you love it best,' Mica said, reaching for a piece.

'Is Big Hunter getting none?' Ripple's voice came from behind, tickling the back of Oiwa's neck with partridge feathers. 'You can share a partridge if you come by my tent.' The feathers touching his nape froze him with pleasure.

'Have a foreleg,' Honey offered.

'Marvellous,' he rejoiced. 'So loose and succulent.'

'Show us your bow again?' asked Mica.

Oiwa stood, turning to get it. Ripple tripped him. He sprawled. 'Oh, Big Hunter, let me help you up,' she tittered, holding out a teasing hand and a feather.

'It's so embarrassing,' Oiwa thought, back in the wigwam listening to muffled mirth. By the time he returned to the fireside, it had dispersed. 'She's gone,' he thought in relief. He sat, picking his teeth with a beaver rib while Honey and Petal sang songs of the geese.

'Oiwa, stand up with your bow against you.' Bark suggested.

'Just touching the tip of your droopy dick,' Mica joked.

'It should be nudging your navel. That bow's too short too,' Tine chipped in. 'You've grown far too much, brother.'

'Your kin are right, Oiwa. You need a longer weapon.' North Star put in. His brothers laughed enormously. 'Stop it, boys,' their father ordered. 'It's not right to tease,' he added, grinning.

The clouds separated. The moon shone on Oiwa. He remembered that stunning face in the water fleetingly. 'I have to choose who to pass my old bow on to. I'll think about that,' Oiwa answered, 'So it's still alright for me to borrow your axe, Mica?'

'Yes, Big Hunter,' he replied teasingly.

The next morning Oiwa awoke in a brotherly huddle on their wigwam floor, remembering how every year they covered the large river pebbles with new clay. Then the hides they slept upon were stretched over it. Their smouldering fire was in the centre, surrounded by scorched stones.

Oiwa went to the bushes and dug a small pit for his toilet. 'I smell beaver,' he said out loud. 'A reminder of his successful hunt.' He covered his traces with loose earth and washed in a small rivulet rising from a bubbling spring. Walking back to breakfast, he passed Tine going to the undergrowth. His sisters returned from their ablutions on another side of the village. Quill had been up long and, like a good mother, cracked stored nuts to have with honey. She crouched, hammer-stone in hand, going through remnants of the previous autumn's harvest. The empty shells gathered in a ring at the edge of her rock anvil. Bark scooped them for the fire.

'We'll slice the rest of the caribou and hang it to dry,' Honey said as she took out her obsidian knife. 'Pelt will guard it.' Their wolvine-brindled dog looked eager. 'Here's a bone,' she called, casting him a shin.

Oiwa crunched his last honeyed nut to lick his shallow wood bowl. He swilled his palate with clear, cold water and cleaned his white teeth with a chewed stick. The sun banished the mist from the treetops and distant mountains before he had gathered his bow and quiver. 'Here's my axe,' Mica said, pulling it from his belt.

'Thanks.' Oiwa touched the keen-edged implement, feeling pride in borrowing it. He slipped it in his belt. 'I'm off now.'

'Come back lucky, Oiwa,' his kin said.

As he passed Ripple's door-flap, her young twins called, 'Big Hunter, can we come?'

'No,' he replied quietly. 'Play with your little sister, be good.' Oiwa walked on. The power of the River Dun was in force. Meltwaters from the mountains rushed to... where? Oiwa knew only from distant legends, telling of its length, strength and mystery.

Oiwa thought. 'I'll go to where I killed the beaver. There are groves of straight trees there.' He strode powerfully through thickets and grassy clearings. He stepped over narrow rivulets and leaped others feeding the Dun. He trekked uphill to a ridge overlooking Mirror Ponds. 'I don't want a sapling. A larger tree, but supple, is what I'm looking for. I see a new bow in every bough. There's a bent one. It won't do. I see that other one breaking. My old bow is elm. I like it: springy yet tough. Search on, Oiwa,' he told himself as he wandered onwards.

'This isn't easy. Wherever I look there's something that's not quite right. There's one that could suit Dad. That kind might be for Honey, but she can have this when I've made my new one,' he imagined, fondling his old bow affectionately. 'Dangly dick indeed. I'll show them.'

Doves scattered from the boughs above. Squirrels slid behind beams. Oiwa was not hunting them. He sat for a while, chewing dried venison. As his saliva softened it, the flavour expanded with each jaw clench. 'I'll have more. I always swallow the first bit too soon.' He remembered, masticating quietly, contemplating his surroundings.

'What's that?' A twig snapped directly behind him. He looked round. 'It's an enormous black cat!' he yelled, leaping up in alarm, spilling his arrows with a clatter. The feline sprang, fur on end, hissing and spraying disgusting scent, then fled.

'Waaaaaaah!' shouted Oiwa, violently coughing up venison. His outburst sparked an uproar: jays screeched; doves flapped in alarm; startled deer rushed unseen deeper into the undergrowth; squirrels squealed in the trees.

'My heart's beating too rapidly. But the cat's vanished, thank Gumar. I can smell its ugly spray. Thank Tumar, it's not over me. It ran right past that tree. Oh! It's sturdy and straight, bark slightly wrinkled: no lower branches. Let me look closer. There's a beautiful bow within. I see it flexing, bending, springing perfectly, in my mind. I must feel it: my new weapon's living in there. Thank the Forest Spirits for great fortune – and my courage scaring off that lynx.'

The beautiful polished axe, flaked from silver-spangled, dark-green stone, had a fine cutting edge. 'Here goes,' Oiwa urged, 'Let's chop. Only the weight of the axe, as father taught me. If I swing forcefully, it shatters. "Not hard son," Dad advised. "Easy, easy. Chip, chip finishes the log. Chop upwards into the wood: then a downward cut at knee-height to meet the first. Chop all round like that."

'This is sweaty work. I'll take my jerkin off. Here, bow and arrows, you can lie on it. Have a quick look round. Make sure that cat won't creep back. Right, chop away. A second round will bring it closer to toppling. Stand back. Look at the stem. Decide where to chop to drop. Just a few blows here will do it. It's creaking. The high branches lean. Stand aside, look up: watch it come down. There it goes, kissing the others farewell. That's a new space in the canopy; and I did it. Great! Just hear it bouncing in the forest litter.

'The trunk's good. I'll take a longer bit than needed. "Measure thrice. Cut once," Dad says. Up to my sternum, I'm certain.

'Right. Brush this bruck off and cut through... Not another lynx?' Oiwa thought, catching a suspicious sound. 'No, nothing. Just an upper branch swinging back? Time to trim and cut the length. It's thick enough to split into several bows. I'll have the best one. Only a few swings. Last chop: done,' he said out loud.

'Time for meat. I deserve it. I'll squat on my trophy and gnash a strip. Such great sport I'll have with my bow,' he mused, chewing. 'My brothers are right, though. I need a powerful weapon. Big game, not just beavers... There's that rustle again!'

Oiwa's heart thumped. '*Aaaagh!*' He was caught by horribly painted arms. 'Leave me,' he yelped, struggling. 'Get off! I'm choking. Get your hair off my face. Who are you?'

'Big Hunter,' he heard whispered hoarsely in his right ear. 'Big Hunter. It's only naked Ripple. Don't fret. I've brought you your flight feathers. Here, look in my hand.'

'Thanks, I've plenty,' he answered, glancing down at them. 'You've smeared dark paint all over my stomach.'

'Oh, poor boy. Let me clean you,' she teased, pulling his breeks out and dropping the trimmed feathers down his torso.

'Get your hot, oily body off me!' he gasped, repelled.

'No. You're mine now. Anyway, we have to retrieve those flights, don't we? Let's delve.'

'Urrrghh,' Oiwa thought. 'It feels like a hairy spider.'

'Exciting down here, isn't it?'

'Leave them alone,' he demanded as she pulled out a knot of Oiwa's new, tightly curled hairs.

'Ouch!' he protested as she tugged repeatedly.

'Oh. Sorry,' Ripple giggled, tugging other ringlets away. 'I'll hunt somewhere else.'

'Oh no, I can't stop it. I've stiffened. She's tickling my balls.'

'I'll just have to grope further. Here's one, Big Hunter. How did it get so far down?' She crooned, deftly stroking him with the plume as her left hand untoggled his belt. 'Down come your furry troos. We will see so much better.'

'She's pushing them off, but I'm not moving. It feels fantastic. Eeek. My pee-er is caught. She's shoved me forward. Right. I'm kicking these things away. She's still got me. I feel her greasy belly on my bum. But it's great. She's twisting me. Her round face, it's covered in green lines? Most of her is in dappled brown shades. A great white oval is painted round her crotch, her hair's red ochre. Ripple's inside legs are reddened with hematite: bloodlike. It's her invitation to mate.'

'Aren't you going to do anything, Big Hunter?' she teased. 'Your arrow sticking out tells me you'd like to stick it in?'

'Yes,' he grinned, thoughtfully scratching his bum, making his arrow wag. 'My first time. What a wonderful surprise. Great!'

'Come here,' beckoned Ripple.

He felt her breath on his chest. Her red nippled breasts swayed. He grew even stiffer. Ripple dragged him to the mossy ground with her black hands. 'Oh gosh!' he thought. 'She's waving it on her wet crotch and shoving my foreskin further back. It... It, it is so, so... good. Ooooooooh...' Ripple pulled him inside. 'Let go,' he groaned. 'I can do that myself.' He lurched forward.

'Wow,' he gasped as Ripple's hips rose. 'That amazing sensation down in my guts. It's like yesterday when I shot the beaver, but far more intense. Now I pull back as men do. Shit! Too far: I'm out. Where's that glorious place? Missed.'

She grabbed him again, shoving him back in. 'Deeper, Oiwa,' she was saying, 'Don't slip out again.'

'I'll show her how far I can push. There, right in: in to a place of red glory. Pull gently back, not so far this time. I'm shaking.' His knees wobbled uncontrollably and Ripple clenched his backside down.

'Steady, steady. Make it last,' she whispered.

'I'm not in control,' he thought as she shoved him further into her. His balls squashed into her wet crotch. 'Oh... Oh, I'm going to cum.

Pull back?' Ripple was pressing him in deeper. Her nails dug in his buttocks. 'Too late,' he thought as he came. 'Wonderful, oh, so, so... w o n d e r f u l.

He lay on Ripple, trembling, her paint slippery with his perspiration as the last three weakening shots left him. She patted his scrotum gently, and then grabbed him, pushing him back up inside her. 'I understand,' he thought. 'Do it again. Here goes. Oh, but it's sore: Magnificent a moment ago. Now it's painful pleasure. I don't think I can do this. She's moaning and moaning, revolving my hips. She's squeezing my man in her: he's going floppy. Ugh... She's stopped. I can lie still.'

'Wow.' Is that all you can say?' Ripple complained. 'This moss is cripplingly uncomfortable. Off you get.'

'I can't move,' he replied, feeling his calf spasm.

'Yes you can.'

'Ow! Ouch! It's cramp. I'm stuck.'

'Why get cramp now? You stupid limp imp,' Ripple chastised him, trying to wiggle him away.

'*Aaaaaaaah*. Stop!' Oiwa appealed. 'It's aaaaaaagony.'

'Well, I've got a fucking pinecone up my backside, mate... Off!' she screamed, pushing him up.

'*Ah ah aaaaaahhhhh.*' Oiwa yelped, gasping and threshing, his left leg bent in agonised contortion.

His erection collapsed completely as he hopped on his good, right leg. His chest was cov-  ered in Ripple's paintwork. Smears of red from her nipples adorned his own; his flat stomach was a muddy brown mess; a stressed and tangled feather was stuck to his inner thigh. Two dark handprints adorned his backside. Around his glistening penis, smudges of Ripple's white and red dyes mixed to a fleshy pink. Dewy pearls of semen dribbled to the moss as he hopped about.

'At last,' he said. 'It's clearing. I can ease my leg.' His penis tip receded within its protective foreskin. 'Better now, Ripple. I can wriggle my toes,' he reported, massaging his painful muscle. 'It's okay. My cramp's gone.' he repeated. 'It's better. Where *are* you?'

The Big Hunter stood alone, naked in the bright forest light, searching. 'She's gone. Disappeared. Not a sign: vanished.' He wondered, amazed, staring into space. 'What a mess,' he thought, looking down. 'Where are my breeks? Oh. There, upside down on that bush.' He put his good leg in first, then slowly eased the cramp-stricken one through the other leather tunnel. He hitched them up, remembering when they were forcibly lowered.

His bow and arrows still lay on his jerkin, with Ripple's flights scattered over the quiver. He found Mica's axe stuck in the tree stump. The stone head was cold on his hip as he tucked it back into his belt. He found his knife next to the soggy venison. He sheathed it, balanced the trunk on his shoulder and set off, contemplating his first genuine orgasm.

There was no sign of Ripple's tracks, nor a whiff in the air. He felt clumsy in his gait, making too much noise for a Big Hunter. 'I'd better be ready.' Oiwa thought. 'I'll notch my last quartz-tipped arrow in my bow and pull it tight.'

As he approached the Dun, he could hear the meltwaters tumbling. 'That sounds just like new quartz pebbles rumbling along the bed. We'll get them when the river is down to make fresh heads,' Oiwa thought. It was another reason why they returned there.

'I reckon Ripple will appreciate another partridge,' he thought excitedly. 'Maybe I can prong one on the way back. I'll follow the sloping banks of the river to the gravelly ridge further down. They go there for gizzard grit near dusk. There I'll wait, silent under the willows.'

Catkins brushed his jerkin, leaving scented yellow pollen. He practised pulling on his bow to see which twigs moved or didn't. The river tumbled by just yards away. Wagtails and dippers worked for their livings on the wet rocks of the rapids. The Dun was over an arrowshot across. The river narrowed, deepened and slowed near the

Goose Clan's village. 'I wonder if the fish traps have been seen to?' he wondered, waiting. 'Bees gather nectar in the crocuses over there. Perhaps a hare might drop by to the nibbled turf?'

He felt pins and needles like ants in his cramped leg, and wiggled his toes to relieve it. 'Mustn't rustle the leaves,' he warned himself. 'Ah... there's the whiff of vixen. Is she waiting for a bird too? Yes. Wingbeats. Here they come...'

Dark shapes sped through the evening sky, landing on the shingle bank. Scanning round nervously, they began to peck at the sharp damp grains.

'Dang,' thought Oiwa. 'I want to pee. Can't. Now it's a fart. Clench it back. Shhhhh. Let them get confident. At last: draw your old bow, Oiwa. Quiet. Don't shift a leaf...'

His triangular point touched his tense knuckles. A partridge scraped away happily. Oiwa checked the trajectory. He heard the birds' beaks and claws scratching, kissed the bowstring and let go. The partridge heard it, but too late. The arrow transfixed her, trussing her nest mate too. Oiwa swiftly loaded another arrow, and released it. A third bird fell thudding the ground as the rest flew off squawking in alarm.

'Good,' he commentated loudly as feathers floated. The nest mate was still twitching, so Oiwa wrung its neck, taking care not to break the arrow. A sad vixen slunk stealthily into the undergrowth.

'Brilliant!' thought Oiwa. 'I'll take the skewered brace to Ripple and just drop the third as a by-the-way from the Big Hunter.'

He shouldered his bow wood, crunching proudly from the rapids towards the camp. A kingfisher darted from a stump to the rushing water.

Oiwa passed the first tent in the ring. The North Star glimmered above. There were welcoming nods from his clansfolk as he displayed his double hit. Ripple's wigwam loomed. The twins were outside yelling 'Big Hunter,' in welcome. Oiwa, smiling broadly, reached the hide opening. The door-flap shifted. He displayed his offering. A

head moved from behind the moose-skin. Oiwa stepped forward, the partridges dangling. A long eagle feather loomed from behind the doorway. Beaneath it stood Barb, Ripple's man. 'Good evening, Big Hunter,' said Barb gruffly.

Oiwa gasped, not realizing Barb was home from the hunt. Dropping his prize, he hurtled to his own tent in shock. He entered the darkness. His family were all there. 'Welcome home, Big Hunter,' they greeted him.

Speechless, mouth agape, he dropped the bow wood. His untrapped wind answered them audibly.

'How has your day been, Oiwa?' asked Quill from her crouching position.

He said nothing.

Bark stood. The black embroidered goose on his jacket moved as he breathed. 'Barb brought you these from Ripple.' Holding his hand over Oiwa's head, he released a flutter of arrow flights. Oiwa blushed his reddest, grimacing while awkwardly shrugging his shoulders. North Star was the first to laugh. Quill shook, followed by his sisters, who were giggling outrageously. Mica and Tine joined in loudly. Bark waited, watching Oiwa's face as his ability to speak returned. He put his arm round his brother and said, 'Poor Oiwa. It's okay. We put her up to it. You don't even have to tell us about the cramp.'

'I thought it was all so marvellous,' he said almost cheerfully.

'Oiwa. Young brother.' Mica put in. 'You have grown and achieved much. We reckoned it would be good for you.'

'That beaver was great,' Bark said. 'We enjoyed it. You did well, Big Hunter. It's our way of saying thanks.'

'So you set me up,' Oiwa said, shaking his head with a shy grin.

'Well. It would've happened soon,' Tine said. 'Ripple was determined to get you, you know.'

Bark grasped Oiwa's shoulders and explained, 'She does it with most of the growing lads,' flicking his nose lightly in a very friendly way. 'You get to mate with her once. She only does it when she is safely giving Moon Blood.'

'Yes, son,' Quill concluded, 'There has to be a first mating. Ripple enjoys her role. Barb understands. He just acts gruff.'

Honey and Petal shifted poignantly as their mother explained, 'We all love mating, but don't abuse it. If we didn't couple, there'd be no infants. You wouldn't be here, nor me.' She and North Star looked over her brood proudly. 'We know when we can mate for children, and when purely for pleasure. We understand when not to be mated with too.' North Star nodded, twitching his long, whiskery chin.

'I gave birth to you all. I lost two of you. That is plenty of children to bear, but I wanted you. I love you all. I want you to grow, being good people. Mica will be taking his woman from the Caribou clan soon; she will live in our band. You, Bark and Tine have women waiting somewhere.'

'Sons,' said Quill. 'You've all cuddled and mated. On your travels you will caress and join with the womenfolk. The clans of man are wide and broad, the way Gumar and Tumar ordered it. If it is Gumar and Tumar's wish that you give fertility honourably as you journey, then let it be so.'

A long, thoughtful silence reigned round the glowing embers.

Chapter 9

*

Sweat Lodge

'**G**ood morning Big Hunter.' Ripple called out. 'Stripping the bark off, are we? Pussy got your tongue too?'

Embarrassed, Oiwa searched his pouch for bone wedges. Ignoring her, he tried to tap one in across the heartwood.

'Big Hunter.'

Oiwa hit his thumb. 'Bugger!' he thought. 'That's it. I'll go and speak.'

Ripple stood, holding her youngest to her breast. Milk dribbled down the baby's chin.

'Oh no. I'm getting a stiff on,' he thought, making to turn away.

'Oiwa,' she said kindly. 'What we did in the forest won't happen again between us. Whilst I'm suckling my child here, I cannot conceive. Oiwa, Big Hunter, for a big hunter, you are. You well deserved my favour. I reddened my legs to invite you. I stalked you. I even saw the big cat. It vanished, like a spirit, at your tree. I watched you fell it. You moved beautifully. You never saw me. I creep more quietly than any lynx. Ghost lynx or not.'

He had felt cross, frustrated and embarrassed in turns. He was calming down now, but he didn't find it easy.

Fixing him with her glance, Ripple continued. 'You were a lad. You're greater now. You left life's moisture in me. Now you know what it's like to achieve that. The mystery, revealed for you. You will grow. You'll understand breeding is important, special. It is not just for fun. There will be times when your urge is to mate. Remember my words. Ask yourself, is this right, now?'

'Okay,' Oiwa said hesitantly. Touching the babe's cheek, he turned and left. At his fireside he tapped his wedges, lengthening the lesions. Soon he had four fine bow lengths.

'This piece is perfect,' he decided. 'I can dress it with my basalt scrapers, leave the handgrip thick and whittle long, willow leaf-shaped arms. I'll whip it below the string notches, with sinew and thong to prevent splitting. I can make a fine crosshatch on the grip and up the face of the bow and inlay it with hematite. Then I'll oil it with goose fat.'

'You are doing that extremely well Oiwa,' said North Star. 'Here, use this lynx gut. It's the best bowstring you'll ever get. Use reed-seed oil for eternal suppleness. Yours will be the best hunting bow ever.'

'Thank you so much, Dad. I'm really proud now.'

'Good, son. You should be. Can I knot the loops?'

'Yes. I'd be honoured.'

When finished, Oiwa flexed his bow, feeling its strength, remembering forever the beautiful twang. 'Was that really a lynx spirit guiding me?' he would often wonder as the gut touched his lips.

Mica came by with Bark. Tine was away, meeting folk. 'Try this heavy caribou arrow,' Bark offered.

'Thanks, Bark. I'm itching to use it. I'll shoot it at the rotted larch. I'm not pulling my bow hard yet. It needs seasoning.'

'Right, Oiwa. Twenty paces to test.'

'To the woods, then.' Oiwa fitted his arrow and drew back the lynx gut, feeling its smooth, tense strength.

'Don't hit the bees' nest.' Mica said to put him off.

'Thank you,' Oiwa answered awkwardly as the gut touched his lips. Time stopped with the resounding twang. His arrow struck home. Chips of bark and rotted wood exploded as the stopped bolt vibrated.

'Well done, Oiwa. What are you going to call that amazing beast?' asked Bark.

'I don't know yet.'

'Right.' Mica said. 'Give us your weapon and we'll test it gently while you think.'

'Halloo there,' Tine hailed. 'I've brought Lichen and Rush from the Caribou clan.'

'Its lucky Oiwa didn't pin you with his new bow then,' Mica called back.

'We've got a fallow deer and a hare,' he said as they ran towards them.

'I think we can see that, dear brother,' Mica answered.

'That's the name.' Oiwa realized impulsively. 'Ziit. Ziit: the sound of the arrows. It's perfect.'

The two visitors caught up, puffing with their loads. 'Hello, I'm Rush, this is Lichen.' The dark-haired young men bowed, introducing themselves.

'This is Ziit. Listen,' Oiwa said, plucking his string tunefully. 'I remember you. It was when our clans met some seasons ago as we moved camp.'

'Yes, that's right,' answered Lichen.

Oiwa mused silently. 'I remember how different they are from our Goose clan. They've no face hair, unlike my brothers. They constantly pluck and trim with obsidian razors. Others grow them, threading beads. Mine's only downy yet.'

'We'll carry your small burdens to the clan ring,' said Bark. 'There you go, Oiwa. Pick them up,' he joked. 'We'll go straight to North Star's wigwam.'

'Greetings, young men.' North Star said, wearing his impressive bone and antler necklaces, his grand feathered headdress making him appear taller than ever. 'So, you have come to court our girls, I believe?'

'Thank you for your welcome,' Rush answered shyly. 'Here's a block of razor stone from our mountainside, and bears' teeth from...' Rush stuttered. 'One of our bear's heads, I suppose.'

'I'm delighted to accept.'

'Lichen, what wonders have you brought?'

'Pink salt from our cliff and panther claws… from one of our panthers… It limps now.'

'Come,' invited North Star. Honey opened the flap. 'Be seated. Petal, pass the tray around.'

'It's sliced caribou,' she explained. 'I've beaten them out thinly then rolled them round crushed pine nuts and grassy onion leaves mixed with poached liver pate. A Goose clan delicacy. Mother skewered kidney to the slices of tongue.'

Oiwa loved it when visitors arrived.

'This night.' North Star announced, 'in our guests' honour, we shall enter the Sweat Lodge. Oiwa, tell Greyling it's his chance to heat the stones.'

'Right, father,' he said. Taking some skewered kidney and gripping Ziit, he walked over to Greyling's wigwam.

'Greyling,' Oiwa said as he was invited in, 'North Star wants the Sweat Lodge tonight.'

'Yes, he did mine last time. My sons are away hunting down the Dun, but I can cope. You could help me now, though. Come to the clan fire.'

Beside the clan fire, in the centre of the plaza, was a smaller area of burnt stones. From there a cobbled pathway led down to a hemispherical dome of stretched skins. Its door gave on to a round, clay-lined pit.

'We must heave the old stones out, Oiwa, and shift them up the gradient to the fireplace.'

It smelled of juniper inside. Oiwa loved the mystical, spiritual atmosphere of the place, the polished log benches and the fireside elk-skin water trough. A cloven bear's skull and a goose-shaped ladle hung over a sturdy leather bucket.

'We will fill that down at the Dun. First we collect tinder then stack it, piling the stones amongst it. You fetch a brand from my fire, shove it deeply in and set it to smoulder. We heap wet leaves over everything so it burns slowly and the cobbles won't crack with the heat.'

The pair carried the bucket to the river.

'Ah,' said Greyling as they arrived. 'That must be Barb's new canoe.'

Oiwa, embarrassed, lowered his head. 'Let's get this filled,' he suggested shiftily, narrowing his pale eyebrows.

'Done,' Greyling said after several trips. 'Now we cut juniper and pine for the pit and fill the grease lamps. You light the wicks. That'll warm the place. Then we steep fronds in the pit.'

'Where's Ziit?' Oiwa thought suddenly. He banged his head on a dangling stone lamp and tripped on the moose antler stone shunts before realising with relief that his bow was propped behind the juniper at the door.

The first bat coursed the cooling air, inviting its fellows to chase moths. Oiwa returned, hearing news from the Caribous. When it was time to enter the Sweat Lodge, Greyling greeted them in his feathered finery. His quill-breasted waistcoat shimmered in the dark. Smoke from the stone clamp drifted, sometimes obscuring his painted face, but two luminous white streaks constantly shone on his cheeks. His leather-clad nephew Tuft was his assistant. 'We've greased the cobbled path. Don't slip,' warned the youngster.

'Please enter,' North Star invited. He sat at the back of his lodge.

'This is all new to me,' thought Oiwa. 'Life is changing.'

'Be seated,' came his father's voice. Oiwa watched his brothers remove their clothes and sit. He did too. He saw the small stars at their hairlines glittering in the lamplight. His father's glowed brightly.

It was cool in the lodge, despite the lamps. Oiwa felt his goose pimples rise. Rush and Lichen removed their neatly stitched buckskin clothing, folding it carefully. Everyone remained still and silent until North Star began to drone softly. He nodded slowly, his wispy beard occasionally touching his wrinkled chest. He wore no adornment. Mica, Bark and Tine had tooth pendants glistening on their sternums. Lichen wore a knotted cord with a small, perforated stone, and Rush a thin sinew holding a drilled cobnut. Oiwa wished he had a token to wear. All he had was an annoying flea. 'Got you,' he thought as he popped it between his nails. 'That's my blood you're bleeding now, dead pest.'

North Star's drone had ceased. The door flapped open, and in shot a hot rounded stone, followed swiftly by Tuft, who had pushed it along the path with a moose antler. As it dropped on to the soaking mattress, the steam exploded. The smell of broiling juniper and pine filled the air. Oiwa felt his pores open. His scalp oozed. More fleas fell on to his shoulders. Soon they were all crushing fleas. Rush was catching Lichen's for him. Tine was squirming. 'They don't like this juniper much, do they?' Oiwa thought.

Mica was standing with the bear's skull, dipping it into the water tank. The lamplight rippled over him and around the ceiling. Tuft rolled another rock into the basin. Mica tilted the skull so that water ran from its eye sockets on to the hissing stones. The room filled with intense heat and pungent steam. Oiwa's lungs filled with damp forest essences. His nose was running. So was North Star's. He flung the snot into the pit, and Oiwa copied his action.

'Rush,' he said. 'You've got fleas escaping from your armpits.'

'You too, Oiwa. You catch mine, I'll get yours.'

They all changed places, and he found himself sitting next to Tine. How the sweat gushed from his golden oxters.

'What do you think of this, then, brother?' Tine asked.

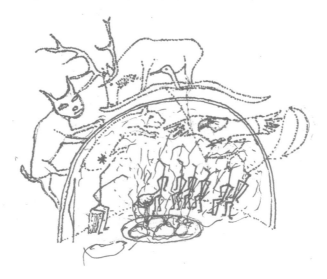

'It's amazing. It's like I'm becoming new inside.' Tine nodded, sweat running from his elbow onto Oiwa's thigh.

Bark rose, bellowing, 'Two more?'

'Here they come,' screeched Tuft. The stones rattled past Rush and hurtled into the pit. Bark held the bucket above his head and quenched the stones. The door flap descended. They were invisible again in their tight capsule. Sweat poured from Oiwa's locks. He leaned his head back, breathing in the wonderfully pungent atmosphere.

Oiwa's mind wandered. His head seemed to rise far above the lodge. He could see the clear stars.

Tine laid a wet juniper branch in the pit. The sensation increased. Oiwa's dream went on. He heard the swishing of powerful wings flying past the distant moon. They beat the droning rhythm of North Star's dirge. His arms stretched out, and he felt the drag and lift of feathers. Eye-level with the Great Gander's skein, he flew across the night sky. Far below, the dark world of forest shimmered under the moonlight. The rivers shone. The moon and constellations looked back up from the marsh below. Behind was the vast ocean they had flown over. Silvery sparkles flashed from the waves and an ermine edge beat the shore.

'Where have you been, Oiwa?' North Star asked quietly from the as Mica cast another skull-full on the steaming stones.

Oiwa stared over his bill to focus on his father. The beak slowly dissipated as the steam began to clear. 'I have flown with my family of geese,' he replied. 'I crossed a wide ocean. I landed with them in icy waters. I came back through the river tunnel under the earth to here.'

North Star's drone slowed, and then quickened. A low tremor from deep in his chest rattled like dry branches. He directed his glance to one of their guests. 'Where have you travelled, young man?'

Lichen's head turned and looked through the dark forest. 'My breath forces clouds of mist into the cold, clear night. My hinds nibble on low branches in the clearing. I move towards them. My antlers rustle the lower twigs. Ice beads, bright and hard, cascade on to my hide. My hinds turn their nostrils. They sniff my warm scent.

My presence reassures them as they graze. I look up through the clearing at the stars. A dark skein passes high above.'

Greyling slid another great pebble into the pit. Mica scooped the yellowed skull.

Lichen looked down at his cloven hooves as they reverted to pulsing, veined hands. 'I took my hinds to new pastures in the forest,' he continued. 'I mounted my hinds. My fertility wet their wombs. They will drop their fawns when the sun allows new succulent growth.'

Mica stood. His head bent beneath the skin membrane which connected, yet separated them from the world. He pushed back his light, matted hair. His small white star shone. He moved behind his young brother and leaned Oiwa's head back on to his stomach. Oiwa gazed up to him as Mica took a sharp bone splinter. He punctured Oiwa's forehead with tiny, deep pricks in a star pattern, wiping the blood down his young brother's cheeks. The members of the circle watched as he jabbed the same emblem below Oiwa's navel. Mica then placed his thumb into an open nutshell where the glistening powder that shared his name was kept. He plied the mica deeply into Oiwa's belly wound and then into his upper forehead. 'You have the Star now, brother,' he whispered.

Mica's voice took over from his father's drone. He stood behind him in the glow of their solitary lamp. Bark took the skull, applying water. Mica gently massaged his father's neck. He coughed to clear his throat to begin a familiar legend. 'Many, many winters before my grandfather's father's father was ever born, we lived in another land. That place, like this now, gave us all we needed. That other place was taken from us by the great, rising water mountain. We could live there no more.' He gazed ahead, his hazel eyes, saying, 'Only a few of us remained. We followed the geese that lived in that land, for they went somewhere good. It was a long, long journey. We came here at last.' He breathed deeply, wiping perspiration from his chest.

North Star slowly raised his head, saying, 'It is tradition to send a party of young men to revere the geese's first landing. You, Oiwa, will join your brothers. You have shown great skills and are an example to others.' North Star searched the faces of Lichen and Rush. The lamp flames shifted the shadows on his as they flickered in the steam. Bark plied another cranium of water. A wave of heat swirled beneath the stretched hides. From above, hot rain fell.

'Our guests here will take two of our clan's daughters as wives. First they must learn more of our ways and history. You, my sons, will take them on your great journey. You will meet our sacred familiars to gain wisdom. When you return you will be great men, leaders. Mica, Bark and Tine are already, for they've been before.'

Bark sat. North Star plied water over the hot stones with the goose ladle. Mica crouched beside Bark. He held a tiny, polished bone cup that shone in the lamplight. It brimmed with a clear, thick potion that smelt of the forest's treetops. Mica sipped. The potency soaked into his tongue. His mouth felt hot. He inhaled a great lungful of sweat-lodge steam. His limb, covered in thick brown and golden fur, entered the cold, starlight forest. 'My paw is growing its dark claws again and becoming swathed in hair. I stalk in the ether of the night. My claws scratch my dark, shining nose. My great teeth shine yellow, reflecting the moon. I prowl in the shadows to climb the summit of my rocky tor. There, bears before me stood and roared through time. I command the sounds of the night. My echoes return from distant mounts. My eyes shine white as I see through the deepest dark.'

Soundlessly he placed his talons back through the lodge membrane to sit beside Bark. His claws receded beneath his clear nails. His palms throbbed. 'North Star, I have travelled as Urs the Great Bear.'

Bark took a sip of the ambrose. He leapt like a lynx through the pelt screen. 'I'm lapping from a clear pool. I see my whiskered face and shining eyes. Other lynxes press their red tongues into the expanding ripples. The stars shake as we lap. Our strong feline aroma pervades the night.'

Tine removed the last ambrose drop. He rose, and looked past the stretched hides. 'Far below I see our circle of tents as my vast wings spread. My hooked beak and beady eyes search the darkened land. The mountain's snowy peak rushes towards me, shining with the stars. I make for Black Crag where I force my wings to slow me. My mighty talons touch the eerie. I perch, observing. They spread again. My left talons close on a downy twig. I circle and glide back to where steam dreams and reality meet. These talons slide through the leather roof. I perch back on my log. My murderous beak fades. My arm plumage dissipates. There's a furry stick between my toes. Father, I have flown far this night.'

North Star looked at Rush. The goose ladle poured its clear contents in a long stream. The bubbling and hissing seared round that hothouse. Rush leaned his dark haired head sideways: 'I walk to the great river and take a canoe. I float downstream. A feather tickles my back through my clothes. My chest itches painfully. I rise from the boat and speed up to behind the moon.'

Rush's companions looked to where he'd sat. They saw a bright light rise as though it were a star shimmering in the mists.

'Where have you been, Rush?' North Star asked.

Rush looked to North Star, unseeing. 'There... Not back.'

Chapter 10

✳

River Journey

'Widgeon's my favourite, Rush. It's the way she moves, sits and looks. When she offered me those huge hot wood grubs warmed in honey, and licked her fingers coyly, I loved her. There was absolutely no other choice.'

'Well. I'm in so much love with Teal, Lichen. Remember? We met her ages ago. We were only knee high, but even then she struck me. I thought of her for long after their camp visit. Those stuffed linnets she roasted were *so* wonderful.'

'Yup, Rush. I agree. We've seen many young ladies. I think we are lucky. That one called Sage-Tip? She's odd. Did you hear what the other girls said?'

'No?'

'I overheard. She told them, "Those two, especially Rush with his round face and stubby nose, just fail to see my inner beauty. He's welcome to Teal! I'm going to dig clay anyway."'

'No!'

'Yes, cousin.'

'I'm so glad we are going to be alone with them, Lichen. This is a wonderful wigwam to be in together. Are you going to feed her those grubs from your lips again?'

'Yes. And I'm going to roll them in milled hazels just for her.'

'Please show me your splendid fish traps, Widgeon,' Lichen asked after their sated sleep.

'Of course,' she beamed. 'Let's hunt grubs too,' she suggested, closing the tent flap behind them.

'I'll lean my spear over the door, Lichen added. 'I don't want Rush and Teal interrupted.'

'This is what I've been waiting for,' Teal whispered by the hearth

'And me. Ever since we met at the clan gathering.'

'Yes, Rush. You showed me how to dredge for gudgeon in muddy backwaters and cook them on hot stones. I do that so often.'

'I love how your lips move when you speak,' Rush heard himself say.

'Can we fish together?' Teal asked.

Rush leaned close, trying to say, 'Of course.' He faltered, trembling. Looking deeply into Teal's eyes, he put his lips to her forehead.

Teal whispered, 'You leave tomorrow?'

'Y-yes,' he stammered.

In their treasured privacy, they gently removed each other's clothes. It seemed so right. In the sunlight glowing through their hide cocoon, they caressed. Rush felt Teal's passion. They held tight in long embraces. Teal hummed sweetly, swaying against his skin. Rush's knees weakened. He felt Teal's breasts on his as she pulled him closer. He stiffened. They kissed. He caressed her spine. She leaned back. Rush felt her. They stood blissfully, moving like waving moonlight. Rush pressed forward, feeling fathoms of emotion. Teal held his dark head to hers, sharing his bursting gift.

'Of course we'll fish together, my beautiful Teal,' Rush whispered, united in the warmth of the smouldering charcoal.

'Ziit flexes easily, returning well, Honey. These new arrows are splendid,' Oiwa said, stroking the flights gently. 'We'll need fishing lines, a long length of net and harpoons.'

'Okay, Oiwa, let's gather,' she said. 'I'm looking forward to the splendid fiesta tonight before you all leave.'

'So am I. I can't wait. It will be such an adventure.

'We have a very long journey,' Mica said by the Goose clan's central fire. 'First we paddle downriver. We'll eventually get to where she flows extremely rapidly through amazingly deep clefts. That is Gunnal's Gulch. Deep down it, the Dun divides through rocky gorges and caverns. One chasm widens like a bowl, worn by years of tumbling currents. There's a shingle beach on the right. There we pull our boat in. Tine, Bark and I have done this before. It isn't easy. It is essential we land there,' he said, gazing into the flames. 'The Dun gets far too fast and treacherous beyond. The cliffs narrow even more. It's treacherous. Nobody survives that.'

North Star repeated Gunnal's legend, chewing on a quail. 'Gunnal, the ugly giantess, lay over rivers, tempting men. All who entered were consumed with fire. She spat them out like cinders. Once Farrnar rowed down the Dun on his iceberg boat. Gunnal's legs opened wide for him. The rocks squealed. They were as high as he could see. He sped his iceboat, paddling ever faster. His friends the bears pushed him too. He hurtled between her knees, entering her great, oozing cleft. The dark tunnel shone brightly with the ice. Farrnar's iceboat stuck tight in her womb. She froze! Farrnar escaped through her innards, casting his clothes away because of the stench. Gunnal retched, vomiting out the naked Farrnar, who spilled from her mouth into a great pool. Cursing, she turned forever to stone. Farrnar delved deep through the eel-filled waters. They covered him in slime, painting him gold like the sun. On the bank he mated with a waiting she-wolf. The undersides of their tails turn golden at night because of the tryst. That was the birth of the Loup tribe. They always help those who suffer Gunnal's anger.'

Mica continued. 'At the cliff-bottom are steps hammered out by Farrnar's children. There's a hawser to pull canoes up. It's a high climb. We carry our craft along the clifftop and look down into Gunnal's Gulch. Rivers foam into her where the Dun disappears inside. At

Gunnal's Navel there's a weird spy-hole. We can look right down it. Then we climb Gunnar's Paps.' Mica paused, fanning his brow. 'Then we march, carrying our boat to her shoulders. Below them is Wolf Lake. It is an easy descent. We can watch Gunnal's Falls spill into the waters far below. It's awesome.'

Steaming, pit-cooked meat was brought from the ground. Bats whirled, catching moths, fatally attracted by the fire-glow. It was a great feast, with dance, leaping fire, acrobatics, and shrilly performed legend songs.

Oiwa woke deep in the night, listening. 'Mica?' North Star asked quietly. 'When you get to Goose Landing, please ask the Innu if they've heard more of my old, old cousin Weir? He was a very fine man, but at the end of our journey to the Whale Geese, he changed. He was drawn away from us. He vanished. I've never understood why. If there's news, please bring it. I asked when you went before. Tales can take years to travel.'

Oiwa cupped his ear to listen. 'The last we heard was that he'd seen the Glowing Mountain. He followed the flights of geese past Warm Waters. We know no more. If he's alive, or found the Old Lands, we'd somehow surely get word?'

'Yes, Father, I'll ask and bring what news I can.' With that, they entered and snuggled down. Mica rose moments later to quietly cross the plaza for a naked goodbye with New Moon and her cakes.

Oiwa awoke at dawn, keen to examine Heron's Tooth again. How beautifully she was made: her double-stitched leather hull, stretched over a rigid bentwood frame, shone brilliantly after Honey and Petal's polishing. She would be so fast. Five plank seats were fixed between pairs of rigid spars; Oiwa was glad they were hide-padded for comfort. After a while, though, he realised he must go back. Teal was cooking gudgeon in nut flour. Rush would be delighted.

'Right,' Mica told them, 'I will be in the prow watching currents and keeping an eye out for obstacles. Tine, you're behind me, Bark and Oiwa together in the middle. Lichen, you go behind them. Lastly, Rush in the stern to steer and fish. Do you like fishing?' he asked the keen, nodding young man.

'I'm so proud for you, Rush,' Teal told him afterwards. 'Here's a pouch of bone and thorn hooks.'

'Thank you, Teal,' he replied, kissing her.

'And a drawstring bag of snails too. Wonderful bait, Rush.'

'Thanks so much,' he said, kissing her again.

'For you, Lichen, a bone and antler harpoon,' Widgeon said lovingly.

'It's wonderfully murderous. I adore it. The carved and polished shaft is splendid.'

'Right, men. Carry the Heron's Tooth to the shingle bank. Everyone will be there waving us off.'

'There's Ripple and Barb. I don't mind now. I feel rough, tough and ready.'

Oiwa's sisters loaded their weapons. Teal and Widgeon placed the folded net at the stern with a couple of bones wound with lengths of gut. Quill carried two rolls of leather and extra clothes. These tucked neatly into the sides of the Heron's Tooth. 'Mica,' North Star said, 'here's a pack of moose pemmican. You never know when you'll need it. All of you, give your mother and me a hug before taking your paddles.'

'I blow you a kiss, Widgeon.'

'A hatful from me to you, Teal,' Rush added as they pushed off for the middle of the Dun.

'At the first bend,' Mica commanded, 'turn and wave. Listen for the cheers, and then bang your paddles on the sides in farewell.'

To the sound of clattering oars, they slipped out of sight of the onlookers. 'At last!' Mica rejoiced. 'We're off. Right men,' he ordered. 'Even though we're going downstream, it's still a few days to the dreaded Gunnal's Gulch. Paddle hard. Let the Heron's bow bite water.'

The Dun wound round hills, between rocks and over rapids. She bent east then west, but her direction was forever northwards. They travelled through familiar woodlands first then passed rocky, shingle-bound islets. Waders watched as the Heron's Tooth sped by.

Rush looked at the riverbank. Turkeys scratched on a gravelly beach. He tapped Lichen on his shoulder, pointing. 'Later,' Lichen said, 'later.'

Not too much later, Rush hoped.

The Dun widened, flowing round a wooded hill, the right bank a treeless plain. The current slowed. Rush fished. He fitted a large carved moose vertebra from his tackle bag over the wooden stern-peg. It was wound with a strong gut line that spun easily through the hole from which the spinal cord had been sucked years before. He fitted a sinew trace and took one of Teal's hooks, whipping it on tightly. He crushed a snail in his fingers and threaded it on the hook. 'That'll do,' he thought, unravelling several yards of line, tossing the bait to one side and watching it float.

Mica leaned over the prow, eyeing the water. Oiwa paddled, contemplating his surroundings. Above, buzzards soared in thermals, watchful for prey. A falcon perched low in a tree. It leaned forward to glide silently across the river. Its talons spread, it dropped on to its furry quarry.

The Heron's Tooth carried them effortlessly. Mica navigated round boulders and shallows. Rush fished, and was diverted by a heron throwing its head down to take a large dace. Then something tugged his finger. He gripped the line and jerked his left hand. 'Hooked!' he shouted, gripping the taught cord in his right hand, playing the fish. 'See it leap. It's shaking its head.' He spun the backbone to wind in slack. The Heron's Tooth glided on. 'It's tiring. In you come, my fine trout. Over the side. Got you.' He bent the fish's head and sensed its spine cracking. It flapped furiously on the boat's bottom and lay still. 'Dinner for one.' he shouted.

'Me, please?' Oiwa called above the sound of paddle strokes.

'Come on, Jasper,' Rush said to his sharp knife. 'Let us cut these fins off and bind them above the hook as a lure and then shove a new snail on. Good, now for a proper cast. More gut, whirl it round my head and let go. Excellent, it's gone far. There's the splash. Drift down with us and I'll keep an eye on your snaking line.

'There's the heron flying by. Ah! That's a big swirl by my bait: A hungry fish? Ouch! The line's tightened round my fingers. Strike... It's a big one, chaps. It needs more line. It's headed upstream. Turn the boat.'

'Aye, Rush.' Mica responded. Paddles splashed. Heron's Tooth spun, facing the oncoming water. 'Upstream. Follow that fish.'

'That's better. Lichen, help me. Grab the line too.'

'Sure thing, Rush. Shift over.'

'Ning! It's changed its mind. He's making for the bank towards the roots of that wide willow. No you don't,' Rush yelled. 'Back-paddle, Mica. Pull with me, Lichen. It's going to leap. Look at it flying under the tree. It's a beauty. Strike again,' he shouted. 'Did you see those silvery sides? The water's stilled now. We've turned it away from the roots... Shite!' he shouted moments later. 'Lost it. The line's slack. But did you see it flash just then? Paddle quick,' he yelled. 'It's running downstream. Faster. Follow it.' He screamed. 'It's decided to hide way over there. Catch up with it... Stop the boat,' Rush suddenly urged moments later. 'Lichen. Draw line in. Tighten on its jaw. There it leaps. Haul!' he instructed.

'I'll harpoon the brute,' he shouted, reaching for his new weapon. 'There it goes,' He cheered, hurling it. 'Bugger. It's cut the line. It's free,' he feared for an instant. 'No! Yes. I've hit it. Gone right through. It's writhing in the air. Take the harpoon cord, Rush. You pull it in.'

'It's a whacker, Lichen. Help me haul the writhing monster in. There, over you go. Into the boat, you giant. How violently you still protest.'

'Here, Rush, take my axe,' Mica offered. 'Swipe its brains with that.'

'Thanks, Mica. Become dead... now... fish.' He brought down the implement, splitting its skull. Then he sat back, shaking, stunned at his catch, nursing his blue fingers. He slowly wound the tackle back on the bone reel, knotted the line and disgorged Teal's treasured hook from the monster's gullet.

Lichen cut his harpoon from the fish, regarding his cousin's silent gaze.

Mica broke the trance. 'Paddle on. There's far to go yet.'

Chapter 11

*

River Meeting

'There's an exercise we must master.' Mica said seriously. 'We have only one chance to land Heron's Tooth in the Gulch. We must train. When I command, 'Right, beach,' jab your paddles in on the *left*. Turn as sharp right as possible. We drive her on to the shingle shore. We leap out immediately, beaching her. Then lash our gear inside for porting her up those steps.'

Soon Mica spotted a landing place. 'Pull to the central flow,' he commanded, thinking, 'This will be excellent practice.' Suddenly he yelled, 'Right, beach,' pointing his paddle to the small strand he'd seen. 'Aye,' the cry went up. The Heron's Tooth turned. They stroked forcefully, compensating for the Dun's flow. Heron's Tooth crossed it, nudging the sand. 'Ashore sharpish,' Mica commanded, leaping out and taking the prow. Tine, Bark and Oiwa stepped into shallows. They gripped the sides of their canoe, beaching her as Lichen and Rush leapt ashore.

'Well done,' Mica said. 'We'll practise and get slicker. Back in the boat.'

Downriver they went. 'This is wonderful,' Oiwa said to Bark.

'Yes. It sure beats home. I love hunting in the mountains, but this tops it. Look, Oiwa. An osprey. It's swooping. Watch its talons open to meet a scaly back. There it soars again with a wriggling fish.'

'Smoke downriver from a knoll on the right bank. We'll call in.' Mica announced. 'Wait for the command... Right, beach.' Their paddles splashed. The Heron's Tooth jutted with the effort. She bounced into the rapid stream and was crossing it. 'Fuck!' Mica shouted. 'Log coming at us! Pull harder.'

'Ah! It's hit!' Rush and Lichen warned, feeling the brunt of the crash.

'The stump's punctured Heron's Tooth,' Oiwa moaned as she slewed.

'Paddle! Paddle! Paddle!' Mica yelled, striking the surface with terrific force. 'She's turning. The log's crunching into shallows. The tear is widening. She's taking water.'

'What's up?' they heard shouted from the bank.

'Struck a trunk. That's what's bleeding up,' Mica returned.

'The log's rolled, pushing her under. Catch the harpoons – they're floating out.'

'Grab the trout,' Rush yelped as it bobbed alarmingly close to the side.

'Get her off the log,' Mica bayed, leaping from the prow, waist deep. 'I'll lift the stern and pull her round. Keep paddling. She's pushing me under. I'm shifting,' he spluttered, righting the boat. 'I've got her. My feet are dug into the gravel, but she's still sinking.'

Two men splashed next to Mica. 'Fall, Rail, where have you come from?'

'Hunting, visiting and now rescuing.' Fall answered.

'Marsh too.' Oiwa said, as another of Greyling's sons balanced on the stranded trunk. Then he bellowed, 'Ziit's floating out! Grab him, Marsh.'

'Okay. And your quiver... the harpoons too. I'll hurl them to the bank.'

'Terrific,' Oiwa spurted as he too sank with the craft.

Rush let a curdling yowl, seeing his huge salmon's chin nudging the side of the boat. 'Don't let it escape,' he screamed, jumping behind Mica, grabbing its gills, miraculously dragging it ashore.

'Keep hold of your paddles.' roared Mica while catching Rush's.

'Oiwa, out quickly,' Marsh commanded. 'Here! Help shift the root out.'

'Lichen. Rescue everything?' Oiwa pleaded.

'Now. We must turn the root and push the boat away. Shove like shit,' Marsh shouted. 'Pull the root back. It's tearing. Never mind. Push. She's coming loose. Pull the hull towards the sloping bank. Her nose is tipping. The Dun's water is running out from her.'

'Stop that net,' Rush hollered from the bank.

Mica took control. 'Roll her over gently. Don't let anything else escape while she empties. Then we can carry her to Fall's camp up the track.'

They followed the masses of animal footmarks to the knoll where the fire glowed. Water ran from every seam of their clothing.

'Put her by Scoula,' Marsh suggested. 'And mind our game.'

'Nice beast,' Oiwa commented, seeing a hind slumped ready for grollocking.

'First we must think about fixing our boat. Who's got resin?'

'I've a little,' Rail offered.

'Not enough. Fine crew we are. Totally unprepared. Oiwa, go to those larches and tap some. Here's my axe. Take the baler to gather it.'

Oiwa nipped off to the clump in a vale. He chopped a V-shaped cleft into several trunks. By the time the last was cut, a run of thick sap flowed down the bark. With his grey knife, he scraped it on to the scooped wooden vessel and went the rounds until he'd collected an ample supply. On his return, he found that Rush had been busy too.

'Help me with this stone slab,' he called from the riverbank. 'I've just hauled it out.' Together they carried the heavy rock. 'I've already set three stones by the fireplace. We can aggle this on top and make a fire under it. Then I'll cook the salmon.'

'What about our deer?' Fall protested weakly.

'We'll have the liver and kidneys. You can stash the rest for later. Oiwa, help me gut the fish. Here's your trout... Catch. Hold Uncle Salmon up by the gills and I'll run my shiny blade down its belly. We'll cast the entrails and heart into the Dun as thanks. It will feed an eel or three.' As they hit the water, Rush suddenly felt that sharp itch he'd experienced in the sweat lodge. He stood, chilled, momentarily.

The friends ran back to the fireplace. Bark and Tine marked round the punctures in the Heron's Tooth. Their toolkit was rolled open beside them. 'We'll make leather patches,' Bark said, 'bore holes through and do the same in the Heron's wall. We can stitch patches each side of the rents. We've plenty of needles. We can do it together. Rush is heating up that stone. I'm going to melt Rail's resin on it and blend it with Oiwa's. We can fill the patches when they are almost sewn. Stitch the last bits. Squash them together and, swift as a bison's fart... Finished.'

'Do you want that stone heated quicker?' Marsh asked.

'Yes. How?'

'We've rolled the thighbones in fat to burn for Tarune and Barouci, the deer sprites. We'll do it on the stone and speed things up. They'll reek enough to get shot of the midges, aaaaand... keep the marauding beasts at bay. What do you think?'

'Since you put it like that, why not? But don't crack the stone.'

'We've grollocked the deer. Fall's wrapped the flesh in its skin. We're scoffing the liver and kidneys before having the salmon anyway.'

'Okay,' Marsh said. 'We can shovel ash over the stone to spread the heat with the deer's shoulder blade.' Then he remarked, 'Look, here's burnt bones from a past feast and a busted blade. I'll keep that. It might come in handy.'

Rush thought of Teal. Carefully he took his jasper knife from its padded sheath. 'I'm going to cut my salmon's tail off. A Greyling brother can give it to Teal for me. She'll know it was her hook that caught it and she'll dry our fine trophy.' He looked around apprehensively. 'I just feel we're being watched. But I see nor hear nought.'

'By the gods, those bones don't half smoke,' Tine said.

'As usual,' Bark put in as they worked the patches. 'That's the terrible beauty of it all. The animal's offering crackles and spits. The femurs glow and turn white. The gnats go. The scavengers leave us alone. The thighs collapse. We pushed the thick ends together. The gods are sated and we cook our resin.'

'Right,' Mica said impatiently. 'Fan those embers. Let's boil the glue and thicken it.'

'That's it. Done.' Mica said in relief after they'd squeezed the blister patches. 'Look, the resin's oozed out by each stitch and sealed them. It should make flexible, watertight mends. They'll be tested the morn anyway. Maybe now we can taste that liver?'

Rush took charge of his range. 'Hand me the offal,' he said to Fall. Everyone circled the stone hungrily.

'Here,' Fall answered as his blooded hand passed the limp organs.

'Kidneys first. Strip the suet off,' Rush said to himself. 'More fuel under the stone. That's it. Heating up nicely. Resin's dried, now for more sizzling fat. I'll halve the kidneys. Don't they smell great? Now for the liver. I'll slice it on my knee. Never mind the bloodstains. Take what you want, men,' he said as it curled temptingly on the slab.

'Now for the salmon,' he announced, straining to hold it up high.

'Wonderful.' Oiwa cheered as warm hind blood ran down his cheeks, 'This is so good. How do you do it so well?'

'Watching with mother. That's how. Mind out, the fish is going on. First I must spread more fat over the stone. There, help me on with it, someone. The lower side will cook. Then we roll the fish over. Mica, Bark, will you do that with your axes please?'

'Just tell us when,' they replied.

'About ready,' Rush instructed when he smelled well-cooked salmon. 'Axes wedged under the side. That's good, now heave it over. The skin will stick to the rock and all the cooked flesh will be revealed. Lichen and I share the cheek. Hunters' privileges, you know. Then you can all get stuck in.'

'This is wonderful, Rush,' Tine remarked as flesh slid from his slate knife into his mouth, the juices trickling into his growing stubble. 'How long until the other side's done?'

'When the spine's been picked clean and peeled away, I expect,' Rush replied. 'Would you like the eye before I turn the other cheek, Tine?'

'Give it to Mica, he's the lookout.'

'Mica, An eye for you...'

'Thanks, Rush. You enjoy the other.'

'How's your expedition been?' Mica enquired of Fall.

'Great, in fact brilliant. We lived a few days with the Stork clan and shared many of our kills. I've fallen in love with one of the chief's daughters, Gale. Here's the knife she gave me. See, it's polished basalt with a bear-fang handle.'

'That's awesome, Fall.'

'Yes, Gale's lovely too.'

'Oh, shut up,' his brothers said. 'All he can do is go on about his new love. It's sickening.'

'You stop it. I'm going back for her.'

'It'll cost you more bear's teeth than you'll ever hunt,' they jibed.

'I can...'

'Shut it!'

'You're jealous.'

'Pfffffffff.'

Fall changed the subject. 'So, Oiwa, you have the North Star tattoo. Well done.' He brushed back his light hair back to reveal his.

'Gale saw plenty of your other star too,' Marsh sniggered as he dumped salmon flakes into his mouth.

Fall ignored his annoying brother. 'It's healing nicely, Oiwa.'

'I'd forgotten about it,' Oiwa replied, pushing his hair back and rubbing the tiny scabs away from the glittering specks. 'It was terrific in the lodge. We became our Spirit Familiars. I went far on my wings of the night then flew back to where I received my stars. I feel different now, like I've grown.' He scratched under his trousers to free the star's scabs there.

'Mine was like that. I'm a heron. That's why I love fish. When you return, we'll have a big sweat. But you'll experience Buzzard's lodge. He's Gale's father.'

'Quiet,' Marsh warned.

'Has everyone had enough?' Rush asked. 'The salmon's nearly gone. Any venison, Fall?'

'Not for me,' he burped politely.

'Your trout, Oiwa?' He shook his head dreamily.

'Listen,' Bark said, pulling his damp trousers tight. Stretching a leg high, he squeezed his stomach tightly and farted musically. 'Sufficient food for me too.' This brought screams of laughter.

The distant northern mountains glowed in the sunset. 'Let's put the boats together on their sides and shelter between them.' Mica suggested. 'Forked stakes holding a ridge-pole will support our leathers. One end open to the fire, and it will be cosy.'

'I'm nearly dry. Let's stoke the fire and steam off before dusk.' Tine suggested.

'And drag a couple of small fallen larches for the fire, Rush,' Oiwa suggested. 'I'm almost dry too. No point in changing – all our other stuff's wet,' he added. 'We'd better hang it out,'

Rush sniffed the air. 'Could rain? We'll hang it anyway. It's soaked now, if it wets again, it will just be fresh wet, won't it?' He was still wondering about the odd presence he had sensed.

'Reasonable thinking,' answered Oiwa.

Another fire burned beautifully beside the cooking table. Oiwa and Rush hung the wet things on stick frames. Evening drew in. The band crouched, swapping news. 'I'll tell you all a fascinating tale about Ripple,' Bark offered.

Oiwa realised that all eyes were on him.

Cool air wafted from the Dun. The river could be heard passing, passing... passing. Stars appeared one by one. A thin cloud cut a rising moon. Owls hooted. Distant carnivorous nostrils smelt the acrid warning of burnt bones.

Marsh shifted on his haunches when Oiwa's Epic of Ripple had concluded. 'It's strange,' he said when their laughter subsided. 'We had a great time with Buzzard's Stork clan, but something worrying is up. Three folk are missing. Birch Skin, one of Buzzard's many nephews, and his bydie-in, Snaaaaar. They assumed hunting. She hurried back for her daughter, then cleared off with his weapons.

'Odd,' they all thought.

Marsh, picking his nose thoughtfully, continued. 'She's a tiresome varmint. Nothing's right for her. She'd had a series of men, but only bore this one girl, Dew. You'll hear about it there anyway. But the short story is, Birch Skin was found murdered with a stinking vulture ready to scavenge him. He was bare-naked, hunting knife busted off in his breastbone and his prick sliced clean off.'

'Horrid,' thought Oiwa, wide-eyed, wincing and furtively covering his sacred area.

'You'll hear when you stop by. They're pitched downriver. Buzzard asked if anyone sees some suspicious woman and girl about, bring them back for questioning.'

They swapped news until Rush eventually said, 'It's got cold. The sky is filling in. Rain is coming. Let's bring the gear inside and huddle down.'

'I'll bank up the fire,' Fall offered as the first heavy spots arrived.

They crawled together on a groundsheet. Rush hugged his salmon tail and curled up. The raindrops hit the hides and ran down over the canoes.

'So it's a hunting trip, Mica?' Marsh asked in the deep snuggle.

'More than that. We're off to Goose Landing to pay reverence. I've been before. I'm taking a wife when I return. I'll be chief when Dad goes dead. '

'Fall's got his nuts twisted over Gale. He'll have to take precious presents to Buzzard, then bring her home to make her into a proper Goose clan woman.'

'Aye. This trip's for Oiwa, Lichen and Rush's initiation. Our Caribou guests will become family by taking Widgeon and Teal.'

'Those two. They're nice ones, I must say. What about the ugly cousin?'

'She left in a huff, talking about "Inner Beauty", Marsh laughed.

The rain poured. The fire hissed. The drops pelted on their hide roof. They were warm and snug within. Rush let a long, silent break of deadly wind.

'Who's guilty?' Tine enquired.

The cook kept quiet and went to sleep, grinning.

In the rain, a pair of sly ears listened. A wet, slightly bent nose sniffed the steam from the stone. Two bulging grey eyes stared at the shelter. The bedraggled intruder slunk back into the gloom.

Day broke. Rain ceased. The Dun roared.

Mica shook drips off after his morning pee. He'd clambered over his tent-mates to wee and crap then washed in a grassy puddle. 'Rise and look stupid,' he encouraged briskly. Slowly they followed.

Their campfire was a wet mess. Rivulets ran through the ashen hearth. The embers beneath the range still lived.

'It'll be a hard paddle upriver,' Rail remarked, cleaning his teeth on a chewed stick. 'The current's strong.'

'We'll have to port Scouler until slacker water,' Fall suggested.

Rush crawled out with his salmon tail. 'Fall?' he asked confidentially. 'Would you take this to Teal? It's just, I lay awake much of the night thinking of her. I love her. Tell her I'm thinking of her? And say that when I return, we'll fish together.' He rubbed his dark eyes.

'Of course, Rush. I hope you don't get teased like my ugly brothers tease me.'

'Thanks. Thanks,' replied Rush. 'Here it is. I'll give it a kiss first. Take it.'

'Well. It's onwards and upwards,' Marsh said as they broke camp.

'Stow everything carefully in the Heron's Tooth,' Mica said. 'It's time to move.'

'No breakfast?' Rush asked.

'That's right. Nothing. We're well fed from last night.'

'Hugs all round, chaps,' Tine said.

'Don't stop any arrows,' Rail added.

'We won't if you don't,' came the standard reply.

The Greyling sons carried the Scoular, venison inside her, over the flat river plain to meet the Dun upstream.

'Okay... Time to test our mends,' Mica stated. 'Same positions. This'll be practice for approaching Gunnal's Gulch. The Dun is running fast. She'll be doing just that when we near her gorge,' he impressed on the crew. 'Rush, hold the stern as we embark. Jump in after. If you miss, we'll try and come back for you. If not... swim,' he added fondly.

Rush leapt into his seat. 'Off we go,' he said.

'Paddle on. Check those patches. Watch for leaks,' Mica spelled out.

'Can't see any,' Bark reported.

'Me neither,' confirmed Oiwa. 'We'll keep looking, though.'

'We'll do the Left Paddle manoeuvre later. Strain into midstream. It will be bumpy, but fine.'

'I'm glad of these padded seats, Mica,' Oiwa pointed out.

'Me too. Paddler's backside's agony.'

On the left bank the light woodland continued. The right bank was still, grassy plain. The Dun cut deeper, narrowing slightly. This made her faster and even bumpier. 'How are those mends?' Mica called.

'Just fine,' came reassurance from the stern.

'I can't see a practice beach yet. Better speed on,' Mica said.

'Bison scent,' said Bark urgently, looking to the banks. The river swung. Ahead was a turn. The current took them to the high right bank. The Heron's Tooth careered round as the side heightened. Eroded loam slipped from it, clouding the water.

'There,' Tine said. 'Ahead, on the bank. Grazing beasts. They are watching us.'

'We're going right beneath,' Oiwa whispered. 'Look at that huge curling tongue gripping the grass above. I can hear the bison's front teeth shearing it from the roots. See their reflections, Bark? They're like a vast, chewing hedge lining the bank.'

'Yes. Amazing. There's our reflections too: As though we're right in the middle of them. I've never seen the like,' came Bark's reply.

'That herd's vast. The biggest I've seen,' said Lichen, looking upwards.

'Smell their breath,' Oiwa remarked. 'It stinks of putrid grass.'

'And their extraordinary flatulence,' added Rush with an air of authority.

'I'm desperate for a pee,' Lichen announced as soon as they'd passed the herd. 'Can we steady the boat?'

'All pee.' Mica commanded. 'Let's get it over with. Either stand up, or do it in a bailer. Anyone for anything else?' Mica queried when all had done.

'No. Not yet,' came the reply in unison.

Not long afterwards, Mica surprised them with the barked command, 'Paddle left. Beach!' They came ashore on a small wooded island, disturbing the nesting storks. 'Excellent,' Mica remarked. 'Now disembark. Stretch your legs.'

'Where there's storks, there's fish,' Rush thought. 'I'll wander along the backwater with my harpoon. There are big river perch gliding between the roots of overhanging bushes. Their spiky fins radiate like arrow fans. Come closer.' He whispered to them while crouching on spongy moss. Come perch; come,' he willed. 'Account for refraction... hurl. Hit it!' The water clouded muddily as the perch struggled. 'Come on perch, I'll pull you out.'

'Right, men, we've rested up and stretched. On with our journey,' Mica said as Rush reappeared.

'Might I mention breakfast, perhaps?' asked Rush. 'We could cook this before we go.'

'No. Fillet it. Eat it raw.'

'Okay. Not much between six anyway.'

'Embark. Same drill. You last, Rush,' Mica commanded.

The river rejoined, the storks settled awkwardly. Heron's Tooth sped as the sun climbed. Wooded hills rose on their left; to the right, grasslands spread.

'No more stops,' Mica informed them. 'With good headway, we'll be with the Stork clan by early evening.'

Vultures circled, searching for a crippled animal. The scarlet irises in their balding heads noticed two land-bound travellers east of the immense bison herd. They appeared too healthy for further scrutiny.

'Paddle on,' Mica decreed. Their arms powered the rhythmically dipping shafts. A pleasing white bow wave appeared at the prow. The centre of the river flowed fastest. Mica steered into it. The craft bumped, reaching the turbulent current. A breeze caught Oiwa's hair as he paddled eagerly. They gained speed with every dip and pull. The crew chanted, their voices strong above the sound of speeding water. It stopped their hunger as they raced between the banks.

'I smell bison again, but on the other side,' Rush remarked some hours later. 'There are more vultures too. Maybe there's been a kill?'

The sun was sinking when Bark spotted a lone hunter. 'Wave our paddles to greet him. He's raising his long spear in welcome.'

'There's a column of smoke... and another. At last: signs of civilization!' Tine exulted in relief.

'Round another bend, closer to the rising hills,' Mica reminded Bark and Tine. 'See the white mountaintops in the far distance. I don't want to mention it, but that's where Gunnal's Gulch delves.'

Heron's Tooth scraped her keel lightly on sand. 'The Dun widens here, becoming shallow,' Mica warned. 'Take the deeper channel by the left bank.' As they dipped into faster water, the long canoe lurched left around a bend. A stretching quartzite sandbank and a great pool came speedily into view. Boats were drawn up on the bank. Children played and fished. They shouted and waved excitedly. The Heron's Tooth had brought them to the Stork clan.

Chapter 12

*

Buzzard's Welcome

'Hard left, beach,' Mica instructed. 'Swing round, point to the shore, glide across the slack pool and arrive gently, kiss-like, on the sands. Me out first, then Tine. He holds the painter for Bark to alight. Oiwa follows.'

'Me after. Hurry up, my arse is so painful, even on that cushion,' Lichen complained.

'I'll stand in the stern pushing Heron's beak higher,' Rush added, 'She'll pull further up so I can step on to dry land.'

Clamouring children surrounded them. Their mothers appeared with dried washing from the bushes. 'Lovely ladies,' Mica remarked. 'Unload Heron's Tooth,' he said, pulling in his stomach and standing tall.

'Whoop, whoop,' Buzzard greeted them. 'Meet my wives. Here's my family running to greet more Goose clansmen. Welcome. Have you come to woo our women and take them away?' He laughed broadly. 'You can – it just depends how many bear's teeth you can afford.' He took Mica's hands, shaking them. 'And two black, spiky-haired Caribous. Your fine round faces give you away. Come to my house,'

Buzzard invited. 'Your things will be brought up by the youngsters. They'll want to nose in it anyway.'

'Be careful with my bow, and those arrows,' Oiwa said to the excited children. 'I'm keeping an eye on you,' he added as they tugged his trousers while he followed Buzzard's huge footprints along the gravelly ridge. The Stork village was unlike theirs. It was haphazard, with no circle, only a rough oval, a mix of teepees and skin-covered wicker huts. There were fireplaces everywhere, with a massive heap of wood stacked roughly in the middle. Were they having a fiesta? Oiwa wondered.

'Meet two more of my wives,' Buzzard said, smiling broadly. 'This is Gale, a fine daughter.' She sat by the door burnishing a pot. Others lay beside her with patterns carved through the polish. She raised her head in greeting. Her trailing black hair shimmered in the slanting sunlight. Her face was long and elegant, her dark eyes shone clear and bright. She laid her pot aside and stood to receive the visitors.

'She's as lovely as Fall told us,' Bark saw, as did the speechless Tine and Mica.

'Welcome to my father's house,' Gale said, brushing the clay dust from her tunic. 'One of my mothers will fetch a drink.'

'How many wives does Buzzard have?' Oiwa asked.

'That you might never find out,' Gale answered, smiling. 'I have many, many brothers and sisters. Stand aside. Some of them will put your gear in Buzzard's house. Prop their harpoons and bows against wigwam sides by the doorway, you young,' she instructed. 'Come in, be warm by the hearth.' Buzzard's place was evident: a great leather floor-cushion on the rush matting had a huge depression forced by his considerable weight. Around the fire, polished logs served as seating too. A curtain of white stork feathers screened the way to the adjoining chamber.

Ember entered, standing tall after ducking through the flaps. 'Cool honey water?' she offered, handing one of Gale's pots to Mica. He sipped and nodded a thank you over the brim. He handed it on to Bark, wiping a small petal from his top lip. Bark noticed dried rosebuds swirling in the bowl. He passed it on to Oiwa, who strained some of the fluid through clenched jaws and handed it to Rush, pink petals stuck to his white teeth. Ember giggled. Rush raised it to his lips, feeling the incised design on his fingertips. Plover, a further wife entered with a second crock. They felt the reviving honeyed water settling in their stomachs. Hunger pangs dissipated.

'Good. You've had something,' Buzzard said, entering with style. 'Now. Tell me about yourselves?' He grew even more in the confines of his home. His dark, long hair, plaited with contrasting white stork feathers, rested on his shoulders. His suede jacket sported bear-tooth toggles. The slightly open neck revealed darkened skin with a hint of a red tattoo at the top of his sternum.

'I'm Mica, of North Star, and these are my brothers Tine, Bark and Oiwa. These two are...'

'They can speak for themselves,' Buzzard said, delving in his pouch for birch resin. 'Well, young Caribou, enlighten me.'

'My name is Lichen, a son of Otter. He is next to our leader on the...'

'I don't want a family history,' Buzzard interrupted, turning to Rush.

'Rush. Son of Puma,' he blurted. A pink petal slid from his chin.

'Good,' Buzzard said. 'That's got the formalities done. In your honour, I have ordered a feast. It is good having visitors.' Ember and Plover nodded happily as Buzzard bit off small chunks of resin. 'What brings you this way – a hunting trip?' He handed a piece to Mica.

'Not a hunting trip. We're travelling to Goose Landing.' The gum softened beside his tongue. Buzzard listened with interest. 'It's part of Oiwa's initiation. Rush and Lichen are taking two of our clanswomen, so they come to earn them.'

'You'll be going through Gunnal's Gulch again?'

'Aye,' Mica responded.

'You Geese-folk are brave, maybe too brave. The Dun's still high with rain and meltwaters. You should bide here a couple of days and pray for sunshine and no rain. Think about it. We've plenty to keep you amused.' He smiled, passing the rest of the resin round. Mica chewed happily; the dried, minty herbs in it released their flavours. His mouth freshened.

Ember and Plover noticed Buzzard begin to rise. They helped his hefty bulk up. 'Come see my village.' They stooped to leave, following the chief of the Storks.

Behind Buzzard's house stood a tall meat-drying rack, surmounted with horns. Eye, their brindled dog, guarded it. He chewed a huge shoulder blade noisily. Most of the odd dwellings had meat frames. There were skins stretching too. Some had piles of wooden trays waiting to be polished. The doors of the structures were set in all directions. Outside, things were being made or mended. Everyone looked busy.

'Two more of my wives live there. Not all of their young are mine. We had a rare visitor from the Innu. He's responsible for twins. Talking of offspring, Gale is spoken for by Fall, one of your clan. He'll need to bring good gifts when he comes for her.'

'We met him and his brothers way upriver. We camped together. You'll get excellent presents – he's smitten,' Mica replied.

'Good,' Buzzard beamed, rubbing his ivory toggles. 'I'm longing for more bear fangs.'

As they toured, Rush noticed burning, bits of curled, singed hide, smashed pottery and the remains of a central fireplace and ruined stone tools. He looked closer.

'That's all that's left of that evil bitch's hut,' Buzzard cursed, spitting venomously. 'We torched it.' He shook his head gravely. 'We'll speak later.' Ashes blew in a slight breeze. Burned bone beads fell to powder. They followed Buzzard, his mood more serious. Later he said, 'There's been a successful hunt this morning. Two good buffalo. There's enough for my whole village.' The sun was setting. Fires were revived. Menfolk appeared from tents and huts wearing furs against the cooling evening. 'Follow. We'll get ready.'

A three-quarter-moon rose. Oiwa pinned his hair back with heron feathers, showing his Star. He rubbed grease on it from the side of his nose and it sparkled. He tugged his short, soft beard, hoping it was a little longer. His brothers' whiskers grew quicker.

Gale lent them elegant furs. 'How is Fall?' she asked

'He's great. He spoke wonderfully of you,' Oiwa answered. 'His brothers tried to shut him up, though. Maybe jealousy? He's so proud of your knife.'

'I'm glad. I miss him. He's returned for bear's teeth. That'll settle any bargain with my father,' she added. 'Let me place this beaver wrap over your shoulders. You will look good in it.'

The Goose journeyers filed to the arena. Buzzard, sitting on his big log drum, said, 'Meet my brother, Catfish. Sit in the circle of seats. I'll bang mine.' It resounded loud and long. Catfish bashed his too. The young men's eyes opened, awed at the sounds. Oiwa sat patting one. 'Nice,' he thought.

In the centre lay polished trays of rolled raw buffalo fillet stuffed with dried mushrooms that moistened in the blood. All was covered in scorched plantain seeds, sprinkled with rock salt and garnished with salsify. Ember cut them into round chunks with her magnificent dark carving knife. Rush drooled.

'Dig in, men,' Ember said, taking some.

Catfish's chief wife, Stella, joined her. 'Lovely meat,' she commented. The troupe agreed with their mouths full.

Catfish turned to Mica, asking directly, 'Did you blokes see anyone on your journey?'

Mica swallowed prematurely, hurting his gullet as the hunk descended. 'Only Fall and his brothers,' he managed, reaching for a drink before adding, 'Yes, there was the hunter. We waved shortly before we arrived.'

'Nobody else other than Hoof Tracker, then?' queried Catfish. Mica shook his head. 'Did none of you notice anybody or anything strange?' They shook their heads, not knowing if Catfish was pleased or no.

Rush pondered as he and Oiwa took more meat. Their eyes gazed heavenwards as they chewed. 'I'll note the ingredients,' Rush thought as the others dipped in. The bowlful shrank until only blood remained.

'I'll have that. Chief's rights,' Buzzard said, draining it.

A chorus of girls swayed past singing as Catfish asked sadly, 'Did you hear of my boy's murder?' Tine nodded while biting into another hunk.

'Yes. We we're very concerned. Do you have news?' Mica asked.

'Absolutely,' Buzzard put in. Catfish spat in the fire; an ember darkened as his phlegm bubbled. Buzzard explained, 'What we know is, it's bizarre that that woman, Snaaaaar, went hunting with Birch Skin without weapons. He'd been very tolerant of her temper and her demands for ages.' Catfish frowned, coughed and spat in the fire again.

The smell of food grew as a cooking pit was opened. A vast hunk of roasted hindquarter got speared and lifted from the charcoal on to a huge tray. Gale scraped the ash as it wobbled slightly, steaming aromatically.

'She, vile bitch, left her daughter Dew to go in the hills with Birch Skin,' Buzzard told them. 'She returned, collected her, and gathered their bows and arrows. She hurried off, saying cheerily, "Birch Skin's found game, back soon." and hasn't been seen since.'

Catfish coughed again. Stella slapped his back. He spat mucus through his curled tongue into their fire. The moonlight shone brightly. Gale carved meat, passing it round on an arrow point. Catfish chewed, saying, 'There's more. Hoof Tracker, who you waved to, was suspicious. Next day he left to follow her and the daughter. He found their traces going in a completely different direction from what he'd expected. They were easy to follow first, then they vanished.' Catfish put more meat in his mouth, sucking the blood.

Buzzard carried on. 'Hoof Tracker returned and followed his earlier hunch. Although faded, he found traces of two adults going in one direction then it looked like, one person, Snaaaaar, had hurried back.' He leaned forward, belched, wiped his chin and reached for more meat. His knife slid through it, peeling off a juicy slice. He continued. 'Hoof tracker searched the wooded hills, and came upon a mossy clearing.' Buzzard shifted awkwardly. 'There he found Birch Skin's murdered corpse.'

Catfish shook, enraged. 'Birch Skin was my son, made by my second wife,' he remonstrated emotionally. Stella soothed him.

'Hoof Tracker saw the wounds inflicted on my boy. He'd been stabbed and slashed over and over. Hit with stones and bashed in the eyes.' Stella cuddled her grieving husband.

Buzzard continued. Catfish wiped his eyes. 'Hoof Tracker was terribly upset. He rolled the stiffened body of his friend and saw how viciously he'd been attacked from all round. Then he noticed the broken obsidian blade, its murderous black end between Birch Skin's ribs. His poor mouth, agape, shocked.' Buzzard paused, inhaling deeply. 'Hoof Tracker vomited. He turned aside so as not to spray his dead friend. He coughed, choking at the edge of the clearing and finished throwing up. That's where he found the bloodied bone dagger-handle. He stooped to make sure, and discovered worse... His manhood! It had been severed. A horrid mess. Balls and all.'

The friends were shocked. Their meat lay cold in their hands. A tray of spit-roasted quail followed. Trembling fingers reached for the small birds.

Catfish uttered. 'She mutilated him, she did,' pausing in revulsion. 'We know it was Snaaaaar. It's her stinking knife.' He pulled a wing off his bird, sharing it with Stella.

Buzzard took over. 'Hoof Tracker lifted his mate's corpse over his shoulder to carry him home. Slowly the body bent at the stomach as he made his sorry trek back. We sent out hunters to find her, but she's clever. There were false trails, then a decent trace, then none at all. Hoof Tracker later found the right one.' Buzzard swallowed some quail breast. 'He followed those two to the hills. Just at the edge of the trees he found their shits.' He shoved more in his mouth, explaining as he chewed. 'The both of them squatted and crapped, concealing their mess under pine needles, then vanished into the rocky lands. The rain of the other night obliterated any signs in the open. She could have crossed the Dun way upriver at the ford, where the herds go.'

'But can you be sure it was their shits?' Rush asked seriously.

'Yes!' screeched Stella. 'They were pure white and stank of lilies.' With her splendid sarcasm, they fell into staggering fits of amazed laughter, breaking their gloom. Buzzard tried to add to the mirth, but couldn't, holding his belly to stop it exploding. When the outburst subsided, he finally he whispered bits of of what he meant to say to Stella, still holding his sides.

Stella translated Buzzard's comment bit by bit. 'And they'd – wiped their – arses – with pure swansdown.' Her shoulders shook, her mouth hung open, tumults of mirth ringing in the night air. The rest of The Stork clan came to hear the crack. The joke was repeated many times, dispelling the lurking sadness.

Oiwa picked up a beat on his drum. It circulated round their ring. The nubile chorus returned. They ate until weariness got them. Stifled yawns and Oiwa's chin drooping to his chest told their hosts it was time for their guests to sleep. Gale showed them through the door to their curtained room. She'd lit lamps of fat-filled river mussels. Round the walls, sturdy upright frames supported horizontal poles. Over these were thick hide beds. At the far end was a huge litter, where Buzzard perched. He would come through later, or sleep elsewhere with another wife.

In the centre of the oval space was a skin-lined pit. Water covered the bottom. Large, burned river stones were piled at its side. This was Buzzard's sweat lodge too. A low hum came from Rush's direction.

'Salsify makes him fart too,' Lichen remarked.

Chapter 13

*

Buzzard's Lodge

The travellers woke late. Light penetrated their room. Bed frames creaked as they moved in their cosy bunks. Nature called. They left the warmth, visiting bushes.

A dish of crushed nuts, dried fruits and maple syrup awaited them; chunks of Buzzard's violet-flavoured tooth-cleansing gum too.

The Dun had quietened. Gale worked on her pots. 'What's that carved pattern mean?' Oiwa asked, impressed

'The V shape's Gunnal's Gulch, the wavy lines, the Dun. The stick-stabbings show the rapids you shoot; those needle impressions are the Heron's Tooth. It will be fired by your homecoming.'

'Thank you, Gale. I'd better look more closely at clay pots in future.'

They met Buzzard at the river-brink. 'Level's dropping. If no rain it'll be okay tomorrow afternoon, perhaps. Rest now, before braving Gunnal's rapids.'

'Great,' said Bark. 'We're itching go.'

'When you're in the ravine, watch the rock pictures,' Buzzard went on.

Amid all this, Oiwa thought, 'Ziit needs exercising, I'll fetch him.'

Entering the tent, he spotted Buzzard's weaponry. His arrow-points were sharp. He touched a tip, pricking his finger. The tent darkened with a heavy sound behind. Oiwa spun, facing Buzzard.

'You like my arms?' he challenged.

'Aye,' Oiwa answered nervously.

'Well, we'll examine them.' Oiwa relaxed, realising that Buzzard's gruffness was teasing.

'My quiver of points.' he said, handing it to Oiwa. 'The flights are goose. The heavy arrows slaughter buffalo. The shaft's much heavier, denser wood. This head's special.' He placed it in Oiwa's palm. 'My quartz point. It's long – the sides swing back.' Oiwa slid his finger along its sweep. 'The shaft's oily for deep killing.' He flexed his bow. 'My sons and me have lain up crags, knowing buffalo will pass. You hear and smell them a long way off. It's height that's advantageous. You loose arrows to them; the weight does it. These ones penetrate their hides between the shoulders, striking their hearts.' Oiwa gazed admiringly at Buzzard. 'I once hid in a tree to get one there, he dropped, stone-like. The arrow sunk to its flights... wonderful.'

'Let's look at your bow outside, Oiwa. Give me an arrow.'

'Here's a jasper-tipped deer shaft.'

Buzzard strung it, pulled, turned to the drying meat and shot. The pierced slab of meat spun. The dog leaped bush ward and retrieved Oiwa's missile.

'An excellent weapon, Oiwa. What's its name?'

'Ziit. The sound of the flights.'

'Give me the arrow, Eye. Good dog,' Oiwa said. He fitted the arrow and shot through the same piece of dangling pemmican.

'Ziit's like you, Oiwa; young, strong and clever, but still strengthening.' Then he asked, 'Are you worried about your journey?'

'I daren't think about it.'

'You should. Danger lurks, waiting for false steps. Be wary.' Then he asked. 'Do you have children?'

'No,' Oiwa exclaimed.

'None on the way, even?'

'None. Well, probably not,' He stammered, tugging his soft moustache.

Buzzard grinned. 'You've sexed, then?'

'Well, sir, I was almost raped,' Oiwa confessed.

'Tell me? I promise not to laugh.' They sat by the drying meat. Eye gnawed his bone. Oiwa luridly acted his explicit tale. Buzzard didn't make fun, but they ended in excruciating laughter. Their stomachs ached like the night before, when Buzzard couldn't tell his swansdown joke.

'You and Ziit have done much together,' Buzzard observed. 'I'm going to advise you.'

Oiwa acknowledged the huge man, noticing again the red tattoo topping his chest.

'You're a handsome young man. I've seen the daughters of my village look at you. You're shy yet; that will fade. Your brothers too have a presence. Your two friends, who are spoken for, are very happy. That's good.' He paused momentarily. Oiwa scratched his nose and shifted his chewing gum from the right molars to the left. 'You, Oiwa, have a great life ahead, I can see. It's your spirit. You have qualities for sharing. Women see this.' He paused for thought. Oiwa slid the gum behind his front teeth and squeezed it with his tongue. 'They'll want to mate with you. If they have a child from you, it will have advantages over other kids. Mothers like this.'

Oiwa's jaw dropped. The gum fell to his hand from the tip of his tongue while he considered his body and just what it could do.

'Oiwa. In my village our families are well mixed. It's good; we don't make jealousy. We have respect and love for each other.' He doodled in the dry ground with his heavy arrow. 'When an interesting man stays with a clan, females might want to *borrow* something by mating. It's fine.' Oiwa scratched his chin and leaned on his log drum. 'If you don't want to breed, polite refusal can be given.' Buzzard leaned back, adding, 'You should never mate with someone you aren't happy with. The outcome is usually bad. And you should certainly not mate with a woman who does not wish it, for that's worse.' He finished, saying,

'Breeding is an art. Be comfortable; be stunning. Have another chew of gum.'

Oiwa flicked his old gum into the bushes. 'Thanks, Buzzard. That's been helpful. I hope it'll be useful. I'll mind on.' They stood and walked, Oiwa mopping sweat from his brow.

Rush and Lichen wandered with Bark and Tine. Mica was telling a group of squatting children tales of adventure. They listened avidly with their mothers. Hoof Tracker's hunting band returned with their booty. Their hunting paints dried and cracked on their faces. Roasting pits were prepared to receive their haul. Mica's story finished. The youngsters ran to the river to see if their fishing lines had profited. They gleaned from their traps. Silver fish flapped into their baskets. Jay screamed out from the other side of the sandbank. 'My canoe's gone! I hauled it right up last night. Who's taken it?'

'I haven't,' whined a boy.

'I know that, stupid. You're here.' Jay's eyes flamed. 'I'm aiming to see about this.' She raged up the beach homeward. 'Dad, wake! You've been hunting. This is an emergency!' Jay's arms flew. Her tantrum was heard over the whole village.

'Jay, calm. Let's go and look, dear.'

'It's been thieved,' she screamed.

'There's my post, Dad. That's where I tied it.'

Scale knelt down among the other craft and examined the post. 'It's only kids' footprints in the sand. The rope's unleashed, that's drag marks to the Dun. Well, Jay, I hope it's returned soon,' he said, rubbing his chin. Hunt paint flew dustily in the air. 'It took us a while to make, didn't it, my pretty angel.'

'Yes.' Jay moped. 'I got sore punching holes and sewing hides on its frame.' Scale ruffled her long, dark hair. 'It'll return,' he reassured her.

Rush and Lichen sat amongst young women and girls who liked their spiky hair. One asked Rush, 'Why is your face so round?'

He grinned back. 'My mother expected to give birth at new moon. I wouldn't come. I waited for full moon. Mum said that's why my face is so round. She was going to call me Moon Face, but named me Rush instead, because I was so slow.' They laughed. He added, 'But she actually sat and squashed me.' They shrieked out again.

'Lichen, do you put egg in your hair?' another enquired. 'It's so spiky.'

'No. Our hair sticks out like this. It's a clan thing. We do our hair by pushing through bushes in reverse.' They giggled.

Oiwa strolled up. 'Your hair's a mess,' someone said, 'It's light like sand. Why's that?'

'It's a mess because I haven't done anything to it for ages. As for colour, our clan's mostly like that; it's our breeding. Some of us even have red hair.'

'Ooooooooooohhhh!' the girls said.

'My brothers have the same. You've seen us Goose folk before – you know fine what we are like.'

Moss, his teasing inquisitor, said, 'Let's do his hair, girls. Jump on him, sit him on the ground, pin him down'.

Oiwa feigned struggling for a moment, then relented. 'Okay, okay, I give up.'

'Good. Sit. We will get our stuff. Sleek, make sure he doesn't move.'

Sleek obeyed. 'Here,' she said. 'Perch on this log.'

Moss returned with friends. 'We've got combs and bowls of scented water. Head back,' she demanded, pulling stork feathers from his tangles. 'Sleek, hold a bowl of water behind his neck and I'll soak his disgustingly matted head.' Oiwa grinned at the attention. 'What's that floating in the bowl, Sleek? Pour. Wash his scalp.' Sleek obeyed. 'Uuuuuuurgh. It's gone murky. Get fresh.' Moss rinsed. Sleek held a fresh bowl for her.

'Right, girls.' Moss directed. 'Comb from the ends up. Don't tug his pretty locks.'

'I like your Star, Oiwa.'

'Thank you. It's Moss, isn't it?'

'Yes. Do you have any more?'

Oiwa blushed and didn't answer.

'Be still. There's loads of ugly knots,' Sleek warned.

Gradually Oiwa's hair untangled. It reached his shoulders in waves. He noticed something warm and smooth being rubbed into his scalp. The combs slid through his hair more easily. He then felt a cool, runny sensation. 'We are going to knead this all through and massage your scalp too,' Sleek told him.

'What is it?' Oiwa demanded.

'Duck fat and egg, you goose. Now sit still.' They struck a sharp flint flake each and trimmed his ends over their fingers. A growing circle gathered. Oiwa's hairdo was the centre of attention.

He looked down and watched the barbers' feet astride him, working in rhythm. They straddled him as Moss and Sleek attended around his ears. He could feel their breasts brushing his shoulders. It felt lovely. Then they combed his hair right over his face. 'That looks better,' they said.

Were they twins? Oiwa wondered.

'Right, you little girls, each of you gets a thin length of his hair. Start at the crown and work round and down in a spiral.'

'Are you listening, Moon Shadow?' Sleek called out.

'Yes, Sleek,' she responded, trying to stop giggling.

Moss explained. 'I want you to plait your lengths. Sleek has beads to thread in. There are little bird bones that look good too. We're watching, so get it right.'

'Take it in turns,' Sleek added. 'Try not to pull his hair too hard.'

Sleek whispered to Moss, 'He'd look very pretty with his other hairs taken in hand, wouldn't he?' They giggled endlessly.

Dusk descended. Fires glowed. The travellers gathered with Buzzard and some of his wives and children. He signalled his guests to be seated. All admired Oiwa's hair. He spun his head. Beaded plaits flew out. 'I'm delighted with it,' he beamed. The turfs from over the cooking pits were dragged away. Large bundles of long, steaming waterweed were hauled out expectantly. The parcels were slid on to the trays, carried to Buzzard's party and placed before them. The steaming bales smelt of river and bird.

'Share it out, Mica,' Plover said. He peeled back the hot shroud;

inside was a cooked goose. 'Wonderful,' he said, eyeing it delightedly. 'I'll get my axe. Legs first. They ease off nicely,' he reported as he twisted the blade. 'Wings next, and then the succulent breast.' The band devoured voraciously, goose-grease covering the brothers' stubble.

'It's an honour having goose,' Tine told Buzzard as Hoof Tracker passed.

'Join us, please?' invited the chieftain. The sinewy man sat on a vacant drum. He observed everything and everyone as they spoke. 'The geese are excellent.' Plover said. 'You were away really early?'

'We left afore dawn for the North Marshes. Crept through bordering trees and silently waded towards the goose nests. If you do it right, they think you're moose. We wore antlers and masks.' Nobody interrupted this softly spoken man. They ate and swallowed silently. 'At light we were so close you could almost touch the birds. The mist lifted.' He tossed a bone to Fang, his dog. 'We selected geese where they slept. We shot our bows. Lots woke with arrows in them, making terrible noises. Others charged with wings open. We shot them too. That's one, see. A hole in the breastbone.' Rush pulled out a busted bit of flaked stone.

'When we'd got enough, Fang killed any wounded ones and carried them to our base. We collected the eggs of the dead. Oiwa, you've got some in your hair.' Buzzard's children pointed and shrieked at him. Oiwa swung his plaited locks, twisting his head rapidly.

'Hoof Tracker, would you like to join us in a sweat later tonight?' Buzzard asked.

'No. I have to track early; I will need my energy.' He stood, tapped his drum seat in thanks, bowed his head in respect and quietly left.

'Absolutely great,' Oiwa thought. 'A sweat, a cleanse, and a long sleep before an afternoon's sailing. Perfect.'

A procession of youngsters carried water through the shadows to the pit in Buzzard's house. Rolls of matting were placed round the room for seating. Lamps were lit and the first hot stones were hauled and dragged on steaming wet mats through his doorway.

Conversation lapsed; Buzzard bid them entry. 'Undress, then go through.' Steam filled the atmosphere as they stepped into the sweat lodge to sit. Buzzard faced the ring from the far end beside Plover. A floor lamp lighted him.

They sat inhaling deeply. Buzzard's legs were parted. Tattooed from his pelvis upwards, they observed an exaggerated penis. Testicles were etched into his inside legs. The organ's staff reached his chest. The red ochre dome they'd spied at the summit of his sternum was the enlarged tip. Their jaws dropped as they stared at the imagery.

'You approve of my tattoo?'

Stammered yeses with shaky nods assured Buzzard they'd noticed it. His actual member dangled from where his pubic hairs were expertly styled.

'When I became chief, my wives did this magnificent artwork for me. It's our custom that when I can no longer give them pleasure, they will club me to death, skin me and use my tattoo for a drum skin.' Mica and his band listened incredulously. 'Long may I be fit and fruitful and not be a drum too soon!' He pinched Plover playfully. Stones splashed in. Steam obliterated the potent design. Oiwa and Rush shook their heads, amazed.

'I don't want to be chief.' Rush whispered. The message was passed on. Humour replaced awe.

Oiwa stood, getting steam around himself. His lower star glittered visibly for the first time. Sweat escaped him in tiny rivulets. His hair felt glorious draped on his shoulders. Plover scraped Buzzard's perspiration with a moose rib. Oiwa swept the sweat from his body and crouched again. He took a rib to scrape Rush's back, then Rush did Oiwa's. More of Buzzard's brood entered, bringing oils and scents. They massaged Mica and scraped him down to his great pleasure. They sat, relaxed in hot mists.

Rainbow, mother of two from Buzzard, entered holding an oval tray of hot, fried elvers. She passed them round. In turn the company tasted them. Heads back, they dropped the tiny eels into their gaping mouths, enjoying the crispy sensation. Rainbow stroked Bark's pubic star.

In the mists, a drum-skin was brushed in rhythmic flow. Lizard Toe, who massaged Lichen, left to fetch dried fruits. She had two daughters and a son... only one from Buzzard. Her boy came from Innu and a daughter from the Lynx clan. Thus the Stork clan grew in strength and variety of bloods. She returned with her basket of dried fruit and berries. A wondrous painted bowl of thick maple syrup bound a mass of crushed fried nuts. She dipped her fruits in on spiked sticks to tempt the young men.

Bruised fennel seeds and new pine needles were cast into the water hole, creating a sensual atmosphere. 'Would you chaps drag the cool stones out and make room for hotter ones?' Plover asked. 'There are long tongs by Buzzard.' The exertion broke more sweat as several boulders came forth, clacking as they rolled out. They stretched their limbs after the long pull. The tree tattoo on Lichen's back shone, as did Rush's of a full moon. They sat and tasted fruit from Lizard Toe's skewers. She moved to Buzzard and plied his red tongue with sweet morsels. Plover produced a white crane's wing and stroked his thighs. Bark watched as Buzzard's natural organ stiffened.

Lads dragged red-hot rocks in on drenched mats that plunged into hissing water. A noisy smell of splitting stones filled the chamber, mixing violently with herb and pine aromas. Reeking steam obscured Bark's vista of Buzzard's swelled tool. He wondered why he actually needed that exaggerated tattoo.

Lizard Toe placed her lithe self above Buzzard's reaching member, carefully lowering herself over him. She moaned gently. As she took him in, the mists closed.

Rush and Lichen climbed to their bunks where the atmosphere was even hotter. They were trothed. So too was Mica, though he was happy to remain prone on his comfortable mat to consume the delights of the Buzzard's sweat lodge.

The grass curtain parted like Oiwa's locks. He saw two white, luminescent figures enter. They resembled long-billed storks with feathered costumes hemmed at their hips. Their elegant legs were painted with red, stork-like scales.

They parted, moving in a slow dance in and around the bathers. Their arms flexed as white wings fanned the swirls of rising clouds. Bark saw Lizard Toe moving gracefully on Buzzard's thighs. The stork dance revolved and quickened. Oiwa watched it attentively with wild pleasure. The feet and wings maintained a rhythm of complete unison. A feeling of extreme excitement developed in his stomach's pit, where a dark heat breathed. Lichen and Rush looked down on the arena, remembering loving Teal and Widgeon. They felt blessed by their bonding.

Two voices sang as conception began with Buzzard and his next mother. That warm, intimate aroma of fertilized baby glided among the scents of herbs, fruit, fish and sweating bodies. It lingered and hovered to give truth to the blessed friction of mating. Buzzard would keep his skin for another year.

Oiwa wiped sticky nut honey from his groin. He licked it from his wet finger. As it touched his lips a feathered wing brushed his perspiring back. A soft hand took his from his mouth. The bill of a stork fell over his nose and touched his chin. He saw pert breasts through the open costume. The dance continued, and the fleeting peck sought another male.

Tine's crouching form glistened in the glowing wicks. He enjoyed caresses from the plumes. His toes curled over the rim of the steaming crater. He was gently urged back from behind. He reclined. The white wings touched the soles of his feet and then caressed his ankles. The feathers stroked his calves, knees and thighs as the winged dream placed a feather beneath his relaxed scrotum, stroking exquisitely.

The stork moved to Bark. Tine lolled his head dreamily in his brother's direction. Bark's testicles descended in the heat. They lolled between his open legs. A loving beak stroked them. His penis rapidly covered his shining star. His eyes opened smartly. Blood pumped through his arteries; his heart thumped as he lay mating.

The other winged creature alighted at Oiwa's feet. He lifted his relaxed head and pulled his plaited hair from the floor. He raised himself to where his dreamy eyes discerned Moss. She knelt over his open knees. She took off her feathered dress and placed it where Rush had lain. She crouched back on Oiwa's feet. Oiwa looked along her legs. Her eyes summoned his glance. He extended a toe. His hard nail discovered her warm, soft haven. Moss gazed upward, his toe delved deeper. He prised himself up on the rolled mat, his tight erection concealing his star. The low light showed Moss sitting on open, bended knees. 'My toe is exactly where my penis should be.' Oiwa, quite naturally, thought. He licked his lips as he proposed that very move.

Moss wanted the same. She moved. Oiwa's wet toe became naked, exposed and suddenly cool. Moss leaned forward and pulled his elbows away. He flopped back. His plaited hair hit the rug with a thud. His pelvis became utterly prone. They gazed at each other. Oiwa trembled. Moss moved forward. Her neat, pert breasts poised themselves over Oiwa's nipples. They touched. A shot of hot feeling welded that moment. Her dark hair encircled his brow. His stars glittered.

Oiwa clenched his buttocks, which had been thrust up by the rolled mat. This purely instinctive move was apparently the right one. With extreme pleasure he protruded his extended penis further. It touched the area where his toe had caressed. Moss kissed his tip with her vaginal lips. Oiwa's eyes rolled in his skull. Swaying slowly, she gradually engulfed him. Oiwa felt every slight move. Moss pushed down, Oiwa rose. They felt their pelvis bones meeting. Moss explored the full sensation of him being inside her. She wanted to share a part of Oiwa. She had teased him just for this. Her motive was pure. She moved upwards as Oiwa sank. His eyes looked to hers and he stretched his arms around her, stroking her spine. She moved forward. Oiwa rolled with the mat. This forced his organ deeper. Moss exerted more pressure and felt Oiwa's stem grate somewhere wonderful. This was their moment. It lasted as they mated for sheer joy. Oiwa felt his orgasm grow. It met with Moss's. A great wail of climax welled from the depths of his being. Moss squeezed further down. Her voice shook. They moved and rolled, joined in bliss. Hot stones were missed and languid bodies moved from their gyrating path. Oiwa pressed in and Moss responded. They kissed and smiled and hugged. Together still, Moss scratched his bum and back. His plaits ringed her forehead. He moved inside her, giving a deep a kiss when the last beats of his sperm flowed.

Their total oblivion ended with Buzzard's loud handclapping.

Mica had intended faithfulness, but had just spermed, siring twins with Sleek.

Bark was barely aware of Buzzard's applause. He'd been taken by one of his wives. They were standing together, prior to mating.

Plover watched Tine. He lay extended by the steaming pit. He felt her glance and stood. He moved over. It was soon to be full moon. She welcomed him in as a lovely man. He mated with her as a lovely woman.

Chapter 14

Entering Gunnal's Gulch

The sated brothers slumbered indecently long. Rush and Lichen woke early. They stowed the Heron's Tooth, carefully not disturbing their relaxed comrades. Rush thought only of Teal. It was a fine day. The Dun was lower.

Oiwa opened an eye where Moss had left him. He yawned, struggled up then yelled in pain. 'Craaaaaaaaaaaaamp!' he screeched, hopping. He stumbled into Tine and crashed to the floor. This explosion ruined the tranquillity. His kin rose reluctantly to help Oiwa straighten his contorted limb. He yelled, gritting his teeth until the spasm finally eased.

'Seems regular, this cramp?' Tine observed as he dressed

'Not that regular,' Oiwa returned, searching for his clothes.

'When was your last attack?' Tine joked.

'Shut up,' Oiwa warned, shoving the afflicted leg carefully into his breeks.

'Look, young brother,' Tine sniggered, pulling his jacket on. 'I'm showing I care.'

They emerged through the feathered curtain and met Gale. 'Here's breakfast. Duck egg and kidney puffed omelette. Dad's favourite.' It rested on a warm stone. Her beautiful mixing bowl contained a willow whisk bearing traces of beaten white.

'It's marvellous,' Bark said for them all. 'The crispy outside hides this bright yellow middle flecked with verdant sorrel.'

Buzzard made his entry. He was accustomed to that sort of night. 'It's a fine day to set off. Are you glad you stayed?'

'Yes. Thanks so much, Buzzard,' Mica began. 'Last night's mating has set us up perfectly for the journey. Thank you. And for Gale's marvellous omelette too.'

Rush and Lichen entered. 'Risen again,' Lichen exclaimed, mockingly. 'And what was that yelling about?'

'I got a touch of cramp.' Oiwa admitted.

'Hmmmmm,' mused Rush. 'That breakfast was good. I'll cook that one day.'

'We'd better go soon,' Lichen ventured.

'Sadly, you are right,' Mica responded, turning to Buzzard. 'We thank you vey much indeed for your amazing hospitality, Buzzard. Gale is splendid. You have wonderful wives. You are a great chief. May you live long and breed many more children.' They cheered wholeheartedly. Mica meant every word.

'Thanks.' Buzzard replied. 'It too has been a very great pleasure for me and my people to have you. Please stay on your return.'

'Absolutely,' he assured, hugging Buzzard's broad shoulders.

They reluctantly walked through the village to their boat. Moss and Sleeke ran up. Sleeke kissed Mica, remembering fondly their embraces. Moss made for Oiwa's side. He smiled brightly at her. She clasped his hands, pulling them to her breasts. 'Your hair's a mess,' she commented, then hugged his neck and pulled his head to her shoulders. 'We must do it again when you return. And you'll need your hair done again too.'

'Oh, Moss. Thank you. Of course,' he said as they walked hand in hand to the Heron.

'Stop a mo, Oiwa. I want one of your plaits.' She took from her pouch a tiny, white blade, severed one and shoved it in her belt.

Oiwa brushed his locks back and hugged her tightly. 'It's the best hairdo I have ever had. I love it, and I love you.' They ambled inevitably to the Heron's Tooth. Plover joined them, as did more of Buzzard's retinue.

Little Jay tugged at Rush's jacket, asking, 'If you see my pretty canoe, will you send it back to me?'

'Of course. What's it like?'

'It's short, just room for Daddy and me. She's called Otter. She has an otter's head painted on her prow. Daddy had just finished it. I painted the whiskers. He said, 'That's beautiful. Those whiskers are so real that we could even shave them in a few days.' He thinks I am very good at painting, my Daddy does.'

Rush stooped and reassured her. 'Your Daddy is right. You must be a wonderful painter. We'll keep our eyes wide open for the Otter.'

Jay squeezed his hand. 'Thanks. I know you will.' The child ran off, calling, 'Daddy. Daddy. Daddy.'

Loaded with extra supplies, Heron's Tooth slipped into the water. Moss moved close to Oiwa, saying, 'Here's a hatchet. My father says it's for you.'

He smiled again at Moss with a deep thrill as he stepped reluctantly towards the boat. The grey, sharp head of the hatchet shone. The polished antler haft fitted his grip perfectly. With tight throat he croaked, 'Thank your father very much. It's so beautiful... I must step aboard and take my seat.'

Bark's weight tilted Heron's Tooth as he boarded to sit by Oiwa. Tine and Mica assumed their positions. Lichen sat behind. Rush held the rope then hopped in and pushed off. The crew thrust the paddles, making a strong wake.

'Don't stop any arrows,' they heard from the shore as they found faster water.

'No chance,' they laughed back. 'Now lift our paddles in farewell then beat them hard on the water,' Mica said needlessly. White storks flew from the overhanging branches. A blue heron glided to the far bank. The Dun turned and they vanished. Moss kept waving to the final glimpse.

The crew paddled in silence. Each had his thoughts. Mica piloted and signalled which current to take. Shingle banks appeared. Dippers scoured them for hatching flies and pupae. They steered to the deeper channels.

Rush fiddled with the long net. He tied an end to the stern-peg, where his reel had spun. He imagined there might just be a fishing opportunity. 'Teal will have my salmon tail by now,' he thought, as his toe twiddled with the other end of the net.

Lichen pondered. 'I could make a hood for Widgeon for clan occasions with a feathery stork-skin.'

Oiwa considered his new hatchet. 'Perhaps Moss's family hope we become related?' Oiwa dwelt long on the prospect. 'I'll ponder until we return.'

Bark paddled in time. 'I could make shit-hot flutes from goose wing bones as gifts. Stork wings would be good too, and there's heron's legs as well.'

Tine could not forget Buzzard's generosity. 'I mated his wife. What an experience. I'll find something special for them.'

Mica piloted and paddled with something on his mind. 'I might ask for Sleek. I'm tough – I could have two wives.'

Afternoon drew to evening. They made excellent progress.

'Right. Beach,' Mica called. The prow touched the sandy bank. Mica hopped ashore and stretched. His crew disembarked, and hauled their boat to safety. They made camp. Mica got his fire-kit. 'This dry grass is good. I just need twigs.' Oiwa read his mind. 'Set them there, Oiwa. Wood now?' The others put the boat on her side and fixed their lean-to shelter. Rush took a harpoon, the net and North Star's strung bag to the Dun. Mica struck his flint core against his firestone. A grand spark arched, drifting into the grass. He picked it up and blew. He sheltered the fiery glow within. He blew again softly. A tiny flame kindled. Mica held the bundle up. The fire grew in his palms. He placed it quickly in the bundle of twigs and puffed rapidly. 'Fire,' he shouted. 'Thank Grool.'

Rush searched the river. A gigantic eel poked its head from its dark lair. Rush probed his harpoon behind its gills and shoved. A large rising moon reflected in the ripples. 'I've got him!' he yelled in excitement. He could feel the eel's slow, powerful resistance beneath the water. It struggled, coiling up the shaft, trying to squirm from the deathly teeth of the weapon. Rush felt the creature tiring, and wrenched the harpoon up, gripping it further down between the writhing, slimy coils. 'Done it,' he gasped. He flung the harpoon up the bank and leapt after it.

'Am I being watched?' he wondered momentarily. He could see nothing: just the evening landscape. Nothing moved. then a covey of distraught partridges took flight, their moon shadows flitting over the ground in racing dots. 'Perhaps one of us raised them?' he considered.

He left the eel impaled the jagged spike and looked for a calm pool in that backwater. Emptying North Star's drowned bag of pemmican, wrapped its contents in netting, and sank it in the pond. Who knew what would be in there later?

Returning to camp with the eel, he pushed his harpoon through the beast's jaw and staked it to the turf.

'What a catch!' Lichen exclaimed, handing him his knife. 'Lets cut it into chunks.'

'I'll gut it first,' Rush said poking the entrails from the pulsing flesh with his fingers. 'Look, the stomach had a small string of tiny mussels, some snails and sticklebacks. I'm not sorry for you,' he told the eel, ramming it on sticks to cook.

'That'll be a fine supplement to Dad's dried meat.' Mica said.

'What dried meat?' Rush asked.

'I assumed you were bringing back a partridge, Rush,' Mica asked.

'No. I thought maybe you had.'

'Not us,' Oiwa said as he twisted his eel round in the heat. 'A fox?'

'Didn't smell fox,' Lichen added.

'Marten perhaps?' Tine suggested.

'Possibly,' Rush put in. 'It was something.' He tested the eel on his tongue. His eyes rolled back with delight.

When they'd finished, Tine said, 'I could still do with some of that pemmican.'

'Oiwa, come with me.' Rush said.

'Where to?'

'Never mind. Follow me.' They went off in the moonlight. Rush had the bag. They found his net. 'Help me heave this out, Oiwa.'

'Wow.' Rush exclaimed, 'It's full of crayfish.'

'They mustn't escape. Stick them in the bag, quick.' They worked fast, getting their fingers nipped at times.

'Dad's caribou meat,' Oiwa said, seeing the remnants.

'Yes. It's put to better purpose. It got soaked anyway. We can sling this net back for the morning.'

'Sshhhhhhhhh,' Oiwa said. 'I heard something.' They listened.

'What was it?' Rush whispered.

'I don't know.' He felt for his axe. 'It came from those bushes.' They stole towards them. Oiwa swiped his chopper into the shrubs. A swarm of sparrows flew out in terror. 'Can't have been in there, then.' Oiwa said.

'Let's set the net.' Rush suggested.

'Okay.'

They left. Oiwa bore in mind Buzzard's words. He looked back. The moonlit landscape revealed nothing, but he didn't like it.

Rush gathered a huge armful of dry pine needles. 'Crayfish,' he announced and dumped them on the ground.

'Crayfish!' the rest exclaimed delightedly

'I'll pile the needles and make a wide pit into them to put the darlings in.' He tipped them out and shook the bag. He turned it inside out to pull off the hangers on. The wee lobsters began to bury themselves in the bed. 'Cover them, Oiwa. I'll light the needles with a firebrand. There it goes, burning fast and hot. That's the Caribou way to cook crayfish! Tuck in when they cool,' he said.

'I love peeling the hot shells and scoffing the tails,' Mica said, cracking claws in his teeth to get the more succulent flesh.

'The heads are so good too,' Bark remarked. They peeled and

chewed through the entire haul until Bark, reaching into his provision bag, said, 'Buzzard's honey and maple gumballs. Here, hand these round. There just right for afters.'

Their meal eaten, Rush thought lovingly of Teal. 'Fall will have delivered my message and salmon's tail by now. I'm sure Teal's put it somewhere special. That comforts my yearning for her.' His mind drifted as his friends told tales of yore. He gazed at the rising moon. As if in a dream he was back in North Star's sweat lodge, feeling that great heat within him. His pores opened. Perspiration ran under his clothes. In trance, he flew again from his body. The feeling came violently to him: it was as though he had been punched sharply below his right shoulder. Then another blow hit him close by. It knocked his breath away. He panted and saw he and his comrades below as he streaked skywards. Briefly his own image peered up to him. Their campfire was a mere glowing dot on a vast, darkened world.

Rush's sweat cooled on his body. His dream sped him towards the shining moon. It was easier to draw breath as the silver orb grew and the stars took different perspectives. His dream flew him behind the moon's face. He looked down on a darkened world with orange light shining behind. He felt at utter peace there in company with other spirits. The bruising pain in his back cleared. His dream took him further past the moon. He saw the path of the silvery Dun as his dream took him closer to his world.

Rush felt his soul rejoin him, seated by the fire. He drew a great breath as his eyes popped wide open. He felt as though his heart had ceased beating, but began again with a great thud in his chest. The cold sweat left... he warmed again. He pushed his gum round his palate with his tongue. His round face was blank and pale.

'What's up?' Lichen asked his cousin.

'Nothing,' he replied quietly. 'I remembered the dream I had in North Star's sweating house. It startled me.'

'Yes,' Lichen replied. 'I was a caribou. I made mating for new life.'

'I went to the moon and returned. I have just been there again. It was strange. I'm back. Now I know I am real.'

Oiwa joined in. 'I was a goose flying by starlight over the vast ocean. I landed on a silver lake.'

Mica added, 'I was a great bear with claws so sharp.'

'I was a yellow-eyed lynx. I would have mated again in a cave, but I had to return.' Bark reminded them.

'You are always going to mate with something,' Tine added. 'But I was a soaring eagle in the mountains.' He yawned as he spoke. The yawns caught. They felt it was time to bed down.

Rush lay between Lichen and Oiwa. He felt cold again, sleeping fitfully. He listened to the night sounds as his friends snored. Bark let wind. Mica grumbled. Rush thought he heard another sound. Was that a sharp intake of breath? A stifled sneeze, or a muffled yelp of pain? he asked himself. He wriggled out of the huddle and stood in the open to listen. The night was clear and cold. The stars shone; the moon too. Nothing moved. He walked round the Heron's Tooth, scanning the landscape. The sound of the Dun rippling and rolling formed a background to the land's silence. Rush looked up at the moon's face and silvery halo: it glared back. He turned to go to bed. He felt a presence, but could not discern what.

Cold shivers went through him. 'I need to pee,' he thought. He paced away from the Heron, and pushed his bladder hard. He admired the arching shadow of his urine in the moonshine. The fount sped into a clump of frosted grass. The icy droplets crackled with the sudden heat.

Abruptly, Rush heard a violent, high-pitched scream. He leaped into the air yelling. A petrified hare shot up from its hide in the tuft. It jerked in terrified somersaults. Rush's arms flew out in distress. His urinating continued unabated, but inside his trousers. The hot fluid stung his cold legs.

A commotion began under the awning. The hare, still snowy white in its winter coat, arched as if in anguished, slowed time. A blood vessel, deep in its brain, burst under the extreme pressure of trauma. It descended from the zenith of its flight into Rush's outstretched arms. They both landed with a thud on the frosty turf. The stricken rodent lay gasping over Rush's forearms. A wet eye and steaming lashes looked up at Rush as the hare's head lolled, dropping further as its steaming breath slowed. Its legs attempted flailing running motions. Its front paws twitched as Rush felt its pulse slacken. Cooling urine ran round his ankles. The hare's mouth opened, her tongue quivered with the final beats of a stricken heart. Rush felt he'd seen this before. He did not know where.

'What's up?' Rush's fellows asked, scrambling. Their hands felt for their knives. Oiwa grabbed his axe. They fell out in a tumble from their warm ambience and struck the cold air. They spread out to face any attacker, eyes wide in the low light. They saw Rush collapsed in the moon glow. They approached as though he'd been murdered. He shook. He couldn't speak. He let the corpse go with a limp flop. His ear turned as he thought he heard another footfall.

Mica looked on the soaked face of the hare as Rush crawled up and looked down his sodden trousers. Mica glanced into Rush's eyes. 'I, I, I, must have k-k-killed it w-with m-m-my p-p-pee,' Rush stammered. Mica's jaw opened in surprise.

'Good shot,' Oiwa remarked respectfully. Lichen picked up the hare. It stretched long and limp. He displayed its anointed head.

'Some weapon,' Bark remarked in wonder. 'No wound. No blood. Just piss.'

'How do you perform that feat, Rush?' Tine asked.

'With this.' Rush exclaimed, hopping, pulling his leggings off and pointing to his willie. 'I pissed on it.'

'Oh, what a dangerous arrow, Rush,' Mica remarked.

'Let me help,' Lichen offered, doubled with laughter, but couldn't. He tried to point. His hand merely gesticulated as he creased up again. Laughter tore through the group as Rush's pants came off. 'I'll hang them up, cousin, and get you dry ones,' he just managed to articulate.

'I'll gut your hare,' Oiwa put in. 'The liver is yours: the killer's honour... Here.'

Rush put his shaking palm out. He removed the bile duct and ate the soft delicacy in pensive silence. Lichen rekindled the fire.

'Hare for breakfast, chaps?' Mica added.

Oiwa stripped off the white pelt. 'I'll burn the thigh bones with kidney fat for Tarune,' he said. 'That'll stop the hare's spirit biting your dick off, won't it?'

They squatted for a while in the fresh glow before retreating to the cosiness of the awning. Rush changed and crawled in. Eventually, he slept.

The morning was misty. Oiwa woke first and squeezed out from between Mica and Tine. He chewed on his old gum to clean his teeth. He drank from the Dun and gathered branches for the fire. Rush yawned and stretched his stiff legs while the others rose, remembering. He had dreamed of Teal, and didn't wish to move. Oiwa tossed his dried breeks to him. He sat up reluctantly.

Oiwa jointed the hare with his new axe.

'Come on Rush.' called Bark. 'Get out here and pee on a buffalo, will you? We need more meat. That hare won't keep us going long.'

'Rush,' Tine added, 'if you drank more we'd never go hungry.'

'You are so right, Tine. As soon as nature allows I'll piss on lovely strawberries just for you. Then I'll pee on thee. You'll make rotten eating, though.'

'Oiwa, come to the net,' asked Rush. They hauled it from the shaded water. 'There's hardly anything in it.' Rush complained. 'There were lots last night. There should be more. Something's not right,' he said as they folded it carefully. 'I don't know what, but this just isn't proper.' They returned to camp dejected. Bark was seeing to the hare. The others stowed the Heron's Tooth. Mica checked the mends. He was satisfied.

They crouched around the fire. Bark stood, handing round hunks of hare. He coughed for attention. 'Those heights over to the northeast are like a slumbering body. That's Gunnal.' He chewed his foreleg as they peered. 'She's slept for scores of decades. She can only be woken by her lover, but even so her sleep is angry.' He fondled his spear, arranging the feathers below its deadly head, to let his words sink in.

'The Dun here's quiet. Soon she'll bend towards Gunnal's Ankles. There are trees at her toes; we sail between them. As we go through her ankles, the Dun darkens and deepens.' Bark removed the protective felt sheath and tested the sharpness of his missile's point. Its flaked surface glinted. He glanced at Oiwa, Rush and Lichen. 'You've not been before. We have.' He iterated while having a mental flashback of climaxing with Plover. He forgot where he was. He coughed. 'Err. When we reach Gunnal's Calves, the trees vanish. The ravine rises steeply.' He looked up to illustrate. 'Rugged scrub hangs over it like torn hair.' He shifted, swinging the lance. 'Her thighs rise and narrow. The walls are worn smooth.' He shoved his weapon up for attention. 'High on her stony skin you'll see her pictures. Her tattoos.' Rush, Oiwa and Lichen watched Bark, holding their hunks of hare and gazing in wonder. He seemed commanding and different. Mica was usually the speaker; Oiwa appreciated their equality.

Bark drew a deep breath. 'At Gunnal's Bairn the Dun divides. It's a rocky island. Gunnal gave birth when Farnar's great ship of ice wedged itself deep inside her. She froze. Her baby waits.'

Rush fanned his face.

'We land and give the baby honey and milk. Plover handed me a bladder of it. We pray. This gives us safe passage. After the libation we paddle on to enter the –' he trembled at the notion – the great cleft. He leaned his spear, 'There we are, lads.' Oiwa took his axe, placed the hare's head on a branch and split it. He shared it with Rush, making sure his friend got the eye he'd peed into. Oiwa's portion of brains had a blood clot. He didn't notice when he sucked them from the cavity. When Rush finished, he rubbed the hare's pelt with ash and rolled it up. 'Another trophy for Teal,' he mused.

They were ready. Oiwa checked Ziit was safe. Before launching, Rush looked over the grasslands. He found partridge feathers. 'Maybe it was a lucky fox?' he hoped.

'Are you killing game over there?' Mica called. 'No,' Rush thought as the vision of the shining moon flashed through his mind.

They boarded. Rush was coxswain. The net lay folded at his feet. He attached it to the stern-peg, just in case. Lichen took his place in front, Bark sat centre left with Oiwa right. Tine settled in behind

Mica at the prow. They pushed off into the flow and were quickly in deep waters.

Oiwa leant to Bark's shoulder as they paddled, remarking. 'I didn't know about Gunnal's Bairn.'

'No. We didn't tell you everything.' They fell silent, paddling to Mica's piloting. 'Faster. Stronger,' he called out. Oiwa glanced at his bow, feeling pride. Mica beat time on the prow with his axe's shaft then took his paddle, pulling hard. 'We spent too long splitting hares at breakfast. We must make up time,' he panted, and pulled harder. 'The Dun's slower – paddle fast.'

The crew toiled as one. A tributary of the Dun joined, as did others. The river widened and deepened as small streams poured in too. The oarsmen sang to keep rhythm.

River life went on, ignoring them. The caribou felt no fear; these men were not hunting, they sensed. A brown bear looked idly on at their passing, as did the coypu, otter, stork and eider.

The banks closed: a strata of rock, like worn toenails, had been eroded by the Dun's power. On either side quartz outcrops glowed as they sailed over worn veins. Heron's Tooth rose imperceptibly. The water quickened. This was just the beginning of their river race. They passed Gunnal's Toes. Spruce woodlands gave way to rocky scrublands, bare, exposed. The river narrowed. The Heron leaped up another foot as the water bulged in forced waves. An outcrop of black basalt formed Gunnal's bony ankles.

Mica whistled shrilly to signal for careful paddling. He conducted their course with hand signs. His crew acknowledged each movement. Their paddles dipped accordingly.

The bright sun sent a golden sheen over the strong waters. They saw joining currents as they tumbled into one shifting flow. Small whirlpools and strong eddies tugged the Heron. Mica paddled and signalled, skilfully guiding as Rush steered from the stern. The Dun narrowed at Gunnal's Calves. Heron's Tooth hit the turbulence of the swirling, backed-up river water. It rose, waiting to descend into the Calves' Pool. The Heron's prow left the surface and splashed down with a shudder as her stern tipped upwards, throwing Rush into the air. He landed back on his seat, paddle still in hand. His feet caught in the coiled net. He found his balance as Lichen glanced back at him, alarmed. The Dun, constrained by the climbing, narrowing cliffs, flowed more swiftly, darker and deeper. Rush peered down into its racing depths, as did Oiwa. They sped over unseen boulders. Below them, barbel sucked the rocks for lodged carrion and river slime.

Lichen looked up to the heightening cliffs. Scrubby trees hung, roots exposed like arteries pulsing for grim life. Veins of red granite slanted within the exposing cliff. Banded with crystalline darts, it resembled severed flesh. Mica shouted loud. The raw cliffs echoed back over the rumble of water. 'Look, her Knees.'

'*Her Knees, knees... ees,*' the cliffs replied.

Mica shouted again: 'Her Knees.'

'*Her Knees... knees... ees... ss,*' the echo repeated as he pointed to each side. Two huge eagles flew from the towering basalt caps. The crew gazed amazed as they glided by. Above, in reds, whites, blues, bright greens and yellows, the paintings began to appear. Tall men and women fishing, hunting, mating, climbing trees, porting boats, casting nets and diving into the deeps were all magnificently depicted. Birds, fish, bison, all manner of animals were there. On each side of the canyon, pictures looked down to them.

'Paddle left,' Mica shouted.

'*Dle left, left, eft, ft,*' the paintings called back. Heron's Tooth slewed away just in time, and rounded a rocky outcrop. 'Baby's Vomit,' Mica called out over the splashing. 'Best to avoid that,' he shouted.

'*Vomit, vomit, vomit,*' the cliffs chorused.

'Paddle right.' Then,'Back paddle left,' Mica commanded. 'Don't look up.'

'*Up, up, up,*' Gunnal's Thighs retorted as the echo rang over the cascading torrent.

'Pull hard left. Hard left again. Hard left. Left. Left. Left!' he repeated urgently, as did the adorned rocks. Then he shouted, 'Again. Again. Once more. Another time. Do it. Do it. Paddle left.' His voice cooled.

They were in slack water in midstream, and Heron's Tooth relaxed. Her hides and frame stopped straining at every jerk the Dun delivered.

'Right men. We are in the shelter of Baby's Vomit,' Mica announced.

'*Vomit, vomit, vomit,*' the rocks tediously chimed.

'Now we simply paddle downstream to two short promontories coming from a small, rocky island. Those are the Baby's Legs.'

'*Legs, legs, legs.*'

'Between them is a large, slowly flowing whirlpool.' He paused as '*Pool, pool, ool*' faded away. 'We paddle to the right heel and the current will carry us to a sandy bank called Baby's Bum. There we beach.' The crew ignored the echoes 'Now paddle to the far right of the pool.'

Heron's Tooth caught the fringe of a huge eddy and was pulled towards the left. Mica allowed her to be dragged round. A small, sandy bay lay on their right between the smooth Legs of Gunnal's Bairn. 'Beach now. Paddle fiercely,' Mica coaxed. Their craft turned from the swirling pool and nosed into the crisp sands. Mica hopped swiftly ashore. His crew followed, pulling their boat well up to the sloping rocks.

Oiwa's toes dug into the reddened sand as he lifted Heron's Tooth with the others. Fine lines of stranded quartz and agate graced the Baby's Bum. The crew's toes and heels scattered them as they ran up the shore. Dippers fed in the waters that lapped around the Bairn's Toes. The rocky outcrop, no more than 60 paces long, rose towards its head. Oiwa wondered at the shape of this islet. He looked up to the glowering, dark cliff walls, some hundreds of feet apart. The huge paintings looked down and across at them. 'Who made them?' he asked Mica.

'Some say it was the River Spirits, others blame it on Gunnal's Lover, who does it to tease her. Buzzard says he gets his women to brush them up and paint more.'

'Look. Up there, Oiwa,' Rush pointed to a vast skein of geese flying in frozen formation.

Tine spoke. 'They're us: they were painted generations past when we first came this way.'

'There, see, packs of wolves,' Oiwa said.

'They're the Loup-Folk who bide below Gunnal's Head. We'll meet them at Wolf Lake,' Mica answered.

Oiwa wondered at the reflections of those pictographs. 'They drift and ripple on the surface and penetrated the depths. Perhaps they live another life beneath with the barbel, salmon and trout?'

They stepped over the Baby's Belly. Oiwa glanced down and spotted a small pit graven into the low bulge. It was filled with still water and red weed. A single snail sucked its side. Oiwa nudged Tine. 'What's that?'

'It's the Baby's Navel.' Oiwa felt for his in sympathy. 'There's more.' Tine pointed to the child's chest. 'A nipple!' Oiwa shouted.

'*Nipple, nipple, ipple, ple.*' came the cliffs' answer.

'There's another.'

Bark made for the Baby's Head. He stood on its eroded chin. The crew gathered round. Oiwa saw scraped contours of a face, eyes, nose, ears and a gaping mouth; the lips desperate for a mother's breast. 'Who carved this?' he asked Bark.

'The locals claim Gunnal's midwife did. Look, there's a painting of her.' They all turned. 'That tall figure in white. See her red arms crossing her belly, and her triangle breasts. The insides of her thighs are streaked red too. But the Goose clan has a different story. We say it was Gumar and Tumar, Gunnal's ancestors, Mother and Father of all clans. Look again at the Midwife. See there. Look hard. She's painted over two other faded figures.' They stared. Oiwa began to see, in faint ochre, two naked people, hand in hand. Gumar's rounded breasts were faintly picked out in dark manganese. Her pubic forest grew in worn shadow. Tumar's penis was accentuated. As they looked, a flight of rock doves emerged from Gumar's cleft.

The over-painted Midwife looked down with her slit eyes. She nursed a suckling baby. 'We must feed Gunnal's Bairn,' Mica remembered. Bark held the bladder. Together he and Mica squeezed it between those lips. The sticky yellow fluid dribbled into the rock as the flask was wrung. The Midwife's gaze seemed less severe when they looked back up at her. 'Now. All kneel around the kid's mouth. I'll utter the prayer. 'May this ambross keep you until your mother awakes. She'll suckle and you'll walk from the river. You will grow strong. You shall be the Great Hunter and sire many to follow. These are the wishes of Gumar and Tumar,' Bark said. 'Now rise.'

'Hungry kid. I hope it doesn't throw up,' Tine remarked. Rush giggled: his first happy moment since his moon dream.

'Tine, it was my turn to crack that joke,' Bark complained.

'You should've been snappier then.'

Oiwa peered downstream. The Dun took a right turn to disappear into a deeper, darker ravine. He gazed at the precipitous cliff wall on the Dun's left. There, a gigantic, multicoloured man was depicted clearly, crisply. The black manganese shading, with ochre on the contours, made him real. He too stood and faced the river. His hips twisted in silhouette. He wore a raptor mask. The beak protruded from above the giant's nose. Outstretched arms supported vast wings. Down his back draped a feathered cloak. His feet pointed downstream. The torso supported his stiff phallus, which disappeared round the river bend. On his wrists, magnificent armlets dangled.

'Look at that!' Oiwa shouted.

'That must be Buzzard,' Mica exclaimed. 'He said to look out for him. I didn't expect that.' He trod from the Bairn's forehead. Dippers took flight and a redshank darted off. He moved carefully to the slippery left ear. They all followed.

'It's Buzzard all right!' Oiwa said. 'Remember his sweat lodge. How *huge* he grew.' They nodded in wonder. Oiwa felt the twinges in the pit of his stomach again, just thinking of being with Moss. He tugged a lock of his hair and grinned. He recalled Buzzard's advice about mating, and verses from the Gumar and Tumar legends.

The water ran fast. 'See – up there. A bloody dangerous sling... Just hanging from the clifftop,' Lichen pointed out. 'There's women in it, possibly Storks. They're painters... By Gumar, I wouldn't like being up there.'

'It's lowering... Ooops. It bumped!' Tine cringed.' Amazing. They've swung to the tip of his prick.'

'Looks like they're about to daub it,' Mica observed. He cupped his hands to his mouth, calling, 'Is that Buzzard?'

'Who else? We've left the potent bit to last,' came a distant reply.

'Can you paint mine?'

'Come up here then.'

'On the way back?'

'Sure thing, Mica,' they called

'Woooo,' Tine flashed to a smirking Mica. 'Your reputation's gone before you.'

From the clifftop shouting, waves and laughter got confused in the echoes. Mica and his band waved back, blowing kisses. 'Time to press on,' Mica said. He led them past the Bairn's lips. The libation had vanished.

'Don't puke, little one,' Bark said. Rush noticed how Oiwa's traveller's beard had thickened, as his brothers' had. A great diver disappeared into the huge eddy as they manoeuvred their boat towards the slow current. Before boarding, Mica informed them, 'We follow the flow left of the Bairn, pass its lug, and paddle right below its head to the mainstream.

'There are countless paintings of snakes, birds, strange fish, the stars, the sun and the moon. Spirits, symbols of our ancestors, and other clans. The Dun's too fast and treacherous to look up at them. You might catch a glance. Don't be distracted, or we'll be ancestors quicker than we want.' He met everyone's eyes for acknowledgement. He got it.

'Keep your paddles ready. Listen. Soon we'll enter Gunnal's Gulch. It is a huge fissure in the mountain. Way up, part of it is blocked by a massive rock. We go beneath. It's her lover's foreskin. The noise is tremendous there. *You will all have to watch for my signals.* At times it will get dark, even though it's midday. The Dun divides, careering into different ravines. *We must keep right.* We will come out where the ravines reunite. It'll be turbulent.' His eyes widened as his team stared back. For Tine and Bark it was a rueful reminder of what they had achieved before. They were glad of Mica's words. 'As I said, there's a small protected beach, which will be on our right. Paddle swiftly on to it, hauling up below the hewn steps. We climb up with Heron's Tooth on our backs and our tackle strapped in.

'I will repeat: we port our canoe over Gunnal's Belly. There's a sheltered valley between her paps where we can camp. Tomorrow we make for her shoulders where Gunnal's ugly head is propped. The Dun spews there from a vast cavern as a wonderful waterfall into Wolf Lake. We can climb down the side of the falls, relaunch and meet the Wolf clan.' Then he added, 'See. It's simple.' His crew shifted anxiously. He finished, reaffirming, 'We must not miss the beach.' He took a deep breath and warned, 'Nobody has gone past there and lived.'

'I feel sick,' Oiwa thought. 'What if we get it wrong? There will be no future! It's just here and now, then nothing if we fail. My guts feel wobbly, like they want to empty.'

White-faced, he glanced at Rush for reassurance. He and Lichen trimmed off strands of jet-black hair. It was a Caribou sacrifice, asking for protection from the River Gods. Oiwa took his jasper knife, severed a lock with a red shell bead on it, and cast it on the water.

The diver reappeared, waving a small fish. 'A sign of good fortune?' Oiwa hoped.

'Embark,' Mica bade. In trepidation they took their positions and paddles. They dipped them in the river to move with the whirlpool of Bairn's Toes, meeting the current that would draw them into Gunnal's Gulch. The diver flew off, landing on Vomit Rock to digest its catch. They paddled from the whirlpool's gentle pull and rounded the Bairn's Toes. It took them past its chubby legs. Their speed increased as they sped by the ribs, where a rough arm seemed to slide by. An otter pulled up with a silvery dace and watched the Heron's stern vanish round baby's head. Two sandpipers dibbed as the captain called, 'Paddle hard right.' The boat responded, hitting the rushing flow. Her prow jutted through the tumble of water. Spray splashed their faces: A last wake-up call. 'Hard right,' Mica shouted. They plunged their paddles vigorously. She leapt to another baulk of careering water. 'Ride the waves,' Mica encouraged them. She slewed; a wave hit broadside on. Oiwa got soaked and the Heron's Tooth took water. Spears floated in their ties. She righted herself. 'Bale!' Someone shouted. The women up high yelled farewell. The crew raised their paddles in salute, then plunged them deep to guide their craft. The artists watched their progress down into the ravine, wondered who it was that went before.

The Heron bounced. The Dun boiled beneath. 'Hold her steady,' Mica called. Their paddles went in. They held firm and level. The canoe veered round an awkward twist. The river suddenly widened to a great pool. The cliff painters watched the men enter. At the far side opened the enormous cleft of Gunnal's Gulch. There the river plunged to the roots of the mountain. The pool was water in waiting, putting off being swallowed into the mountain chasm. They saw the awesome basalt pillar that had crashed into her crevice: all that remained of her lost love.

The water in the centre of the pool dipped to a lower level. The

Heron was inexorably drawn, pulled faster. The darkened cavern narrowed frighteningly. The painters in their distant cradle peered as the tiny stick, with six good men in it, was drawn to that gulch. Oiwa felt the prow dip. Mica ducked his head in reverence as the Heron commenced her plunge. Rush wondered why his life seemed to be drawn out of his control. The darkness cast by Farnaar's Foreskin was chilling. Ahead, a silvery light loomed. The tumble rocked Heron's Tooth. Oiwa bounced alarmingly. Rush pushed himself tightly in the stern. The boat lurched and listed terribly. Oiwa looked into the deep current as water flowed into their skin craft. Mica signalled urgently to right the boat. Paddles dipped the other side and the Heron righted. She sat lower in the water. Ziit floated. 'Bale!' came the command again. Tine did what he could. Chasm walls flashed by. Then suddenly, they emerged into blinding, silvery light. Sunbeams shone in a watery arena. Spume and foam flew. There the Dun divided.

'HARD RIGHT!' Mica screamed. Instantly the crew worked as one. Heron's Tooth's prow looked to its course and entered the tossing torrents. She bounced towards her destined ravine, hitting the side as she entered. Mica was thrown forward. Tine leaped and caught his leather belt, hauling him back from certain ruin. The Heron's stern washed across the current. She listed seriously. Oiwa back-paddled hard; Rush followed, as did Bark. The Heron's scraped prow looked down the Dun and slid over the waters as if naught had occurred.

They rounded an angle, where the sun barely reached. Huge icicles, like ogre's hands, clung to the slimy walls. Oiwa felt the chill batter his face. His nose froze. The ravine widened. Gunnal's rocky flesh appeared redder. She closed in through dark veins of cruel igneous rock. The Heron jerked in the narrow straight's thundering rapids. Her mends held, though water bounced between stern and bow as she tipped fore and aft.

It seemed like a lifetime, fleeing down the tortuous canyon. Vague slits of grey light showed them the way. 'Get ready!' Mica called. 'Soon, soon.' Then, 'Very soon now!' The Dun veered left and daylight streamed down as they shot from their course to enter a splendid, golden pool. The canyon came back together again. *'Paddle right. Beach!'* Mica finally commanded.

Heron's Tooth grounded. Mica prepared to leap to the shingle. 'Look,' said Rush. 'Under the steps. There's Jay's canoe. That's smudged whiskers on the otter head.'

Tine moved forward, wiping his brow after their fearsome escapade.

From a dark cleft overlooking the beach, Snaaaaar hushed her child. She pulled hard on her bowstring, her buffalo arrow aimed at Mica's spine. Rush stood to cast the rope to him as she uncurled her fingers. Her missile sped. 'Here, catch, Mica.' Rush called. Mica had one foot on the shore when Rush leaned forward. Lichen reached for a hand-hold to disembark when the arrowhead struck Rush just below his right shoulderblade. He only felt a dull punch. He sat heavily down in his seat. This caused the Heron's prow to rise. Water ran to that end. The Heron's beak shifted and lifted from the shingle. She refloated.

Snaaaaar angrily took another missile and pulled again, saying. 'Shit! Missed the fucking bastard. He'll have this one instead.' Mica heard the arrow flight and leapt backwards on to the shingle. She loosed another projectile. Mica looked in her direction and saw the woman's raging eyes. He arched backwards and fell. The arrow passed his throat, a flight feather nicking his windpipe.

'Back! Back!' he yelled. The arrow splintered behind him. He jumped into the escaping prow. 'Paddle fast! Down the Dun, Now!' he yelled. Rush reached for his paddle. The arrow-shaft stopped his movement. He tried again, feeling an awkward discomfort.

'Fucking bastards!' Snaaaaar screeched, fumbling for another murderous point. 'I have to kill *him*, not that hare pisser!' She strained her string and aimed for Mica's nipple. Rush, deaf to the commotion, stood to get his paddle. His buckskin shirt tightened. He glanced at his chest and saw the shiny black point sticking through. His fingers went to touch it, but his pierced scapula denied the movement.

Lichen and Tine grappled furiously with their paddles as Heron's Tooth shifted in the current. Mica heard the arrow, and saw a second lethal stone erupt through Rush's shirt. Rush sat down with a thump, his breath rasping.

'That little shitty bastard!' Snaaaaar screamed. 'Ruining my shots, the weasel. I'll kill that fucker yet!'

'Dew! Follow me.' She sent another arrow to shatter on the cavern ceiling. Gunnal's Gulch swallowed the Heron's Tooth. Dew stood in shock. 'Come, Dew, my flower. Follow Mummy.' Dew did what she always did through fear and loyalty: she followed.

'Leave the kid's boat. Run. We'll see their stinking corpses float on Wolf Lake beneath the waterfalls.'

'What waterfalls, Mummy?'

'Shut up. Carry these.' She passed her quiver.

'Paddle down the middle! Use your ears. Keep heads low. Fend off the edges,' Mica yelled. 'Don't get your brains bashed out.' It got pitch dark. The reflections vanished from the turbulent waters; they used the sounds and echoes to judge where the cavern walls were. Mica held course in the central flow, past hidden rocks. Racked with pain from the arrows that skewered his torso, Rush breathed shallowly to preserve what life remained. He wondered if they could be snapped off or pulled out, but realised this was not the place. There was no time.

Mica commanded his crew as best he could in the dark torrent.

With his right hand, Rush checked that his precious net was tied to its stake. It was. When he'd recovered from the twisting movement, he painfully reached for the net's other end and wound it tightly round his left ankle. He removed Teal's fishhook and threaded it in the mesh, tying its sinew trace to secure his lifeline. He sat back, careful not to scrape the arrow flights or nudge the shafts. He rationed his shallowing breaths. He did not want to cough to cause more internal bleeding.

They arrived in an immense underground lake, where the current slackened. They could judge the scale of the space by the echoes. Lichen spoke first. 'What's happened to Rush? Is he hurt?'

'Yes, badly,' replied Mica. 'He's been struck by two arrows. I don't know if he is alive or not.' Lichen reached round to his dear cousin and clutched his knee. Rush moved it to let him know he was still with them. He took Lichen's hand and slowly lifted it to the arrows, so his cousin and friend knew exactly how he was. Lichen wept. His cries filled the great cavern.

'Paddle on,' Mica said calmly and rationally. 'Follow the flow.' With every dip of Lichen's paddle, his heart felt like bursting. Oiwa turned to comfort his friend. 'Sssssshhhhhhhh, Oiwa!' Mica called back. 'Paddle on, young man.' Oiwa dipped his paddle. His arms felt frozen. Bark patted his shoulder in comfort and reassurance. Their peril sunk in.

After a distance the cavern opened. A shaft of silver light shone on the black water. They sailed towards it. Rush's head arched back. He looked dimly towards the glow. As he slipped into it, he saw a patchy full moon looking down on him, and remembered his dreams. The crew gazed back at his sad features in the moonlight. A great island of ice loomed in the distance. It reflected what light there was as they paddled by. Far-off shafts of silver light beamed on the subterranean lake through the pierced roof. Rush bent forward, keeping focused on them.

Mica glanced at Rush. His dark form contrasted with Farrnar's isle of shining ice. He waved his arm, indicating a course to the right. 'Paddle right,' Mica said. Rush, unseen, nodded.

Mica headed for the furthest right-hand exit. Eroded pillars held up the cavern's opening. There the Dun tumbled from its darkness for an instant. On either side, rocks piled the edges of their branch of the river. The Heron's Tooth bounced and tipped. Rush was in agony. He felt the netting on his feet. He breathed in long and slow. He saw two pointed rocks, like petrified twins, looming. This was his moment. Rush drew his feet up under him: The rocks closed in. He leapt. His final force landed him between the megaliths. The snapping arrows wrenched his lungs.

Heron's Tooth was caught in the rapid cascade. She sloped alarming-ly to another dark abyss. 'Hold on tight!' came Mica's scream over the crash of water. Spray soaked them. Tine was flung upwards, landing in the Heron's bilge among the spears. Oiwa was nearly thrown over the side. Bark caught him. Lichen bent in weeping misery as the Heron's Tooth lurched, wailing when Rush vanished. Suddenly, Heron's Tooth veered towards the bank, striking jagged boulders and throwing Mica headlong on to wet rocks. She burst her prow, and the current took the stricken canoe towards the dark cave. Mica raised his grazed head, watching, knowing they were doomed. 'Great Goose of our clan! Save us!' he shouted. No one heard.

As the Heron's Tooth and her precious cargo careered downstream, Rush's netting uncoiled. Wedged between the boulders, Rush felt the first tug on his foot. The tie on the stern-stick had held. He felt his leg extend. A loud bang within told him of the dislocation of his hipbone from his pelvis. Heron's Tooth slowed. Rush's knee joint sprung, but held. The knot tightened, and the Heron's Tooth jolted to a stop. Rush's leg swivelled freely. His knee stretched further. So did his ankle. Rush looked down. Blood flowed from his lips. He coughed; the arrows splintered, puncturing his diaphragm. He thought of Teal and mouthed her name. His tongue relaxed and hung from his mouth. The tiny ball of gum he'd kept in his cheek slid from behind his canine tooth as he died.

A rising spirit looked down, seeing a twisted corpse. It hovered momentarily, then rose spiralling over the desolate torrent. Fraught figures struggled as another was washed deep underground. The soul slanted away.

On its passage to the moon, it saw Teal's small teepee engulfed in an aura of moonlight. Then two dim figures on a barren landscape.

Chapter 15

Aftermath

'I'm hungry, Mother.' Dew protested, struggling behind Snaaaaar.

'Keep up, dear. We'll stop between those hillocks.'

Dew plumped down, glaring at the Paps' exposed summits. In the dell between, stunted trees huddled for shelter.

'Have we any crayfish?'

'No. All gone. And you ate the meat Mummy got. You do have an appetite, don't you, my petal?' Snaaaaar answered, racing far ahead.

Dew saw smoke rising from the scrub and stumbled on. Snaaaaar warmed her hands as she approached. 'See what a lovely fire I made for you, my buttercup,' she said as Dew's bare feet crunched through the coarse undergrowth.

'Yes, Mummy, but I'm hungry,' she whined, flopping beside her.

'Tend the fire. I'll find something good to eat.'

Dew sat contemplating the flames, casting dry leaves on them. They curled, glowed and became ashen membranes to rise and drift. Her eyes followed them to notice vultures circling high in the distance. Far further, snow-covered mountain peaks shone with the declining sun. Behind her, the moon looked over Gunnal's desolate landscape.

Dew's precious moment broke. Screeching nesting birds, white, like phantoms, arched and wheeled round Snaaaaar's dipping head, angrily diving at her. Snaaaaar paid no attention as she robbed their downy craters.

'Here, dear...'

The hysterical birds plunged, mourning their lost clutches.

'I've got eggs.' She shook one at her ear, listening to the movements inside. Her sharp fingernails rent its shell. Mouth wide open, she emptied the egg in. She shut her mouth. Poking her tongue through the rich yolk, she tasted, swirled and swallowed. Her slate eyes rolled in gratification.

She shook another speckled egg by her opaque lug, where dangled a dainty straw earring of a wee bird. It went so nicely with her hairband, she imagined. Snaaaaar listened. The swirling sound within it was not so pronounced.

'Here you are, dear. Open wide.' Dew edged to her mother's side, jaws apart. 'Put out your tongue, my little one, and I'll crack it.' The egg's contents slipped in. 'Shut and swirl.' she heard her mum say. Dew closed her eyes, trying to wriggle her tongue. She found a lump and choked.

'Swallow, darling. Swallow,' Snaaaaar shouted.

'Can't!' Dew uttered through slimy lips. 'Can't. Can't!' Her teeth bit the diminished yolk and she gagged.

'Come, my bluebird. If Mummy can, you can... Swallow.'

Dew tried with difficulty.

'Finish it!' Snaaaaar snarled.

'What, Mum? Even the beak?' She spluttered then spewed over her mother's lap.

Snaaaaar lurched back, hissing. 'Just like that stupid Birch Skin. No bleeding guts.'

Little Dew cleaned her mother's front and curled up where it was least cold to sleep.

The Heron's Tooth halted in the rapids and swung towards jagged rocks, the net tearing horribly on Rush's limb. Their canoe belted its nose on the boulders, crashing smartly. Mica was hurled on to them, his left ear and temple smashing on the sharp edges. He lay stranded in a wet heap, motionless amongst a litter of rough stone.

Bark was flung face forward into the wrecked prow. Tine was cast half out, legs and feet strewn over the side in the racing waters, his arms flailing as he righted himself. Oiwa, still seated as the impact reached him, saw Lichen fly, yelling, into the treacherous currents. He hit the torrent and vanished, to be hurled down a thundering cataract. Oiwa landed among their cargo of sodden weaponry and stores.

'Grab what you can!' Tine roared over the tumult.

'Ziit first, then his arrows.' Oiwa knew instantly. 'Grab the spears. Blast! Dropped the paddle and the pemmican satchel. There goes the rope, floating off. Snatch it quick, before it vanishes. Got it!' He hurled it ashore, where it landed on Mica's body. Bark was bent over him. 'He can't be dead?' Oiwa thought bitterly as he stamped from the stricken Heron.

'He's alive!' Bark called out. 'Tine, help me up with him. Get him on that ledge under the cliff. We'll drag him under those ferns. It's more sheltered there. I'm going down to help Oiwa rescue our stuff. You stay with Mica. He's moaning. It's a good sign.'

'Good man, Oiwa' Bark said as they retrieved what they could.

'Rush leapt out!' Oiwa told him desperately, 'We've lost Lichen too. Flung from our boat... washed down the Dun. There's no saving him.'

Bark slapped his forehead in remorse, then controlled himself. 'Stack what's left against the cliff. We'll have to stop here. We can't go on until Mica's fit. It's late. We're exhausted. That's two of us we've lost. It's tragic.'

'Aaagh. This is terrible,' Mica grimaced in agony, feeling the bloody mess dangling from his lobe. 'Are we safe?'

'No,' Tine answered. 'Rush flung himself out, saving us. Lichen was hurled into the river. Heron's Tooth is fucked. It's just us, stuck here.'

Mica lay trembling in a vast, vertically sided, collapsed cavern, sharp rubble strewn where it fell, the Dun, scoring channels through it. Downstream a gaping chasm swallowed the powerful waters, which rapidly thundered in a vertical drop over which Lichen had vanished.

The sun moved upstream. Its late-in-the-day beams rested on an obscured cliff. A vast icicle, like a gigantic hand, adorned this precipice. Rush lay face down between his rocks, still anchoring the Heron, his body cooled under that frozen spectre. Each day, the afternoon sun made the icy wrist minutely thinner. The meltwaters trickled down, to refreeze on the huge knuckles of the spreading hand. The sun hid behind the high horizon, and darkness closed on the crater. Only silvery reflections revealed the hanging form. The weight of the massive hand became too much for its dwindling arm. Minute fissures filled with weakening, running water. The iceman's arm parted, and the fist fell.

The survivors looked round, terrified, as the icicle shattered in bright cascading shards on the rocks. Rush's rigid corpse was dislodged from its stone vice and careered past his comrades in the crystalline torrent. As Rush's net slackened, the Heron's smashed nose was yanked from the bloodstained rocks. The brothers looked on agape as their canoe was drawn inexorably into the flow, following Lichen. Her broken prow raised in salute as she vanished.

Rush was towed into the flow. His rigid body spun. His arms raised and dipped as he passed his comrades. 'He's swimming,' Oiwa called out. Bark held him firmly.

'He's not swimming,' Bark said quietly. 'Just wave him goodbye.'

Oiwa lifted his hand limply, not really comprehending. He felt a great lump rising in his throat like an immovable flint nodule. The four survivors looked around. The only shelter was the inhospitable grotto itself, eroded by millennia of water. There was no obvious way out. 'We can't scale the cliff,' Bark announced. 'It's too sheer.' They looked up into the sky, where vultures wheeled, eyeing them for fresh carrion.'

'We must have fire,' Bark said. 'Oiwa, find fuel.'

Oiwa gathered wood splinters lodged in the rocks and threw them to Bark, before searching the cave floor. Rounding a corner, he found

himself standing on the brink of Gunnal's Guts, the appalling precipice over which Rush and Lichen had plummeted. The cave went on.
Blocking it was a great barricade of stranded tree trunks and branches, washed there by earlier spates. Oiwa pulled at a whitened bough,
and the pile shifted. A finely balanced trunk dislodged and fell into
the mighty current. Others followed as the dam loosened.

Oiwa was assailed by an overpowering stench. His throat ached,
and he gagged as the rotting head of a bison rolled at his feet. As
the dam of wood and decomposing meat collapsed, a volley of bats
flapped past Oiwa's face, and he screeched in terror. Dragging the
wood behind him, he ran back to his brothers. Shaking, he opened
his mouth to tell them what he'd seen. Nothing emerged but harsh
breath. He dropped his branch. Tears broke. He shook. Tine wrapped
him in his arms. Oiwa sank to the cavern floor, convulsing with each
burst of grief and terror.

Tine gathered him up carefully, asking softly, 'Where did you get
that wood?' Oiwa pointed. 'Show me. We need more.' Oiwa limply
turned in his brother's arms and led the way.

'We'll drag the branches out,' Tine said as the stench of bison
greeted them. 'Don't you come near, Oiwa. That foul carcass is about
to shift. You've had enough. Just haul some wood back.'

'Okay,' Oiwa nodded bravely, but with a smashed heart.

On their return, they found Mica clutching his ear, rocking with
pain and chanting to relieve it.

'We'll get the fire blazing. Night's closing,' Bark said as their world
shrank to the fire-glow. Stars shone. The silvery waning moon gave
Oiwa strange comfort. He tried to hum a tune, but nothing came.
Bark heated wet moss until it steamed. He applied the poultice to
Mica's swollen jaw. Mica moaned painfully.

'Can you pee?' Bark asked.

'I already have.' Mica answered through his clenched jaw.

'Can you again? It will stop infection.'

'I think so,' he replied.

'Then piss on this moss. I'll bathe your lug. There's grit, slime and chunks of rock in there. Your ear's actually hanging off. I'll have to remove it. This might hurt.'

Mica nodded. Tine took his flint blade core from his pouch and pressed a sharp flake with his axe butt. The translucent sliver fell into his palm. He sliced the swinging ear away.

'When are you going to do it?' asked Mica abruptly through the gap in his teeth.

'It's done,' answered Bark.

'Really?'

Oiwa sat trembling by the fireside. Tine gripped his hand. 'It is so hard,' he said. 'Goose journeys have never been like this. It's all gone so menacingly wrong.'

Oiwa nodded grimly. His throat ached. Only the glimpse of the moon soothed him. He buried his head in Tine's breast, shaking. Bark nursed Mica. They watched the fire. Tine's chin dropped and Oiwa lay down. Bark shifted, allowing Mica to rest on his chest. They slept. The moon slipped by. Clouds obscured the stars.

Oiwa dreamt of someone far off. She gazed at him through a shimmering veil. He woke and rekindled the fire. Mica tried a yawn. His jaw remained locked. Grey streaks of daylight saw the last black bats flap their leathery wings back to their cavern. Oiwa tried to say, 'Good morning.' His mouth moved, but silence came. Instead he picked up a stone and flung it at the rock face. It shattered, but still he couldn't speak.

The crack woke Tine. He groped in their sodden supply bag for dried meat.

Oiwa shared some in silence. The food pushed against the stone stuck in his larynx. The meat sat coldly in his stomach. He moved from the fire, where his dark thoughts lurked, and ventured away to look at the speeding waters. Then wandered towards the bats' retreat. Midges buzzed around the strewn carcases of the bison. Behind the collapsed barrier, a dark path wound. Oiwa held his breath and ventured into the tunnel, towards the bats' roost. He could hear their distant chatter and their dry wings fluttering. Maybe they could escape that way. He struck his bow on the rock-face to get his brothers' attention, pointing Ziit in the direction where the bats had gone. Mica stood, saying painfully, 'Follow Oiwa.' As they made for the cave, the sky darkened. Sheet lightning flashed, crashing behind grey clouds. The first heavy hail was forced down by quickening wind.

Oiwa took his quiver, Bark, the spear and Tine carried the rope and bags. They held their breath and climbed the slumped tangle of boughs into the unknown. 'Forward and inward,' Oiwa wanted to say. He just looked back with his hazel eyes and blinked. Mica understood Oiwa's command.

'Follow,' Oiwa signalled as he clambered over the flotsam-strewn floor. Bones, antlers and horns of drowned beasts were littered around. They picked their way until the cave turned into utter darkness. Oiwa stuck out his arms, stopping his brothers. He ushered them back to the light. He gripped his new axe and ran to the bison. He took a huge breath and looked inside the rotting rib cage from where its offal had spilled. Dangling under the spine were the huge, fat-encased kidneys. Oiwa bent in, severed them then ran as the bison slumped, nearly enclosing him.

He flung the fat at his brothers' feet, returning for strewn femurs and a loosened horn. Back with his kin, he chopped off the ends of the bones and stuffed the fat inside. Tinder lay at his feet. He pushed it into the lard. Bark understood. He took his firestones and struck. Sparks flew through the gloom to the dry fuel. Oiwa blew. Small embers grew, then flames melted the grease. Soon a bright torch flared.

Mica forced his mouth open a little, spluttering, 'You're brilliant, Oiwa. Show us the way.'

Oiwa was feeling better, despite everything they'd been through. 'Right. Onward into the dark,' he resolved.

Their path weaved. The cave roof lowered. They stooped. Later the ceiling became so lofty, it escaped the light from Oiwa's torch; Mica carried the spares. Inexorably, their trail descended.

Oiwa sensed it first; a strange odour. Underfoot it was peculiarly soft. Overhead, things shuffled. Oiwa peered, clicking his tongue.

'Bats,' Tine said.

'Yes,' Oiwa nodded excitedly, signalling Tine to bend over. Handing Bark his torch, he mounted Tine's back. Reaching high, he gently picked two bats like ripe plums. He passed them to Mica, who clubbed them with the butt of his green chopper. Oiwa harvested a dozen. He climbed down and signalled to go, tucking their next meal in their battered jackets.

'Gather wood if you can,' Mica said as they moved on, as though reading Oiwa's thoughts. Later the cave opened into a vast gallery. Water dripped from above. Their torchlight shimmered from wonderful yellow and green streaks sparkling in the stone.

'Let's cook,' Mica murmured as his jaw relaxed. They made a fire. Oiwa pushed an arrow through a bat. The smell of singeing fur filled the still air. The leathery wings crisped and he crunched. The fragrant flesh warmed beneath the fine skin and loosened from the light bones.

'I've not eaten bat,' Bark remarked.

'Me neither,' Oiwa gestured.

'Nor I.' Mica added.

Tine shafted another. 'My second ever bat going down. Small but tasty.' Their fire comforted them. Smoke rose to the high roof, leaving the air crisp. Tine sang a soft, serenely echoing song before they explored the cavern.

'Look there,' Mica pointed. 'In the middle. It's a small pool of the clearest water.'

Oiwa approached it warily, examining the stumpy stalagmites that surrounded it. Their tops had worn hollow and nursed polished, conical pebbles, shining in their fonts like eggs in a coot's nest. Their torchlight flickered in reflected glory. They stood at the pool's edge where the ceiling's reflection looked up. Veins of sparkling golden stone shimmered in its depths. The stillness was profound. They looked up, pointing to flashes of shining brilliance, then leaned over and saw themselves framed in the glorious light.

'This is the most beautiful thing I've ever seen,' Mica whispered reverently, watching in wonder his brothers' reflected gazes. He glanced again round the sanctuary of beauty. Then... he quietly said it. 'We have to move on.'

'Lets embrace and seal this moment forever,' Bark suggested.

'Yes, and then we will drink from this wondrous pool,' Tine added.

Stooping, they drank deeply from the brilliant water. The ripples made great play of the torchlight on the glittering rock roof. Oiwa imagined a familiar face glancing back at him.

'We must trace our path where the cave narrows again,' Mica told them reluctantly. 'There's a long log across it.'

Mica was about to speak, but Oiwa hushed him. Nervously he took hold of the horn he'd found, and placed its open end directly on the cave wall, pressing his ear to it.

Oiwa looked at them in alarm, mouthing the word, 'Run!' and hurtled on.

'Follow Oiwa,' Mica yelled. Terrified bats flew past into Oiwa's flickering torchlight.

Bark caught up, 'Light my torch, Oiwa,' he asked as more bats darted past in a fearful cloud.

Oiwa sprinted ahead. 'There must be a way out. Follow the bats!' he indicated

They ran through the dark. A distant grey light appeared far ahead. 'Make speed,' he panted. 'I know the peril they flee from.' The light ahead was dimming, and the flying creatures careered up the beam. Oiwa saw the opening. He turned as his brain screamed, *Hurry!*'

They reached the light amid swarms of ascending bats. Bark bent. Mica jumped on his back and shinned up the rising tunnel. Oiwa scrambled up Bark's spine and crawled on to the ledge where Mica had perched. The tumultuous roar of tumbling water that Oiwa had heard became deafening. Tine leaped on Bark's shoulders. Mica dropped his bone lamp. It fell past Oiwa and scorched Tine as he scraped on to the ledge. He leaned down, grabbing at Bark's outstretched fingers. The torrent gushed at Bark's ankles. Oiwa reached down too. Bark's face came into the light as a log struck his knee and dragged him under. Tine could not hold on. In one terrible instant, Bark vanished.

Chapter 16

Scoured

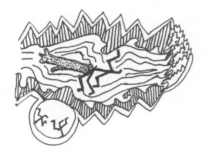

'No! Not now!' Bark thundered, as the speeding trunk smashed his joints. He gulped as he foundered. 'Keep my head up!' he told himself. 'Swim! Save myself!' The flume curved along a quartzite curtain, which split into arches. As the torrent propelled Bark through one of them, his head caught in the narrowing point. He felt the base of his skull separate from his stretching neck. In those final moments, he felt warm breath enter his nostrils. Before his ears ceased hearing and his heart crashed to a stop, he found himself looking deeply into the eyes of a large mother cat.

The lynx's stripy grey face licked his cold one. He felt long whiskers caress his temples. Bark noticed his body shrinking. The cat's teeth softly gripped his furry neck. She swam with him. They saw a familiar broken corpse slip from a rent in the quartz curtain to wash from sight. The new kitten emerged into a starry night high on a mountain cleft. There he suckled with his new brood of brothers and sisters.

Oiwa was frantic. His torch spluttered out as he scrambled up the steep flue. Panicking bats shat on them. Tine's spear clattered down the shoot. Mica slipped as the air, pushed by the flash flood, blew his hair up in front of him. Oiwa gripped where he could and sat in a depression, splaying his legs on to the walls of their tunnel. His slight beard blew over his chin as the last escaping bats scraped past his face.

Tine felt a shunt of debris elevate him. Oiwa cast the rope to Mica, who slipped. The rising flume forced his head up to Mica. Tine's head sped between Mica's legs as the rising tide forced him up. Tine's shoulders met Mica's rear as he rose to face his navel.

The plug of water and men ascended. Mica's head crushed into Oiwa's scrotum. The water ripped over Tine's head, as a hunk of rotting bison mashed under him. The power of the speeding haunch forced the trio violently upwards. They hurtled through a crevice to find themselves sprawled on a cold platform. There they lay, hearts pounding, temples thumping. Mica moved first. Tine felt Oiwa shift. In the all-consuming darkness, Tine spluttered and sneezed. The stench of rotting bison made Oiwa take a hand from his dashed testicles to cover his nose. The intense pain made him speed it back to nurse them. His mute yell of agony was felt by Tine and Mica.

Oiwa panted savagely, curling up against the searing pain. Miraculously, Ziit still hung over his shoulder. He lay crouched as Mica spoke. 'Are we all here?'

'We lost Bark,' Tine answered with difficulty. 'I tried grabbing his hand, but he was swept away.' As Tine's words sank in, the putrefying bison carcase dissipated in the swirling pool, its bones drifting slowly down.

'We lost Bark?' Mica asked in alarm.

Oiwa grimaced desperately. 'I don't know how to cope with this. What is happening to us?' he cried within.

Above, the tunnel curved higher. The bats had fled. Tine looked around, spying a grey hue far above. 'There's light!' he declared urgently. 'Mica, Oiwa, don't move.' He put his hand up, covering the glimmer. He removed it. The light was still there. Suddenly, with hideous belching and vomiting sounds, the column of fetid water withdrew, dragging the buffalo remains like a vile catarrh. The reeking mucus withdrew deep into Gunnal's interior. To fill the vacuum, fresh air was sucked down in a thin, reviving rush.

'We must move. Gunnal may blow her stinking nose again,' Tine warned. 'I'll take the rope, Oiwa. I can shin up further and see.' He edged over Mica's knees. 'Sorry about your ear,' he said as he clumsily bashed it.

'It's fine,' Mica winced, 'Just get up there.' The tunnel narrowed. Tine wedged his feet on each side to scramble up, slipping slightly on bat excrement.

'How are you doing?' Mica called.

'Okay,' Tine answered, banishing thoughts of his lost brother. 'Further yet,' he puffed through cool, sucking air. His head reached to where the grey light eked. His chin edged above a rocky shelf. Far, far above, daylight shone down.

'*Light!* It's *light!*' he called, lowering the rope.

'Are you safe?' Mica shouted.

'Yes. You grab the rope, I'll hoist.' Tine yelled over the noise.

'Okay. Oiwa's coming first.' Mica fumbled in the dark, putting the rope in Oiwa's hands.

'Tie it round you.'

Oiwa moved his hands from the site of the throbbing pain to rope himself, banishing the agony from his mind.

'Up you go,' Mica encouraged.

As Tine tugged on the rope, Oiwa climbed, and found that the effort distracted from the pain in his crushed balls.

'Oiwa's pelvis is bloody hard,' Mica thought, rubbing a painful swelling on his forehead.

Oiwa edged higher to find Tine's ledge, and looked up into the late afternoon light.

'Your turn,' Tine called. Oiwa cast the rope. Mica heard it drop. As he felt for it, he found an arrow. He gripped it in his teeth then grasped the rope. He shinned up the steep flue. Dragging himself up, he squatted next to Oiwa. Fresh blood trickled from the soaked scab round his earhole.

'I'm going further,' Tine announced. 'We'll do what we did just now. Oiwa then you, Mica.' It felt wretched not to mention Bark.

'Oiwa, is your quiver okay? I rescued an arrow.' He nodded in the gloom. Mica found it and dropped it in the empty container.

Tine heaved. 'Come up, Oiwa.' His pain had eased, but he was wary. The light and his heart strengthened as Tine's silhouette appeared. Ziit was scarred but undamaged.

The rope touched Mica's shoulder. His green axe was still in his belt. His mood lifted. 'I'm on my way.'

'The next bit's easy,' Tine said when they had settled. 'I'm going up. The cave's surface has rills. I can grip them with my toes.' Soon he reported, 'I'm up on a wide ledge, startling nesting pigeons. Otherwise it's quite flat. Other tunnels do drop away. I'll crawl and squint down one.'

A cold breeze fanned him from far below. Above, fungi hung like weird ears. Beyond them shone an even brighter light.

'Come on.' he called excitedly. More birds took flight down the other shaft. He felt the rope tighten. Shortly Ziit's tip appeared above Oiwa's shoulders. He rose blinking into the light. His matted hair had few beads left. He coughed. It sounded so different, just a rattle from his chest.

Mica pulled up next. The rumbling of Gunnal's innards threatened. A surprisingly warm draught rose, the fungi vibrated. Squabs in their nests instinctively drew back.

'I think we're safe,' said Mica as he sat by Oiwa.

Tine stooped to peer down the dropping cave. Silvery reflections waved up and down its walls. He craned his neck and looked through a narrow, level cave. The golden light of sunset beamed back.

'Safe. Yes. For the moment,' he added urgently, 'Look down there and listen.' Mica stepped forward. His head brushed the fungi; giant slugs within withdrew their stalked eyes, shrinking alarmed into the crevices. Mica leaned forward and looked down to the silvery flickering light. 'Gunnal's Falls,' he said to Tine.

'Yes. We saw them last time, but from the cliff above.' He inhaled deeply through his nose. 'We're up Gunnal's Snout!' They all looked at each other. 'We can't go down,' Tine warned gravely. 'It's a sheer drop to her gaping jaws and the waterfall. We would just follow Rush, Lichen and Bark. We must explore.'

'Okay, Tine, but the light's fading fast, and we're exhausted. We can actually rest here.' A draught of warm air rising to greet them was their only comfort. 'Look, we've got grub. My bats washed away, but there's pigeon squabs in these ledges. We can cook on a fire of old nests and dry fungus.'

'Cook,' Tine said. 'I've got two drowned bats in my jacket.'

Oiwa nodded eagerly. 'Here,' he intimated, pulling another bat from his clothing. There was enough fuel for a warming glow; one arrow for a spit; one spark from Mica's stones to catch the fungus. Then the old nests glowed. The aroma of roasting bat and fledglings followed.

Oiwa dreamed that the moon was looking down on a craggy mountain. In the mouth of a cave, a lynx lay suckling a human baby. It slowly turned into a kitten. 'I will call you Purrrrer,' the mother cat said lovingly, as her new incarnation reached for a soft, pink nipple.

Dew slumped, crying, 'Can we stop? My feet are sore. My knees shake. I can't go on.'

'Just over the brow, dear,' her mother called back to her. 'Not far now.'

'But it's getting dark, Mummy!'

'Yes my bluebird. The stars will shine and you'll see your way. Come on now.'

The bare, rising expanse seemed endless as Dew followed Snaaaaar's angry quest. She stopped to wait for her little treasure, but on went directly Dew caught up.

Eventually Snaaaaar stopped. Her form, darker than black sky, stood out against her starry background. Her straw headband shone. The tiny, knotted earrings dangled.

Dew met her at the summit of the smooth rock slope. She gazed down the precipitous edge. Far below, an immense black pool was held back in a cavernous mouth, dammed by Gunnal's Teeth. The silver cascade roared over her jutting chin, falling thunderously into Wolf Lake. It swirled deeply down into the darkness of a spectacular pit, eroded over eons. In those terrible depths, barbel sucked on foul bison meat. A fresher corpse was spat out and forced into those depths, to be tossed in the heavy, golden dust that settled at the bottom.

'We are here, Dew,' Snaaaaar softly informed her awestruck child. 'In the morning we shall see them floating like spit on a piddle puddle.'

Dew drew back exhausted. 'I hate this,' she whined.

'You curl up and sleep, dear. You didn't drop any arrows now, did you?'

'No.'

'There's a good girl.' She extracted a morsel of robbed pemmican from her hidden store, 'Here, my little Summer Fruit, have this to help you sleep.'

Her mother then ranted secretly by the precipice.

'Why didn't my dad come back all that time ago?' Dew asked.

'Don't start asking silly questions now, dear,' she hissed.' He probably fell over a stupid cliff on his crazy expedition. How should I know anyway?' Her voice changed from chilling tones to that of sweetness and love. 'Now you curl right up and go to sleep. I'll light a little fire. Have sweet dreams and stop asking awf...' she stopped herself. 'Silly questions, my Tulip.'

Dew's head fell forward in slumber. She dreamed of her father waving to her as he disappeared into the forest.

Muttering to herself, Snaaaaar remembered Birch Skin's last, surprised moments when she hacked the deadly knife into him, snapping it. 'And those other bastards,' she recalled, 'carrying their stupid boat of meat. An arrow in the first one's kidney sorted him. How the second one turned. Smack, right into the bridge of his nose and deep in his dull brain. And the third one who carried that fish tail. Got him in the nipple, didn't I? How they writhed in their unexpected deaths.

Then I carried the meat back to my sweet little Poppy who waited so patiently.'

* * *

The mountain cold penetrated the brothers' bones. Eventually dawn broke. It reflected light up Gunnal's Nostrils; then rays shone along their escape tunnel. They wakened and stretched. Pigeons fluttered. 'Watch out for those sheer drops,.' Mica managed to say. His ear wound hurt. 'And the one behind, into Gunnal's Gullet.'

Oiwa wanted to say, 'I need a pee,' but couldn't. Tine said it for him. They lined up and pissed down the nostrils.

'Eggs for breakfast?' Mica suggested. 'I'll get some.' They cracked them, sucked them out and dropped the shells down the shaft. Alarmed, the pigeons took flight.

The passage was dry. Tine edged along as the noise of the falls from outside amplified. A nesting raven flew from a ledge. He made for there. Two grey chicks waited helplessly. Tine put them aside and rested. He listened to Mica and Oiwa scraping through behind.

Tine moved squinting into the full morning light. Mist from the falls below wet his cheeks as he emerged behind a flattened boulder. He sat; the wind flicked his matted hair. He peered down to Wolf Lake. Oiwa appeared with Ziit's string flicking his ear. Mica followed shortly.

'Look at Gunnal's Falls,' Mica blurted as he emerged, 'That huge cascade, the foam, the swirling, black water.' Oiwa gasped, shaking soundlessly. He pointed below and touched Tine's shoulder. A tiny, bright splayed form floated on Wolf Lake. Tine covered his eyes, stricken, then looked again as Oiwa gripped Mica's hand.

'It's Rush,' Tine said. The situation hit immediately.

'Or it could be Lichen?' Mica added sadly.

'No. There's net tied to his ankle,' Tine observed.

'Why does he look so bright?' Mica asked. 'He seems like he's lit with rays of golden sunshine.'

An osprey clasped a shiny, wriggling fish and rose with it to its eerie.

Oiwa pointed. Another body emerged. Mica shook. 'Bark,' he stated mournfully. They watched in remorse as their brother's corpse spun gently in an eddy. It shone too as it turned on the black depths.

'We must leave,' Mica said quietly, sadly and respectfully, forcing back his tears. Oiwa tugged him, pointing as a third body bobbed up from the dark fathoms.

'It's Lichen!' Tine said. 'He glitters too. Why?'

'He's drifting towards Rush,' Mica added. 'They're going to touch.'

They crouched and gazed down, shocked, over the expanse of water. Their cave hung below a great overhanging black rock. 'A ledge!' Tine shouted amidst the roar. 'It leads down, then round the cliff face.'

Tine stood slowly and moved ahead along the ledge. Oiwa smoothed the flights on his arrow and flexed Ziit. The bow responded to his tired muscles. Mica followed Tine, signalling for Oiwa to wait. He did. He prayed silently for the spirits of a lost brother and two friends.

Oiwa watched Mica round the corner. He waited.

'Come, Oiwa,' he heard Mica call. 'It's quite safe.'

* * *

Snaaaaar looked down from the clifftop in cruel satisfaction. 'That's three of those bastards dead! What about the rest of them? Look, Dew.'

From above the roar of Gunnal's Falls, Snaaaaar heard voices. Mica's call rang in her ears. 'Bastards! Shits! Fucking useless, idiotic men,' she hissed. She removed her curved bow from her shoulder and lodged an arrow shaft at the string. Dew stirred, distressed at her mother's anger. Snaaaaar leaned over the sheer drop and looked towards the falls. A movement below caught her eye as Tine edged unknowingly into sight. Instantly she fully bent her bow. Tine passed behind an outcrop and was lost to her. She maintained the strain as she heard small stones drop as Mica's shoulder edged into view.

'Stop!' she heard Tine call back. 'It's no use, we can't go on. The ledge has fallen away.'

'Just like her stupid father,' Dew heard Snaaaaar hiss. 'Fucking around on a mad, crazy journey. Should have stayed with me!'

Mica's head appeared. 'Do you need any help?' he called.

She tightened the string. 'Straight into his fucking, ignorant cranium,' she thought as Mica turned back telling Oiwa to wait. That move exposed his shoulder. A piece of the ledge dropped from beneath Mica's toe. He pressed himself back as Snaaaaar loosed her missile. It streaked by Mica's stomach, grazed his left shin and smashed into the rock shelf. Another large flake fell to the distant water.

Mica yelled in alarm, pressing further into the rock face. Tine then heard Snaaaaar move above. Scree slipped from her toes to dribble over the edge.

Oiwa pricked up his ears. He felt his body redden inside with blooded anger. He picked his way along the high path. Far above he saw Snaaaaar's head disappear. He pulled the only arrow from his quiver and fitted it to Ziit's string. She vanished, but he heard that scree.

He stole along the ledge. Looking up, he spied her slightly bulging stomach protrude through a deeply cut cleft. From her position she saw Tine. Tine saw her. He realised that there was no escape. The ledge had gone, and if he backtracked he'd be in full view. Hurling the rope behind him, Tine sprang into thin air. Snaaaaar loosed her bolt. He did not feel the arrow; just the rush of breeze as he plummeted.

Snaaaaar's bolt entered the nape of Tine's neck. The point exited through the star on his forehead. The bitter red darkness of death covered the insides of his eyes. His body fell to the water hundreds of feet below.

'Got him!' Snaaaaar cheered. 'Now for that other turd!'

She swivelled, ready with another arrow. Mica was still a viable target. 'I can see his ribs and hip. I'll kill him through his kidney like that other shit.'

Oiwa, unseen, pulled hard on Ziit's string as she aimed her missile at Mica's midriff. He'd edged back, but was still fatally vulnerable. She adjusted her aim. Her belly protruded just a fraction further. Oiwa pulled Ziit back to his fullest. He only had a light arrow, its delicate jasper tip designed for small game. His upward shot was long and high. He strained back a little further as Ziit's string twanged in song. The arrow flew in a near vertical trajectory. Almost at the end of its range, the small point cut into the suede jerkin that hung lightly round Snaaaaar's hips. The tiny barb pinned the loose flap tightly to her belly. It hurt her: burning, like a flying ember. Her bow arm involuntarily tilted as her arrow left the string to fall into the gorge.

Oiwa's shot was not fatal by any means; it couldn't have been at that range. But the jasper head lodged at her pelvis, its small, fiery point scoring the fringe of her pubic curls as it snagged her stomach lining. She stepped back slightly, but her left knee weakened and bent, pushing Oiwa's arrow further into her as its shaft pressed against the rock.

Dew understood her mother's last, venomous tirade. The rounded stone she'd been fondling sped from her hand to Snaaaaar's back. Her mother's right knee buckled, and Oiwa's projectile slid deeper, puncturing Snaaaaar's bladder. Her own weight forced the arrow up through her intestines to her liver. Snaaaaar felt the shaft's relentless, agonising progress. It punctured her diaphragm, then squeaked through the spongy tissue of her lungs as she was forced into a squat. Before her arse touched her heels, Dew's stone struck the back of her head. The arrow-tip emerged behind  her collarbone. She screamed venomously, coughing blood to spiral over the precipice.

Tine's spirit looked up from the depths. It saw a long trail of bubbles rise to where he had broken the surface. Just to one side of it, a distorted form crashed on the water. He swam up through the currents. His new eagle wings broke the surface. He looked into the bulging, unseeing eyes of his deathly assailant as his spirit soared high above Gunnal's Falls.

Chapter 17

*

Wolf Lake

'I'm sorry, I'm sorry. I didn't mean to kill you. But I couldn't let you do it again.' Dew sobbed, looking down to her mother's twisted body by her murderous floating bow.

Oiwa stood staggered at his arrow's effect, hearing Dew above. A flock of doves flew past. Oiwa whistled. The first sound he'd made since his voice left him.

'You saved us.' Mica shouted from around the cliff. Oiwa whistled in answer. The doves flew back, vanishing above. 'I'm going to edge along. Stay there, Oiwa. Keep your back pressed to the cliff-face, like me.' He felt sick. The sight of the minute corpses below accentuated the height. He composed himself. 'It's you and me now, Oiwa. Keep still. I'll come to you. Don't move. The ledge is crumbling. That's another bit gone from under my heel. There you are. Okay?'

Oiwa nodded, gazing blankly down to the bodies of his kin and friends. How placid they looked in their shining garb. Snaaaaar floated in crumpled contrast. 'Come forward,' he whistled to Mica, as the ledge widened.

'Tine had the rope. Was it with him when he fell?' Oiwa shrugged in Mica's arms.

'I'll go and look. Stay right where you are.'

Oiwa nodded, tears dribbling over his cheeks.

'I've got it.' Mica shouted round the crag.

'Throw it up to me,' they heard Dew's small, sad voice cry out. 'I'll help. I didn't do it. It was my mother. She killed your friends. I had to stop her. I had to!'

'Are you all right?' Mica called back.

'No... But I'll help you. Trust me.'

'I'll tie a stone to the rope and hurl it up. Watch out.'

Oiwa edged round the crag, holding a rock. Mica took it. Flaky stone dropped alarmingly from the ledge as he tied the rope round and round the weight. He swung it below, gaining momentum. 'Stand back. It's coming up,' Bark called to Dew.

She stepped back, looking for a good anchorage. There was only a crisscross of worn fissures, eroded by driving rain and wind.

The stone landed heavily on the clifftop. Dew ran to grab it. It bounced, skidded back and tumbled. Oiwa heard her warning. 'The rope's snaking back. Grab it!'

'I'll hold you,' Mica said, gripping Oiwa and leaning into the cliff-face. The rope tore through Oiwa's hands, burning his palms. He gripped harder, and rock stopped. Pulling it back, he swung it again, casting it higher.

'Watch out!' Mica called.

Dew leapt forward, catching the stone. 'Got it,' she yelled, jamming her foot on the rope. 'I'll wedge it into a crack. I'll tell when it's safe,' she shouted. 'I'm securing a boulder over the rope too. You'll be all right now.'

'You go first, Oiwa. You're lightest.' Oiwa looked at his sore hands and tugged the rope again.

'I'm holding the boulder down to stop it shifting,' Dew called out. 'The rope's tightening.'

Ziit's tip emerged before Oiwa's head appeared. He flung himself over the edge. She noticed his empty quiver.

Mica looked up at Oiwa's heels. Bits of crumbly rock fell into his eyes. 'Thank the Spirits he's made it,' he thought. 'He's safe. Now me.'

Oiwa gazed at Dew. She put her hand out to him, but would not leave the rock. Mica began his ascent. Oiwa leaned over the edge. 'He's coming up... That stone under his foot's dislodged! He's swinging freely on the rope. It's twisting at the top. Hold it steady! Thank Tumar he's climbing again. He's not looking down. You can do it, Mica,' he urged in his silence. 'Give me your hand,'

At last, Mica's his fingers felt the top. Oiwa grasped Mica's wrist and pulled him up. What a mercy! Mica scrambled away from the drop and squatted on the bare rock, sobbing in relief and anguish. Dew watched him from her stone, not daring to move.

Oiwa soothed his brother's heaving shoulders then went to Dew. She looked up at him. 'My mother did it. I hate her. I killed her. My stone hit. She fell.'

Oiwa shook his head. He held her trembling hand, mouthing, 'No,' as he touched Ziit's string. Dew stared again at the empty quiver.

Doves landed on the clifftop then flew away to the cave. A skein of geese honked high in the sky.

Mica scraped on to all fours then knelt, watching Oiwa with Dew. He controlled his heaving chest and slowly got to his feet. Unsteadily he went to Oiwa's side. 'Let's get the rope,' he said softly, unable to utter consolation.

'It was the stone I slung. It hit her head and knocked her over.'

Oiwa mouthed 'No,' again.

Mica stepped in. 'Oiwa's right. He wounded your mother. She sank on his last arrow. You probably didn't even see it. Your stone dropped with her, but you certainly didn't kill her.'

'Well, I'm glad she's dead. She murdered my dad. I know she got rid of Birch Skin too. He was lovely.' Dew said as though dazed.

'Take my hand. We must leave this place.' Dew gripped Mica's fingers. He shifted the rock, retrieving the rope.

'We will go down Gunnal's Arm. Look below,' Mica said. 'Large hide boats are sailing across Wolf Lake.'

At the closest prow, Musk stood tall, a wolf skin over his shoulders, its head making a fine cap. He guided his craft to the wreckage of the Heron's Tooth. Rush's net was still tied to the stern, the knotted strands dotted with bright golden specks. Musk leaned over to pull it. The net tightened. Rush's gold dusted body followed, turning in the water. His face gazed up. His tattered garments, floating hair and disjointed leg reflected the in gilded sunshine.

Musk drew Rush's remains to the side. 'Some of you lean away, the others of you pull this good man out.' The stiffened corpse drained. A stream of glittering specks sank gracefully to the lakebed. They laid Rush carefully on a central plank where a shimmering pool gathered. Their hands glistened.

Claw, at his helm, drew alongside Bark. He touched Bark's shining yellow back. His crew drew the rigid body into the boat and watched golden waters leave him to drift, glittering, to the bed of Wolf Lake.

More craft moved towards Lichen and Tine. Another slowed at the side of Snaaaaar's body. Mica watched as her limp carcase was dragged from the lake and dumped in a shapeless heap. Her bird earrings were wrecked, her hairband, gone. Oiwa's fatal arrow jagged up into her jutting jaw, keeping it firmly shut. Thin blood dribbled from a pulseless artery as Bristle's barge began its return to the Loup tribe's camp.

Eyewhite's women rowers retrieved Tine. 'Look at that terrible buffalo bolt sticking through his forehead,' she said to her sister, Pelt. 'But how golden his beard glitters from his sad face. When I saw that wrecked boat, I knew something terrible was happening. It's far worse than I imagined.'

Musk looked pitifully at the smashed arrows protruding from Rush's chest. 'Paddle at once to Gunnal's Hand to meet his company,' he commanded.

'The big craft is turning,' Mica reported. 'The shores here are quite changed. The larch woodlands are gone. That was thick forest last time I was here. What's happened?'

Musk's boat rounded the cliff. A ram's-horn trumpet-blast rent the air. The oarsmen raised their paddles in salute as Zeal's side pressed gently on to the gravel. Mica and Oiwa took Dew down the back of Gunnal's Hand to the shingle. They saw Rush. Musk's crew gathered round.

'We have a victim in the boat.'

Mica looked down. 'He... he saved us,' he stammered. 'He made himself into a human anchor to stop Heron's Tooth so we could escape.'

Another trumpet blasted as Claw's boat drew up next to Zeal. Claw jumped ashore. 'We have one with us as well.' They looked into Long Wake.

'It's Bark,' Mica said. The crew stood in respectful silence. The brothers gazed at the golden forms. Bark's beard seemed thicker and tighter. Rush's dark head of hair was brightly streaked in gold and glittering sunlight, his face in total peace. The bodies lay as dreamlike figures.

Eyewhite's rowers pulled the Osprey shoreward. Pelt blew a peal of reverberating blasts on a bark lur. 'Come with us,' Eyewhite said. Oiwa, Mica and Dew stepped in.

The Osprey set off, and the sombre flotilla began its slow progress across Wolf Lake. Mica looked at the barren hills, which climbed to snow-tipped mountains. He watched the long expanse of water open to a vista of level calmness. Oiwa saw the Loup tribe's encampment on the treeless far bank. Huts, wigwams and turf shelters spread themselves over a grassy rise where an arm of land pointed into the lake. Smoke rose from many fires. Piles of fallen trees were heaped around the village.

Musk guided his boat back. He peered deep into the dark, clear waters. The sunken roots of upturned trees poked about nearer their shore. Fish hid in their waterlogged remains. Herons fished patiently in the shallows.

Bristle's craft reached the shore first; its dark cargo was lifted out as Zeal approached. 'Should we pull that arrow from her?' Heng asked as the wet corpse unfolded on the bank.

'No.' answered Bristle. 'Cover it.'

The Osprey made headway over the lake towards Wolven Den. Dew wondered what would happen to her mother's corpse. Oiwa and Mica sat silently. The women paddled.

Zeal felt sand under her side. Musk hopped out. His wolf's head dangled askew. Long Wake's prow, decorated with eagle feathers, touched the sand. The rowers lifted Bark on his wooden litter and carried him up the shore towards the Resting House. Rush was aloft on Musk's men's shoulders. Tine and Lichen were being carried too. Oiwa and Mica watched, stunned.

'Come with us,' Eyewhite said to Dew. 'You will be cold and hungry.'

The brothers followed their dead remorsefully to an avenue of smooth quartz pebbles. The biers continued up the slight gradient to the raised, oblong building. It had a hide roof with walls open to waist height. It was a quiet sanctuary for the dead to rest before burial. Mica and Oiwa followed the grim procession. The four bodies were placed on the floor while a vast, central pile of quartz rocks were arranged to take them. The smell and sounds of the stones scraping together was like that of life and death meeting.

Musk said, 'Lift your lost ones on their boards and lay them over the stones. They will rest there while we make a proper burial place. My people will prepare and guard them. You shall come and relate what happened.'

Mica and Oiwa shifted the planks. Their fingertips smudged the golden residue. They felt lonely.

Musk led them to his splendid wigwam. It stood among a family of others. Huts and stretched-skin shelters were scattered over the shoulder of land. 'Come in. Sit round my glowing fire in the ring of leather bolsters.'

Eyewhite entered. 'We have been listening to Dew's sorrowful story. She's suffered. She sleeps now. You two have had terrible experiences too.' They nodded to Musk's wife.

Pelt came in. 'Here's food for you. Maybe you don't feel like eating, but it is here. Oiwa reached for the steamed bream, but pulled back. 'Not yet,' Mica replied. The wooden dish was laid on the rush floor.

Mica began their story. Bristle and Claw listened. Slowly the tent filled. Mica's voice related all. Oiwa confirmed with gestures. His throat ached. Expressions of horror at Snaaaaar's venom broke the silent intent of the listeners. Oiwa held his head in his hands during those vile episodes. The people of the Loup clan understood their plight and their quest.

When Mica finished, Musk said, 'We will prepare a place for your honourable dead up with ours. I must explain. Our graves were ruined two years ago. Late rains filled the soil just before the great freeze. During early spring an immense amount of snow fell on the frozen ground. The thaw commenced, the mountains and hills shook. The ground rumbled and the soil shifted. I ordered my Clan to cross Wolf Lake. Its waters shook and splashed as we headed for the other side. We all watched as the whole hillside slid down on to our village. The trees piled up and filled Wolf Lake. Our place was scraped away by roots and shifting mud. Wolf Lake got jammed. It took a year for it to clear. The river that Wolf Lake becomes was dammed. The Dun's meltwaters flooded the whole valley. The forest swirled on its surface. Eventually the dam unclogged. It all gushed along with the raging flood and broke free towards the ocean. Our ancestors got washed into the lake. We moved back when it was safe. We remade our homes and respected our ancestors' new resting place.'

Mica then realised why the place had changed so much.

'Our first newly dead inherited the old place to begin their afterlife. Yours will go there too,' Musk stated.

Mica scratched the scabs around his ear. They cracked and bled. He'd forgotten the injury. Eyewhite whistled. Her dog, wolf-like, bounded in. 'Lick that man's ear,' she commanded. Mica shied away. 'It's all right. He will be gentle. He'll clean it, sooth it, stopping inflammation.'

Pelt spoke to Oiwa. 'You've been struck dumb, Oiwa.' He nodded, clicking his tongue. 'Can I feel your throat?'

'Yes,' he clicked solemnly.

'Open wide?' Oiwa's jaw slumped. 'Say aah?' Only warm breath rasped. 'Let's leave it now.' He nodded, fiddling with his hair, deep in thought. Absentmindedly, Mica reached to the wooden tray with his sore hands. Warm flakes of clean-tasting fish caressed his tongue. It was their signal to eat.

Snaaaaar's corpse was dragged up the valley and hidden in an obscure cave. They dumped ashes over her so no animals would eat her, lest her poison sent them mad. Musk's men stopped the entrance with boulders. He instructed, 'Do not pull Oiwa's arrow out. None should know where she is. Her name must never be spoken again!'

Chapter 18

Burials

Musk and Eyewhite dressed ceremonially. She wore a finely braided skirt and beaded blouse. Her dark-feathered shawl contrasted with her white-painted face. Black hair was piled above her head in a backcombed fan stuck with ivory wolf-headed pins. Strands of red beads dangled from her earlobes.

Musk greeted Oiwa and Mica, his handshake rattling with shining bone bracelets. He wore his wolf cape and carried a long spear. Its great polished head glinted in the fading sunlight. 'Are you ready?' he said through his mask of star-dotted blue paint. His family led them back to the small mortuary.

'Across the threshold we feel death,' Eyewhite said. 'Our quartz pebbles are the seeds of birth. The red stony floor, the blood of life... Enter,' she whispered.

The bodies lay on their pink quartz dais. Rush's golden form rested on a low litter. Lichen, Bark and Tine lay on theirs. The murderous arrows had been removed from their deathly havens. Over Tine's wound a new star blazoned, glistening like sunset gold. Stone lamps, burning fragrant oils, graced their resting corpses; the bodies looked unworldly, beautiful and distant. The river gold from Gunnal's Pit remained like a second skin. Their soaked clothing had finished draining on to the leather surfaces. The glittering silt seemed to weld them to their litters.

Bark and Tine's travelling beards were bound with fine leather tatting. The darkly polished strands made dramatic patterns, terminating in knots under their chins. This tightened their skin, making them resemble spiritual beings. Mica leaned forward and pushed Bark's long, fair hair aside to show his star; his face was clear and distinct in every feature.

Oiwa removed the broken arrows from Rush's chest. He solemnly leaned forward and compressed Rush's ribs. Stale air came up Rush's windpipe as a last sigh. The snapped wooden projectiles stuck up like rounded splinters. He twisted at one and pulled it free. Black, clotted blood dripped on to Rush's jacket. Oiwa pulled the second lethal shaft out. Rush's chest sank, gurgling. His corpse relaxed, his head lolled forward.

Eyewhite and Musk's daughters chanted a slow lament. Their sons beat a rhythm with their spear butts. Eyewhite lit more pungent oil lamps then led her family away. Mica followed into the evening starlight. In the still of the sacred precinct wolves howled and sung. The waning moon shone brilliantly as the canine chorus hit the still night air. Silence struck when Vulpan, the Wolf Captain, growled. His voice evolved into a high-pitched solo to Luna. The moon seemed brighter, renewed with another spirit.

The morning was windy and wet. Musk and Eyewhite's people gathered at the death house wearing their finest clothes and parading their resplendent weapons, despite the weather. They chanted their song of paradise and rebirth. Oiwa mouthed the words, feeling the emotion. Drummers played a heartbeat rhythm, symbolizing a new pulse. The breeze abated and the rain slackened as the procession began.

Oiwa and Mica lifted Rush's bier on their shoulders; two of Musk's men took the back poles. Musk and Claw followed with Bark. Eyewhite led the procession. Dew and Day followed Lichen and Tine's bearers. They left the rose quartz platform and proceeded from the building at the other end. An avenue of low wooden stakes took them up a slope to where the forest had stood. Their feet trod bare rock, where springy moss had been.

The chants continued until they reached a long terrace overlooking the Loup clan's village. The level spit of hillside widened. Five conical stone cairns stood in a close group; by them a, square platform had been prepared for a sixth. The great wolves Vulpan and Scurran, his harem's leader, stood boldly in the centre of the stone quadrant, watching the approaching procession

Musk halted the funeral train. He paced slowly to greet the two ambassadors. They came forward, circled him and sniffed his crotch and anus. They then bade him to caress their necks and sniff noses. Eyewhite joined Musk on the rammed stone surface to repeat the greeting. The wolves sat and bayed. The rain ceased, the sun shone in great streaks through the clouds and anointed the new resting place. Vulpan and Scurran shook water from their fur. Small rainbows shone briefly through the spray.

Musk signalled the procession to advance as the wolves slipped away up the loose scree. In the centre of the platform was a flat boulder. It had been pierced to take a carved pole, decorated with feathers. 'Place the biers by the rock,' Musk said. 'Sons, bring the basket with Rush's net.'

Eyewhite added, 'Take the dead and sit them back to back on the eternal rock.' Her whitened face remained expressionless yet full of calm. 'Claw, come forward with our totem stake and set it in its socket.'

Oiwa and Mica looked at their brothers and friends. They seemed distant. The gold film on them caught the brilliance of the new shafting sunlight. Their rigor mortis had weakened so Rush's leg relaxed. One by one, Oiwa and Mica lifted the bodies and sat them leaning against the feathered pole. They removed Rush's net and wound it round them, keeping them in place. Its gilded knots and dark fibres glistened.

Eyewhite said, 'Daughters, place the bowls of sacred food at their feet. Sons, give them knives, bows and arrows and firestones. Day, put the dishes of quartz pebbles on their laps to symbolise new life and rebirth. I will put their painted leather masks over their faces. Then we begin building.'

'This is like a bad dream,' Oiwa thought. 'Mica says nothing. What is going to happen?'

Many poles had been cut. They placed them like a wigwam round Rush and Lichen, Bark and Tine. They joined at the totem, which rose prominently above them. Musk's team quarried stones from the hillside and began constructing the pyramid. Oiwa and Mica assisted. This custom was new to them, but it felt good. The stones were packed in neat courses. Eventually the top would be reached.

The funeral feast was lavish, lasting well into the night. For Oiwa the worst was over. 'My brothers' spirits are in another place. So are Rush and Lichen's. It's Mica and me now. Where do we go from here?' he thought as he curled up beneath a pile of pelts.

In the dead of night a lynx, hunting to feed her kittens, crept over the low pyramid wall and dragged off a duck that had been placed at Bark's side.

Oiwa's sound sleep restored him. Rising quietly, he realised it was time to move on to Goose Landing. He pulled at Ziit. 'You seem much stronger, Ziit, but you need arrows.'

Mica stirred, stretching and sitting among his swathes of furs and matting. His morning fart erupted.

'Nice one,' Mica commented.

Oiwa's throat pain was less, but he was still unable to speak.

'What's up, Oiwa? Your look is piercing down into my head,' Mica asked, rubbing it.

'I need to talk.' Oiwa wanted to say. Instead he flashed his eyes to their hut door and left. In moments Mica was by his side, brushing his teeth with a chewed stick. 'I have to finish our trek,' he said from within, pointing along Wolf Lake. 'I must go on for the sakes of all of us.'

Mica felt something hurting inside him. He knew Oiwa was

speaking to him, as he had in the caverns. What was he saying? He was pointing to the Wolf Clan's boats, and then to the watery distances of the lake. He was looking up to the rising tumulus for their brothers and friends. Oiwa gripped Mica's head in his palms and turned it towards the vanishing point of the lake. He clicked his tongue and mimed moving forward.' Then Mica realised.

'I'm going back in the tent,' he told Oiwa, shaking a little.

Oiwa followed.

'Oiwa wants us to continue our quest,' Mica announced.

Musk woke, yawning. Eyewhite handed him his leggings, saying, 'Oiwa's right, of course. He feels that after everything, it would be such failure to give up.'

'I just don't know.' Mica admitted.

'We'll talk over breakfast,' Musk suggested. 'Finish your toilet, get yourselves ready and we'll discuss this round beechnut mash and boiled eggs in Claw's teepee.'

Claw and Peach Leaf sat drinking thin meat broth. 'Welcome, sit,' she said. They bowed gently and squatted. Eyewhite and Musk joined the circle.

Wooden bowls of warm beechnut mash with toasted pine kernels and dried apple were handed round. The boiled eggs steamed in a coloured grass basket. Oiwa took one of the green duck eggs, nodded and tongue-clicked, 'Thank you.'

'Take more, there's plenty.' Oiwa smiled back at Peach Leaf, taking another. He shelled it and dipped it in his nutty mix. He bit. Rich, runny yolk trickled on to his beard. He dipped again, the nuts soaking up the yolk. 'Delicious,' he indicated, shelling his other egg eagerly.

'I am glad we are met,' Musk said as he convened their breakfast meeting. 'So, Oiwa, the speechless one, told Mica he wants to continue.' He looked directly to Oiwa.

Oiwa answered with a nod and a click.

'That's natural for a spirit like Oiwa's.' Musk observed. 'How do you feel, Mica?'

'I do not know what's best.' Mica began. 'I led and we've lost our brothers. Our parents will be devastated. Those who they mated with will be stricken too.' He rubbed his eyes, gulping, 'Rush as well: he saved us with his wit and brave resourcefulness, and Lichen, horribly drowned.' Mica dropped his egg on the beaver skin at his feet. Its white held as it wobbled, picking up loose hairs. Eyewhite wiped it.

'For myself, I just can't think what's best. I need time.'

Musk looked at Oiwa, asking. 'Oiwa, can you explain how you feel somehow?'

Oiwa made little balls of yolk and nut granules, arranging them thoughtfully in a neat circle round his bowl.

Peach Leaf quietly passed round fine, ivory-coloured pottery cups of Claw's soup. Oiwa set one by him. 'I'll stand,' he thought. 'The effect will be better.' He opened his mouth: Closed it and shook his head. Mica gazed up to him. 'Compose yourself, Oiwa,' he told himself, clasping his hands where his heart rattled. He stared past the teepee skins, miming distance with paddling motions. He stepped forward, pointing to illustrate the immense range. He spoke loudly and shrilly in his own head. Oiwa shaded his eyes and squinted to an imaginary, far-off place. He turned behind to indicate his lost brothers and friends. He mimed shaping the construction of their pyramid. The words inside him said, 'I have to go on! I have to complete my destiny. I must find out why, who we are and who I am. My feet are set on this trail. I cannot stop.' He sat and reached down for his soup. It tasted of the full essence of life.

Musk breathed deeply, blowing on his broth. 'Mica. Do you have anything to add?'

Oiwa stared at his brother's brow. Mica's head ached with confusion.

Mica began, 'From what Oiwa demonstrated, he obviously needs to...' His own words ended abruptly. In their confused place Oiwa's thoughts, lodged in his head, came tumbling forth. In Oiwa's voice, he repeated exactly what Oiwa had said in his own mind. 'What did I just say?...' Mica asked his listeners slowly and blankly, directly he'd finished.

'You spoke Oiwa's thoughts most eloquently,' Eyewhite observed. 'He might have lost his powers of speech, but when it's vital, he summons another power, which we modern folk have begun to lose.'

'I've given this great thought,' Musk began, 'You and Mica should honour the Whale Geese.' He popped a dove's egg into his mouth after rolling it in his nut mix. 'My reasoning is that Oiwa is positive what he should do. Mica is not.' Musk swallowed and drank broth. 'Mica feels responsibility and his leadership has been shaken. What happened to you was not accidental, it was brutal *murder!*' He sipped again. 'You could not stop that, so you are not blameful, Mica... It was not your fault.'

Peach Leaf handed beakers of rosehip tea as Musk gathered his thoughts. 'Mica, it would do you good to accompany Oiwa to his journey's end.' He paused thoughtfully. 'Oiwa, what do you think?'

Oiwa stood tall, his face unburdened. He smiled, gripping his axe, wiggling his toes and feeling good.

'That's decided,' Musk concluded. 'Here's the plan. We'll kit you out with new arrows, clothes and supplies. Claw's going to the end of Wolf Lake in his log canoe, Evergreen. He can set off tomorrow and take you. His boat's heavy, but once she gathers speed she's unstoppable.' He sipped hot tea and swirled it round his teeth.

'Thank the starry spirits,' Oiwa felt inside, tingling with emotion.

Chapter 19

Onward

It was strange walking past the empty burial house as he and Mica strode to the cemetery. 'They've left here,' Oiwa thought. 'Building their tomb helps free them. I can travel my trail and remember,' The bodies were undisturbed. Vulpan and Scurran had guarded them, only condoning the theft of the dried duck because they knew the mother lynx was nurturing Bark's new life in one of her kittens.

Marten, Claw's nephew, greeted them. 'I've been quarrying.' Oiwa regarded his contemporary as he spoke. His bare feet sucked tightly to the rocks. 'I've cracked the stone with fire. It makes it easier. We have put more supports inside the chamber too.'

Oiwa looked at the banded strata of pink granite. 'The flesh and bones of the mountain to house our dead.' he thought.

'I am devastated about your terrible ordeal. The best I can do is crack stones and help build with you.' Marten said.

'Thank you,' Mica replied as he looked at the fresh courses of stonework being laid by Musk's clan.

'Their facemasks are good,' Oiwa thought. 'I can remember them as they were instead of in death's changes.' He lifted a stone, placing it looking towards Wolf Lake. 'I'll scratch eyes on it so they can see where I'm bound,'

As the mists dissipated over the lake below, the building rose. The space within became separate from Oiwa's world with each new block added to the pyramid. He looked down into the sepulchre and saw Rush's feet in shadow while other hands packed the granite chunks together.

Mica and Oiwa worked with the team until they finally placed a capstone on top of the monument. 'Time to leave,' Mica said. They walked downhill. Marten followed. His slim, light build belied his strength, born out of natural knowledge and wisdom. His buckskin clothing flopped easily about. His necklace of bone beads rattled harmoniously as he moved.

With the mists gone, the tranquil waters of Wolf Lake reflected the mountains and blue, cloudless sky. Dark trunks from the landslide trees poked out in places. Occasionally one dislodged to float with the slow flow. Dippers and flycatchers fed on the muddy carcases.

Musk said, 'We've packed for tomorrow's voyage. If there's anything you fancy, let us know.' Oiwa mimed chewing and ran his tongue round his teeth. 'Yes, there's gum.'

'Here's some.'

Oiwa nodded thanks, enjoying the caraway flavour. Musk seemed to hear Oiwa's words in his head.

'Would you come with me to set my sun-sticks, Oiwa?' Marten asked.

Oiwa nodded, wondering what was up.

'I'll fetch them,' he said eagerly, returning with a bunch of thin, short stakes bound with cord. He also carried Ziit.

Oiwa clicked a thank you and strung the bow deftly, mouthing Ziit's name affectionately. He pulled on the tight gut. Ziit responded as he let the tension go, springing back to his original faint arc. 'That's better,' Oiwa thought contentedly.

'I'm going to set my sticks in the stone,' Marten said. 'The sun is nearly over Rut Mountain.' Oiwa looked across the lake to a black, pointed summit where the sun approached. It was a stunning sight, framed by a golden aura.

Marten loped down to a grassy plain by the shore, stopping at a black stone slab. Oiwa followed. In the centre of its level surface Marten stuck a single stick into a water-filled hole. 'I drilled this with my stick and bow, Oiwa. It took ages. I used really coarse sand to grind them out.' Oiwa looked over the surface. There was a ring of holes round the central one. Each was filled with water, reflecting the sun as golden discs in the flat, black rock.

He inserted a stick in each of his thirty-two other holes. Rivulets of shiny water trickled from Marten's wells as he shoved them in.

The shadows formed an ellipse. Oiwa realised, They also touched the opposite sticks at different heights. Tiny golden sunlit lines of shining water radiated from Marten's circle.

'Lovely, isn't it?' Marten commented.

'Yes, like the shadows from our village I saw whilst gathering honey from the tall pines. My wigwam's shadow became part of an ellipse.' He mused, nodding.

'See my engraved lines, Oiwa. They've filled with water and reflect the sun.'

Oiwa looked into Marten's face. His lightly scarred cheeks were sucked inwards in concentration. The scars resembled the spirals of a whirlpool. They were filled with a faint blue dye, the colour of compressed arteries.

'My main line is scored directly towards the mountain peak. It crosses my circle and continues on either side. All these other lines go to fixed points like the North Star and Gunnal's Falls. With the sun being above Rut Mountain now, I know its position for late spring. It will be there earlier and earlier and higher until midsummer, and then begin to come back and go down as the year goes on.' He leant back and looked at Oiwa. 'I can check its rising and setting positions too. As for the moon; well that's something else entirely.'

Oiwa understood. But Marten hadn't finished. 'There's so much more! I've discovered...' Eyewhite rang her stone chimes and called them. Marten left his sticks. They walked towards Eyewhite as Marten began again. Oiwa chewed, trying to understand.

Musk's family sat round a clay brazier. On its raised points rested a shallow pottery dish painted with a zigzag design. Duck fat sizzled within. Hundreds of plump white grubs wriggled in a hide bucket. Eyewhite poured whipped eggs over them and stirred. Oiwa and Mica licked their lips in anticipation. She spooned some out and fried them rapidly, saying, 'The dead trees are full of larvae. It's wonderful,' adding, 'When they stop wriggling, they're ready.'

'Marvellous,' Mica exclaimed as the first ones popped warmly in his mouth. Oiwa agreed, nodding.

'There's plenty of fish hiding amongst the roots too,' Marten explained as he fetched a large perch. 'Lots to be thankful for.' He placed the fish over another fire. Its fins burned off slowly and the aroma of deep, dark waters wafted past.

There was little for Oiwa to do. The sun was high and warm. With a full stomach and a feeling of ease, he lay down and snoozed. Marten returned to his sticks. Oiwa's sleep became profound. In a faraway dream, he looked over the side of a canoe into dark water. His reflection stared back from the ripples. Under the chin was an egg. He saw himself curled inside it. In his sleep he reached for his throat.

It rained heavily in the night. Gunnal's Falls spoke loudly as her spout grew in power. In the early morning, Claw's head appeared where the brothers slept. 'Time to go,' he said.

The waning silver moon dipped as the night sky lightened towards the east. The night shift of wolves and owls finished. A blue jay hopped about the muddle of huts and teepees as Marten joined them. 'I'm coming too,' he said

Evergreen lay in a cutting that dipped into Wolf Lake. Her smooth, pointed nose touched the water. Oiwa saw her heavy load of skins, bags of moss-green stones, bundles of furs and baskets of grub chrysalises. 'The Bald Heads of Lake End love our chrysalises,' Marten said. 'They don't have the green jadeite there, so we can trade.' Oiwa listened as he placed Ziit and a quiver of new arrows into Evergreen.

Mica pushed the stern. Claw guided Evergreen's prow into the black water. He and Oiwa hopped in, then Marten and Mica. Musk and his family waved them off from their dugout canoe. The craft rolled slightly as the crew got used to their positions. Short plank seats were wedged into side slits. Leaning on them were strong wooden paddles; they dipped them into the lake. 'Pull hard,' Claw called, and Evergreen's nose cut the sun-drenched ripples. 'Paddle steadily. Increase power as she speeds up,' Claw instructed them. 'Soon we just dip paddles to keep the momentum. It will seem effortless. My boat cruises well. We're avoiding the shores. Keep to the deeper waters. I'll watch out for floating or submerged trees, but there won't be so many out there,' he stressed, pointing to the middle distance.

Marten and Oiwa paddled in the stern. 'I've got thirty-two sticks in the ring,' Marten began, 'but it really doesn't matter how many you have; it just means that you can make different observations. If you have an even number it is easier to divide the areas up into squares or oblongs with fine twine.'

Oiwa's ears seemed to close over as Marten went on. 'There are so many applications I can create.' He continued energetically as his paddle dipped into the dark lake in time with Oiwa's. 'You see, I can actually peg them out on flat ground with the aid of a string tied to the centre one.' Oiwa's mind drifted as he feigned interest. He thought briefly of his dream, recalling his reflection. 'And then,' Marten energetically explained, 'by knowing when it is midday, I can tell you exactly which peg is my north' Marten paused for Oiwa's reaction. There wasn't one. Marten nudged him with his paddle.

Woken abruptly from his daydream, Oiwa nodded. Marten began again. 'When I have north, I can plot east, west and South. Then, with some thought I can tell...' Oiwa's head began to ache slightly as Marten rattled on about his sticks. Oiwa nodded wildly to clear the dull pain in his forehead, but it just moved to the back of his cranium. Marten's lecture flowed on. 'Oiwa,' he confided, 'I can also put on two centres some way apart and, with the aid of cords, arrange my sticks in a perfect ellipse!'

Oiwa shook his head. Marten took this for Oiwa's sheer amazement.

He leant forward, saying confidentially into Oiwa's ear, 'That means that I can...'

'LOG!' Claw shouted. 'Hard on the prow! Paddle left,' he commanded. Evergreen turned and rolled slightly as they passed a nearly submerged trunk. 'That was close,' Claw said to Mica.

'Yup, if it weren't for those dippers landing on the tiny knot sticking up, we might not have seen it.'

'I wanted to travel at night, but if there's no moon it's dangerous,' Claw commented. 'Gather speed,' he called. Their paddles dipped as Claw and Mica looked out for flotsam.

'There won't be a moon tonight,' Marten assured them.

'Claw?' Mica asked. 'I forgot to enquire earlier, but is there any news of Weir?'

'That was a long time ago. A very long time,' Claw said as he paddled. 'All we heard is that he went to the Lands of Steam and as far as Fire Mountain. He left there in a boat, and that's all we know.'

'Thanks, Claw. It is just that our father still wants to hear if there is anything new?'

'He sired two children with us: a boy, Cedar, and a lovely girl, Hazel. They have wedded children now. Is that any help?'

'Well, we knew, but thanks.' Mica remembered their stay in Buzzard's village, and wondered if he'd sired too. 'Thanks, Claw. I'll tell Pa there's nothing new.'

No further log alerts interrupted Marten's endless stream. Oiwa could not answer, nor change the subject. He tried making the best of it when Marten did wild calculations in his head and explained his theorem of Time and Distance. Oiwa thought of starting a paddling song, but that wasn't possible. He beat a rhythm with his paddle on Evergreen's side as he dipped it in and out, but it didn't catch on.

Evening moved closer. The dipping sun turned the waters golden. Evergreen eventually bumped the lakeshore. Oiwa took gum to chew while they erected a small leather tent along Evergreen's length. She was bone dry inside and was a fine place to sleep. Claw pulled out dried venison, and there were hard-boiled pigeon's eggs in a grass box. It was enough.

Chapter 20

The Bald Heads

Morning mists hung over Wolf Lake; the water was dark as ever. Oiwa stirred in the hollowed trunk. Mica breathed slowly. Marten slept, flopped over the rolled hides. Claw slept sitting at Evergreen's prow. Oiwa lifted their skin cover. Light crept over the canoe's sides. He slipped out on to the moist shore over the stony beach, feeling sharp grits scrape his soles. Soon the softness of saxifrage soothed his toes as he meandered up the bank.

A hare dashed from behind a boulder as Oiwa posed to pee. He jerked inside, remembering Rush's hare. The purple-flowered saxifrages wiggled as his torrent dashed among them. The crew gradually rose and flung the cover aside. Oiwa found a hollowed stone filled with clear water and washed sleep from his face. The crew made for the springy verge where a waterspout charged down the slope. From this they drank. 'Hurry,' Claw called.' The sun is creeping through the mist. We can be there for evening if we shift.' Oiwa went to the boat in the refreshing cold mist, chewing his tooth-cleaning gum.

The day sped by. Marten paddled, mercifully for Oiwa, deep in thought. Claw chanted in time with his paddling. Duck rose from the water; geese gaggled on island nests. Evergreen's wake spread behind. The lake widened and the far side was out of sight.

Evergreen slipped easily through the rippled surface as she headed for a bank of fog. The murk glided gently before them. Gradually the mists burned away. A backing breeze urged them forward. Wolf Lake roughened. Evergreen rode the waves. The crew paddled strongly and evenly, keeping her steady. A spit of land poked out into the lake. Claw signalled to make for the lee of it. The sheltered waters were easier and safer. The signs of wrecked spruce, larch and pine had diminished. Though the banks were bare of forest, ferns, buckthorn, knotgrasses and flowering saxifrage were beginning to reclaim the land.

Keeping time to Claw's voice, they became as one with Evergreen. They felt a glow in their muscles as the water sped beneath. Marten worked out his mental puzzle with a satisfied expression. He moved his arms gracefully in an effortless flow of paddling.

'Mother of Gods!' Mica shouted, pointing forward and to his left. 'It's Heron's Tooth.'

Oiwa tried to say, 'She's just drifting skin and busted spars. Look. Air has caught under the leather; there's the mends we made.'

Mica poked one with his paddle as Evergreen took them slowly past. 'The bubble's moving and wobbling along under the hides,' he reported. It reached a great tear and burst out like rumbling flatulence. Evergreen turned and glided steadily on as the Heron's Tooth's flabby remains finally sank into the depths.

Mica shook his head, bewildered, and looked to Oiwa. The memories returned like an evil flood. Claw noticed and took up his tune loudly. Oiwa gripped his paddle. The rock in his throat hardened as he bent to his task.

After some hours, Evergreen felt a slight current. It drew her into a flow in the lake. The bank turned ahead, creating a distant barrier.

'Lake End,' were the first words Oiwa was aware of after his trance-like paddling. He'd been remembering their ordeal. Marten was aware of his state and kept his silence. He could feel the darkness of Oiwa's inner soul. 'Lake End,' Mica repeated as he pointed to the black line of land rising at each end to meet the hills.

Beyond the water's edge were more distant mountains. The sun shone warmly on the paddlers' backs. Glaciers dripped far away, sending their tears down to an unseen ocean. Geese gaggled on marshy islands. Mica and Oiwa's Whale Geese were some distance yet.

Claw heard the welcoming rattle of paddles from ahead as a long hide craft appeared. Oiwa came suddenly to his senses. He stepped over their precious green jadeite cargo to Mica and gave him a brotherly kiss on his neck and hugged his shoulders tightly. Mica heard Oiwa's voice deeply inside him saying, 'It will pass as we go forward.' Mica noticed Oiwa's beard's matted tangle. He nodded, returning the affection.

'Claw,' a voice called, 'It's Char. Have you got our rocks?'

'Yes, Char: And your grubs. How's your father?'

'Well dead!' Char answered from his painted prow. Their crafts closed in, bumping gently. Char leaped into Evergreen. He wore the scantiest of clothing. Around his thick waist he sported leather shorts with beaded string tassels. He had a plaited belt of dyed hide tied at his left. Flapping from his muscular shoulders was a red-lined waistcoat of rattling quills.

The friends banged foreheads loudly in greeting. Claw's shiny black hair contrasted with Char's polished bald head. Swathes of colour enhanced his cranial dome. Thick stubble jutted from his temples and a long, tight plait whipped in the momentum of his leap. His tight leather clothing emphasised his muscular frame.

His crew of five braves stood in the Salmon's Fin. Their toes mingled among their silvery catch. Each wore similar garb. Their muscles shone in the reflected light from the lake.

'What happened?' Claw demanded, shocked.

'Fucking murdered by those shit-eyed bastards up at Warty Hands,' he returned. His forehead smacked against Mica's, who'd forgotten the painful greeting. 'Mica!' he exclaimed. 'About three or four springs since we met. And who buggered up your ear? Some pup of a lobe-sucking bitch?' he suggested rudely. He looked towards Oiwa and hurtled to greet him.

'Good. Jadeite, lovely,' he laughed as his brow clashed Oiwa's white star. 'I need some to carve the old man's bleedin' death mask for when we stuff him underground.' He looked directly at Oiwa. 'You're new. Quiet bastard, aren't you?' He cracked Oiwa's brow again before he could shift.

'Ouch!' Oiwa thought, pulling back, feeling if his skin had been split.

Char lurched past Oiwa and grabbed a green pebble by Marten, who held his paddle behind, slowing Evergreen. Marten had been here before. 'I'm not getting brow-beaten,' he thought. As Char lurched forwards, he moved back and raised his paddle in front of his forehead.

'Shit!' Char yelled, tumbling on his knees. 'What a wanker's way to say hello.' His crew looked round at the unexpected spectacle. Char aimed to punch Marten's testicles. Marten deftly placed the paddle in the way. 'Bugger him!' Char shouted, nursing his bruised knuckles.

Char's mates in the Salmon's Fin screeched with laughter. 'What a perfect twat,' Cod's Eye called from the stern.

'For fuck's sake, where did you learn that stinking trick?' Char moaned as Marten placed his paddle back.

'Mother's advice,' he replied.

'Well, you get first chew of smoked eel when we get back,' Char announced, regaining his dignity. 'It's a reward for remembering vile tricks.'

'What happened to Smolt?' Claw asked as Char recovered.

Char shook with rage. His plait swung violently from the nape of his neck.

'My dad was ill. He'd scoffed something that was off. He had the shits for days. Well, he decided to go out. He was feeling better. He sorted his tidal creels. That's when he got cut short. Limpet saw it all. She was going down from Salt Slap to help. That's when she saw those two young fuckers from Warty Hands.' Char sighed as the

Evergreen began drifting towards the town. 'Pa stooped for a poop behind the rocks. When he stood after wiping his arse, one of those smelly turds pulled back his bow and sprang his shitty little arrow into Dad's throat!'

'Smolt was fucking raging. He didn't need that filthy arrowhead through his windpipe. He was a fighter. Those two virgin wimps stabbed him in the guts, laughing deliriously. Limpet snuck back to us. We crept over the boulders to the ebb. Yeah, they'd gutted him, the mean bastards. The shits took his liver for a trophy and humped off with it, if you please.' Char spat yellow phlegm over the side in disgust. 'But we followed.'

Claw remembered the shocking hostility between the Bald Heads and the Mouflons of Warty Hand Hills. Char ranted on in his tribe's customary abusive manner. Oiwa was staggered at the string of expletives exploding from his lips. It was all returning to Mica too.

The sun dipped behind them as Salt Slap came into view. An incongruous copse of tall pines stood uphill above the stone walled huts, wattle houses and wigwams. People came to the shore in greeting and fires began glowing.

Oiwa saw that Salt Slap was sited on a broad bank separating Wolf Lake from the sea. To their right the current ran through a breach in the bank where it spilled to a tumble of rocks and gravel banks. Then it ran in through a deep trough to the hidden sea.

Char finished his tirade. Evergreen's helm bumped the gravel bank, 'We followed that two mountain farts and spotted them climbing small cliffs to their home. Me and my brother, Sether, fitted our arrows. We shot them just below their fucking shoulder blades, into their spines. Our arrows hissed like piss from a rutting wolf. They thud through those crappy swines' shirts. Their bleeding poky little black eyes must have fairly popped out shocked when they felt our arrow-tips. They fell, dropping Pop's liver.'

'I don't know about these Bald Heads,' Oiwa thought as he helped tie Evergreen to a fish-shaped post. He sighed and rubbed his rump to ease the discomfort of his hard seat. The soft aroma of pine wafted in evening mists. The babble of the Salt Slappers' welcome surrounded him. Oiwa stood and looked. 'I'm getting used to being mute,' he thought. 'I'll just have to walk tall and be mysteriously silent.' Mica strode ahead with Claw. Char greeted Sether with a smart tap on the skull. Marten followed with his bundle of sticks.

Sether put a curling ram's horn to his mouth and blew across its pointed end. The note began with a tremble, growing to a tremendous blast. He wrenched the horn from his quivering lips when the note was at its height. The roar of it rang around the echoing mountains and across the silent water.

'Fucking show-off,' Char called back.

'These are *very* challenging people,' Oiwa thought. 'I had better rise to the occasion and pull myself out of this depression.' He looked back at Evergreen, and decided to leave his feelings there on its hard seat.

Oiwa swaggered up the shingle to the scrubby turf, where more carved posts stuck out. Some represented strange distorted humans, others birds and animals. One had a vast eel writhing round it with garish yellow eyes. Another, a dismembered human body, chilling dark eye sockets staring from its severed head. Each sculpture was a remarkable feat. Oiwa looked back for an instant to the cavernous eyes, then turned to meet Salt Slap's welcome.

Mica chatted with folk like long lost friends as Char took them to his building. It was dug into the rising bank, with a low masonry wall at the front. This held a wooden framework covered with thick hides. Outside in the evening glow, Limpet crouched over a steaming pit. She greeted Char, her man, as a crowd gathered. She hauled out a thick bundle of dark, slippery, broad-leaved vegetation. It smelt salty and had an essence Oiwa had never sniffed before. In the chilling air too, there was a different aroma and a huge sense of space and distance.

Limpet signalled the visitors to sit. Yodelling, her three daughters appeared from the house. Her two sons followed with skins of fragrant water. Gneiss, the elder, poured into bowls for the girls to offer. Oiwa accepted his from Thrift. It was a strange vessel; like bone with a smoothed edge. She smiled.

'Thrift,' Char shouted, 'Get Marten the smoked eel. He deserves it. Won by the depth of respect he showed me..' His mates screeched with laughter.

'Thank you,' Marten said, accepting the compliment meekly. Thrift returned quickly with a yard of it. The smokiness wafted into Oiwa's nostrils as Thrift nudged him in passing.

Limpet opened a long parcel from the cooking pit. Oiwa savoured the amazing aroma of cooked meat, like the sweetest pig. Voices behind began an excited chorus while Limpet handed the first steaming pieces to Char. The girls passed hunks round. The  brothers served more drinks. 'Have some eel,' Marten said to Oiwa.

'Thanks,' he signalled. He held the tender meat by its protruding bone. As it cooled he bit some off and rolled it on his tongue. It was just like tender young boar. Cooking it in wet leaves clearly made it even more succulent. Forgetting his woes, he soon found he'd finished, except for the bone, on which he gnawed greedily. Other hunks of meat rose from the pit in swathes of steaming weed.

'Was that good?' Gneiss asked Oiwa.

'Yes,' he nodded eagerly.

'More?' Gneiss asked politely.

'Yes,' he wildly clicked as meat slid from a rack of ribs on to his lap. Oiwa looked to Mica and smiled delightedly.

'I'm so pleased to see you happy,' Mica said.

Thrift sat between them to share water from her shining bowl As he gazed upwards, Oiwa noticed the stars coming out brightly.

'What's that dog growling at in Char's house?' he questioned with a furrowed brow. 'Something's shuffling about too.'

'Don't pay any heed,' Thrift remarked. 'That's just Shit Eye, our bitch. She always gets excited when there's folk about.' Oiwa remembered their dog as he watched Thrift disappear into the house. 'Stay and guard,' she told Shit Eye. 'Here's a bone.'

'Thrift,' Limpet called. 'Bring that nice shoulder out. We can put it in for later.' She arrived with another bundle for the pit and sat next to Oiwa again.

'The feet are a real treat, but they take a lot of baking.' Oiwa nodded knowingly, remembering the trotters he'd chewed with his family. Drumming and singing took his mind away as a spectacle of acrobatic dancing and leaping the fire-pit commenced.

'Where would you ugly sods like to sleep tonight?' Char asked his guests. 'It's either in our place by the fire or one of the wigwams.'

'I prefer the sound of your hearth,' Claw answered. Mica signalled approval while sucking a vertebra. 'Delicious. I love the spine marrow,' he remarked, reaching for his toothpick. They continued supping as the other daughters prepared bedding. Thrift, a hefty individual, served strips of smoked fish and ice-cold aromatic herb tea. Her shaven head shone. Small shells dangling from her ear piercings sparkled in the light of the rising moon. Oiwa heard distant water tumbling from Wolf Lake. There was another rhythmic flow too, but further away. Oiwa could not understand it. He stood in the fire-glow listening.

Thrift rose too, putting her broad face close to Oiwa's. He looked round. She made a welcoming gesture of rubbing noses. Oiwa responded. She pulled her head back slightly, then swiftly struck his forehead with hers. 'Welcome!' she screeched with a wail of infectious laughter. Oiwa's head reeled. His silver star swelled. The inside of his head thumped. Everyone laughed, clapped and sang. During the clamour he felt Thrift's hand take his. She pointed to the sound of the water. He looked down to her leathery cuffs and the tiny jadeite discs sewn in a line up to her powerful shoulders. A dark leather choker with a finely carved stone roundel glinted as she moved. She pointed again to the running water and tugged Oiwa's fingers, saying, 'I'll take you... there, Oiwa.'

Before he knew, they were far from their firelight. 'Just follow me,'

Thrift urged. He looked down her strong, broad back. Three tight plaits swing to her ample waist, which was drawn in by an elaborate woven belt. It caught the light of the distant galaxies in its brilliant polish. Thrift's skirt moved over her powerful muscles. From her high hem a curtain of soft grass tassels swung to her knees. The small black shells, which weighted them clacked as she moved.

'We're going to the Viewpoint.' Their path seemed warm under his bare running feet. The tiny shells on its surface prickled his dry soles. Oiwa's matted, virtually beadless hair bounced around his ears. The path took them higher on the undulating terrain. They saw the moon-lit silver of Wolf Lake spreading. It reminded him of the dream when he landed as a goose on to shining water. They stopped. He went to speak about it to Thrift, but not a sound came forth. He looked to her and she responded. Oiwa immediately struck her a violent blow on her forehead and mouthed the word, 'Welcome.' Thrift laughed, and it was the first moment for seemingly black years that Oiwa laughed himself: Even without sound, the humour engulfed him.

Chapter 21

*

Salt Slap Salts

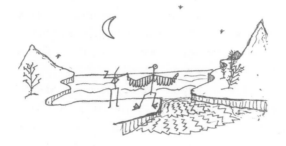

'Take my hand,' Thrift asked warmly, 'We'll go along the ridge.'
To Oiwa's right Wolf Lake spread; on the other side, far off,
he saw, for the first time, the Ocean. The moon shone on the
incoming tide to a vast arm of the sea. Waves broke like swans' wings.

Thrift pointed to still, green pools, shining in the night air. The
same green as her choker charm, the hue of her eyes and the emerald
flash of the dipping sun. 'Our salt ponds,' she said, taking a tiny birch
capsule from her belt bag and unscrewing the tight lid. 'Taste,' she
said proudly.

Oiwa licked his finger and fitted it in. He touched his tongue with
the rough grey crystals. They slowly dissolved as he cracked one with
his white teeth. 'How highly salt's valued at home,' he mused. 'Our
scarce pink rock-salt is so different.'

'Come to the outflow where white waters roar. Listen. The wolves
howl to the moon from the slopes. This is a place of change,' Thrift
explained, pointing lakewards. 'From there everything is landward.
This outflow is land's gate to the Ocean, where it all changes.'

'This is amazing,' Oiwa thought. 'It's nothing like the Dun or the
lakes. It's powerful, living water.'

Thrift continued, 'When all the trees slid from the hillsides, they backed up here like a mountain and jammed up this entire bank. They froze solid. Ice built behind, until finally the lake exploded with underwater pressure. Wolf Lake spat the trapped trees into the sea, taking them to who knows where.'

Oiwa gripped Thrift's meaty hand. She grasped his with undulating fingers, flowing with tidal rhythm. Oiwa gazed, pondering. In his head he heard gaggling geese. His toes curled and clawed the gritty soil; they spread, web-like, under him. His skin turned bumpy. His neck grew. His eyes pierced the dark of the hillsides. The gaggle amplified, filling his ears with the call. He saw waves below as he flew. 'That's where I'm going,' he said in an avian voice.

On the rim of his brain he felt the guidance of a power attached to all things. He saw under the moonlight nests of his goose familiars, then a vastness beyond comparison. Oiwa looked down over the endless sea. A voice rang in the plumage of his ears, stately, powerful and prophetic. 'Your earth spirit's destiny, Oiwa, is almost boundless. You will venture to far places, revealing what life will bring you, those whom you travel with, and those you leave behind.'

Oiwa's wings faltered momentarily at the words in his head. He then turned in the night air and saw himself talking with someone far below by the water's edge and water's beginning. He flew back over the icy ocean and down to rejoin his human host, becoming absorbed again within its skin and bones.

Oiwa blinked as the sun rose. Time had played tricks on him. Thrift took his hand carefully, leading him back to Salt Slap while morning duties began. Mica awoke as Oiwa came to their hearthside and lay down by the ash-grey embers. He dreamed of distance and time. He dreamed of faces reflected in pools. He saw crowds of people, then vast fields of beings from different ages, past, present and future, in multiple ranks, like terraces up a hill, each level a generation, like great wing feathers working in unison. In front was his figure, clear and distinctive. But behind those levels of humanity, his own face looked straight back. He gazed deeply into his eyes and saw... With that, his dream ended, but the images remained clear. He slept undisturbed until the following day.

Oiwa woke to Sether's horn. He felt different, taller. His body moved freshly, as if he had shed a cumbersome skin. Shit Eye growled again at the muffled rustle as Oiwa took Ziit and made for Char's doorway. Sether stood in the sunlight with his wife.

'Good day Oiwa,' Sether said, enjoying the shattering effect of his horn. 'Sound sleep is good for youths. Here's Birch Twig, my youngest wife.' Oiwa bowed and looked into her eyes. 'Birch Twig is a granddaughter of Weir. Hug your distant cousin.'

'Astonishing!' Oiwa registered, opening his arms to embrace and rub noses with her.

'Sether and I have children. Weir's blood runs within them,' she said.

Oiwa looked deep into her face. He recognised the familiar features. Her plaits were lighter, with a reddish tinge, quite unlike Sether's black ones.

'Oiwa,' Mica shouted. 'You awake? I hope you had sweet dreams.' he remembered immediately, and stood, slowly taking them in. He noticed that urgent rustle again. Shit Eye barked angrily.

'Hallo, Oiwa,' Thrift called and thumped his back. 'I'm taking you sightseeing, lazy bones. Look lively, drag your ugly feet.' Still winded, Oiwa gripped Ziit and waved to Birch Twig. They walked off round Char's house, which was cut into a grassy mound of clipped herbs and juniper. To one side was a heap of old refuse that birds pecked.

'We're going to the Last Pines where we perform certain rites,' Thrift said, taking Oiwa's hand. From Char's midden they climbed a buckthorn slope. The shadow of the Last Pines met their toes as Thrift led the way to the quiet space. The tall copse felt different from the rest of the hillside: still and timeless. 'Here we do our dead ones,' she said, pointing high into the branches.

Oiwa looked up. A tall, dangling body was suspended under its shoulders by taught leathers. Stones drooped from the ankles.

'That's Smolt. My granddad,' she grumbled. 'Killed. Arrowed dead by those sneaking, greasy turds.'

Oiwa was not accustomed to foul language, but he supposed it was the Bald Heads' way. He stared at the pendulous corpse as it twisted, creaking, on the plaited leather cords. the spear up its spine held his shrinking head high. The dried skin glistened, and precious beads hung from the stitches that closed the fatal wound.

'We salted him after those cockless shits gutted him. The rocks stretch him.'

More corpses, old and young, hung in different states of preservation. Oiwa stepped forward. His foot found something in the pine needles. He kicked casually. 'Ah!' he choked as a desiccated hand flew out.

Thrift grabbed him, saying, 'This is how we do it. Don't be shocked. We face death like life. It's all one for us. It's how and when dying happens that's horrid.'

Oiwa stared at the withered fingers. They landed by a fine stone axe with a wonderful haft; beads and broken pots were scattered nearby. Clothing hung like bats in the branches. Deceased remains of tight skin on bony frames cast fleeting shadows.

'Follow me,' Thrift urged, pointing to the edge of the clump.

Relieved to be leaving that place, Oiwa did not glance back. The couple emerged overlooking the sea, and ran down a grassy slope towards the shore, where they came to a low cliff.

'What are those?' Oiwa thought in amazement.

'Seals, silly.' Thrift replied.

'But I can't speak,' Oiwa tried to say.

'You can, Oiwa. I saw you become a goose by Land Gate. You spoke; as a goose you flew away, but your image remained. We stood until dawn. You told me all. Not with words, but I understood. You endured terrible events, but you had good times with fine matings. Your Goose Spirit returned and filled you, but I still hear what you think.

'Yes,' she continued, 'They are seals. Their skins make good clothes, their fat, wonderful lamps, and their meat's gorgeous. Watch them lollop into the water.'

'They are amazing.' Oiwa thought.

'Now, Oiwa, follow me along the cliff and round that bluff. There's a tall cleft up in a crag.' As they ran, more seals vanished into the surf.

A small oval hovel stood at the crag's base. Strings of drying fish swung under the eaves. Old Skellig crouched at the doorway. 'She's older than the rocks,' Oiwa thought.

'Be quiet,' Thrift told him.

'Announce yer bleedin' selves,' the crone screeched as she tried to get up.

'Thrift and Oiwa.'

'Too soon to bring Smolt here,' she moaned. 'And who's this fucking imp Oiwa?'

He noticed her shiny head, 'Maybe her hair fell out naturally,' he thought. Then he saw a bedraggled grey plait sticking out from behind a waxy ear.

'He is a traveller and deserves respect,' Thrift put in.

'Respect, my arse,' she sneered. 'Want a lamp?'

'Please, you twisted old bitch,' Thrift answered.

'Got something for one?' Skellig demanded.

'Here.' Thrift pulled a seaweed parcel from her skirt pocket. 'Stuff that down your shrivelled gullet.'

Skellig sniffed, smiling a nearly toothless grin. 'Smells nice. Very, very nice. Here're two whelk-shell lamps, fatted and wicked.'

Skellig crouched by her door, undoing the package as Thrift led Oiwa towards the cavern. A narrow path led up to the jagged cleft. Stunted bushes and spiky shrubs endured meagre lives in the fissures. The sides of the ravine narrowed. Buzzards screeched, circling above. Their pathway was worn and smooth. Small offerings lay on stones. Odd empty bowls leant among the rocks. 'Was it the buzzard or Skellig who emptied them?' Oiwa pondered. They turned a corner. The pathway delved between polished, living rock. Thrift's hips rubbed the smooth sides as Oiwa followed, watching her contours change as she pushed through.

A high cliff appeared in front of them. Below it, the path widened into an open precinct where pots and baskets lay strewn. Stone tools, wooden mallets and stakes lay scattered. Drums hewn from tree trunks waited to be played. A human skull lay partly on its cranium, its eyes staring emptily upwards. Oiwa picked up a mallet and struck a drum. The sound boomed and echoed round the courtyard. Starlings flew

out of a narrow cave at the base of the cliff. Thrift led Oiwa there.

They stooped to enter. 'Their shadows blanked out the light, but a flame flickered ahead of them. Sleeping bats shuffled. Oiwa and Thrift stretched tall as the ceiling rose. They picked their way through more votive litter. The cavern echoed as fragile objects snapped underfoot. Oiwa reached the torch. Thrift handed her lamp to him. He touched her wick to his flame. They walked on under their lights. The cavern was adorned with paintings of people that seemed to move in the weaving glow. Some wore horns, some masks, others... nothing. Further in, pictures of seals appeared, with an image of a man with huge tusks in a sealskin. On the gallery roof was a dance circle under the moon and the stars. A central triad held spears and a bow. Oiwa felt for Ziit. He was there.

Thrift led him further into the hill. Another entrance opened to their right. The rocks shimmered in the flame of Oiwa's lamp. It warmed in his grip. They bent and crept through the smooth rock passage of worn painted images to stand again in a wide hall. Oiwa held his lamp high. He pulled his breath in sharply. A leaning skull with dry, flaking skin suddenly returned his glance. He turned. His elbow struck something hard, yet brittle. 'Be careful!' Thrift shouted. Oiwa turned and Ziit caught in an open rib cage. A body began tumbling from its shelf.

'Stand still,' Thrift warned urgently. Oiwa froze. She unhooked Ziit from the jutting bones. 'Calm down, Oiwa,' she said almost gently. 'This is one of our sacred places. Only special visitors come here. Follow me slowly – and put Ziit down before he does any more damage.'

Thrift held Oiwa's hand as she took him forward. They arrived at a rounded entrance to a further chamber. An aroma of pinecones and juniper wafted from it. They edged through. Thrift took her lamp and lit others in the gallery. Slowly the glow permeated the domed chamber of light pink rock. Standing on a low shelf, all the way round the wall, leant stiffened bodies. Each had a jadeite claw hanging from under its chin.

Oiwa was no longer startled. He was getting used to surprises in this death hall,

'My ancestors, Oiwa. We care for them. Over there is a son of Weir. He's an ancestor of yours called Elder. He had many children here. He travelled too.'

Oiwa looked up at the strange shrivelled face. Elder's lips had stretched and thinned. His teeth jutted. A salty sheen shone on his body. A sealskin hung down his back. At his feet were hammer stones, an antler and an obsidian blade. Oiwa tugged his beard and gazed at his dead relative.

'He never knew Weir, but his mother, over there, always spoke beautifully of him. Weir journeyed on, never returning.'

'This is tremendous.' Oiwa thought, gazing round the tomb. He listened to Thrift's tales of the departed and how their spirits lived there and came out into the world.

'There's one last place I must take you,' Thrift said. 'Come.'

She led to a tall slit in the rock face. They squeezed through a translucent hide that divided from the floor up. Thrift led Oiwa in, holding out her lamp. 'These are our chiefs: men and women. This is their place. Smolt will dwell here when he's dried.'

Oiwa ogled the huge death-claws. Ornate spears leaned beside their owners. Shields, masks, carved staffs, huge shells, headdresses and baskets of clothes lay at their feet. Their totemic jadeite jewellery hung profusely. The ancestors' eye sockets had shells placed in them, helping them to observe. Their plaits hung proudly over their shoulders. The salty crust on the flesh glittered. Oiwa turned to Thrift. 'It's wonderful,' he wanted to say. She nodded and looked back at him mysteriously in the lamp glow.

'I have to ask something of you, Oiwa. I am to breed soon for my first baby. My mother and Birch Twig suggest I take one from you.' Oiwa's eyes opened widely. 'You're smart and good-looking. They know you'll be something big in the world, but you're passing through like Weir. They say we should mate together.'

Oiwa's eyes bulged; his jaws parted. He looked at Thrift. 'She's strong and interesting. The very thought's making me hard.'

'I don't want one off Marten. He's clever, but I couldn't cope with a child that went on about sticks and time forever. If I pull one from you, I would be really happy. Even if I never saw you again.'

Oiwa mopped his brow. The hot breeding pit in his gut was growing. he had to mate.

'Just think, Oiwa. If you make a baby in me, it might become a leader and then be in here forever.'

Oiwa realised he hadn't had a mating thought since Rush was hit by the arrows. He inhaled the pine-scented air. Not a single urge... until now.

Thrift glowed in the lamplight. A rich tingle shot from deep inside Oiwa's belly to his throat. She undid her salmon-skin belt and felt Oiwa's passion. Her skirt slipped to the cave floor. Her jacket's toggles loosened from their leather nooses with silent ease. Oiwa moved, taking it from her shoulders, casting it on a heap of ancestral gear. He looked up to 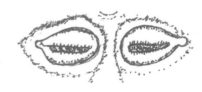 shell eyes, and then kissed Thrift's neck as his clothes rubbed against her.

She fumbled for his belt-fastener, deftly slackening it. Oiwa helped. He shook off his trousers with a couple of kicks and felt his penis touching her navel. He stepped back to doff his skin jacket and felt liner then returned for a naked embrace. He tugged at her plaits, pulling her head back. They kissed, passionately sucking tongues. Thrift's breasts rose; his slim form sunk between them. Oiwa felt her moist hairs against his shaft. Thrift rose gently on her toes. His tip flicked to her warm, wet vagina.

Thrift felt his potent point touch a spot just within, making her glow deeply. A simultaneous thrill streamed back to the pit of Oiwa's stomach. They stayed there joined, hardly moving while those mollusc eyes watched. Thrift's toes relaxed. She felt Oiwa's penis slant directly in. She pressed down and Oiwa's hips pushed up. Thrift's heels raised themselves as Oiwa gently dipped, careful not to lose his place while he enjoyed his arrow being caressed by those inner lips. They moved thus. Oiwa counted the gentle strokes. He felt Thrift's thrill and grip on his stem as she moved. He knew he could come at any time, but wanted to preserve that moment for Thrift. Her movements became wilder as she clenched him. He held her close with his strong arms as she cried out in pleasure. Her warmth ran like hot liquid down his crotch as a great space opened up within her. Oiwa pressed his hips, thrusting deeper. This was the moment he came. He shook. He felt life spring from him in that place of the dead. A new being beginning as the long beats of sperm flew out from his engendering nib.

The two stood together hugging, feeling the wondrous warmth of each other. Oiwa's erection remained, and he played with Thrift's plats. It was such pleasure. While he fondled her hair, he moved out a little. Thrift moaned deeply. Oiwa pushed in and the sound continued. He partly withdrew again. Thrift pulled him back in. That deep feeling within Oiwa began again. His head swam as he moved back and forward repeatedly in ecstasy. Thrift's passion climaxed, as did Oiwa's once more; his male thrill deepened in his second coming. After, they stood motionless together, holding each other, feeling as one, as the hard part of Oiwa slowly began to soften. They felt they could begin to move apart. There was a new smell developing in that ancestor cave: the smell of Thrift, Oiwa and infant.

The flickering lamplights bathed them in a warm glow. Their breathing gently subsided as they looked into each other's eyes. Thrift moved first. Oiwa experienced the cooling of his member as she came off him.

Oiwa swung round to look into the eyes of the dead watchers. Shadows and glimmering reflections came from them as though they blinked. He turned away. The muscle in his left thigh tightened. The sudden contraction gripped down his calf. If he could have screamed, he would have. All he could do was hop and try to straighten his cramped, contorting leg. He fell writhing on to his jacket. Objects crushed beneath him. His head struck ancestral feet during his collapse. The perished cord that held those remains to the wall snapped. Oiwa looked up in agony as the stretched mummy tilted, tottered, turned on hardened heels to tumble directly over him.

The sound was new to him: breaking bones rattling in dry skin. His spasm intensified. This did nothing for the condition of the corpse. Oiwa inhaled mummy dust from the bouncing body. He choked and coughed, tasting the preserving salts. His leg was shackled in pain, when Thrift came to rescue him.

'The damage! The damage,' she shouted in shock. Crushed pottery jabbed into Oiwa's ribs as he rolled. 'Fire!' Thrift yelled, as Oiwa's lamp caught fragments of fabric. 'Put it out!' she demanded. Oiwa rolled again in panic under the ancestor. Thrift picked up her skirt and flailed at the sparks by Oiwa's side, stamping out flames. Bone and skin crushed underfoot.

Slowly the terrible muscular grip in his thigh eased. He lay there and gradually extended his leg. Thrift pulled the smashed body from his chest. His head poked up between the corpse's legs and he blinked. Dust covered his face as he looked over the busted spine. The dead head lay, eyes down between his feet, glaring up his bared legs.

Oiwa tried sitting. The ancestor's legs lifted on his shoulders as a trickle of bone beads fell from above. Thrift looked deeply into the eyes of the father of her first child and laughed and laughed and laughed. Oiwa chuckled inside. His tight stomach jerked. To their sheer mirth, the dead spine slid gently from his navel on to the stone floor.

It took time to dress before emerging from the sepulchre, where slanting light dazzled. They looked in Skellig's croft on the way back to hand in the shells. They enjoyed a romantic feeling between them as Skellig screeched out knowingly, 'It's a girl. She will live for 92 years. Watch that cramp, boy. You can do a lot of damage like that.'

'Oh no,' Oiwa thought. 'I feel so embarrassed.'

'Pretty prick you got, though,' she added with a lurid cackle as her wrinkles spread. 'I seen it through my spy hole.'

Oiwa automatically covered his genitals.

'Too late for that,' Thrift added, 'but I told you, you're fucking special, Oiwa.'

The couple went on towards Salt Slap. 'See the salt ponds? Well, we let the seawater in. Then we block them off and it dries up. When that grey salt sticks to the edges, we trade it. It's good for cramp. You should have some. It would stop you buggering up our bodies. It's right good for preserving fish and healing wounds too. And I hope Skellig's right that you made me pregnant.'

'I'd rather not go back through the copse of corpses,' Oiwa thought.

'We'll return along the shore,' Thrift said. 'The sea goes everywhere. There's no bounds to it once you get up the inlet.'

'Where's Everywhere?' Oiwa wondered.

In the town, folk heaved salmon from an ice-pit. They sliced it with long flint blades.

Limpet was laying out swathes of broad kelp for wrapping meat. Shit Eye snarled in his guardroom as Oiwa and Thrift arrived. Mica was drinking warm honey water with Marten, who had his sticks out. Claw was telling Sether and his young brood exaggerated adventures.

'I'll put Ziit away,' Oiwa decided. Shit Eye grumbled while Oiwa passed. 'I'll make myself presentable. It looks like we are having a feast. Where's my gum?' He brushed his hair with his hands and got the chew from his pouch when he heard a terrified yell and a violent struggle. He ran to the cell where the commotion was. Round the narrow door he saw Char in front of a writhing man hanging upside down from the rafters. Shit Eye stared obediently upwards. The victim's head dangled at Char's chest. His arms were roped behind.

Oiwa advanced.

'Stop, Oiwa!' Char said. 'Watch.' He took a long serrated blade from a shelf and put it on the throat of the struggling man. He grabbed his hair to stop him swinging and bent his head back. Shit Eye bristled expectantly. Before Oiwa could blink Char slit that exposed throat. The man's torso convulsed wildly. His blood sprayed around the slaughter room. The rope tying his feet twisted as the naked man spun.

Like Oiwa's cramp, the spasms slowly decreased as the blood rhythmically pumped out. It drained down the dying chin into the gaping mouth, then over his horrific face and hair. When all was still, Shit Eye licked the blood off the dripping head. On the man's final twist, Oiwa spotted a snapped arrow surrounded by swollen bruising just above his twitching shoulder blades.

'I feel disgustingly cold with jellied guts.' Oiwa thought, quaking inside.

Char opened his victim's stomach with one swift gash. Guts tumbled. Char reached in, severing the intestines. His sons carried the flopping body outside to Limpet for butchering. 'Good carcase, well bled,' she said as she wrapped joints in the seaweed.

Oiwa ran retching into the salmon pit. There he felt Thrift's breath. She put her arms on his shaking shoulders. 'We do this,' she whispered. 'We eat our enemies when they harm us.' Oiwa heard as he looked down at his bile seeping into the crushed ice. 'Them fucking bastards murdered my grandfather.' Thrift waited while Oiwa stopped vomiting. 'It's justice. You drank from an enemy's cranium.' Oiwa shook his head between his knees. 'If those stinking Mouflons had a chance, they'd have dragged Smolt off. Instead all they could get was his sodding liver for their cunt of a leader up at Warty Hands.'

Oiwa turned and glared at Thrift. For a split moment she saw a huge gander standing in front of her. It vanished as Oiwa cut himself off from her. 'Oiwa. Wait. You don't understand. If we get an arrow in the backbone below their shoulders they get paralyzed from hips down.' Oiwa strode off in front of her. 'They live longer, keeping their meat fresh. If it goes bad, it can send you blind,' she shouted as he stormed away. She ran and grabbed his wrist. 'Another thing. When we've scoffed them, we shit them out. Then they can't do more harm. You shat some out today.'

Oiwa spun and looked at her. Her stance was less bold. He sent one thought to her: 'I don't do your shitting for you. Neither does my daughter.' He turned and walked back to Salt Slap to squat by the fire pits. He signalled for dug-up fish.

Thrift squatted near, but not too close. 'Dug-up fish too, please.'

Chapter 22

Solan

Guiltily, Thrift confessed to Limpet and Birch Twig about the smashed ancestor. Word spread like wildfire. A seething mob arrived at Char's house, filling his precinct. 'Oh no!' Oiwa thought, jellied with fear. His hackles rose. Sweat poured down his spine.

'Oiwa,' Mica warned. 'You could end up cooked in kelp too if this goes badly.'

'Thrift, tell this story publicly,' Char ordered.

Bravely she stood with Oiwa and repeated it. Oiwa faced the crowd, trembling in the night air. Their jury's faces flickered unnervingly in the torchlight. Finally Thrift finished. Silence prevailed. Two hands clapped.

'A terrible portent,' Oiwa judged. Ominously a drum struck. More hands clapped and Thrift's sister, Spark, choked then laughed simultaneously. Sether attempted blowing his horn, but failed. He burst out laughing too. The Bald Heads' funnybone had been struck a mighty blow. It was so hilarious they could barely make a sound. They slapped their sides and pointed at the couple. Others collapsed weeping in mirth.

Oiwa and Thrift stood in bewilderment as the racket grew. Marten dropped his precious sticks and clutched his stomach, hopping. The more surprised the pair looked, the more the cackling chorus grew. They gripped hands and gazed at themselves. Oiwa kissed Thrift tenderly on her neck. This made the crowd gather in momentum. Oiwa and Thrift grinned and shamelessly giggled. Oiwa's silent mirth made it all the funnier.

Folk mimicked mating and cramp attacks. Others tumbled like mummies on to the stricken. Then Skellig appeared, thanking Thrift for the baked Mouflon foot. It all got funnier. The old woman related the lurid spectacle she'd spied from her secret viewpoint in the upper cleft. Her ribald commentary on the mating received resounding applause.

When Char was finally able, he banged his drum. 'Thank you for the best tale in years. I pronounce you Heroes of Salt Slap. I name Thrift's baby Skellig.'

The feast commenced. It was a magnificent affair. Oiwa and Thrift stuck to fish. They were handed huge steamed oysters to swallow. 'I've never seen these before,' Oiwa thought as he watched others slide them down their throats. 'Quite magnificent.' Mica sucked a gristly kneecap knowingly. 'Any feet left?' he heard Skellig ask.

'You'll be off soon, Oiwa, won't you?' Thrift asked. He nodded back with wide, moist eyes. 'If that's so, will you come again to make sure of this little girl inside me?' she implored. Oiwa grinned. Thrift led him to the gate where the land ends and the Ocean begins. The moonshine witnessed their deep tryst.

'It's only a couple of days by sea canoe to the Whale Geese,' Mica told Oiwa the next morning while he massaged his thigh by the fire.

'Okay, I'm ready to leave,' Oiwa thought, looking up and nodding.

'We can soon. Claw and Marten will wait.'

'Here's gum,' Oiwa wanted to say. He passed Mica a lump, indicating agreement.

'Char has salt and a vole skin hat for Ugruk, the Innu chief. He's lent us clothing for colder conditions and a boat.'

Oiwa wondered why the Bald Heads didn't wear much. But then Thrift felt so naturally warm, he realised.

She came bustling in with a birch-bark box of salted meat with honeyed fruit and nuts. 'Here you are,' she said. 'It'll keep you going. The meat's mountain goat, not mountain man, Oiwa.'

'We will escort you,' Char said. He and Mica walked ahead by the salt ponds.

Oiwa and Thrift followed, talking privately together, then slipped aside. 'One more time? Let's make really sure,' Thrift suggested. 'I know you should be coming back, but I feel you won't.' Oiwa looked to her; his face gave nothing away. He held her gently as he entered. They heard Mica calling. It made no difference. They emerged later, dressed, from the reeds. Oiwa felt his axe from Moss wedged in his belt. His index finger tested its sharpness as they meandered past pools. 'We take our dead ones to soak in brine here before we hang them.' Thrift informed her stud. He glanced over the thick solution and wondered if there was any one in there. 'I expect Old Skellig will pickle soon, but she's salty enough already,' Thrift joked weakly. 'Oiwa, I'm sorry you're moving on. Maybe that old crone was right. If so, I'll have something of you with me forever.' Their palms met with passion. 'A strong child makes a mother attractive to other men too,' she admitted.

Oiwa suddenly stopped. The pain seared up his thigh. 'If mating does this every time, I'd better stop,' he thought as he hobbled along.

The sea breeze caught Oiwa's hair at the nousts by the shore. 'Here's your canoe, Barbel. It's walrus hide.' Char said.

'What's walrus?' Oiwa thought as the muscle tension subsided. Mica recognised the musk-ox rib and bentwood frame. 'Your other clothes are in that,' Limpet told them, pointing to a sealskin case, with walrus-tusk toggles. 'You'll find good parkas in there,' Char added. 'Ugruk's stuff is inside too. If you find him, split his forehead for me, please.'

'Certainly will,' Mica joked.

Marten watched them from where Oiwa and Thrift had mated the night before. He'd noted the days were lengthening and the moon waning. The sun rose further round the rim of the world and set further along it. His mind considered a concept. He sucked in his spiral-tattooed cheeks thoughtfully.

The brothers settled on the Burbot's seats.

Marten observed seals lollop across the stony beaches into the gently breaking waves. He watched gannets diving like darts. Cormorants flew parallel above the ripples. Eider duck and ducklings swam in flotillas. They braved lines of surf, always appearing behind them further out to sea. Marten watched the Burbot's first paddle strokes, taking them north-east, where the Ocean's arm bent. The water darkened in the deepener channel. He was jealous.

'Hug the north shore,' Mica called. 'See that snow-capped mountain? We're heading the other side of it.' Oiwa nodded. The Burbot rose to the waves.

'Those legless seals look so weird lolloping down the shore,' Oiwa thought to himself. 'But they swim wonderfully.' He nudged Mica to watch them watching them. Mica smiled and paddled harder. Disturbingly, though, Oiwa found that the Burbot rising with the swell affected him. The unsettling motion increased. 'Oh no. I feel sick,' he wanted to say, gripping his paddle and looking to Mica. There were two Micas glancing back. It was worse. 'I must stand,' he thought. 'Oh. I'm so giddy.' He burped noisily: The taste of his last meal burned in his throat. 'I'm going to throw up.' Bile shot to his mouth from deep below. He hurled himself to the Burbot's side. The dark sea got the hot contents of his retching stomach. The stench ran through his nostrils. His nose gushed. A stream of stinging mucus linked him to the yellow bile passing beneath. Oiwa's belly spasms continued uncontrollably. His head reeled. He looked into the depths. 'I wish I could just sink into them,' he thought as he collapsed against the sealskin baggage. He glared up to the shifting clouds. 'Oh. I feel so wretched,' was all he could think as he shut his aching eyes. There he languished until Mica eventually beached.

'Wake up, Oiwa!' He heard Mica bawl.

'My guts feel terrible.' He burped again. 'But my head's not spinning. I'll try moving.' The boat tipped as he lurched to his knees. Oiwa sprawled on the wet, weedy shore. He shook himself as a flight of white terns swooped screeching towards them.

'We'll stay until the tide can take us further.' Mica said, looking at the mountain; its paps were covered in cloud, but he could see the snowline and the ravines cutting darkly into its side. Geese honked, but not their geese yet.

'Gather driftwood,' Mica suggested.

Oiwa searched fuel for Mica's blaze, and then returned to the water's edge, watching the surf coming up the flow. He heard the seals singing on an islet. It was all new to him. Seaweed waved in the currents. Small snails sucked the stones. He grabbed a handful. 'I'll take them to Mica.'

'Buckies,' he said. 'Here, watch this.' Mica pulled some fire away and said, 'Get some of that kelp. It's what Limpet wrapped that Warty Hands man in,' Oiwa dragged a great swathe of it to the fire. 'We lay some out, put the winkles on, then fold it, shoving embers over.'

The smell of ocean wafted in the breeze. Later, he swept the fire off and revealed the steaming shells. 'This is how you eat them,' Mica explained. 'Get your toothpick, shove it under the cap, there, and twist them out. They're great.'

Oiwa copied him enthusiastically.

'I'll show you what else we can eat,' Mica said. 'Look, over there: clumps of mussels. Bring them to the fireside. We can cover them with seaweed, then heap fire over them. They cook in moments.' Steam rose, the weed spat, crackled and shrank in the scorching heat. 'Ready. See them opening? Watch me,' Mica said as he sucked the body from a bivalve. 'Delicious.' Oiwa joined in. 'Use the empty shell as a pair of pincers, grip another, part its shell and down it.'

Oiwa learned. 'My guts feel better after that,' he thought, 'The stomach's accepting this shore food.'

'Lets have that fruit and nut mix,' Mica suggested.

Oiwa got the boxes from the case. They sat and enjoyed the fire, the beach and the food. But despite the hot food, Oiwa realised he was getting cold. The breeze quickened as he untoggled the case and pulled out two pairs of tall leather boots lined with fine plaited grass. Used to bare feet except in the coldest weather, he had never seen the like. He slipped a pair on and fitted his trousers inside.

Mica went over and pulled his on too. 'Here's a pair of salmon skins. Tie the sinew loops round your knees and over the tops of your boots, like this.' Oiwa copied him. 'That will keep water out if we get into choppy seas. Here are the parkas – made from split seals' guts,' Mica told Oiwa as he pulled one over his head. 'They're watertight and windproof.'

Oiwa had never seen clothing like it before. He could see Mica through the stitched translucent membrane, but his voice was muffled. Then his head popped up into the fur-lined hood. 'My turn,' thought Oiwa. He pulled his parka over his head and down to his shins. The mounting breeze had no further effect. 'Wonderful,' he thought.

They hauled the Burbot up before the tide rose. 'I'm going to sleep in the boat, Oiwa. We set off when the tide's come right in. Hopefully you'll get your sea stomach and stop puking.'

Oiwa pondered as he stamped about the beach, watching the rhythm of the ebbing waves. 'I can't understand why I got so ill. I went through the Dun's rapids and down Gunnal's Vulva. I never felt the least bit sick.' He then wondered, 'What's this tide anyway?'

Misty clouds obscured the other side of the inlet. He lifted rocks to catch elvers in his hands. They tried slithering away so he strung their heads on  twine with his bone needle. They wriggled into a writhing knot as he hunted more. The breeze never affected him. The boots felt strange, but warm. He built up the fire and waited, watching in amazement as the water returned slowly over where they'd gathered shore food.

It was mid afternoon when Mica stirred. Oiwa anticipated it and broiled the young eels in seaweed for a snack. As soon as the tide slackened, they paddled off. The outgoing waters sped them on.

The breeze felt cold on their faces, but they kept snug in their new clothes.

'Those Bald Heads,' Mica stressed, 'are amazing. They never feel cold. It must be their blood.' Oiwa nodded. 'And the way they dish up their neighbours. Last time I had heart and kidneys. Maybe that's what keeps them so hot.' Oiwa blinked, feeling ill again. 'How they keep their victims fresh is cruel. But at least the Mouflons have nothing against us. Just don't let them know we've eaten any if we should meet.' Oiwa got queasier. 'Lovely girl for a Bald Head, Thrift is. North Star's Clan will enjoy that story. It's even better than the wood sprite epic.'

Oiwa nodded, holding back vomit as he looked ahead, wondering what lay beyond.

Marten decided. 'Claw, there's something I have to do,' he said. 'I know exactly where they're going. I'll catch up and come back with them.' Claw knew there was no stopping him. His eagerness was formidable. 'I'm borrowing Gneiss's kayak.'

Thrift approached Marten. 'Take this to Oiwa please.' She handed him a small, flattish green pebble. 'He can burnish his leather with it,' she said coyly.

He set off that afternoon on a falling tide, well equipped with dried food and his astrologer's sticks.

Mica knew the way. The Grey Mountain changed colour as they got closer. The bottom of the snowline undulated around her lower contours. Deep crevices still contained shining snow. The honks of the Whale Geese sounded as though they came from the mountain's spirit.

Inexhaustibly the brothers paddled as the evening light stretched. The backing breeze sped them as the southern mists cleared. Oiwa discovered an energy he'd never experienced. His arms gained power to paddle with the surf. The sea was like wind; it carried them. The cold air sliced like a cutting edge, which seemed to pare the skin from his face, making it feel new. His soft beard enjoyed the salty spray as they crashed through waves they overtook.

The first stars and moonlight shone as day slipped into twilight. The sun slanted below the western edge with dignity. Her last rays pinkly lit the undersides of thin cloud. The sun finally blinked from view. The jade flash sparkled fleetingly. It struck Oiwa in wonder. The days were lengthening.

A leg and toe extended from the Grey Mountain into the open Ocean. They paddled into the sheltered ankle, where they made camp. 'Early in the morning, Oiwa, we will sail round that promontory to meet our familiars,' Mica told him.

A cold breeze blew all night. The sea drenched the Grey Mountain's toes. Starlight glittered in the shortening northern nights.

Marten, a tide-flow behind, watched the starry hunter in the sky and the progress of the waning moon. His camp and fire was in the leeward of a low hill of old shells and ashen dumps. As he watched the galaxies, he ate pickled char and smoked eel with sliced seaweed. He too would arise at first light.

Oiwa woke uncomfortably on a stone boring into his hip. 'I wondered when you'd wake,' Mica said quietly. Oiwa yawned, shaking, in the bitterly cold shadow of the Grey Mountain. He sprang up and leapt about for warmth. They chewed dried goat, launched the Burbot and paddled to the pointed toes of Grey Mountain. Seals sang on her polished nails as Oiwa heard a great roar.

'Walrus,' Mica said. 'They're gigantic seals. They make wonderful boats, like this, and their tusks are solid ivory; great for harpoons. You should never get between them and their pups – very dangerous indeed,' he added.

Oiwa took it all in. They rounded the rocky toe. The walrus roars amplified along with the high-pitched shrieks of terns. The dark waters turned suddenly golden as they rounded the first toe to the screech of gulls. The light of the low, rising sun was blinding. 'Hug the toes,' Mica told Oiwa. 'The current will take us into the open sea if we don't paddle hard and keep close to the shore.' Oiwa nodded and looked away from the bright sun. As they rounded the toes, seals slid into the glittering water, their backs gleaming golden in morning glow. The walrus roared, rearing aggressively at the intruders.

'Paddle harder,' Mica shouted. Oiwa, though distracted by the wonders, dipped his paddle and pulled forcefully. The swirling currents eased as they entered stiller waters. Oiwa looked back to seeing the sea heap up where it rushed round the foot. Mica spied the long bay. The broad beach sloped gradually to the sea, the white sands tinged with pink gravel and grey shingle. Above, a ragged edge of grasses spilled over the dune. Mica pointed to the middle of the bay, where the sands joined a rocky shore covered in seaweed. 'That is where we land.'

They paddled across the lapping wavelets. The gathering breeze blew them shorewards. The Burbot's sides kissed the soft slope. Cormorants lifted their wings and flew just above the sea to rocky vantage points. The seals watched. Walruses settled their mounds of blubber on rocky slabs.

'Pull the boat up, Mica whispered as they touched the shore. They stepped silently from her bow and carried the Burbot over the sand to the tattered edge of the dunes. The light brightened into full day. The final star vanished as the sky donned her morning mantle.

'Take Ziit, Oiwa. I will bring my weapons. This isn't a hunt – it's security.' The two climbed the slipping slope of blown sand, grabbing tough grasses that rooted in the fragile terrain. As they rose the wind blew harder. They pulled on tussocks and gained height with the force on their backs

This land was so different. The gale and the sound of the tide filled Oiwa's ears. Gradually they reached the crest of the long dune. As they peered over, a deafening roar of gaggling geese erupted.

They looked down over the vista to a wide plain of pools and grassy marshlands. A winding river cut through it. Dotting the estuarine landscape were hummocks of grass, like a million warts on a rough hide. On each one, a goose sat.

Oiwa glanced to the base of the dune where dark heads of goslings poked out from under their parent's wings. He edged forward; a rivulet of sand ran down. The guardian geese raised heir black heads in alarm. Oiwa and Mica were spotted. The goose chorus rose to a trumpeting tumult. They all stood to face the intruders with wings raised and outstretched necks. The look of the plain changed. Geese rose, their black webbed feet and claws digging into the matted roots. The goslings' heads disappeared behind their parents' wings. They trumpeted in a violent racket, alarming Oiwa to his liver.

'There they are,' Mica said. 'The young have hatched. We were delayed, but that is okay.' Oiwa couldn't hear him above the tumult, but felt it. 'These are spirits of our past and future souls.'

Oiwa stared back as the hullabaloo rocketed.

'Now we go down there.' Oiwa looked back in blank disbelief as Mica squeezed his hand and urged him forward. They crawled over. Geese from the distant river joined in the rallying call, drowning all sounds of sea and wind. The vanguard of angry birds spread their wings, hissing violently as they descended the slope. The reek of digested grass hit like a hot blast as they neared the fierce phalanx. Maddened terns buzzed.

'Put your bow up, Oiwa, or they will peck your head. Keep your hood on. Go forward slowly.' The front line of whale geese advanced, leaving their young to scatter. 'Put your arm out. Point at the nearest birds. They'll think it's an outstretched head. Now look into their eyes and walk towards them. Hiss if you can, but make no aggressive moves.'

Oiwa stood tall. He stared, pointed and breathed in deeply, exhaling through his teeth with a loud *Hsssssssssssssssssssss*. He stooped level with his adversaries. Ziit jutted forward like an outstretched beak over his hood. His short, pointed beard wagged from his chin. His steamy breath jetted another hiss. The geese widened their wingspans and ran directly at him to stop suddenly short, jostling his bow-point. Oiwa hissed as he fixed the closest protruding head with his glance.

The birds stopped. Oiwa felt the heated breath of a mother goose on his brow. He blew gently on to the protruding black beak. She moved her head back and clacked her bill. Oiwa saw her wet tongue. Shining spittle rimmed her sharp, jagged jaw.

The racket subsided. Oiwa looked to his brother. Mica's feet had changed. He could see him, but he was different. He'd become two figures, one rising from the other. A large feathered bird stood within Mica's skin, then stepped forward.

Oiwa became aware of himself too as a beak clacked against his. His beak rubbed down the neck of his erstwhile foe and preened its wing. He received a similar greeting across his tight feathers. Oiwa stepped with the goose to a shining pool, where he settled and floated. His webbed feet paddled. He followed his guide, watching her tail wiggle. Tiny whirlpools from her feet welled up behind her as Oiwa kept up the pace.

They swam past tranquil nests and waddled over beak-clipped hummocks, then followed narrow rivulets in a maze of tangled waterways. Oiwa saw dark goslings nibbling at the shortened grass. Others went with their parents towards the river. He turned his long neck and thought he could see Mica in his plumage amidst another huddle of whale geese.

Oiwa followed, squeezing through a narrow gulley, which divided round a distinct mound surmounted by a great, downy nest. On top stood the mighty Solan.

'So, Oiwa. You have come to see me?' Solan said clearly in Oiwa's head. 'You've had a very hard journey,' said the Great Goose. 'You have travelled far from *your* nest.' Solan's voice was loud and clear, each word perfectly formed and distinct. 'It seems a very long time ago when you flew with me and my brood from your father's sweat lodge. Does it not?'

Oiwa turned and looked into Solan's deep red eyes. 'Yes. A very long time,' Oiwa answered.

'Come on to my island and squat with me.' Solan moved sideways to make room. Oiwa's clawed toes touched the submerged matted roots of Solan's nest. As he began to mount the turf hummock, Solan's mate, Solange, raised her head from behind him. 'Welcome, Oiwa,' she said.

Oiwa dipped his beak in acceptance. Five goslings poked their heads up from their warm den. Oiwa felt his plumage drain as his breast rose from the water.

'I am going to take our young to the beach to feed,' Solange told Oiwa. 'You can keep my place warm.' They slipped into the gulley and made their way to the ocean's shore.

When his brood had left, Solan said. 'You have far to go yet, Oiwa, and much to accomplish.' He gazed at Oiwa. 'Yours will not be an ordinary life. Your destiny will touch and affect more of your human kind that you could possibly imagine.'

Oiwa listened in silence as he tried to absorb what his familiar was telling him.

'Weir was like you, only he perished.'

'How?' Oiwa asked.

'You will find out in time, Oiwa. Now, Goose, look into my eyes and gain from me what you can.'

Oiwa swallowed spittle down his long neck. He fixed his glance on those shiny irises. Within them he saw the night sky, just as he had from his father's sweat lodge. He and Solan were high above the world, which curved at its edges. He blinked. As his eyes shut, a star and moon map set hard in his skull. He moved his head, but the image did not turn. It remained like the heavens do as you walk, sail, or fly.

'Now you have our chart, Oiwa. My goslings have it from my milt.'

'Solan, thank you,' Oiwa responded. 'I can see a dark space in my head. There's a skein of us far ahead in the night sky. We are guided by the stars. Now I see daylight, but I can feel the heavens and the moon. They guide me, Solan.'

'That's correct,' the Goose King replied. 'This is how we travel our vast distances. As you journey onwards, you'll have to do it as a man does. With man's impediments and man's skills.'

'So I am going on, not back?' Oiwa asked.

'Oh yes, Oiwa. For you a very long distance, and further after.' Solan ruffled his plumage, and then nibbled short blades of grass. Oiwa did the same. They tasted succulent. 'We geese mate for life. Our families are strong. We travel from here to where your ancestors came. We live in harmony there and feed to return here to nest and give birth.' Solan looked towards the river and the sea. 'Here we have everything to bring up our young. We cannot fly during much of this time. We've shed many of our feathers to make our nests. We watch our goslings feed on the fast-growing plants and grasses. We take them to the shore, where they dive for seaweed that sways in the depths. Their small wings are like the flippers of seals, and their feet propel them down to snatch the succulent algae from the rocks.'

Oiwa's head filled with goose lore as Solan continued. 'Our young rapidly grow big and strong, as we ourselves replenish our migration fat and flight feathers. Then we fly back to that wonderful land for the winter, where there is little snow and plenty to sustain us.' Solan paused as Oiwa took it all in.

'Now for you, my man-goose. Your human voice is gone, but your inner one remains. Some men-folk may hear it. You will find ways of hearing others' inner voices. This will show you the truth.' Oiwa listened, saying nothing. 'Your journey is necessary, but it's for you to discover what it will bring. There will be many risks and much to overcome. I hope you fare better than Weir.'

'Thank you, Solan. I knew there was more for me than just returning to my clan. I will think deeply on all you have told me,' Oiwa said in his own clear voice.

'Then let's spend some time with you being a Goose,' Solan replied. 'Then we will go to the shore.'

Chapter 23

*

Ugruk

Later, Mica joined them. Solan led them to the river. Oiwa felt comfortable as they bobbed down its last few yards to cascade to the sea. Other geese and goslings fed in the salty water. Oiwa dipped his head below the surf, seeing goslings flying underwater, tugging at the masses of nutritious plants. He tasted the swaying fronds, feeling, 'I know that flavour.'

He paddled, at home amongst his huge family, each goose, an individual as a human. He drifted, watching Mica floating up the shore. He paddled to meet his brother. He turned his head and looked. He was distanced from his flock. His scaly claws touched the shingle beneath as he watched Mica waddle, then stand as a man. Oiwa trod from his fading Goose reflection to walk the incline. His wings grew transparent, his arms solid in his seal-gut parka. His booted feet crunched shingle. Mica's hand reached. They embraced. Oiwa heard his soft words: 'Now you know what and who we are.'

'Yes, Mica. We're different from other people. We're part of something else. There's so much to understand. I've grown. I'm fuller. My head has new wisdom. I must discover all that's locked in it. I'm tugging my beard, ensuring this real. I know you can hear me, Mica.'

'I hear you, Oiwa. You are new and changed. This is why we come here.'

They looked along the shore. Gravel crunched under their boots. The dune rose beside them. By the Burbot, smoke from a small fire crept skywards. A thin figure waved. 'It's Marten, standing by a circle of sticks. He's coming to meet us.'

'Here, Oiwa. A gift from Thrift.' Marten's outstretched hand opened, revealing the green pebble.

'Thanks.' Oiwa nodded, remembering their togetherness. 'It's so smooth; lovely to touch. I'll cherish it.'

Marten spoke of sticks, 'The further north I bring them, the more the shadows change. I could draw you a diagram in the sand...' But he noticed a difference in the brothers and stopped. They sat by Marten's fire. He said, 'My calculations demonstrate it will be light all the time in seventeen days.'

The three sat in silence. Mica listened to the waves and birdcalls. Oiwa removed his polished stone from his pouch to warm it in his hands. 'There's a flaw on its edge. Slight silvery specks, like cold moonlight, shine from within it. I'll get my axe and place its sharp edge gently into the crack and set the pebble on a beach stone.' Mica watched as Oiwa pressed his axe blade into the fault. He raised them slightly then brought his chopper down. The pebble split neatly in halves.

Oiwa spent the rest of the long day meditating while rubbing the two halves until they shone. He rummaged in his pouch for a ruined quartz arrowhead. With its jagged edge he drew a flying goose on the smoothed surfaces. As he drew he saw a face shine through. 'Who is she?' he wondered as he skilfully scored the sparing lines of his emblem, powerfully emboldening it.

Oiwa thought of his future while carving. 'I remember all that happened and how changed I am: my gains, my losses, my loves, my dislikes. I know the sweetness of mating. But that great rock is still in my throat. Turning back with Mica is wrong, no matter how it hurts to leave him. All I see is my journey to the unknown, and that someone there. I hear voices of geese telling me how to follow. I curl my toes in my boots to feel if they are goose. They aren't now.'

He looked to Mica, who was talking with Marten about theories. The fog of words wafted past as he spied Gneiss's kayak. 'I need time to gather physical and mental courage,' he realised.

His own words rang as he listened to Marten's final conclusions, 'If you travel far enough you will arrive back at the place where you began.'

'That's completely crazy,' Oiwa thought as he stood and looked out to the horizon, imagining the utter impossibility of Marten's words.

As Oiwa's eyes strained, he spotted a flotilla of craft approaching. Oiwa nudged Mica and pointed to the canoes. 'It's Ugruk and his clan,' Mica explained. 'Build the fire up.'

Ugruk's fleet made for their smoke. The skin craft nudged the shore. Mica walked down as the chief advanced to greet him. Ugruk shoved back his parka hood and hugged Mica. He was short, with dark scrubby hair and a thin black moustache. Ugruk's power wasn't in his size, but in his intellect, serenity and knowledge. They crunched their way up the beach to Marten's blaze.

'Ugruk. Here's the vole hat from the Bald Heads, and salt.' The hat made Ugruk laugh at a private joke between him and Char. 'This too,' Mica added. Crack! went his brow on Ugruk's forehead.

'I let you do that!' Ugruk blurted, rubbing his bruise.

'Bring the seal meat, Sgeir,' he asked his wife. Her young fetched rolls of flesh, dumped them on a skin and cut it up with sharp ulus. Ugruk passed some to Mica. They ate. Mica admired Ugruk's garb as he chewed. His jacket was seal suede trimmed with arctic fox. The chest fasteners were tiny carved ivory selkies, his hood lining white hare's fur pulled in by wolf-bone toggles. He sported a necklace of engraved bear's teeth over his inner vest. The red trim of his caribou calf trousers stretched tightly on his legs.

They swapped news. Oiwa listened. Marten explained about his sticks to the young.

'We are hunting walrus. Will you come?' he suggested.

Oiwa looked the other way, pretending interest in Marten, but desperately feeling the pull of his calling. 'I can't stop myself. I'm standing to walk shorewards. I'll turn to wave. But he's deep in plans for walrus hunts and what they'll do with the tusks. "A fine gift for Buzzard," I hear him say. They discuss killing, weapons; how they'll stalk and have hides for boats; feasting on flesh, and mating after; lamp blubber; bones for tools and whiskers to string beads. "Oiwa could make Moss a fine bracelet from polished flipper bones," says Mica. My heart sinks. I would love to mate with Moss again, and Thrift, but no! There is another. I'm certain now.'

Mica heard Oiwa's voice scream in his head. He stood facing him, shocked. 'I am not going back!' he heard Oiwa yell. 'I'm following the geese. I am going to discover what happened to Weir, and what happens to *me*.' He ground his feet into the shingle. He thrust his hand into his pouch. 'Here's my talisman. Take it from my open hand.' Staggered, Mica gripped Oiwa's palm. Oiwa squeezed the intaglio deep into Mica's palm until the bones separated. Mica had never seen his brother so troubled, yet so empowered. He leaned back, looking into his face. He saw the change; the resolution set firmly there.

Oiwa sprinted to Gneiss's kayak. He laid Ziit in it, along with his arrows and what few belongings he had. Bewildered, Mica looked the goose carving swelling on his palm. The gem was beautiful. He ran to Oiwa as he climbed in the boat. 'Don't go,' he prayed.

Oiwa looked at Mica.

'I will come with you then,' Mica implored.

'*No!*' he heard.

'Our parents? Our clan?' Mica shouted as Ugruk's people gathered round.

Oiwa's voice hit home in Mica's head: '*My life! My destiny! My future!*'

Ugruk clenched Mica's arm as he tried to pull Oiwa from the kayak. 'Let him go. Don't hold this young man back.'

Oiwa stood, hugged Mica firmly and pushed off. Ugruk held Mica as Oiwa paddled across Goose Landing's river. Geese honked tumultuously. Mica shouted Oiwa's name frantically, knowing there'd be no answer. Other ears, in a distant archipelago, listened to that name from the depths of a waking dream.

Dense mist descended over the ocean.

Oiwa had vanished!

The end of 'Skara: The First Wave'.

To be continued...

Bibliography

*

Plants at The Edge: An amazing book on Arctic flora.

Arctic Clothing: This book shows the wonderful craft and artistry of clothing for survival and ritual in the Arctic.

Dawn of Civilisation: A great volume with aspects of life in the early stages of civilisation.

Many volumes of *Archaeologia Cantiana, proceedings of The Kent Archaeological Society*.

Symbols of Power: A wonderful book brought out by The National Museum of Scotland. It deals with the richness of symbolic artefacts of the time of Stone Henge.

Rising Tides: A book on Orkney's eroding shorelines showing the wonderful discoveries to be made and the irreparable damage to Orkney's Archaeology.

Wilder Mann: This volume illustrates the costumes stretching back millennia that are still used in pagan rites today.

The Piercebridge Formula: Although discussing Roman waterways and canals, it has much relevance to earlier times.

The Brendan Voyage: The recreation of St. Brendan's cow skin boat, which is thought he sailed to America.

Fauna and Flora of Canada: Invaluable information on Canadian plants and animals.

The Bog People: This is by archaeologist Peder Glob. It deals with pre-historic preserved people from Danish bogs.

And so many other books, too numerous to mention.

NB. I read Homer after finishing *Skara*, and went back to my book and put in the parts about the burning of caribou and ox femurs etc. I feel this actually has relevance to Neolithic Orkney, looking at the lack of femurs from certain sites.